Highland Romance

Elspeth

A beautiful favorite of the English court, Elspeth Lamond came home to the Highlands unguarded against treacherous clan intrigue . . . or the dangerous longing that besieged her heart.

MacHugh

The Chief of Clan MacHugh, a rugged lord among men and unscrupulous with women, was strangely gentled by the spirited lass from London.

Kate

She embraced her new-come rival with a cruel betrayal befitting her jealousy.

The Earl of Argyll

Elspeth's cunning and powerful uncle would sooner destroy MacHugh than lose the gold that Elspeth's titled suitors offered.

> "Here is the MacHugh's world
> in which he is supreme and the beauty, danger,
> thrill and torment of it is well represented."
> *Library Journal*

BRIDE
OF THE
MACHUGH

A NOVEL BY
JAN COX SPEAS

AVON
PUBLISHERS OF BARD, CAMELOT AND DISCUS BOOKS

AVON BOOKS
A division of
The Hearst Corporation
959 Eighth Avenue
New York, New York 10019

First Avon Printing, January, 1978

AVON TRADEMARK REG. U.S. PAT. OFF. AND IN
OTHER COUNTRIES, MARCA REGISTRADA,
HECHO EN U.S.A.

Printed in the U.S.A.

For my mother and father

BRIDE
OF THE
MACHUGH

❧ 1 ❧

THE dawn was slow in coming. Against the pale sky the mountains were tall and sullen, holding back the day. An uneasy wind stirred in the black trees by the loch and moaned restlessly through the castle parapets, but in the high upland corries there was only the silence of night.

Elspeth Lamond stood on the steps leading down into the courtyard, waiting. She struggled against the panic rising slowly in her throat. Dawn would surely come. Even this awesome corner of Scotland could not cling forever to the ominous concealment of night. The gray day would soon creep down the flanks of the mountains toward the high towers of Duncraig, and the night mists would swirl away to the sea. And surely, with the cold light of morning, the strange sense of foreboding would cease to threaten her. It would retreat with the stealthy night which fostered it, with the wild unearthly night cries and the clammy mists and the restless wind.

She pressed her chilled hands against the warmth of her body beneath her cloak and reminded herself that panic was a thing she had known before. Loneliness gripped her, and if she came perilously close to fright now, it was only that she stood in a strange country among strangers.

Below her in the courtyard grooms with blankets and saddles moved among the horses. An impatient hoof pawed at the cobbles, a metal bit clinked, a yawning stableboy clapped his arms together to stir his blood against the autumn chill. By the light of the kitchen fires Elspeth could see the men sent north by her kinsman Duncan Campbell to escort her to Inveraray. They had finished their meal of ale and meat and were standing about the yard, impatient to be gone with the day. The red of their plaids showed black, but when the firelight touched an ugly broadsword the metal twisted and moved like a thing alive.

They were not Campbells. They were MacHughs, and they had ridden into Duncraig the evening before bearing a letter from Duncan Campbell. Elspeth was to place herself in their hands; she was to entrust them to take her safely to Inveraray, the destination of that lengthy and dangerous journey she had begun so many weeks before in London.

It was of some assurance to know that Duncan had received her message telling of the furious storm which had driven her ship north along the coast, when she had intended to step on Scots soil from Loch Fyne, with Duncan and Inveraray Castle waiting on the shore. But Duncan did not know, for she had not thought to distress him, that her maid and only companion had fallen ill of a fever aboard ship and refused to travel another league. Without her maid, Elspeth was quite alone, and alone she must ride south with the silent MacHughs gathered below her in the courtyard.

She did not relish the prospect. It was the MacHughs who came near to spoiling all her fine courage. Not the grim mountains, nor the rain and mists, nor the cold wind which cried over the land like a desolate whaup. It was the dark arrogance lying on the faces of the MacHugh clansmen—as if their very souls were as fierce and wild as the land they lived on—it was their arrogance that unnerved her.

The dawn was not far away. The castle would come alive, the clansmen would mount their horses, and she would finally ride out from Duncraig and discover what lay beyond those dark hills. But still she stood, her eyes on the pale sky and the fretted parapets.

She could not tell when she first knew she was not alone. The eerie sensation began to tingle unpleasantly at the ends of her nerves; she felt a sudden urge to turn and flee up the stairs. But she forced herself to stand quietly, lifting her eyes to the black depths above her. Then she turned her head to see the length of the stairs leading downward.

She surprised the man and their eyes met without warning. He stood directly below her, his shoulders against the keep wall, one boot on the cobbled floor of the courtyard and the other propped against the stone stairs.

He returned her stare impassively, without turning away. Elspeth recognized him as the MacHugh clansman who had brought the message from Duncan Campbell, and she remembered him for the odd way he had stared at her as he delivered the sealed letter into her hands. His face was now in shadow, but she knew how the thin white scar curved from his left brow to his mouth, giving him a slanting, devilish look.

Standing in the great hall beside her Campbell host, Elspeth had been mildly amused by the man's close scrutiny. Faith, she was more than accustomed to men's stares, and a man was much the same here in Scotland as in London. But now she was not so confident, and scarcely amused.

She said at last, "Do you wish my leave to speak?"

"I've nothing to say." His voice held no insolence; the words were there, brief and indifferent, for whatever she could make of them.

"Have you no chores?" she asked, holding her ground. "We should ride within the hour."

"I've men to handle the chores," he answered carelessly.

She wished she could see his face. She did not like his manner of speech, and she did not like to be stared at from the darkness.

"I came out in search of privacy as well as fresh air," she said. "Please be good enough to leave me."

She noticed that he wore no tartan, for even in the dim light she would have seen that glaring MacHugh red. His clothes were dark, and angrily she thought that he might have been standing there, deliberately concealed, since first she crept down the steps to await the dawn.

He shrugged and seemed about to speak again, but just then the tall doors above them creaked open and a yellow shaft of light fell across the stairs. For a brief instant Elspeth saw the long scar and the flicker of his eyes as he dropped his lids against the light. Then, without haste, he turned and sauntered across the courtyard toward the horses, his cloak, as he walked, turning back to show the edge of his scabbard.

She watched him disappear in the crowd of clansmen and grooms. The yellow light was all about her, and the cheerful, harsh voice of Sir William Campbell roared over her head and echoed back from the castle walls like a cannon salute to morning.

"Miserable morning to ride abroad, Mistress Lamond," he shouted. "You'll find yourself with the ague."

Even the company of the dour MacHughs was to be preferred, Elspeth reflected, to another day of Sir William. Lifting her face to the light, she said courteously, "Duncan will be anxious. You'd not have me linger now that he knows I've landed."

"Aye, he'll be more than anxious, and nae doubt he's had time to regret sending those black MacHughs for you." Sir William's crimson face moved and shook, etched into plump wrinkles. He laughed at great length and the wool of his plaid stretched near to bursting. "But like as not he intends to keep the lot of them out of mischief. 'Tis a good trick; I'll not deny it."

"Are they not friends, these MacHughs?" Elspeth asked. She looked below her; the MacHugh who had spoken to her was standing beside his horse, paying close attention to a girth. "Do you have reason to trust them?"

"I'd not presume to quarrel with Duncan's written word. But it makes no odds. They'll see you safe to Inveraray, mistress. Duncan will hold them to account for you, and that's fair enough." He chuckled, then restrained himself. "A sore trial to the man, with a lass like yourself set down in the hills alone. Must keep his wits about him."

Sir William studied his guest surreptitiously, noting with pleasure the fair unruly curls, touched lightly with copper and shorn close to her head like a lad's after her recent bout with the fever; the eyes blue as a Highland tarn under a summer sky and framed round with lashes thick as feathers; the lovely slim look of her that took a man's breath away, even one so stolidly advanced in years as Sir William. He felt an abiding sympathy for Duncan Campbell of Glenurchy, who would soon discover that a fair lass in the household was much like a tempest in an alepot.

"Is it so dangerous to ride abroad in Scotland?" Elspeth asked slowly. "Lord Argyll assured me I'd find it most peaceful." She added, watching Sir William, "He thinks to keep it so, now he is the King's Lieutenant in the West."

It was enough. She had only to mention his name, Archibald Campbell, Earl of Argyll, and it seemed to shake the very foundations of the earth beneath her. Sir William turned pale indeed; he seemed to have great difficulty with his throat.

"I trust you'll remember me to his lordship, mistress. You've been as safe as a bairn behind the walls of Duncraig, and I'd see you to Inveraray myself if I could be spared from my garrison."

Elspeth stifled the contempt in her voice. "His lordship will be pleased," she murmured.

She liked it little. It was small pleasure to claim kinship with Archibald Campbell; it was even smaller comfort to know that his powerful ire might so easily reach into this remote corner of western Scotland, so distant from London that it might be a foreign land. God's blood, she had thought herself well quit of him, but she should have reckoned he'd not allow her out of his reach.

She straightened her shoulders and walked down the steps to the courtyard. A groom brought a horse to her side, a chestnut mare of good height and condition, and so she found it possible to give Sir William a gracious smile.

"You are kind, sir," she said. Lifting her heavy velvet skirts, she accepted his boost into the high sidesaddle and settled her great cloak to cover her properly. Around her the MacHugh clansmen mounted their sturdy horses; the man who led them swung into his saddle and moved his horse closer.

"Gavin MacHugh," Sir William said brusquely, "I know you, and I hold you in charge here. Will you see this lady safely to Inveraray?"

"I've had my orders," the man said. "She'll be safe enough with me."

There was no disrespect in his voice, but neither was there an ordinary courtesy; and his answer did not precisely match the question put to him. Elspeth noted the wicked scar curving his face and wished she could be certain that because he looked so much a villain and knave he could not possibly be.

She inclined her head slightly to Sir William, touched her whip to her horse and moved toward the open gates. Behind her the MacHughs fell into a column and the man Gavin rode abreast. She was away then, riding out into Scotland, and if it seemed a wild and uncomely place, she had only herself to blame. She had left London of her own choosing, had indeed persuaded her guardian Argyll that it would be quite safe for a lass of twenty to travel alone in the modern world of 1614; and now she must bear the burden of whatever might befall her. This western coast of Scotland, with its wild granite peaks, bleak moorland and glens, its rough clansmen who stared curiously and spoke in an unfamiliar tongue—she must show no fear of it, else all would be lost before it was well begun.

The man riding beside her did not speak. He wore a broad bonnet pulled well over his face, hiding his red hair, and, although she studied him openly, his profile remained as cold and imperturbable as ever. Gavin Mac-Hugh, Sir William had called him; Elspeth thought him an uncouth and tactless fellow and wished Duncan Campbell had seen fit to send her a pleasanter companion for the ride.

It was exceedingly difficult to keep her resolve, not to feel very young and lonely and forgotten. The world had narrowed down to the melancholy sky touching the tops of the mountains, those great squat monsters shouldering one on the other as far as the eye could see, and the grim MacHughs who rode beside her as strangers.

But she had not long to feel sorry for herself. They had ridden less than an hour when the man Gavin drew rein beside her and turned in his saddle to face the men behind him. Elspeth looked at the fork in the track ahead, then at her companions; she swallowed to ease the sudden constriction in her throat.

"We part company, lads," Gavin MacHugh said. "You know our plan, so see to it."

The MacHughs filed their horses past Elspeth on the narrow trail. Gavin HacHugh rested his elbow on his saddle and waited for them to pass.

Elspeth looked at him. "Have you made a change in plans?" she asked. "Do we ride to Inveraray without an escort?"

He did not speak. Elspeth tightened her gloves on her reins and lifted her chin. "I doubt Duncan Campbell will be pleased to hear of your discourtesy."

He turned to look at her for the first time, his face showing the slight trace of a grin. "Duncan Campbell has no idea you are in Scotland, mistress," he said briefly.

It was a full minute before the import of his words reached her mind and began to take on a dreadful sig-

nificance. And in that moment Gavin MacHugh had
taken her reins and tossed them over the mare's head.
With the same swift motion he brought his hand down
on the mare's flanks and spurred his own horse. Elspeth
clutched the pommel of her saddle, almost losing her
balance; they were away at a gallop, taking the track
which led away from the disappearing MacHugh clansmen.

Elspeth could do nothing. Riding sidesaddle, with
the heavy velvet gown flapping about her boots, she
could not hope to kick free and drop to the ground
without mishap, and in any event she preferred to take
her chances with the horse. The trail was uneven and
strewn with sharp boulders, and the man was driving
the horses at a pace to take away her breath.

They rode at a full gallop for what seemed like endless miles along the trail, which dipped steeply to a
river, then curved upward between the hills before
returning to follow the river bed again. Now and again
they dashed headlong through birch woods, dripping
with rain, and the wet branches caught at her hair and
clothes as if to tempt her to take her hands from the
pommel.

Finally they crossed the river at a shallow ford. The
water splashed up and stained her russet skirt and she
knew a moment of panic when her horse scrambled
wildly over the rocks, losing balance and recovering
it an instant later. The man waited for her on the opposite bank. The sudden silence was broken only by
the harsh breathing of the horses as they stood trembling and quiet, their flanks wet and dappled with
lather.

"The trail grows narrow from here," the man said
abruptly. " 'Tis rough riding for a lass. Can you walk
in those clothes?"

Elspeth stared at him, too astonished to answer.

"Come, mistress," he said impatiently. "Will you
walk or ride?"

She could not speak. It was incredible that the knave

should address her so, as if she would go with him docilely; he was daft, else she had gone daft herself.

He shrugged. "Hurry with it," he said, "unless you've a mind to crawl, with my sword urging you along. We've a good distance to travel yet."

Elspeth drew a deep breath. "Where are you taking me?"

"Does it matter? You've no choice in it." He had taken her reins; now he tossed them to her, a small gesture of great mockery. Drawing off his leather gloves, he flexed his fingers.

Elspeth felt a hot anger. "I'll not walk and I'll not ride."

"I've no desire to hurt you, but I feel capable of giving you a hard slap or two. Stubborn or frightened, 'tis of small interest to me. Come along now, like a good lass, or I'll show you the way of it."

"Touch me," she said, "and I'll show you a thing or two. You're a fool."

The man threw a boot over his saddle and slid to the ground. "I can see you're not frightened," he said flatly. "You're the fool then, not I."

Her heart pounded thickly in her throat; her hands grew clammy and wet beneath her gloves. The man had the truth of it: she was the fool. She had not had the wit to be frightened before; she had been too pre-occupied with keeping her seat. But now as she looked at him she felt faint, suddenly remembering the way he had stared at her in the dark hour before dawn.

"You can swoon when we're there," he said curtly. "I'd lose my head if I brought you in across my saddle like a bag of wet barley. Take a deep breath and hold your head down."

But suddenly she was too angry to faint. "What happened to the Campbell who rode to Inveraray with my message for Duncan Campbell?" she asked sharply.

"A fool," he said, "and a featherbrain in the bargain. God's foot, I've no time to haggle over your questions. If you've settled your stomach, we'll move on."

Elspeth wished she might lay her whip across his face. She was fairly caught, but not so much a fool as he thought. "I'll ride," she said shortly. "Walk yourself if the trail is too rough for you."

He mounted quickly, turning to speak over his shoulder. "You'll find the riding easier," he said, not unkindly, "if you'll tie up your skirts."

He wheeled his horse and spurred into the stand of firs bordering the river. Elspeth looked down thoughtfully at the sodden hem and torn fringe of her velvet gown, and, taking the full skirt at the side, she drew it up and secured it with her belt. Her boots were then exposed, and a wide border of petticoat, but she felt vastly less encumbered.

She rode slowly up the bank and her companion led the way without speaking again. Soon the trees began to thin and a brown ridge rose directly before them, backed by other hills whose summits were hidden in the ragged mists. The way grew steeper and choked with boulders which must have fallen from the heights above, and the tough grass beneath the horses' hoofs sprang back and showed no sign of their passing.

The clouds darkened and it began to rain, a cold biting rain which shut out the sight of the gaunt hills. There might have been no other person in the world but the two of them, no world but that of the massive boulders, streaming black with rain, the soggy turf which smelled damply of peat, the occasional cry of a lonely whaup in the low-scudding clouds.

Elspeth tried not to sway in the saddle. It was a bleak and cheerless prospect which faced her, but she had sensed that all was not well before she left Duncraig and she deserved no better for not heeding the warnings in her mind. Indeed, she had feared the journey was a wild and foolish undertaking even before she set sail from England, but one could not lightly break a promise given the dying.

It had begun from so tiny a thing, the incredible change from the gay court of Queen Anne to this miserable and barbaric track in the dark hills of Scotland. It had begun the day her mother had hawked in the rain and returned home with her satin habit muddied and her face flushed despite the wet; the hot fever had come in the night and stifled the very breath of life before the week was out. Elspeth remembered how swiftly and carelessly she had given the promise, thinking to ease the burden of a beloved one who lay ill. But even as she lay wan and ill herself, fighting the dread fever as her mother could not, she had known that the promise to go to her mother's Campbell kinsmen in Scotland had been more binding and sacred than an oath sworn before the altar.

And it had brought her to this. She was aching and sore in every muscle, her body chilled with the bitter rain until she despaired of ever being warm again. But she feared above all things that she would soon weep, and despised herself for a weak and spineless lass, and so rode on with her back as stiff and unyielding as she could well hold it.

Presently the horses began to descend into a wooded glen, and the heavy branches loosed showers of moisture on her head and slapped wetly against her face. It was a dark and sunken place where nothing stirred but the slow rain. The man Gavin dismounted and led the horses along the shore of a small loch where the water was black and bottomless and ferns drooped over banks of peat moss.

They came out into a cleared space where the trees were held back by scattered boulders, and the man said, "We'll wait here. Can you come unstuck from your saddle?"

Elspeth stretched her cramped legs and slid from her horse, but she had not reckoned on the solid granite of the ground or the weakness in her muscles. Her legs gave way beneath her and she stumbled against him.

"It was a hard ride," he said, steadying her, "and I'm sorry for that. But you lasted as well as most men, and there's much that's worse than an ache or two."

There was a grudging respect in his voice, but he took his hand away from her arm at once and tethered the horses at the edge of the clearing. Elspeth wavered to a flat boulder and eased herself down to it, little caring that her skirts dragged in a pool of water. She had never been so wet, or so weary, or so bedraggled and unkempt, and it was a matter no longer worthy of note.

"It will take more than your threats," she said, "to force me into that saddle again. I'll gladly crawl the next fifty leagues."

He did not answer. He held his head to one side, listening, and Elspeth caught the faint sound of hoof-beats, muffled in that drenched world as if the horses rode on blankets.

"I'm to be rid of you sooner than I thought," said Gavin MacHugh.

A few minutes before Elspeth had been certain she would be unable to stand again, but now she struggled to her feet and stood there unsteadily. "Who comes?" she asked, vexed beyond measure that she could not raise her voice above a whisper. "Why are we waiting here?"

He unfastened the silver flask from his belt. " 'Tis the Chief," he said imperturbably, "else something has gone sorely wrong with our plans. Even so, I doubt you'll find them Campbells." He held out the flask to her, and the suspicion of a smile touched his cold eyes. "I've yet to deliver you to the MacHugh all of a piece," he said. "Take a good draught. From the look of you, you have more need of it than I."

She downed a goodly portion of the contents, realizing too late that it was not the wine she had expected. The fiery liquid burned her mouth, bringing quick tears to her eyes, and she gulped desperately to keep it down.

The unseen horses came nearer and the beat of their hoofs was relentless and persistent, louder now and mingled with the low rumble of voices and an occa-

sional burst of laughter. Elspeth pushed a strand of
wet hair from her face and lifted her shoulders, feeling
her clothes hang like a dead weight to drag them down
again. The man beside her was silent. Nothing stirred:
The trees seemed to stiffen with expectancy, the mists
hung motionless over the black waters, the very rain
grew hushed and foreboding.

She knew a great need to hear the reassuring sound
of her own voice. "I would pray," she said, "but I've
forgotten all my prayers."

He looked down at her. "You're a comely lass," he
said dryly. "It'll stand you in better stead than a prayer."

Then there was no more time for words. The clearing erupted with horses and mounted men, milling uncertainly in the small space before the loch. A sharp
command rang out and the horses faded back into the
woods as abruptly as they had come, a trick which left
Elspeth with the childish urge to rub her eyes incredulously.

An enormous black stallion remained in the clearing,
but his rider did not dismount. He sat easily in the
saddle, his hands careless on the reins; then he leaned
forward, resting one arm on his saddle pommel, and
spoke to Gavin MacHugh.

"God's mercy, Gavin," he said, "did you bring her
from Duncraig so quickly?"

"I saw no cause to linger," said Gavin. "She still has
life in her."

The man's face was shadowed by his helmet, but the
amusement in his voice was frank and undisguised.
"I'll wager she has," he said. "You've caught yourself
a Lamond, Gavin, and God knows I've yet to see one
yield graciously."

"I had to threaten her a bit," said Gavin, "else she'd
have read me a sermon on my ill manners."

The newcomer did not take his eyes from Elspeth
Lamond. "You're a lost soul, Gavin," he said lightly,
"and stand much in need of a good sermon. I doubt
it would have harmed you greatly."

Elspeth struggled with a quick flare of temper. "I tire of standing in the rain," she said, lifting her chin. "What do you want of me?"

There was a lengthy silence while the man continued his slow deliberate appraisal of her. "My pardon, mistress," he said at last. "Allow me to present myself." He swept his plumed helmet across the saddle and his voice took on a hard metallic ring that quieted even the restless horse beneath him.

"Sir Alexander MacHugh," he said, and the black stallion with its black-cloaked rider seemed to tower like an immense shadow against the dark silent woods and the stormy Scots sky.

"I do not know you, sir," she said scornfully. "But I shall mark the name well."

" 'Tis of no matter," he said. "You'll know me better before we've finished."

Looking up, Elspeth held his stare until she thought her chin would break from the strain. There was nothing about him that was not dark and hard, tempered with as ruthless and dangerous an edge as the sword he wore at his side: his tanned face, the stubborn line of his chin, the high cheekbones, the dark head set proudly on the powerful width of his shoulders, and the clothes as black as night. Beneath his cloak he wore a leather jack, and boots spurred with heavy silver reached almost to his hips; even his gauntlets were of supple leather.

"So you would know what we want of you," he said thoughtfully. His eyes swept over her again, came back to her face. "Let's be to it, then. Gavin, see to her horse. I'll take Mistress Lamond."

She was lost, without hope, knowing only the immediate need to hold her shoulders straight and proud in the face of his insolence. The words caught in her throat, but she managed at last to speak. "Is this place not suitable?"

"Suitable for what? 'Tis a damp and unholy place, mistress. I doubt you'd find it in the least comfortable."

He walked the stallion toward her. Elspeth retreated, step by slow step; she could not restrain her wayward feet, although with each step she threw away more of the small pride left to her. A lump formed in her throat and came near to choking her; she knew her eyes must be wide as saucers with her dread of his laying hands on her.

"Take care," he said. "You'll wet your feet in the loch."

Indeed, she might drown herself in the black waters before he reached her, but she'd give him to know she'd not once considered it. "I'd not be so fainthearted," she said coldly.

He grinned down at her. " 'Tis out of fashion," he remarked agreeably, "and damnably final. I'll not hold you to blame for choosing the easier way."

At that he leaned from his saddle and took her arms, lifting her so easily that she might have weighed no more than the mists touching the treetops. She found herself on the saddle before him, held secure by his left arm, and it was so deftly done that she had no time to resist. He turned his horse toward the trees and the gloomy darkness beneath them, holding his arm before her face to protect her from the wet branches.

On and on they rode, through the dripping trees, following no trail and leaving none. Suddenly they emerged from the woods and faced the rock-strewn emptiness of a high moor which sloped upward until it seemed to touch the very sky, so low were the gray mists.

Then the stallion turned sharply to round an out-cropping of stone, and the moor was no longer empty. It was alive with men and horses and small fires defying the rain and long streamers of smoke which drifted up to merge with the mists; and everywhere was the blazing MacHugh tartan.

The MacHugh dismounted and lifted her to the ground, and a clansman led the black stallion away. Gavin was already on his knees beside a fire, coaxing the flames higher. Elspeth thought that nothing before in her life had seemed so precious as the meager comfort of a fire on a wind-swept, rainy moor.

"Sit down, mistress," the MacHugh ordered and, when she could not command her feet, led her to a small rise of ground and left her. "Hurry with it, Gavin," he said curtly. "I'll see to the men."

Elspeth did not watch him stride away. Her clothes beneath her cloak were damp and clammy against her skin, and she could no longer control the shivering which engulfed her each time a bitter gust of wind flung more rain in her face.

The MacHugh came back and stood above her, the rain streaming down his face, seeming as tall and dark as the hill behind him. "You look chilled to the bone," he said. He took her hands and pulled her to her feet; then he unclasped her cloak, tossing it to Gavin. He carried a large plaid over his arm and he wrapped it around her until she was completely covered, with only her face to meet the rain.

"It'll serve to keep you dry," he said, amused. "I've never seen a lass so forlorn over a drenching."

Anger surged through her blood, warming it to life again. She was well aware of the figure she must make, huddled in a great plaid like nothing so much as a horse blanket, her short curls plastered against her face, the rain dripping into her eyes and down to the end of her nose.

He stood with his boots wide apart and his thumbs in the wide leather belt at his waist. "Are you still frightened?" he asked abruptly. "Gavin meant no harm. He had his orders from me to bring you here, and I'll take the blame if he forgot his manners while he was about it." He grinned again, looking down at her. "But admit it was a ride you'll not soon forget."

She threw back the offending plaid and lifted her whip; she'd warrant she could wipe the grin from his dark face.

He did not move, or lift a hand to restrain her. "I'd not advise it," he said, low.

Her pride, more than his warning, gave her pause; it was a ludicrous gesture, a small whip against this man and his band of uncouth ruffians. It would be far wiser to save her defiance and strength; whatever he intended to do with her, she would need all the courage she could muster.

She threw the whip from her scornfully and turned away from him to sit beside Gavin. The MacHugh sat down, stretching his wet boots to the fire; his heavy spurs gleaming a wicked crimson and the flickering light leaped to the scabbard of his sword and moved along it to the dirk thrust in his belt.

"Are you hungry?" he asked.

"Yes," she said shortly, for she would need food, even if it choked her to take it from him.

"You missed the sport, Gavin," the MacHugh said, pushing back his helmet. "The finest selection of horse-flesh in all Scotland, and we bagged a fair dozen in less than an hour."

"No moonlight last evening," said Gavin. "D'you think you picked the best?"

"His lordship would have none but the best," the MacHugh said cheerfully. "He'll be displeased to hear how many of his choicest mares have strayed from pasture."

" 'Tis Glenurchy will be displeased," Gavin remarked thoughtfully, "now he's made residence at Inveraray to handle the Earl's affairs."

Elspeth stared at Alexander MacHugh. "A horse thief," she said coldly. "Did you also steal the letter I sent to Duncan Campbell? And write the one to me, signing it with his name and forging his own seal?"

"Aye," he said calmly. "We're reivers and abductors, and we don't mind forging a seal or two if it serves our purpose."

"What is your purpose?" she asked.

"We're no' so fond of the Campbells in these parts,"

he said. "It's never hard to think of a purpose to annoy them." He grinned and added, "Now that you know the worst, have you lost your appetite?"

"Hereabouts they call him Alexander Dhu," Gavin said, his attention on the business of preparing a meal. "The mothers all frighten their bairns near to death with the very thought of him. 'Mind your manners,' they warn, 'else the Black MacHugh will carry you away.' "

He did not smile, but the words were so cheerfully callous that Elspeth could not believe him serious. The MacHugh threw back his head and laughed, and it was so contagious a sound that she was forced to control her features rigidly lest she smile in answer.

She had not lost her appetite, but was ravenously hungry; and the plaid cut the edge of the wind and was gradually driving the chill from her body. It was exceedingly difficult to be angry or frightened or scornful when she felt much like a tabby cat, relaxed and sleepy by the fire, breathing the pleasant, mouth-watering odor of partridges browning on their crude spits above the flames.

She looked up to find the MacHugh's eyes on her. "He's a rough lad," he said lazily, "and not too well versed in the art of pleasing a lass. But you'll not find his like again when it comes to roasting a bird to the proper turn."

At the time it did not seem strange that she should nod her head and put her chin in her hands, the better to observe Gavin's way with a plump partridge. It was no more incredible than the rest of it, and so she deliberately closed her mind to everything but the pleasures of the moment.

Never before had she sat by a campfire in the dark rain of an autumn afternoon, with no roof but the sky and yet knowing the vast comfort of becoming dry and warm; never before had she crossed her legs beneath her, like a boy, with her face dirty and smudged and her hair rumpled from the dampness. Nor had she ever reached eagerly for a hot bird skewered on a dirk, grinning her appreciation much later with her mouth smeared with the delicious juices and stained with red wine. One missed a great deal of joy by being circumspect, she reflected; and she found that she was vastly contented with the world in which she had so unexpectedly found herself, where circumspection and convention were dull matters indeed and scarcely to be considered.

"Have you decided my fate, sir?" she asked at last, and then thought it ridiculous to speak of so serious a matter with her mouth stuffed with partridge and barley bread.

But the MacHugh replied gravely, "Aye, I've come to a decision. Have you any means, mistress, or must we beg ransom of your kinsmen?"

"I fear you'll be cheated," she said slowly, "if you think to hold me for a ransom. I've no means, and no kinsmen to stand the loss for me."

"You were riding to Inveraray to visit Campbell of Glenurchy. I hear his purse is a heavy one."

Elspeth did not answer. Duncan might hold a heavy purse, but she could not swear he would part with it for her safety. Her mother's close kinsman, yet Elspeth had not set eyes on him for many years; and affection dies easily, like a candle flame, with naught to keep it alive.

"And my lord Argyll?" the MacHugh asked casually.

She examined his words, but there was no fear in them—only an indifferent, careless arrogance. "He'd not part with a pound Scots," she said then. "I've no such great value for him."

Across the fire the black pupils of his eyes glittered like steel points. "Your guardian, mistress? And you a lass with half the men in London clamoring for your hand?" His warm voice was slightly mocking, warning her that he was merely jesting, that he had no intention of asking a ransom in return for her safety.

"You seem to know a great deal about me," she said, curious. "Argyll intends to have me wed at his convenience once I've returned to London, but I scarce thought it would interest anyone but myself."

" 'Tis a Campbell habit," the MacHugh said, "to use a pretty lass to their gain." He was silent for a moment, toying with his dirk; then he looked up at her and said quietly, "I know of one man who would give his last shilling to ransom you. Have you not thought of Robert Lamond of Rathmor?"

She was shivering again; the wind whistled among the rocks and tossed her wet hair about her face, and the sound of the rain in the wet heather was like a faint weeping.

"You are mistaken, sir," she said. "I have never seen my father, nor he me. I doubt he would care greatly for my welfare."

She was aware that Gavin gave her a quick scrutiny as she spoke, but the MacHugh seemed to expect the miserable thing she had been forced to say.

"Did you not think to see him while you were in Scotland?" He seemed to weigh his words carefully. "His castle of Rathmor lies on Loch Awe, only a short ride from Inveraray."

"I hoped to see him," she admitted, and wanted to curse her voice for being less steady than it was wont to be. Faith, it was her reason for being in Scotland; it was the solemn promise given to her mother, and yet she knew a quick shame that she must admit to a stranger that in all her twenty years she had not once seen her own father.

The MacHugh stood up. "Then you'll not be dismayed if we pay him a visit. See to the fire, Gavin, and call the lads."

Elspeth stared at him. "You jest, sir," she said faintly.

" 'Tis not a lengthy ride," he replied, "and you've a half sister at the end of it who might rub you with ointment to take away the worst of the aches. I'll wager the Lamonds can take as tender care of you as the Campbells at Inveraray."

Her plaid was sodden now, so he put his own cloak about her and lifted her to the saddle. She watched him swing easily to the stallion's back and remembered that she had thought earlier she could not possibly ride another mile. But she kept her hands light on the reins and allowed her horse to follow the stallion's lead.

Faster and faster they rode, across the moorland and through the wet woods, the hills black above them and the troop of MacHughs clattering behind with a sound like thunder on the earth. The rain stung her face and her body felt cramped with aches, and beside her rode the most ill-bred, uncouth and insolent Scot she had ever encountered.

But it was oddly exciting to be free and away, riding like the wind, and she must confess to the strange and inexplicable truth that she had not been frightened for some hours past.

2

THE night came down early, and with it the rain ceased. The mists rolled down from the peaks to smother the earth in a silent, ghostly blanket of fog.

Elspeth sat her horse wearily before the gates of Castle Rathmor as the MacHughs set up a deafening clamor to announce their arrival. Beside her Alexander MacHugh was silent, watching her, but she was scarcely conscious of his presence.

I was born in that pile of stones, she thought, and her eyes lifted to the massive walls rising steeply above her. The fretted battlements disappeared high in the fog; the walls were broken by only a few unfriendly window slits, and the towers guarding the gates scowled bleakly down on her, branding her an enemy, an intruder on the ancient land of Lamond. There was nothing about the castle that was not stark and forbidding, set down by the somber loch with an air as inhospitable and threatening as the hills which ringed it about.

Within it were her father and half sister, both strangers to her, and mayhap more than one Lamond who had known her mother during that long-ago year of handfast. The brief union of Robert Lamond and Louise Campbell had begun and ended in this formidable castle, and now the daughter born to them had come back to stir old memories and open old wounds.

"Take heart," the MacHugh said abruptly. "They'll not eat you alive."

Elspeth watched the iron portcullis as it lifted slowly above the carved arch of the gate. "I did not imagine it would be like this," she said at last.

His dark face was impassive. "Does it matter so much?"

She lifted her chin, determined that he should not guess at the fearful anticipation touching her. "Do you think they'll be pleased with you for bringing me here in such a fashion?" she asked coolly.

"They've known me for a long time," he said, and she saw the white flash of his grin. "Not that I often bring back a lass from a raid, but they'll welcome you all the same."

Elspeth rubbed the back of her hand against her face to remove a bit of caked mud. She did not look at him again. He exasperated her to a furious resentment and came near to making her anger boil over, but she could not fathom the tears so close behind her eyes, nor understand why she was suddenly so unsure of herself.

"You're not doing it properly," he said, and moved his horse toward her. Before she could duck her head he had taken her chin in his gloved hand. Pulling a fine linen square from inside his jack, he went about cleaning her face as though she were a child facing his inspection. "You look like a street urchin," he said cheerfully. "Jean will never believe you've come straight from Anne's court. Has no one ever taught you to go visiting with a clean face?"

She raised her arm and threw aside his hand, but he only laughed and spurred his horse ahead, leaving her to clatter along at his heels. She suspected he had put her in a rage for a purpose: the tears were gone, and the uncertainty. But she cared little why he had done it; it was enough to ride through the passageway to the inner court with a certain angry pride that her seat was as good and her head as high as when she left Duncraig that morning.

She caused little stir in Rathmor. The guardrooms on either side of the passageway through the keep were filled with clansmen at the evening meal, but the MacHughs were evidently such frequent visitors that their arrival caused no disturbance. When she reached the courtyard only one rude Lamond noticed anything amiss; he held Alexander MacHugh's horse and stared openly at Elspeth, his mouth agape.

"Keep your eyes to yourself, lad," the MacHugh said curtly, and the fellow dropped his eyes hastily. "Gavin, come along with the lass. I'll go ahead and give Robert a warning."

He stuffed his gloves in the wide cuff of his boots and ran up the stairs leading to the upper apartments. Elspeth dismounted, every inch of her protesting the misery of moving, and felt an irrational resentment that the MacHugh was so unwearied.

"Can you make the stairs?" Gavin asked at her shoulder. She turned, an angry retort on her lips, but his blue eyes were warmer than before and he was making no attempt to hide his own strain. "We might lean on each other," he suggested. "If I were a better man I'd carry you up, but I'm not so gallant that I can't see where it would end. We'd both go sprawling, and I doubt I could get up again."

She found herself almost liking him. They climbed slowly up the steps, Gavin's hand beneath her arm to steady her, and she decided he was truly not so much a villain as she had first thought.

He paused before a tall door, heavily carved and studded with brass. "This is it," he said. He stood aside, waiting for her to enter.

Elspeth drew a deep breath. "Are you coming with me?" she asked. There was no sound from behind the closed door, no sound from the courtyard below. Only the fierce pounding of her heart filled her ears like the roll of drums, until she was certain Gavin could hear it in the silence.

"Aye," he said slowly. "I don't imagine Alex intended me to leave you alone." He reached for the door and pushed it open, then stepped back. "Go along, mistress," he said, looking as if he might give her a small push.

The room was in near darkness. She walked only a few steps, then paused until her eyes could grow accustomed to the dim light. Candles guttered fitfully in sconces above the enormous fireplace; the fire had died to a bed of coals and black shadows stretched from the far corners of the room to meet across the stone floor. She saw the MacHugh standing before the hearth, a boot propped carelessly against a smoldering log, his wide shoulders turned away from her. He was offering her no comfort or assistance, and she finally looked from him to the man advancing slowly toward her across the interminable length of the room.

He was tall and gaunt, with a face as bleak as granite. That only could she see; the meager candle-light was behind him, shining in her face, and surely it was only a trick of the light that gave him the appearance of towering above her like a dark shadow cast by the dying fire.

He stopped only a few short feet away and stood looking at her silently. The MacHugh's great cloak trailed on the floor about her, almost swallowing her in its folds. She felt like a waif with her torn and muddy habit, her wet tangled hair, her eyes so wide and straight on his that he must be able to see her very soul through them.

"So you are Elspeth," he said at last in a clipped voice quite devoid of any emotion. "Welcome to Rathmor."

She did not dare curtsy for fear she would be unable to rise from her knees again. Instead she lifted her chin higher and clenched her hands beneath the cloak to give her added courage. "Your kindness overwhelms me, sir," she said. "And do I have you to thank for the indignities I've suffered today at the hands of your friends?" She could not be certain, but she thought he smiled faintly.

"Indignities?" he asked. "I'll not make Alexander's apologies for him."

Elspeth shrugged the cloak from her shoulders and let it lie on the floor where it fell. "I would like an ewer of hot water," she said clearly, "and a change of clothes. Then, if you'll be so kind as to furnish me a quill and paper, I'll send word to Duncan Campbell to come and fetch me to Inveraray."

The room was silent. A log fell in the fireplace, perhaps under the MacHugh's impatient boot, and the candles sputtered in the chilly drafts which swept the floor and walls. Behind her Gavin might not have existed, so still and quiet did he hold himself.

"You shall have all those things presently," her father said, as cool and abrupt as before. "Now come away to the fire and let me have a proper look at you. Gavin, see to more candles. It's dark as a tomb." He took Elspeth by the arm and led her across the room. "The last time you were at Rathmor," he said, "I was told you were as red and wrinkled a bairn as these old walls had seen. Have you changed much in twenty years, lass?"

A cold weight settled in her heart. She wondered if she would ever be able to part with a bairn of her own, however ugly and wrinkled and red in the face from squalling.

The MacHugh turned and looked down at her as she reached the hearth. He had removed his helmet and his dark hair was rumpled; he looked as though he were enjoying the situation. "You make a good pair," he said lightly. "I'd have known you for a Lamond, mistress, had I met you halfway across the world."

His words came as a distinct shock. It was the first time in her memory that anyone had considered her as other than a Campbell, despite her mother's stubborn indiscretion in naming her Elspeth Lamond. In London it was the Campbell name that made her acceptable at court; it was Campbell gold that fed and clothed her; it was the power of Argyll that would see her properly wed. She had not once thought of herself, as she did now, standing in Rathmor Castle, as a Lamond.

Gavin lighted more candles about the room, and Elspeth faced her father. His eyes were blue like her own, she saw, and his blunt features might indeed have been carved from Grampian stone. He was not a handsome man, nor could he ever have been considered so; there was something too hard and compelling, too bitter about the lines of his mouth and the square shape of his jaw. But despite his gauntness he was a big man, with heavy shoulders and powerful arms, and he carried himself well.

She wished she could know what he thought of her, but there was no sign in his face. He narrowed his eyes and held his head to one side, as though to appraise her better; then, suddenly, he put out his hand and touched her hair. "You've had the fever," he said.

His touch, so unexpectedly gentle, almost undid her. "My mother died with the fever," she said quietly, for she did not know if he had learned the news.

"Aye," he said, "I know." His voice, again cold and indifferent, was like a door slammed in her face. He went to a table and filled a silver goblet with wine from a tall Venetian-glass bottle. "Drink it," he ordered, handing it to Elspeth. "You're paler than I like to see a lass." He motioned to Gavin, standing silently in the shadows. "Jeannie is below in the kitchens, Gavin. Will you ask her to see to an apartment for our guest?"

Elspeth did not drink the wine. She held the cold goblet between her hands, and the chill moved from her fingers to her blood and so to her heart. There were no tears in her, only a vast disappointment and a despair as clear and sharp as the Rhenish wine.

Her father leaned against the table and regarded her with his level gaze. "And what brings you to Scotland?" he asked.

She looked him in the eye and knew she could not bring herself to tell him. "I came to visit my Campbell kinsmen," she said slowly. "I am to be wed soon, and I thought it best to travel before the wedding preparations began."

He did not seem interested enough to ask the name of her prospective husband. Of course she herself did not know yet, for Argyll had not come to a decision, but she had expected her father to show her the usual courtesy of inquiring.

But he said only, "I hear Argyll has been appointed Lord Lieutenant of the West. Does he intend to join you at Inveraray?"

"I know of no such plans," she said, surprised. "I doubt the Countess could endure the trip in such beastly weather." She added without thinking, "And she'd never let him from her sight to travel alone."

Alexander MacHugh laughed, and Elspeth looked at him. "But the King might order him to Scotland," she said casually. "James is weary of the eternal bickering of his Scots nobles. Some say he will give Argyll letters of fire and sword against some of his more rebellious subjects."

His response disappointed her. He rested his shoulders against the fireplace jamb and crossed his boots, laughter still flickering in his eyes.

"Have you the King's confidence, mistress, or do you quote a bit of court gossip?" The MacHugh grinned at her. "Jamie's rebellious subjects are a long way from London."

She looked at his wide shoulders and the proud arrogance of his dark head, and London and King James did indeed seem infinitely distant.

"Do you give him so little respect, sir?" she asked, ignoring the unbidden comparison in her mind between this man and the cowardly James Stuart. "Surely a king deserves obedience from the most distant subject."

"I've respect enough for a king," the MacHugh said briefly. "As for obedience and deserving it, that's another matter."

Robert Lamond chuckled unexpectedly, and his hard face seemed less austere. "It's plain she's been taught to despise rebels, Alex," he said, "and you're being served notice to mind your manners henceforth."

"He has no manners to mind," Elspeth said. "I learned that much today, if nothing else." She added coolly, "I'll not soon forget the fright I received at your hands, sir."

"You didn't appear frightened when I first saw you," said the MacHugh. "If I remember rightly, you took me to task for letting you stand too long in the rain."

She was spared the necessity of finding a caustic reply. The door swung open behind her, letting in a cold draft of air that set the fire to flaming briefly. Alexander looked over her head and smiled, and Elspeth turned slowly around.

Her half sister Jean was tall and slim, with dark hair like a cloud about her head. She stood on the threshold with a startled look about her, as if she might take fright and flee at the slightest provocation; and the wide skirts with the neat chain of household keys reaching almost to the floor seemed no more than part of a game of make-believe, so young and uncertain she seemed.

"I've made a room ready," she said breathlessly, and her grave eyes came to rest on Elspeth and remained fixed there, incredulous and amazed.

"Jeannie," her father said, "your sister from London, Elspeth Lamond."

The girl curtsied, her skirts like the faded petals of a flower against the old gray stones of the floor. Elspeth handed the goblet to her father and turned toward the door, but his cool voice gave her pause. "I see you don't care for wine," he said idly.

"I don't care for orders," she answered in kind, and lifted her muddied skirts with dignity and walked to the door.

Jean Lamond led her down a long corridor to another door, and they climbed a narrow, winding staircase cut inside the walls of a tower. A fresh wind was rising without, and the candle in Jean's hand gave an uneasy light; they seemed to be climbing higher than the battlements, so steep and endless were the stairs.

I am a prisoner at Rathmor, Elspeth thought. A

Campbell in the stronghold of the Lamonds, like her
mother before her; and her companions were a banter-
ing, ungentle stranger who had forced her to his will,
and a hostile father who cared nothing for her, and a
half sister too shy or frightened to speak. She must keep
her wits about her, and her courage, and show them
she would not be intimidated.

But she found she was too weary now to care about
any of it.

2

Robert Lamond clasped his hands together and
stared into the fire. "God's love, Alex, she's a comely
lass," he said. "I've had frequent word of her from
friends in London, but they neglected to mention she'd
grown so devilishly fair." He added, the words deep
and harsh in his throat, "Like her mother, with a bit of
red in her hair."

"And a temper to match," said the MacHugh. He
sat on the high-backed settle and stretched his long legs
out before him. "I've an uncommon thirst, Robert.
Hand me the wine." He emptied the goblet, throwing
back his head to feel the cool liquid wetting his throat.
Then he said evenly, "You were hard on her, after the
punishment she's taken today."

"Aye," said Lamond, "I intended to be." His smile
had something of pride in it. "She stands up well to
punishment, I'd say."

"More Lamond than Campbell," Alex said, amused.
"Why do you think she's come to Scotland?"

Lamond's face grew intent. "I'd wager my life she
lied about that," he said softly. "You did right to bring
her to Rathmor, Alex. We'll find out the truth soon
enough."

The MacHugh turned the silver goblet in his hands.
"It smells too much of Argyll to please me," he said
shortly.

Lamond nodded. "I've been waiting," he said softly. "The lass stands high in favor with the Queen, with excellent prospects for a wealthy marriage. But I know Argyll too well. He'd not rest content with a marriage contract unless he can skewer me with the same turning of the knife."

The MacHugh looked thoughtful. "You'll be in a damned awkward spot, Robert," he said, "if he persuades the King to proclaim the lass your lawful heir."

" 'Tis lawful enough, without Jamie's approval," Lamond said, shrugging. "A child born from handfast is as legitimate as any, Alex; you're aware of that. God knows there's been enough bloodshed in Scotland over the question."

Alexander whistled soundlessly, his eyes on the fire. "Do you think she knows?"

The room was silent. Lamond's brows drew sharply together in a scowl as he pondered the question; one powerful hand closed into a fist.

"What odds?" he asked at last, bitterly. "The harm will be done, regardless."

"The damned whoreson," the MacHugh said quietly, "using a lass when he's too cowardly to face a man over steel."

Lamond moved from the table to the fireplace; his foot struck a log and the sparks scattered across the hearth. Then he faced the MacHugh, a half-smile on his face. "Well now, he'll have steel enough behind him now he's the King's Lieutenant. I'll make a wager with you, lad. Who'll be first on his list?"

Alexander grinned. "Not you, Robert. I hear the man is so overburdened with debt that Glenurchy has taken residence at Inveraray to tend to the Earl's affairs and feed his retainers there." He crossed his boots and put his thumbs in his belt. "He'll go after bigger game first and attempt to persuade a bit of royal gold from Jamie Stuart."

Lamond regarded the MacHugh with narrowed eyes. "MacDonald is safely trussed in Edinburgh Castle. He'll not be first."

"He's busy plotting devious ways to torment Argyll," Alexander said promptly. "Don't trust him to wait politely in the castle for Argyll to come down from London and put the noose about his neck."

Lamond said coolly, "The man's a fool."

"He's been six years in prison," Alexander said quietly, "on Argyll's false charge of treachery. D'you blame him for preferring to choose his own end?"

"I dislike to see you drawn into that miserable affair," said Lamond.

"MacDonald or Lamonds," Alexander said lightly, "I'll be drawn into it whether I like it or no'. Would you have the Campbell banner over all western Scotland?"

"I'm well aware Argyll intends to fly it over all Lamond holdings under his eye," Lamond remarked, "but you might keep yourself safer if you'll hold your temper and forbear from baiting the Campbells at every turn." He added gravely, "How many choice mares did you drive away from Inveraray last evening?"

"Enough to replenish my stables for a good while," Alexander said cheerfully. "God's foot, Argyll has a sharp eye for a horse." He stood up, stretching hugely. "Keep myself safe, Robert? You make a noise like an old woman."

Lamond sighed. "Take care you keep out of Glenurchy's hands," he warned, "when he discovers you made off with the lass."

"Aye," said the MacHugh, his swift grin flashing out again. "I think I'd best pay him a call. He'll hear the news soon enough from that pompous ass commanding Duncraig, and there'll be the devil's own mischief."

"And a great cursing of MacHughs," Lamond said causticly. "I wouldn't do it, Alex. Stay away from Inveraray."

The MacHugh shrugged into his cloak. "Only a gesture of courtesy, Robert," he said amiably, "to let the man know his fair kinswoman has arrived safely at

Rathmor. By my own escort," he added. "And surely even a Campbell will recognize gallantry when it's brought to his attention."

"I give you up," Lamond said, exasperated. "You'll try Glenurchy's good nature once too often and find yourself in Edinburgh Castle with James MacDonald."

But he knew the MacHugh too well not to perceive the serious resolve underlying the careless banter. The young stallion might be as hotheaded and impetuous as any Scot, but he tempered it with a steady nerve and a cool wit that had no equal in the Highlands. If they would keep the lass at Rathmor, Glenurchy must be appeased; and the ancient clan tactics, to attack by surprise and withdraw to lead the enemy into a trap of one's own choosing, were yet sound enough to be of good service.

"I'll watch the lass closely until I learn what she knows," Lamond said finally. "The longer we can detain her here, the safer our plans."

Alexander paused at the door. "Aye, Robert, you'd best keep a fatherly eye on her," he said over his shoulder. "I give you fair warning, I've discovered a far more interesting reason for detaining her at Rathmor."

The door slammed behind him and his spurs clattered on the stone stairway leading to the courtyard. Robert Lamond sat thoughtfully for a moment; then he threw back his head and laughed.

3

Elspeth stretched her feet into the depths of the enormous feather mattress and withdrew them immediately. The fine holland linen was bitter cold to the touch, and the small fire burning briskly on the hearth across the room did not warm the drafts blowing like gales about the room. She had bathed in a great wooden tub by the fire, but the steaming water had cooled before she had well begun; neither the Turkish rugs, nor the tapestry hangings, nor the walls eight feet thick could keep the Scots chill outside.

The door opened quietly and Jean Lamond slipped into the room, carrying a silver warming pan in each hand. "You should have waited," she said reproachfully. "The beds are always cold until I've heated them properly."

Elspeth got out of bed again, putting about her shoulders a velvet robe Jean had left on the clothespress, and went to stand before the fire. "I was afraid I might collapse before you returned," she said wearily. Her teeth chattered and she hugged her arms around her. "God's love, it's small wonder you Scots are so dour. Do you ever get the chill from your bones?"

Jean tucked the warming pans beneath the vast mound of bedclothes. "We keep this chamber in readiness for Alex," she said shyly, "but he seldom makes use of it. There's been no fire here for weeks."

Elspeth looked about her with new interest. It was not difficult to picture Alexander MacHugh sleeping there, his broad shoulders taking up most of the bed, his helmet with its eagle wing tossed carelessly on the oaken press, his black cloak trailing over the damask stool.

"Does he come to Rathmor often?" she asked casually.

"Aye," said Jean. "He rides in, then he's off again. I've never known him to stay in one place for long at a time."

"Does he live close by, then?" Elspeth asked, and immediately wished she had not.

"His castle of Ardoon lies above us on the loch, but at present he makes residence at Fraoch Eilean." Jean gave Elspeth a grave look out of the dark eyes, flecked now with gold in the firelight. " 'Tis only a stone's throw from Inveraray."

"I shouldn't think he would care for that," Elspeth said candidly.

Jean smiled. "No," she said, "none of us care excessively for the Campbells." She added hastily, "Alex has promised Fraoch Eilean to Simon as a wedding gift. If you're still in Scotland by summer, perhaps we'll be neighbors."

She is too grave, Elspeth thought, too grave and quiet for so young a lass. "And who is Simon?" she asked gently.

"He is Alexander's next brother," Jean said, surprised. "Gavin is the youngest of the three."

It was Elspeth's turn to be surprised; she had not dreamed Gavin and Alexander MacHugh were brothers. "Is Simon your betrothed?" she asked.

Jean's pale heart-shaped face turned oddly radiant. "Aye," she said softly. "Perhaps you knew him in London. James held him in great esteem there, even honoring him as a page when he was a lad."

Elspeth shook her head. "I knew no MacHugh at court," she said. "But I was with the Princess Elizabeth until she was wed and we were not often at Whitehall." She thought that Simon MacHugh must be a handsome devil; it was no secret that Jamie Stuart favored good looks about him more than brains. And he'd be more politic and well mannered than his brother the Chief, she'd warrant, else he'd have been banished from court the same hour he arrived.

"He must be very unlike Alexander," she said without thinking.

"Was Alex very unpleasant?" Jean asked quietly. "Do you hate him for treating you so rudely?"

They looked at each other. "It was unpleasant to be carried off like a tavern wench," Elspeth said at last. Then she smiled ruefully. "But I confess I wasn't ill-used, except for the bruises I acquired on that mad ride from Duncraig." She rubbed the offending spots and grimaced. "Faith, I'm unused to such sport."

Jean's face broke into laughter. "He'll not let you hold a grudge," she said. "He has a way about him, you'll see."

She tilted her head suddenly, and in the silence

Elspeth could hear a great clatter of horses below her
window. Closer, the portcullis strained and creaked,
giving evidence that her bedchamber was in one of the
towers overlooking the gates.

"They're leaving," Jean said, her voice quickening.
"Come away, we'll watch them ride out!" She dragged
a chest across the floor and climbed up to the narrow
window high in the wall, her skirts and petticoats flar-
ing out behind. Elspeth joined her, careless of the cold
casement against her bare arms, forgetting that she
wore nothing but a night smock and a velvet robe.

The wind had torn the fog in rifts and the stars
showed cold and distant in the night sky. Clansmen
stood outside the gates holding huge torches above
their heads; the light fell against Elspeth's window in
great wavering shadows, and caught in the wild Mac-
Hugh tartan like the color of blood.

"Alex sent your luggage to Ardoon until he decided
what should be done with you," said Jean. "He promised to have it returned before day."

Another time Elspeth would have cursed his arrogance, but now her heart pounded and her blood sang
in her ears and she forgot her anger with him. The
pipes were skirling with complete abandon and the
wind snatched at a plaid and held it aloft like a banner; the MacHughs were laughing boisterously, jousting
at one another with rough hands, as if their spirits were
lifted high by the very lilt of the pipes and the cold wind.
The night had come clear and they were riding out
again; and Elspeth, heedless of her fatigue and bruises,
longed absurdly to be with them.

When the men were through the gates, Gavin and
Alexander MacHugh reined their horses and turned.
Looking up at the tower window, the MacHugh grinned
and raised his arm. The stallion chose that moment to
rear his forelegs in a dangerous arc in the air, and
Elspeth was forced to admire the swift and competent
manner in which the MacHugh gentled his horse. She
thought that the man and horse had an identical bear-

ing of latent strength and violence; they moved together in a co-ordination that was beautiful to watch.

The two men wheeled their horses away from the castle, followed by the horsemen behind them, and Elspeth watched the wide leather shoulders of the MacHugh disappear beyond the circle of light. She shivered suddenly, listening as the castle walls held the last echoing hoofbeats; she did not envy the Scots women who spent so much of their lives steeling their hearts against the lonely sound of horses riding away into the darkness.

Silently they climbed down from the chest. Jean went to the bed and removed the long-handled pans, and Elspeth slipped between the warm sheets. She pushed the bolster behind her back and looked at Jean, standing quietly at the foot of the bed.

"I'm part Campbell," Elspeth said suddenly. "Do you dislike me also?"

Jean drew a deep breath. "I've wondered about you all my life," she said, "and yearned to meet you."

"Am I the way you imagined me?" Elspeth asked, curious.

The laughter was very bright in Jean's eyes. "I thought you would be very grand," she said, "and a bit wicked from living so long at court. And Alex once told me that if you ever came to Rathmor you'd hold your nose in the air over our barbaric Scots ways and bore us with tales of London and how you longed to be back there."

Elspeth laughed aloud, delighted. "Did you believe him? Do you take his word for everything?"

"Only when he's serious," Jean said. She placed the warming pans by the fire and returned to blow out the candles on the table beside the bed. "And then," she added, "I always trust his word. As does my father, and Sim and Gavin as well."

"Small wonder he has such a high opinion of himself," Elspeth said. She clasped her hands around her knees. "Is he an important chief?"

Jean nodded. "His clan is an ancient one in the Highlands," she said, "and they give him more respect and devotion than all the royal Stuarts together. Sometimes I think there's a magic in the very sound of his name, the way his men worship him."

"I begin to see," said Elspeth, "that I'd best keep my opinion of him to myself while I'm at Rathmor."

Jean sighed and blew the candles. Then, as the firelight touched the satin quilts with crimson and flickered against the ceiling, she reached out a tentative hand and touched the bed.

"I'm happy it was you who lived," she said breathlessly, as if the darkness had given her only a brief courage to say the words. "When I first heard of the lad who died, I went to the chapel and said thanks that you had been spared." Her voice caught, then steadied. "My father wanted the lad with all his heart, and I think he yet grieves for him. My mother did not give him a son, you see; she died soon after I was born."

Elspeth sat stunned; her heart turned over and ceased beating for an instant, then began to throb unbearably.

"But Rathmor is a lonely place," Jean went on quietly, "with only a great horde of men trampling about. More than anything else in the world, I've wanted a sister."

Elspeth could not find her voice; it was frozen in her throat, an enormous lump choking off her breath. She stared at Jean, and at last her face must have betrayed her shock and bewilderment.

"You didn't know," Jean whispered. Her eyes widened incredulously. "No one has told you about the bairn." She sat on the bed, holding her hands tightly together, her face gone pale. "Elspeth, I beg your forgiveness. I've hurt you by blurting it out so foolishly."

Elspeth said unevenly, "It can't be true. My mother never spoke of another besides myself."

Jean hesitated. Then she said unhappily, "There were two of you born the same night. The boy was the oldest by almost three hours."

"Where did you learn this tale?" Elspeth asked, feeling almost sick from the great thumping of her heart. "Can you swear it for the truth?"

"I bedeviled Ellen Lamond until she told me," said Jean. "She was the midwife for the birthing, and later she stitched the wee gown for the lad's burial. Elspeth, I've no wish to cause you pain. Forget I spoke of it."

Elspeth waited until she could speak calmly. "Do you know how he died?"

"Ellen said she was told he died of lung fever in the winter," Jean said gently. "He lived only a few months after your mother carried you away to Inveraray."

The exhaustion crept through Elspeth's blood until she wanted to cry with weariness. "I've wondered many times why she left," she said dully, "and why my father cared so little that he allowed her to go."

And I blamed him for being coldhearted and insensible, she thought, and never knew until now that it was my mother, my gay and adored Louise, whose heart was so indifferent and craven that she could leave behind a wee bairn of her own blood and body and never once grieve for him.

"I know nothing of that," Jean said. "It was never mentioned before me. I was almost ten before I heard the gossip that my father had been handfast to a Campbell before he met and married my mother. She was a MacLachlan of Cowal, and they were wed in the chapel here at Rathmor." She added contritely, "You are tired, and I've kept you awake with my chattering." She stood up resolutely, hesitating as though she might find some word of comfort. But none came, and she went to the door. "Sleep well, Elspeth, your first night at Rathmor."

Elspeth put her arms behind her head and stared at the shadowy corners of the tall four-posted bed. The fire was dying and the wind beat against the tower with a sound as lonely and wild as the bleak miles of hills and moorland it had blown across.

What fools are women, she thought ruefully, with

their dreams and fanciful whimsies. And I would be the daughter come home from London, and would my father be no longer a stranger, but would forget his hatred and bitterness and ride to Inveraray to drink Scots whiskey with his neighbors the Campbells and speak of matters concerning Scotland and the world. And mayhap one day he would baff his first-born grandchild on his knee and smile at his daughter with affection; and the lost unhappy years would be put away and forgotten.

But old hatreds were not so easily forgotten in this grim land, and bitterness would have been more bearable than the indifference she had seen in her father's face, mocking her, proving that she had no place in his affections, no place at Rathmor Castle.

From a brief handfast she had come, a marriage for a year and a day according to tradition, and if it pleased it became as binding as church law. But it had not pleased. The lady of Rathmor was remembered as a MacLachlan, Jean's mother; and the strange affair of heart between a bonny Campbell and Robert Lamond was long since forgotten and dead, buried like the lad who could not survive the hard Scots winter.

Dreams were frail things, when all was said, and loneliness the only certainty.

⟨ 3 ⟩

"**G**AVIN, you're witless. I'll trap you now." Simon MacHugh studied the chessboard, his head resting on his hands. He was lying on the rugs before the fire in the great hall at Fraoch Eilean; the chessboard with its tiny tallow figures rested between the two men. "That was a stupid move. I thought I'd taught you better."

" 'Tis a stupid game, taking more time than it's worth. I could have ridden to Inveraray and back in the time you've been plotting the move." Gavin stretched lazily and rolled on his back.

Simon hummed tunelessly, concentrating on the board. "You've no patience. God's son, who'd want to ride to Inveraray?" He moved one of the chessmen and settled back, pleased. "Told you I'd trap you."

"You've the brains in the family," said Gavin, yawning. "Keep them and welcome. Alex, where's Keppoch?"

"Stretched across my bed, dead to the world," Alexander said. "He needed a rest after that ride from Edinburgh."

Simon stood up and walked to the window. The sea was a quiet blue in the afternoon sun; below the castle walls the water birds shrilled raucously as they dipped and swirled above the sand. "I thought he was attempting to stay ahead of Campbell of Cawdor," he said carelessly. "He'll lose his advantage if he lingers overlong."

Alexander said briefly, "Cawdor will stop at Inveraray for reinforcements. Don't worry, Keppoch will keep ahead."

"Damn Keppoch! None of my problem if the fool MacDonald thinks to cross Scotland in twenty-four hours." Simon leaned his elbows on the window casement. "I'm only wondering what mischief you're planning for Cawdor. You needn't deny it," he added. "You've been intent at plotting since Keppoch rode in this morning."

"You've the devil's own suspicious nature," Alexander said, grinning.

Simon turned from the window, resting the palms of his hands on the stone behind him. "Jamie MacDonald is languishing in gaol while Campbell of Cawdor makes for Islay to conquer the MacDonalds with two hundred horse and six cannons. He brings his army straight across MacHugh land, with no consideration for your sensitive feelings, and you'd have me believe nothing will come of it." He shrugged. "Don't you wish I were that sort of ass?"

"You'd make less trouble for yourself if you were," Alexander remarked impassively.

Simon's dark face flushed. "Is it because I've been away in London? Do you think I'm of no use to you now?"

By the fire Gavin chuckled. "Only last week you told us you intended to keep the King's favor," he said. "Have you changed your mind so soon?"

"The devil with the King. If you think you're going to have the sport and leave me behind to twiddle my fingers, you'd best think again."

Alexander propped his boot on the table and studied Simon for a moment before he spoke. "I don't think it amiss to challenge a man who takes a small army through my lands," he said. "Either Cawdor loses his temper and we have a fair fight of it, delaying him sufficiently, or else he'll pretend good humor and stop to chat of the weather. Either way he'll be delayed enough for our purposes."

"I'll enjoy seeing Cawdor squirm," said Simon. "But you're allowing them to ride on to Islay? Christ, Jamie MacDonald will scarce appreciate that."

"Keppoch will warn Angus MacDonald of Islay in time to raise a few thousand MacDonalds," Alexander said calmly. "I've no intention of cleaning up their chores for them."

A loud commotion in the courtyard below came clearly through the heavy doors of the hall. Gavin would have risen but Alexander waved him back. "I'll see to it. It might be more word of Cawdor." He walked to the door, putting on his doublet as he went. "Better blacken your face if you're riding with us, Sim," he said, with no trace of a smile. "You don't want the Campbells to know you're being a naughty lad. It might get back to Jamie Stuart."

He slammed the door behind him and Simon walked to the chair he had vacated and dropped in it, sighing. "I hope he knows what he's doing," he said to Gavin. "Keppoch told me the King furnished Cawdor the cannon and soldiers, and offered him all of Islay for the sum of six thousand marks."

"If he can subdue the garrison of Dunyveg," Gavin added laconically.

"The King has chosen sides," Simon said, frowning. "He'll have Alex charged with treason one of these fine days, if he doesn't make his peace with the Campbells."

Gavin looked thoughtful. "Did you know that Argyll himself has been urging Angus MacDonald to raise his banner against the King?"

"It's the usual Campbell policy," Simon said flatly. It was no secret in London that Argyll had a habit of inciting clans to rebellion so that he might then offer the King his services to reduce the unwary clans to obedience; it was no secret to James Stuart, certainly, who saw a certain profit in accepting Campbell aid, even at so high a price, when it kept his troublesome Highland nobles busy fighting one another and out of his way.

"Aye," said Gavin, "and I'd sooner see Alex stand accused of treason than have him make peace with that whoreson of a traitor."

" 'Tis a devilish choice," Simon admitted ruefully. "I don't envy him his position."

"I'd not worry myself about it," Gavin said. He gave Simon an inquiring glance. "Or is it your own neck that feels uncomfortable?"

"Don't be a fool," Simon said impatiently. "He carries a heavy load on his shoulders; I would I could be of some small aid to him."

"He can handle it," Gavin replied briefly. "You'll not find him lying awake nights worrying over it." He rolled over on his side and looked into the fire. "There's no man in Scotland with less to fear than Alex."

Simon looked at the back of Gavin's red head. "You really believe that, don't you?" he asked slowly. "D'you think his head is attached to his shoulders more permanently than yours or mine? God's blood, man, there's a limit to the things any man can accomplish, even Alexander."

"He'd have to go far to find his match," Gavin said flatly.

Simon started to laugh, then thought better of it. "Such brotherly affection," he said. "But stay with him, Gavin. I'd wager you'd even take the point of a sword for him."

"Aye, that I would. Not that I'm likely to see the day when Alex would be in so dire a situation." He added matter-of-factly, " 'Tis a damned secure feeling to be fighting on his right. The only place in the world safer than a man's bed." He corrected himself, grinnig. "By Jesu, 'tis safer, what with wenches the way they are! You know, you'd do worse than to take a few unobserved lessons from Alex."

"Do you speak of his wenches or his sword?" Simon asked. "I'll admit he's in fair practice with both." He said amiably, "You bastard, I'll take a turn with you any time you name, and you may have the choice of weapons. I'll show you who needs lessons."

They heard Alexander's steps as he ran up the stairs; Gavin was on his feet before the door opened. Alexander pushed it closed behind him with his boot; the thud resounded in the room, silent now as his brothers looked at him.

"We'll be riding sooner than we thought," he said to Gavin. "I've given the order, you'd best see to it." He spoke briefly, anger clipping the words. "Ian MacHugh was jumped by a force of Campbells riding from Inveraray to meet Cawdor."

Gavin leaped for the door, grabbing his sword belt and buckling it on as he went. He paused at the door. "Was he alone? Is he done for?"

"A bad shoulder cut, but I think it's high enough to be safe. He had two men with him; one escaped with Ian and the other was left behind, too badly wounded to be moved." Alexander moved toward the turret stairs. "Wear your mail, Gavin," he ordered bluntly. "We'll cut them off before they reach Cawdor, if we make haste."

Simon bounded up the steps behind Alexander. In a few minutes they were both in the hall again, wearing light steel mesh doublets beneath their leather jackets. Alexander checked his long pistols quickly, and thrust them in his belt; he settled his sword on his thigh, after slipping it out of the scabbard a few inches and back again, and attached the sheath of a long-handled dirk to the belt at his right side.

Simon thought briefly of the two hundred hired soldiers behind Campbell of Cawdor, then dismissed the matter from his mind. He followed Alexander down the stone steps to the courtyard.

"Do you think we stand a chance of catching them up?" he asked.

Gavin had brought the stallion Tammie to the foot of the steps; the black forelegs pawed impatiently at the hard dirt. Alexander mounted, then drew on his gauntlets; his face was hard under his helmet. "Aye, we'll catch them," he said grimly. He checked the horsemen gathered behind him; a good three score stood ready and mounted, awaiting orders. "Ian challenged them merely as a precaution. He had no chance to draw back. The entire bastardly company charged him."

Simon mounted. "Showing their ire for those stolen horses?" he asked thoughtfully.

"A fast cattle raid and a deliberate attack are two different matters," Alexander said coldly. He turned in his saddle and made a final survey of his men, noting the angry set of their faces, the emnity blazing in their eyes. Satisfied, he said, "You'll see how we treat a man who draws blood without cause."

He wheeled his horse and cantered through the gates, splashing through the shallow water between the castle and the shore without hesitation. When he reached the track he spurred Tammie to a gallop; like Simon, he thought fleetingly of Cawdor and his force of men, two hundred of them recruited by the King. But he put them from his mind in the more immediate urgency of cutting off the Campbells while they were still in Kinglass. He had no wish to come on them after they had reached the wild pass of Glencroe; even a greatly outnumbered force of men could fight their way backward down the pass, holding until Cawdor could come up at their rear.

They began to climb, the horses slowing on the trail which curved through the glen. The sharp noise of hoofs glancing against the rocky path was mingled with the jingle of stirrups and harness, the harsh ring as targes hit on the steel of sword hilts. The day was growing dark, and the late-afternoon sun was hidden behind the trees.

In a short while Alexander reined in and held up his hand; his men slowed behind him. "We've missed them, lads," he called softly. "They've gone ahead. Fix your targes; we'll have at them from the rear. If you can't overtake a Campbell you'll find yourselves on short rations when you return to Fraoch Eilean." He adjusted his steel-mounted targe on his left arm, as did his men, and drew his sword in readiness.

The distance between the two groups of horses grew steadily shorter; before long Alexander could see the Campbell tartan through the dusk under the trees. They were on a level stretch of ground, rising to a slope at the far end; the Campbells would hope to gain the slope in time, and Alexander spurred Tammie to a last tremendous effort. Gavin and Simon, riding on either side, raised a great shout and plunged ahead, and the Campbells at last turned to make a stand of it.

The horses thudded together in the small space between the hill and the trees. Alexander slashed his sword against that of a horseman directly before him; his blade was locked momentarily and he gave a hard shove and saw the man go over, his horse scrambling to escape the maddened hoofs of the stallion. He heard the Campbell slogan yelled above the melee and added a lusty shout to the confusion, "A MacHugh!", and the cry was taken up all around him.

Swinging his light sword to the right, he met a blade which cut dangerously close, ripping through his leather jack and glancing against the steel mesh doublet. The swords grated together, then Alexander pulled his arm back abruptly and swung with all the power behind his arm. The Campbell sword clattered to the ground; Alexander thrust the point of his sword, meeting the flesh below the mail covering the man's chest. He pulled it free, reining Tammie around the riderless horse, and met straightway the murderous blows of two Campbells before him.

Gavin moved closer, shouting, "Don't be greedy with them!" and engaged one of the Campbells with a swift series of blows made even more dangerous by the press of horses. The shouting, the wild whinnying of the horses, the metallic clash of swords against steel targes, set up so splitting a hubbub that Alexander's helmet seemed to reverberate against his head. But he heard the dissonant shriek of pipes beyond the sloping hill; it was more of an intuitive sense, for he could not be certain he had heard anything above the great noise in the small space of the glen.

He raised his voice in a deafening shout, pulling the stallion backward from the crush of horses, and gave a final swing to disarm the opponent directly before him.

"Back to the trees!" he yelled, and Gavin echoed the cry. The MacHughs backed slowly; the men to the rear wheeled their horses and spurred to the cover of the woods behind them. The Campbells, having the worst of matters, were quick to sense the change of action; they turned and urged their mounts up the slope of the hill.

Gavin prodded them forward with a wild shout of triumph, brandishing his sword above his head before he reined and turned his horse. In a moment he was under the trees, protected by the near darkness of the twilight. He stopped by Alexander, breathing hard, and wiped his sword clean on his breeks.

"Before God, we were having the best of them! What caused you to pull back?"

"Keep quiet!" Alexander ordered bluntly. In the sudden silence beneath the trees the strident tones of the distant pipes were clearly heard; they sounded on the windless evening as if they were no farther than just beyond the nearest hill.

"Christ's blood," Simon said. "Campbell of Cawdor!"

"Half a league away," Gavin said, low.

"Get back to the edge of the trees," Alexander ordered Simon. "If I give the word, ride like the devil for Fraoch Eilean." He indicated the men closest to him. "A fair dozen of you line up behind me. We'll wait and see what Cawdor has to say."

They waited just within the shelter of the trees, facing the clearing. The pipes ceased abruptly; the Campbells had reached Cawdor.

Gavin slipped from his saddle and tightened a girth; when he had mounted again, he said softly, "Didn't Keppoch say Cawdor was a good twelve hours behind him?"

"He could have made fair time if he felt the need for haste," the MacHugh said absently, his head held to one side as he listened. Two Campbells had been left behind; their bloodied plaids made bright splotches of color in the fading dusk of the glen. Alexander heard the men behind him shift restlessly in their saddles; there was a muffled cough, the jingling of a harness, both silenced abruptly.

"There's only a small number," said Gavin suddenly. The sound of cautiously advancing horses came muted and distant, distorted by the rise of ground between. "No more than a score," he whispered, and Alexander nodded, pleased. "I'll wager the greater part of them are still struggling through Glencroe."

A single horse moved a short way down the hill, sending a loose stone bounding to the bottom. It had grown too dark for them to see either the horse or its rider; there was complete silence beneath the trees.

"Give a light, MacHugh," a voice snarled, "and show yourself!"

Alexander grinned in the darkness; it was Cawdor himself, angry enough to bite steel.

"Give your own light," he replied lazily from the trees. "It'd be wise to make yourself known, sir. 'Tis a dark evening for a stranger to be riding through Kinglass."

There was silence again; Cawdor's horse moved uncertainly on the slope and was pulled up immediately. "You're known to me," Cawdor said, "and that suffices." His voice thinned with anger. "You'll have no need of my name when I've finished with you."

"Are you a Campbell then?" Alexander asked blandly. "If you seek revenge for those two cold Campbells lying yonder, you'd best pause and consider their fate."

He laughed shortly. "We care little for ambush, stranger."

Campbell of Cawdor did not answer immediately. He was undoubtedly weighing the truth in the Mac-Hugh's words, for he could not deny the Highland code of reprisal when a clan was attacked without due cause.

"I am John Campbell of Cawdor," he said finally. He hesitated, then raised his voice stubbornly. "You've got yourself more than you bargained for, MacHugh. If you don't show yourself we'll surround you."

Alexander laughed again. "You needn't profess to have an army with you, Cawdor. I've still the use of my ears."

Cawdor moved his horse slowly down the hill, followed by the men behind him, and paused at the bottom of the slope.

"Are you weak-livered, hiding behind trees in fear of your life?" Cawdor jeered. "Show yourself; I'll hold back my men."

"There's no need of restraint," said Alexander, amused. "Light a torch, Cawdor, and your men will see what they're facing."

Cawdor cursed in the darkness. After a whispered consultation a torch was lighted, and Cawdor saw the glinting of steel beneath the trees.

"I'll take you singly," he said flatly, his mouth hard with rage. "It'd please me to wipe some of that insolence from your face." He dismounted; his men moved up in a half circle about him.

"Well, I've no objection to taking a turn with you," Alexander said pleasantly. "The first to draw blood?" he asked lightly, and added, "I'd not like to send you back to Edinburgh over your saddle."

Gavin dismounted and took Tammie's reins; Alexander slid from the saddle, moving his arms to loosen the muscles. He drew his sword and tested the balance; the torch caught the sharp flash of the blade as he held the point lightly, then released it. Neither the Mac-

Hughs nor the Campbells dismounted; they faced one another warily, forming a circle with their horses.

Cawdor removed his jacket. He wore heavier mail than the MacHugh, but his sleeves were of leather and he wore no guards on his arms.

"Aye, first blood," he said shortly. "If it should prove to be your last, you'll have no quarrel with it."

Gavin took Alexander's jack and tried unsuccessfully to hide a grin. Alexander backed a few paces, then halted; the two men faced each other across a space of only a few feet, and the horsemen moved back to give them room.

Alexander studied his opponent indifferently, meanwhile loosening his dirk from its leather sheath and gripping it firmly with his left hand. Cawdor was short and stocky, and heavier than was wise; his reach would not be troublesome. He held a light sword with a curved basket hilt, as did the MacHugh, and there would be no great difference in the length of the blades. Cawdor's only immediate advantage was his savage ire, but that would prove to be a hindrance once his arm began to tire.

Alexander watched Cawdor's narrowed eyes, and so he was expecting the first deep lunge and parried it neatly. Cawdor followed with a quick feint to the left and then came up under Alexander's blade; the steel grated uneasily until Alexander freed his blade, engaging Cawdor with a swift exchange of thrusts which drove him back a few steps. They moved slowly about the circle, the clear ring of steel against steel echoing in the silence. Alexander was content to leave Cawdor the aggressor; he allowed him to force the pace in a furious attempt to end the matter quickly. The MacHugh sidestepped and parried, using his dirk adroitly, greeting each manuever as it came with an easy negligence born of long and expert training.

Cawdor's anger grew rather than diminished; he finally saw the MacHugh's purpose and slowed himself, but he was already winded. His lack of training betrayed itself in his too-rapid breathing, in the sudden sweat on his forehead; he was inexorably giving ground before the unhurried skill of the MacHugh's sword. The Campbells who watched moved uneasily in their saddles; Gavin's grin grew wider.

Then the MacHugh quickened his pace, driving Cawdor almost to the line of horses behind him. He drove his blade suddenly, feeling it slide along Cawdor's arm before it was countered, but he did not make the disastrous mistake of hesitating, if he had touched the skin the men would set up a shout at the first sight of blood. He withdrew his blade with a jerk, cutting with a final, powerful thrust against Cawdor's sword; and the weapon slipped, hitting the ground point first and then clattering against the rocks until it came to a halt at Gavin's feet.

Cawdor stood motionless, his eyes on the MacHugh, and involuntarily his hand moved to his arm. It came away red and wet, and Cawdor's eyes narrowed in rage so burning that he could scarcely speak.

"First blood?" he asked, low. He stared at the small point of the MacHugh's sword before his eyes.

The MacHugh said caustically, "You hoped to run me through before that scratch was discovered." A displeased murmur ran through the men behind him. "Don't cower, Cawdor, I'll not skewer you. I've a more generous nature than yourself." He ran the fine point of his sword across Cawdor's cheek, leaving a thin red line without breaking the skin. "Take care a MacDonald doesn't do the job for me."

He leisurely sheathed his sword and dirk and mounted his horse. Cawdor did not move; his face was a study of violent and conflicting emotions.

"You'll hear from this," he said slowly. "Glenurchy will take it ill that you've murdered two of his men."

The MacHugh laughed contemptuously from his saddle. "Glenurchy may address his grievances to me, Cawdor," he said. "I await his pleasure."

He wheeled his horse and cantered through the darkness, Gavin close behind him, and the men waiting at the far edge of the woods drew in behind them. When they had covered almost a league the MacHugh halted, waiting for the men to come up around him.

"How did we fare?" he asked Simon.

"A few scratches. Nothing serious, except an increase in the size of your head." Simon added affably, "Damn you, you'll outgrow your helmet."

Alexander laughed. "I warned you before you came." He looked around him at the pleased MacHughs. "Robert Lamond promised a good hunt at Rathmor, lads. Which shall it be, bed or Rathmor?"

Gavin slapped his leg with his gloves. "We were cheated once tonight, Alex, when you called a halt to the sport. Let's ride for Rathmor."

The men agreed eagerly; once out in the night it was less troublesome to ride on than to return for a few hours' sleep at Fraoch Eilean. They spurred their horses behind their Chief, beginning to sing among themselves at the success of the raid. Simon pulled even with Alexander and pushed his helmet back on his head to ease the strain of the leather straps under his chin.

"Cawdor was never fond of you, brother," he said. "After tonight he'll be hot at Glenurchy to burn you out of Argyllshire." He added reflectively, "And I don't think Glenurchy believed your little tale about the fair Elspeth."

Alexander shrugged. "Duncan and I have an agreement of sorts," he said. "We take each other's lies with good grace."

It was true enough that Glenurchy's Campbells did not cherish so bitter an enmity toward the MacHughs and Lamonds as did Argyll, and the MacHugh had long recognized Glenurchy's tolerant hand in that pleasant state of affairs. The man practiced his skill at planting fields and rebuilding castles and left the harsher art of clan warfare to others; it was a truce between Glenurchy and the rest of Scotland, and if it seemed an uneasy peace that might not last beyond the morrow, stretched thin as it were on occasion, it was yet to be preferred to the more devious schemes of the Earl of Argyll.

"I trust he'll take two dead Campbell's with the same grace," Simon said drily.

By his side, Gavin snorted. "He'll be grateful for only two."

"Aye," said Alexander, "this affair was none of Glenurchy's. He has little control over Argyll's men, else they'd never have jumped Ian MacHugh." He reached over to give Simon a hearty slap on the shoulders. "You and Robert may put your heads together," he said fondly, "and bleat and blither over my sins. But in God's name, leave me free to enjoy them."

He half stood in his stirrups and called to his MacHughs, laughing, "Come away, lads, let's make a ride of it," and put his spurs to the stallion. His men were accustomed to riding hard; they needed no light to follow Tammie's lead, and their rough Highland horses had been trained to move easily over the most treacherous ground.

The MacHugh could ask no more of life. He had a good horse beneath him, the feel of his sword against his thigh, the scent of a wild, sweet Highland night in his nostrils. It was part of his inheritance, that unreasonable and reckless pulsing of blood; and if it was a simple emotion, it was still free and unashamed, alive with the same passion which had touched centuries of Highland men before him.

It was enough for a man, for the moment. And at the end of the night's riding, the impudent lass from London waited at Rathmor Castle.

{ 4 }

IN the small family room beyond the great hall, Elspeth stood before the fire and considered the vast discomfort of rising before dawn on a cold winter's day. She thought with regret of her warm bed above its silken quilts, and wished devoutly that the Mac-Hughs had seen fit to hunt their stags elsewhere.

There were voices outside the door; then it opened and Jean entered, holding a MacHugh by each hand. Elspeth was suddenly pleased that her velvet morning gown would give her some advantage over the Elspeth of the bedraggled habit and muddy face; it was a slight compensation for the dismal hour.

Simon MacHugh stepped forward. "Your servant, madam," he said formally, bowing over her hand.

Elspeth looked at his dark hair and eyes and thought it small wonder he was held in such esteem at court. She was certain she had never seen him; faith, it would be difficult for any woman to forget that handsome face.

"I wonder why we never met in London," he said, smiling, and she gave him a small curtsy.

"I am desolate, sir," she said, "that our paths never crossed."

"But we're not strangers," he replied promptly. "I've heard your name many times in London." His eyes laughed into hers; she'd warrant he cared no more for formalities than his brother Alexander. "You're the lass who was so fond of Will Shakespeare and his comedies," he said easily. "I can recall the King speaking of it."

Elspeth's cheeks grew warm. She well remembered that ill-advised evening when she and the Princess Elizabeth dressed as gallants and persuaded their escorts to take them across the river to Bankside; all would have gone without incident had the Princess not shouldered her way through the crowd with her customary royal haughtiness, quite forgetting her disguise as an unimportant gentleman, and in so doing received a hot-tempered challenge from an angered young blood.

Simon MacHugh said gravely, "I hear you indulged in a bit of fencing now and then. Did it become the fashion for the court ladies?"

She could not help laughing at the memory of that incredible moment when she had attempted to draw the long rapier at her side. It was a desperate matter if they would keep their identity secret, for a man who did not answer an affront was one to be despised in London, and the crowd stood ready to jeer them for cowards. She had been dreadfully clumsy, unused to the feel of a sword in her hand, and only the horrified interference of her escort had saved her from the most ignoble of defeats.

"I fear the King did not look kindly on our small entertainments," she said, hoping Simon would not see fit to tell his brother of that foolish escapade which had shocked all London.

"But you were greatly missed at Whitehall," Simon said. "I was in London at the time and regretted your long absence."

"Only a month," she said defiantly and looked beyond him to Alexander MacHugh. He was standing behind Simon, appraising her steadily with his gray eyes, and she dropped her lashes and curtsied again.

"Your most humble servant, mistress," he said. He bowed his dark head over her hand and for a brief instant her fingers were against his mouth.

"I am well aware of your humility, sir," she said coolly.

He raised his head and smiled lazily at her. It

caught her unawares and put her in no small confusion. Jean had spoken the truth when she said he had a way about him; Elspeth would warrant he'd learned from experience how to use that smile with such devastating effect.

"You look rested since I saw you last," he said. "Have you spent the entire week in bed?"

She noticed that Jean and Simon had moved away, leaving them alone by the fire. "After your courteous escort to Rathmor," she answered, "I needed a lengthy rest. I find gallantry an exhausting matter in Scotland."

"So you've heard from Glenurchy," he said, amused. "Did he speak of the MacHughs with kindness?"

"He seems to be pleased that I've been treated with such courtesy," she said thoughtfully. From Duncan's letter, it was more than obvious that Alexander had said nothing of the way Gavin had driven her over the hills from Duncraig. But she had not expected it; she only wondered what tale he had given Duncan to placate him so easily. "I think you lie with incredible ease."

"You're too sweet a lass to be treated with anything but courtesy," he said easily. "D'you really consider it a lie?"

"What would happen if I told Duncan Campbell how you brought me to Rathmor?"

He shrugged. "I doubt he'd touch off a clan battle," he said amiably, "but he'd see that Robert and I received our just punishment." He added, propping his boot on the fender, "I imagine he'd demand an apology and then send his troopers clattering to Rathmor to rescue you. Does the thought appeal to you?"

She considered it. "I'd not mind seeing you apologize," she said. "On your knees, mayhap?"

"Aye," he said gravely. "I can see you'd like it. Shall I commence now, before Glenurchy brings me to account?"

He was outdoing himself to be pleasant, as if he intended to charm her with an unwarranted confidence that he would have no difficulty with it.

"No," she said definitely, "Duncan is riding to Rathmor within the week. You may go on your knees to him."

He laughed at that, in high good humor, and Elspeth knew a certain misgiving that she would, within a lifetime, see the MacHugh apologizing to anyone, least of all a Campbell.

"I trust you have a good hunt," she said. "I'll enjoy myself with only Jeannie as my gaoler."

He raised his dark brows. "Gaoler? Haven't you enjoyed your stay here?"

"I dislike being held against my will," she retorted.

He succeeded in looking very innocent. "You've the wrong idea, lass. No one has held you against your will."

"Then I assume I may ride out when I please. I've been longing to exercise my horse." She looked at him from under her lashes and was not surprised to see his face darken under the tan.

"I'd not advise it," he said.

"You contradict yourself, sir," she said evenly.

His gray eyes held hers. "You've been asking a good many questions since you arrived," he said quietly. "You're a slip of a lass to have so inquisitive a nature."

She said scornfully, "Do you have your spies everywhere?"

"You're a stranger here," he said calmly. "A Scot never trusts a prying tongue."

"I've not been prying," she protested. "I was born here, at Rathmor. Who has a better right than I to ask about the circumstances of my birth?"

"I should have thought your mother would have told you everything you deserved to know," he said. "If she did not, 'tis your misfortune."

Elspeth did not miss the dangerous hostility beneath his quiet voice. She shrugged with apparent unconcern and said, "I tire of your disagreeable company, sir," and would have left him. But he straightened and stood before her, seeming even larger than he had when mounted on the wicked stallion, and the white holland cloth of his shirt looked too delicate against the muscles of his neck.

"For your own safety, you'd best stay within the walls until we return," he said bluntly, and the warning in his voice boded no good for her if she disobeyed him. "I'll leave a few of my MacHughs behind to make certain you take my advice."

"You are quite fierce," she said. "Are you as brave when you've no troop of clansmen backing you up?"

Her sarcasm served only to bring back his mocking grin. "The thought fairly unnerves me, lass," he said.

He turned and strode across the room. Calling to Simon, "Robert is waiting," he was out of the door and away, and she heard his spurs clinking against stone as he ran down to the courtyard.

Elspeth did not move from the fireplace. The room seemed oddly empty and lifeless once he had gone; it was as though some part of his nature left a mark on all who met him, so that one was left with a sudden sense of loss when he departed and took with him that intense liking for life that made all others seem dull and pallid by comparison.

But she was not at all certain she cared to have the MacHugh's mark upon her, or to feel anything but pleasure when he had left her.

2

For three days she sat with Jean in the silent rooms of Rathmor, watching as Jean patiently embroidered squares of tapestry, listening as she chatted of children and fashions and the proper method of preserving fruit jams. She inspected Jean's garden, snugly sheltered inside the castle walls, and turned her face resolutely from the high wind racing with the clouds above the parapets.

She began to feel much like a docile chambermaid;

the boredom of walking in the bare garden or sitting in the hall beside a peat fire came near to choking her.

"I should think you'd go daft with the quiet," she said to Jean.

Jean was surprised. "I'm accustomed to it," she said. "I'd rather be here than out hunting with the men." When Elspeth did not agree, Jean added, "It'll not be quiet for long. They'll be back within a day or so, and the uproar will shake the rafters."

It was so; when a messenger rode into the courtyard with the news that the hunt had been successful, Rathmor was stirred into a feverish whirl of preparations. Fires were begun in the great smoking chimneys, and the spits and turning irons were scoured and sanded; cooks, stewards, maids, scullion lads, all began a great scurrying from the cellars to the kitchens, from the linen storerooms to the bedchambers, up and down the stairs much like an army of industrious ants.

Elspeth watched her half sister with amazement as she moved about in the midst of chaos, directing the entire household. "I fear I'm a frivolous person," she confided to Jean, and went at once to her bedchamber to escape the reminder of her domestic shortcomings in the person of capable Jean commanding the household army.

She sat on her bed, chin on her fists, and considered the matter. She was yet a prisoner; she was to mind her behavior and stay meekly behind the walls of Rathmor; she was not to pry into matters which did not concern her. So Alexander MacHugh had arrogantly ordered, and it appeared that in Rathmor Castle, as in his own fortresses, his word was law.

Her mouth tightened stubbornly. Laws were for kings, and whether a king or his laws were more disagreeable she could not decide. As a child she had taught the Princess Elizabeth and the gay Harry, Prince of Wales, to disregard many an edict of their father Jamie Stuart; she did as she pleased and the royal children trailed behind, and when it became necessary she faced up to her punishment with her eyes widely innocent and her closet stocked with sweets and games against the inevitability of banishment.

But I was a willful, rebellious, uncivil brat, she thought; and it is high time I learned to take my elders' counsel and become an obedient and conscientious maiden with manners befitting my training.

But she rummaged through her clothes for a crimson riding habit, and tied a bright kerchief over her hair. No one noticed as she ran down the steps to the court-yard and crossed to the stables.

She ignored the grooms and led out her mare herself, mounting to clatter across the yard and through the passageway below the keep. She called to a clansman wearing the red MacHugh tartan, "Open the gates," and reined her horse.

He looked up at her, puzzled. "I've orders to let no one through the gates until the MacHugh returns," he said, apology making him stammer a bit over the words.

Elspeth smiled charmingly. "I'm only riding to meet my father," she said. "The lady Jean would know how many extra guests will sit at the banquet table this evening."

He did not believe a word of it, but he grinned in answer to her smile. "The Chief gave me orders," he persisted. "I'm no' to open the gates for anyone."

Elspeth lifted her long lashes and dropped them again. "I shall be most desolate," she said. "I've been shut inside these stone walls until I could weep for a taste of fresh air."

He studied her for a moment. "Well now," he said, "I've no wish to make a pretty lass weep. Will ye take a groom wi' ye?"

He raised his hand and the portcullis began to move. Elspeth laughed down at him, and he foresaw he would face the MacHugh's wrath for falling prey to a pair of blue eyes and a smile as sweet as wild honey. But it'd be worth the price, and more; let the Chief give them both a devil's cursing, and who could say when a plain MacHugh clansman would be in better company.

Elspeth was through the gates before they'd scarce opened enough to give her passage. "I need no groom," she called over her shoulder, and struck her horse with her whip.

The day was overcast and cold with the promise of rain in the clouds and a bitter wind to sting her cheeks and bring tears to her eyes. But, oh, it was grand to be outside the walls, riding past the gray loch, past the mountain ash with their branches held like thin old fingers against the sky, along the track where her mare's hoofs struck splinters of frozen earth from the hard ruts.

She entered a stand of larch; and once, when the trail stretched before her without a turn, she put the mare to a gallop and could have laughed aloud with the joy of it. But she slowed her horse at last, remembering she had come out for more than a ride and must not waste her few precious moments of freedom.

She had coaxed a brief description of the place from Jean. The ruins of an old chapel against a hillside, she had said, just before the larch trees thinned to a moor; the plot of ground around the ancient chapel had once been the burial place of the family. Jean knew nothing of the lad's grave and did not wish Elspeth to search for it; but Elspeth would not be dissuaded, for she could no longer deny the strange hunger inside her to prove or disprove the matter for herself.

She came upon the chapel quite suddenly and her mare shied from a leaning headstone almost hidden in the briers. It was a lonely and silent place, and the small building stood roofless to the sky, the arch of its door covered over with creeping ivy. A thin rain began to fall as she sat motionless on her horse, and she watched the old gray stones grow wet and shining, dripping disconsolately in the stillness.

She sat looking about her for a lengthy time, gathering courage to dismount, not certain that she should intrude upon that holy place. And when she heard an approaching rider, it was with a sense of shock, so greatly was she stirred by the air of melancholy which lay over the quiet ruins and forgotten graves. But she came to life again, and turned her horse; she took a tighter grasp on her whip handle and wondered if the clansman at the gates had dared to follow her.

The rider came around a bend in the trail, and Elspeth took one look at the large black stallion and wished she might vanish into the air, horse and all. The hunt had returned then, immediately after her departure, and Alexander MacHugh with it; she would soon learn if an innocent air and a smile would placate this MacHugh.

He rode toward her slowly, taking his time, and she felt certain he had ridden the entire distance from Rathmor in the same leisurely manner.

"I assure you there was no need for you to come in search of me, sir," she said to break the silence. "I've not lost my way."

He did not answer, but rested one arm across his saddle pommel and regarded her impassively. He wore no helmet on his dark hair and beneath the leather jack his white shirt was unlaced at the neck. But the pistols were still at his saddlebow and he wore his sword, as if he had come after her the moment he learned she was not at Rathmor, and his dark face was as inscrutable as the first time she had seen him on the trail from Duncraig.

She knew suddenly that she would never attempt to placate him; her pride was as stubborn and uncompromising as his own.

"You are blocking the trail, sir," she said softly.

"I warned you, mistress," he said at last, and his eyes flickered over her and rested on the vivid kerchief holding back her hair.

Her cheeks grew warm. "And I shall warn you now," she said, "that I do not take orders from you."

He threw a leg over his saddle and slid to the ground.

"Did you find what you came for?" he asked, his voice still lazy and low. Then, with no change of tone, he said, "I should take my hand to you. If you'd had a proper warming years ago, you'd not be such a stubborn little fool."

Elspeth's eyes widened. She stared at him, astonished into silence. Finally she said, "Your insolence grows out of bounds, sir," and wheeled her horse to ride around him.

But he took the mare's bridle and brought her to a halt; then his hands reached up and lifted Elspeth to the ground.

Involuntarily, with the feel of his hands on her, she lifted the whip. Their eyes met and held; and incredulous, she saw the swift flash of amusement in the depths of his gray eyes.

"Do you brandish that whip at every man you meet?" he asked, and his hand closed relentlessly over her wrist. "It seems a ridiculous gesture; I doubt you'd have the courage to use it."

"Are you afraid to give me the chance?" she asked coolly.

"I don't give orders to have them disobeyed," he said, as if speaking to a wayward child. "You've not been at Rathmor long, else you'd have learned that small lesson before now."

"What punishment did you give the poor clansman at the gates? Twenty lashes, mayhap, for not keeping your prisoner more secure?"

"You're not my prisoner," he said carelessly. "When I want to keep a lass secure, I'll not leave her alone to pine by the fire. As for the man who opened the gates to you, he'll have punishment enough before morning."

She felt the anger like an ache inside her. "What will you do to him?"

Alexander grinned. "You'd never have smiled your way past him if he'd not been at odds with one of the kitchen wenches." He shrugged his shoulders. "But she's forgiven him and all will be well this evening, and by morning he will have lost his purse and gained a better understanding of women."

His hand still held her wrist; she raised the other hand suddenly and struck him a hard blow on the face. His hand tightened until the pain spread up her arm, but she did not back away from him. He stood quite still, looking down at her, his eyes grown cold and pitiless, his cheek showing the dull red imprint of her hand.

She could not say why she had done it, why she had so forgotten herself. He would not retaliate by touching her, of that she was strangely certain; more likely he would turn and stride away, leaving her the small victory that had little of triumph or pride in it. And he would have his revenge in his own time, in a way of his own making.

The larch trees whispered faintly above her head as the rain touched them. "Jean told me there was a lad born to my mother," she said, lifting her chin. "Is he buried here?"

Mayhap he would not answer; she deserved no better. But he kept his level gaze on her for endless moments, and at last there was something in his face besides the cold anger.

"Aye, there was a lad," he said slowly. "He lies yonder, beyond the chapel."

The headstone was pitiably small; the rain lay in the carved letters as if the tears were yet fresh and grievous through all the years. DOUGLAS LAMOND, born 1594, died 1595—there was nothing else, no inscription, no final words of comfort for the wee bairn. Only the name and the long-ago dates, and the rain dripping mournfully with the very sound of weeping.

Something inside her caught painfully. "It is foolish to be sad," she said quietly. "It has been so long, and I never knew until now."

"Old wounds are best left alone," Alexander said, and from his voice she knew he would not soon forgive her for coaxing the tale from Jean.

"It was not merely prying," she said without turning.

"I wanted to see it for myself, to be very sure." He would not understand, of course; he would be contemptuous of such sentimental fancies.

But unexpectedly, his hand touched her shoulder. Vital, firm, with a warm pulsing of blood that pushed the past away as if impatient of anything less alive and urgent than his own nature and the time in which he found himself.

"Now you know," he said, "and if you're wise you'll put it from your mind." He turned her toward her horse and held his hand to boost her up. He stood there a moment, looking up at her, and said gently, "Don't weep over it, lass. 'Tis over and done with, and no tears will change it."

Then he swung easily into his saddle, leaving her to marvel that he could so comfort her with a few brief words. But in another moment he had spoiled all her warm feeling toward him.

"Now you've satisfied your curiosity," he said curtly, "and I trust you'll keep your busy little nose where it belongs. You've had fair warning from me." Then, as his eyes moved over her, he added, "And remember, lass, the next time you strike a man, that this is Scotland and not England, and you've no reassurance it won't be returned in good measure." His voice was tinged with amusement, but the look in his gray eyes sent her blood to racing. "If you care to take the risk again, I'll show you what I mean."

Elspeth touched the mare with her whip. The next instant she brought it down with a sharp crack on the stallion's flanks. Tammie reared, his powerful forelegs pawing the air; by the time Alexander had brought him down and turned, Elspeth was several lengths down the trail.

She rode without using the reins, leaning well forward over the chestnut's mane to avoid low branches; and her crimson habit blew against her and billowed out behind like a bright banner.

The battlements of Rathmor were in sight before the

stallion drew abreast, but she noticed from the corner of her eye, with vast resentment, that Tammie would have left her far behind had not Alexander restrained him with a firm hand. They galloped together to the gates; at the last moment Elspeth wheeled her horse, coming to an abrupt halt less than a foot from the open gates. She looked at Alexander, feeling no little pride in her horsemanship.

"With your horse," she said, "I'd have been here first."

She clattered through the passageway without waiting for his answer. Inside the courtyard the throng of clansmen and the great piles of fresh game littering the ground forced her to a halt before she reached the stables. She slipped to the ground unaided and threw her reins to a clansman.

"A pigsty," she said, wrinkling her nose at the smell.

Alexander dismounted. "If you'd ridden my horse in such a manner," he said, "I'd have brought you into Rathmor on a litter."

Elspeth looked at Tammie disdainfully. "I've little doubt he behaves himself as boorishly as his master," she said.

She lifted her skirts to keep them from touching the soiled cobbles and swept by him, her chin high. But he was too odious to leave her alone; he put out a hand to detain her, and then, with his swift way of moving, he swung her into his arms and carried her across the yard to the stairs.

"Unhand me," she said, low; and was answered by his laughter.

"Don't cavil," he said. "I'm only being gallant." The clansmen in the yard were staring at them with interest; his arm held her so firmly that she could not have moved, but it would have satisfied her beyond measure to fly at him with her fists like a child in a fit of temper.

He placed her on her feet on the stairs and took her arm with his hand, and so she was forced to climb the entire length of the steps with him close beside her and his insufferable laughter ringing out above her head.

He pushed open the door to the great hall and Elspeth paused on the threshold, startled by the unexpected confusion. The fireplaces were piled high with blazing logs and the tables spanning the length of the room were swept with dozens of candles; the light was blinding in her eyes, and above the hubbub of voices and loud laughter the drone of the pipes was the most cheerful sound she had yet heard at Rathmor.

Her eyes widened with pleasure. "Faith, you might have warned me," she said, and wished with lamentable vanity that a fairy wand might exchange her riding habit for one of the elegant ball gowns in her clothespress.

Alexander's gray eyes saw into her mind with an uncanny perception. "You're at a disadvantage," he admitted unfeelingly, "but I'd not have missed this encounter for a fortune in English gold." He looked her over and grinned, an infuriating habit to which he seemed addicted. "At any rate," he said carelessly, "your face is clean."

The young woman moving toward them across the floor wore a magnificent white gown embroidered with gold thread, and her sapphire necklace glittered extravagantly in the candlelight. She smiled at Alexander; his hand dropped from Elspeth's arm and he bowed courteously. Elspeth longed achingly to give him a shove which would send him sprawling ignominiously at the woman's feet; God's love, he deserved no better.

But his poise would have done credit to the most polished courtier of Anne's court. He presented them gravely, "Mistress Elspeth Lamond, Mistress Katherine MacLachlan," and his warm voice with its Scots burr lingered over each name in turn.

Elspeth held her ground, smiling politely in the face of the woman's slow appraisal. She admitted reluctantly to herself that the striking combination of deep auburn hair and dark eyes was uncommonly attractive; the slanting eyes gave the woman the exotic look of a foreigner, and the shape of her mouth was surely made to excite a man's imagination.

She is someone to reckon with, Elspeth thought warily; and she is very sure of herself and her beauty, else she would not look at Alexander MacHugh with so obvious an intimacy.

"An honor," Katherine murmured. She said, "Have you been out in the rain?" Thus dismissing Elspeth, she turned to Alexander. "I'm fair starving, Alex. Come and find me a place at the table."

Elspeth dropped her lashes to hide her amusement. So the woman did not consider her a worthy opponent. Well, she'd warrant she might stand on even terms with any Scots woman, despite her shiny face and wet crimson habit.

She put her hand lightly on Alexander's arm. "Sir, you will be kind enough to take Mistress MacLachlan to a chair," she said, raising her eyes to meet his and the laughter she knew she would see there. "She has no partner, and it would distress me sorely to see a guest at Rathmor treated so unkindly. I cannot imagine why the men have neglected so lovely a lady." She smiled at Katherine and saw the woman's dark eyes narrow coldly. "He is a most gallant gentleman, madam, and I'm certain he'll not mind."

She nodded courteously and walked away from them. Despite her black and unruly conscience, she had not been so pleased with the turn of events since she arrived in Scotland.

3

She found her father at the far end of the hall, standing with his back to the fire. He greeted her brusquely and raised a brow at her damp habit.

She gave him a cool stare of her own. "Yes, I've been out riding," she said. "Must I tell you where and why?"

"No need," he answered. "I saw you come in with

Alexander." He looked at her a moment. "What the devil did you say to Kate MacLachlan to give her that look of outrage?"

So he had been watching her, she thought with an odd pleasure. "I bested her evenly and fair," she said, "and it's given me an excellent appetite." She put her hands behind her; he was a tall man and she had to tilt her head to look up at him. "I've not had time to change, as you can see, but Alexander has assured me my face is clean. Will you sit with me at the banquet table?"

If he refused her, with his cool dry voice and the quizzical lifting of his heavy brows, if he turned away from her, she knew she would not try again. But he held his arm for her and said gravely, "I should be delighted."

She sat by his side at the raised cross table and ate her meal with relish, not caring that half the company ate with their eyes on her and made her the whispered topic of conversation the length of the tables. In this land there was little consideration for rank or precedent, and the entire company of guests and clansmen found seats and ate where they pleased; she could see Alexander MacHugh across the room, seated by Kate MacLachlan and Gavin, making a good deal of laughter among the clansmen around him.

It was good, she reflected, to be among the proud Gaels. There was no formality among men here, where a man's pride of race stood him with the most noble company and gave him the air of a gentleman no matter how low his rank or birth. Even his grooms called the MacHugh by the familiar "Alex"; he was Chief of Clan MacHugh, but no feudal lord, and his clan was his family to the last rude scullion lad. Elspeth thought it incredibly heart-warming that men might keep such faith with one another, assuming respect for themselves and giving respect in return; she had lived too long in England, where pride of name and self-respect were matters reserved for only a few.

When she had finished her meal she rested her head against the embroidered Flemish cushion behind her and toyed with her wine, trying without success to keep her eyes from the dark head so close above the auburn one, to close her ears to the sound of merriment from that end of the table.

Robert Lamond followed her gaze and smiled faintly. "Is he too violent a young man for your liking?" he asked casually.

"Our first meeting did not endear him to me," she answered, looking away from the MacHugh at once, "and he's done nothing since to prove me wrong in my opinion of him." She added clearly, "I find him excessively arrogant and uncouth."

"Like myself, no doubt," her father said ruefully, and Elspeth turned to face him, surprised. "I imagine you find us a barbaric people after your years in London. But I'd not have you judge Alex too harshly, lass. He carries his responsibilities well for one so young. He's not yet thirty, and a man of some importance in Scotland."

"And well he knows it," she said.

" 'Tis a deplorable affair when young lads must be weaned to a sword and given the taste of battle before they can scarce reach the stirrups. But Scotland is a quarrelsome place at times, my dear Elspeth, and a man must look sharp to keep his head intact upon his shoulders."

"I've heard it said," Elspeth said incautiously, "that a Scot manages his affairs more by passion and fury than by reason."

Lamond smiled. "Have you become English to the core?" he asked gently.

The faint rebuke in his voice pricked her like the point of a foil. "England is a civilized country," she said defensively, "and yet Scotland has learned nothing from her after more than ten years of union."

Lamond turned his goblet thoughtfully, making small circles on the linen cloth. "England has been prosperous for many years," he said slowly. "But have you forgotten the bloody victories she's exacted from Scotland over the centuries? We've fought England and poverty and intrigues until we've fair bled ourselves to death."

"You're a stiff-necked lot," she said. "Do you blame England for your quarrels and your poverty?"

"Aye," he said promptly. "Any Scot will blame England for all the ills visited upon him." His voice was light, but the chill in his blue eyes as they met hers was not humorous. "Perhaps we are too proud, Elspeth. Our swords are not for hire in Scotland, and we would keep it so."

"By fighting among yourselves?" she asked quietly.

His face was like stone again, and she could have cursed herself for attempting to match wits with him over so touchy a subject. "We know our enemies before we fight," he said, "and we guard ourselves against treachery no matter where it appears."

The strange foreboding in the room seemed to envelop her, muting the laughter, giving a sad, wild lilt to the drone of the pipes. Elspeth raised her eyes and looked at Alexander MacHugh; she realized he must have been watching her for some time, his eyes cool and measuring, the strong lines of his face shadowed in the candlelight. There was something alert and urgent about his powerful body even as he relaxed. Elspeth drew a deep breath and looked away from him, but it did not serve to free her mind of his presence.

She sighed. "You've preached me a sober sermon," she said to Robert Lamond. "Tell me, are you an admirer of John Knox? Do all Scots go to the Kirk now, and pray for their terrible sins?"

Lamond laughed. "We've not all been converted to the virtues of the Kirk," he said. "Would you have us dour and stern with that unnatural religion?" He added, with a shrug, "We make a small pretence at piety, else they'd never leave us alone. But as Alex is fond of putting it, we prefer to examine our own consciences and bear the blame thereof."

"He is not a Papist," Elspeth said thoughtfully.

Lamond drained his wine. "Neither Papist nor Protestant," he said dryly. "Just a MacHugh."

Elspeth laughed, delighted. "Once I read that only two persons in all the world might be addressed by the most exalted of titles," she said. "The Pope and the King." She added, greatly amused, "Now I see I might add another. The Pope, the King, and the MacHugh."

For the first time since she had come to Rathmor her father looked at her and smiled, his eyes grown warmly blue and his face seeming somehow less gaunt than before.

"He has qualities which mark him off from other men," he said softly. "I might say the same of you, lass, but it would be unseemly for a father to be so vain of his daughter."

And Elspeth thought, with an odd catch of her heart, that she would never know if it were the wine that had gentled him for that one incredible moment, or the blood which ran alike in both their veins.

⟨5⟩

DUNCAN Campbell of Glenurchy lowered his brows and scowled about him. "How came you to meet Alexander MacHugh?" he asked bluntly. "And why did you come to Rathmor before making your presence known to me at Inveraray?"

Elspeth studied her kinsman before answering. He had ridden into Rathmor from Inveraray just before the evening meal, and she had been grateful for the short space of time at the table when she could examine him to determine, if possible, what manner of man he might be. Only last evening, at the hunt banquet, she had heard her father speak of the treacherous enemies he must guard against; and she wondered if Duncan Campbell of Glenurchy might be considered among that company. But the Lamonds and Mac-Hughs had greeted him with courtesy and apparent friendship, and there had been no hint of strain or hostility during the meal. He was a short, powerful man, with a crop of gray stubbled hair and a rugged, weather-worn face; and he bore the great hooked Campbell nose and a pair of piercing eyes so shrewd and penetrating that Elspeth was certain she would never succeed in even the smallest lie while facing them directly.

"What does it matter?" she asked casually. "I am here, and now you have come to fetch me to Inveraray. Do I appear ill-used?"

The scowl became a smile. "You're as bonny as your mother," he said. "I can scarce blame Lamond for wanting to keep you at Rathmor." But he would not be put off. "Did you ask the MacHugh to bring you here? I find it surprising you did not send for me the moment you arrived at Duncraig."

"I find Scotland a surprising place myself," Elspeth said. "Is it true, cousin, that your clansmen sleep wrapped in their plaids beneath the sky and melt the very snow away from their bodies? I vow I've never seen men of such strength. Is it your brisk Scots air or the usquebaugh you drink?"

He chuckled and placed his arm about her shoulders. "If you've nothing to say, lass, I'll forget the matter. 'Tis only that I felt the need to examine Alexander's tale a bit. He's a good lad and I'm fond of him, but he has an unco' smooth way of talking." He added thoughtfully, "And a way with a lass, or so the word goes."

Elspeth smiled demurely. "I cannot vouch for it," she said, and deemed the conversation too risky. "Do you count my father among your enemies, cousin?" she asked, watching his face closely.

He gave her a swift, probing glance. "The word is overharsh," he said flatly. "I'd not be here if that were the case."

She held the gold pomander hanging from her waist and flicked it idly against her blue velvet skirts. "To those at Rathmor," she said, "Argyll stands in company with the devil, and his Campbells with him."

"Aye, I know," Duncan said, and his eyes rested on the tall figure of the MacHugh as he led Kate Mac-Lachlan into a dance. "I know it," he repeated, "and God knows they've reason enough to hate him."

"But not you?" Elspeth asked, her voice carefully indifferent.

"I've no desire to own all of Scotland," Duncan said stiffly. He looked at her and said, "Don't worry your head with it, lass. 'Tis no affair for womenfolk."

"I think it concerns me," she said, but she did not press it further. She saw Gavin MacHugh leaning against the wall across the room, and said to Duncan, "You wish to speak to my father, I imagine, and I must say my farewells."

She moved around the edge of the floor toward Gavin, and as he saw her approach he gave her a friendly grin.

"If you intend to ask me to dance," he said, "I warn you I've no patience with such frivolous matters."

"I've no such intention," she said, smiling at him. "You're an ill-mannered, ugly fellow and deserve to stand against the wall."

In honor of the dancing he wore a blue doublet, the same shade as her gown, and she hoped her own eyes were as deeply blue above the velvet. "So Glenurchy has come to take you away," he said. "Are you happy with it?"

She sat on a bench beside the wall and Gavin stood above her. "No," she said, surprising herself, "I don't care to go to Inveraray. I'd hoped to stay at Rathmor till after the Yule. But there's naught I can do about it."

Gavin shrugged; his left hand rested casually on his sword hilt. "I gave you credit for more spirit," he said, "than to go off to Inveraray whenever Glenurchy wished it."

"I came to Rathmor in the same fashion," she retorted. "No one has asked my opinion of a single matter since I landed in Scotland."

When he laughed the curving scar on his face was no longer villainous; he was almost a handsome young man, and Elspeth thought that she liked him exceedingly well.

"Well now, send us a warning when you've grown weary of looking at the grim Campbells, and Alex will lead a fast raid into Inveraray town and bring you home again."

He used the word unconsciously; but it crept into Elspeth's mind and remained, a quiet comforting word that warmed her all over. Home, he had called it, and who was to say differently?

"Gavin MacHugh," she said, "do you always speak the truth?"

"Now and again, when I feel the urge."

"Then tell me if you consider me a Campbell spy."

"I would all spies were so fair," he said, "and all Campbells so pleasant on acquaintance."

"Do you?" she persisted.

His smile disappeared. "No," he said plainly.

"Does Alexander?"

After a moment he answered, "I imagine he knows you better now than when you first arrived in Scotland."

It was not precisely the answer she had hoped to hear, but it was better than none. She considered her questions carefully before putting them to him, for she did not yet understand her odd concern for these men who had been strangers to her only a few short days before.

"Does Alexander stand in much danger from Argyll? And does my father? Will they raise their clans to fight him when he comes down from London?"

"They've known the same danger since they were born," said Gavin, "and their fathers before them. If not Argyll, it'd be another Campbell."

"He'll come armed with letters of fire and sword against the chiefs who would oppose him," Elspeth said. "The King will call them rebels, and their clans will be harried out of Scotland."

She knew that much for the truth; Argyll had spoken of it to her one night when he had returned from Whitehall, in great spirits over his appointment as Lord Lieutenant of the West. She had regarded his boasting with a weary dislike; even now she could remember the way he had stood in the drawing room of his Strand mansion, still wearing the fashionable embroidered doublet and jeweled sword he had donned for his audience with the King, his unpleasant smile gloating over

the enemies so neatly within his power for all of an
hour past.

He was her guardian, Archibald Campbell, Lord
Lorne, Earl of Argyll; yet he seemed little suited to
bear that noble name. He was a peculiar figure of a
man, and Elspeth had good reason to suspect that the
muscles displayed so fashionably in the thin hose were
composed of padded silk. It had amused her to hope
that one day a sword might puncture the Earl's vanity
and betray to the world that the great Argyll bled silken
padding instead of red blood. But one did not often
laugh at the Earl of Argyll; and now, in the great hall
at Rathmor, Elspeth could still feel the calculating chill
of his eyes. Something about them did not match the
rest of him, did not belong to the thin face and the
stooped, narrow shoulders. They could take the nerve
from one's body with a single glance; they could bring
a shiver up her spine all the way from London.

"Do you think to warn us?" Gavin asked quietly.
"You're a good lass, but we've known his plans for
some time. He's been hovering over Alex like a hawk,
waiting the proper time to pounce, and Robert Lamond
the same."

"Why did Simon leave London?" she asked. "I
should think he would have done you better service if
he'd stayed at court and curried Jamie Stuart's favor."

"He thinks to keep Alex out of mischief," Gavin
said. "And he'd like to be wed in the spring. But if
Alex rides with James MacDonald against the Campbells, there may be no wedding and a good deal of
mischief in its stead."

"Do you think he'll join MacDonald?" Elspeth
asked slowly.

Gavin hesitated, then said simply, "I don't know
yet, nor does Alex himself."

Elspeth thought of the long months before spring
and hoped that Jeannie might have her May wedding,
with the thorns showing their delicate white plumes on
her hair and the skies above Rathmor matching the
shy blue of her eyes.

She stood up, watching Alexander stride toward her. "He thinks my curiosity the result of a busy nose," she said lightly to Gavin. "Here he comes to put a stop to my questions."

Gavin met her eyes and smiled slightly. "I trust you'll be as curious among the Campbells," he said. "We could use an ally in the enemy's camp. As for the questions, I don't mind telling you the truth when I know the reason you ask."

And so she knew that he understood her concern and approved of it; it gave her an odd sense of fellowship with this laconic MacHugh.

The fiddles were scraping into a wild, foolish tune, a country dance much like a dissipated galliard which delighted the clansmen at the village fairs. Across the hall Jean Lamond took Simon's arm and watched Alexander as he spoke to Elspeth.

"He thinks to provoke her before all the guests," Jean said, dismayed. She had long since discovered that decorum was not a word to be easily associated with the MacHughs, and she knew quite well that Alexander had requested the tune.

"I imagine she'll prøve a match for him," Simon said. "We'll watch this, Jeannie. I'd have walked the length of Scotland to see him bested by a lass."

Jean was not reassured. "I pray he doesn't humiliate her," she said. " 'Tis a wanton dance, scarce the thing one would learn at court."

Elspeth was feeling no humiliation. Alexander looked most elegant, she thought, with his crammesy velvet doublet and white linen shirt. He wore no jewels, only a single gold chain about his neck which supported a round medallion, and Elspeth had been told it was a golden pendant bearing the Thistle of Scotland, given to Alastair MacHugh by James IV of Scotland just before the tragic battle of Flodden and found on his body by a MacHugh who had followed his Chief into that bloody battle.

He was intending some mischief; she could see it in his slow grin and in the way his eyes laughed at her.

But she held out her hands to him and observed his steps closely until she had grasped the proper rhythm, and his hands touching hers sparked a small flame inside her which stirred her blood and quickened her feet to match his.

The fiddlers increased the tempo until it was as boisterous as a reel; Alexander began to swing her around the floor faster and faster, whirling her so that her skirts flew high above the floor. They were the only dancers on the floor, and indeed it was an abandoned dance which no proper lady would perform before a company of dignified guests. But Elspeth thought she had never before tasted such joy of movement, and she laughed at Alexander each time he whirled her around to face him.

The music came to a final wild crescendo, so urgent and contagious that they seemed to spin in a continuous circle, deep blue against crimson, like two jewels blazing in the candlelight. At the end, Alexander lifted her high in the air above his head, and the irrepressible laughter caught again in her throat till she was almost choked with it. He whirled her once more before he placed her feet on the floor; but he did not relinquish her hands and they stood laughing at each other in the center of the hall.

His eyes were still warm with the beat of the music. "I think you've no maidenly reserve, lass," he said softly, and flashed her the swift smile which so charmed her. " 'Tis a discovery which pleases me."

Because his steady gray eyes had not left her face, she said the first words which came to her mind. "Why does it please you?"

"I was once told," he said, "by a gentleman who should know of such things, that a man has only to watch a woman dance to predict her skill at other pleasures."

Her eyes widened. "You've an uncivil tongue," she said.

"Well," he said gravely, "it'd fair stagger a man to

learn that a lass like yourself is no' so accomplished as it would seem."

A vast number of people were staring at them. She smiled at him courteously and said, "You delight in insulting me."

He bowed. "I confess I've been striving to meet you on even terms."

She longed to put her fingers in his crisp dark hair and pull until he begged for mercy. But he was smiling, and she forgot the irritation of his teasing and thought only of the intense delight of dancing with him to a gay country tune, while the candles along the walls reflected in his eyes until they glittered darkly and she discovered that his was a mouth much accustomed to laughter.

"Come away," he said, " 'tis much too close in here. Wouldn't you like a bit of fresh air?" He took her arm without waiting for an answer. "We'll give them something else to gossip over."

"I'm warm for the first time since I came to Scotland," she said. "I don't need any fresh air."

He grinned. "Don't worry, lass. A dozen Lamonds patrol the walls, and I promise you'll come to no harm."

Jean Lamond watched them leave the floor. "She is very bonny," she said to Simon, "and very wise to treat him so."

It had given Jean a strange feeling to watch them dancing, completely oblivious to their amazed audience and the disapproving glares of the older women sitting by the fire. It seemed for a moment as if the very breath of the night had penetrated the thick walls of Rathmor; as if the high ceiling had been a wild sky with the clouds blowing across the stars and the night wind bending the trees. The tapestried hangings might have been the encircling forest, the fiddles the high skirl of pipes, echoing across the dark hills as free as a hawk before the wind. It was something between the two of them, barely concealed beneath the velvets and satins, something which came to life when they danced and carried them away into another world which none of the others could know.

Simon must have felt it also, for he whistled between his teeth and his dark eyes were thoughtful.

"Aye, she's bonny," he said, "and someone should warn her that Alex is not so easily handled as her polite London gentlemen."

"I think she knows," Jean said quietly. "She's very like him, Simon."

"Two outlaws," he replied dryly, but he smiled at the thought. "The winter looks to be entertaining. I only hope one of them keeps a sober head and remembers the irate Argyll, else Alex will pay dearly for his sport."

Jean said nothing. She was not thinking of the Earl of Argyll but of Katherine MacLachlan, standing against the wall with her dark witch's eyes slanted in her white face and her hands oddly still as she watched Alex lift Elspeth above his head with his brown hands circling her waist and his laughter meeting hers in that reckless, exultant way.

2

It had begun to snow, immense white flakes sifting down from the dark sky. The night was still and bitterly cold, and Elspeth pulled her cloak with its marten sable lining closer about her.

They walked along the north wall, looking through the parapets to the black loch waters below; and there was no sound in all the muted world but the tramp of the sentries as they made their rounds. Elspeth stopped and leaned against a stone embrasure, looking out into the darkness that stretched to the northward as far as the mind could follow.

"What lies beyond Scotland?" she asked, wishing her geography were not so vague.

"The Atlantic," said Alexander, "and the North Sea. A million miles of cold water, lass."

"I've heard of the Orkney Isles," she said. "I once met a man at court who claimed possession of them. Are they far to the north?"

"Aye, the very top of Scotland. That would be Robert Stewart, doubtless, and he'd claim possession of all Scotland if anyone would listen."

"Do you know him well?"

"I studied with him in Paris. He's a good lad, but he's had a pitiful time of it attempting to regain his islands." He added briefly, "They've been forfeited to the King, and Robert is to be executed for demanding their return."

Elspeth knew Jamie Stuart and his rages. He might be all Scots, that unnatural son of the lovely Mary Stuart; and yet he had no understanding of the wild moor and hill country which fostered so arrogant and Gaelic a pride in its sons. He could not bear that any man but a royal Stuart should know such independence and temerity of character, that any portion of land should receive more fealty and homage than a king. Jamie Stuart preferred his subjects respectful and servile like the serfs of England.

She said, "You studied in Paris?"

"And Italy also. We're no' so uncivilized as you'd like to think." Mockery emphasized his soft Scots burr, and Elspeth changed the subject quickly.

"Where are the Hebrides?" she asked.

"Once they were thought to be the edge of the world. They lie to the west, facing the sea, and the poor Scots there still believe they'll fall over the curve of the earth should they sail too close to the horizon."

The snow fell against her face; his dark hair and cloak were thickly white with it. She did not know why it was suddenly so easy to talk with him; they might have known each other for a lifetime, so close and warm the sense of companionship between them.

"Would you care to leave Scotland and see all the

strange things in the world? Do you want to see America?"

He did not answer for a long time. "Aye," he said at last, "I'd like to see America. Once, when I was a lad, I thought to sail with Raleigh or Cavendish would be the height of a man's life." He smiled faintly. "But I've not sailed so far as the new land. Perhaps I never shall."

"I should like to see the savages," she said. "Bronze men with emeralds in their noses and gold cloth around their waists." Her voice grew quiet and wistful. "They say the savages brought to court by Raleigh were more than seven feet tall, with a bearing as majestic as Queen Elizabeth herself. D'you think they were really kings, kings of all the new America?"

"I imagine they thought themselves kings."

"But they could speak nothing but an uncouth language which no one understood. And Raleigh reported that the land stretched for miles away from the sea, nothing but wild forests and rivers. No cities, no roads, only a wilderness."

" 'Tis no so difficult to believe that they looked upon Elizabeth and her court as savages, living in a strange land cluttered with foolish buildings and dirty streets."

Elspeth sighed. "I would like to see a land with forests which have no end and rivers which flow to the sea from miles away." She added, "I've seen Paris, but I was still a bairn and didn't have the proper appreciation. All I know is London, and a small memory of Edinburgh."

"I think you would like Italy," he said, "and the blue Mediterranean."

"I've heard the sea there is a magic color, so blue you'd not believe it."

"I'll show you a Highland tarn, lass, when the sky is reflected in it, and you'll see the same blue."

She laughed. "Or a Scot bluebell. Is that what you were thinking when you sailed on the Mediterranean?"

"Aye," he said. "I had been too long in a hot land.

The skies were always blue and one never escaped from the smell of flowers. I'd have given my life for one clean smell of peat bogs and heather after a cold rain." He grinned and shrugged his wide shoulders. " 'Tis a contradictory thing. A man longs for foreign places, yearns for the roll of a deck beneath his feet and the feel of the sea wind, and when he has it he's still not satisfied. A Scot never loves Scotland so much as when he's away from it."

"I can understand why all this—" and she made a wide sweep with her arm—"would draw one back." And the words amazed her because she suddenly realized the truth in them.

"There is an old Gaelic saying," Alexander said, "that once a man has known either Scotland or the sea, there will always be something about them to tempt him back."

She looked at his strong profile outlined against the dark sky, and thought that the ancient Vikings who were his ancestors might have gazed at the horizon with the same distant, restless look about them.

"I did not imagine that you were also a sailor," she said softly.

"Only for a short while," he said, and did not explain beyond that plain statement. "All men are many things, lass."

"I think you are first of all a Scot," she said, "and all other matters must come behind."

"I find it a bonny enough place, with no lack of entertainment."

"I imagine so," she said idly. "Why fight the savages in America when you can fight the Campbells in Scotland?"

He laughed at her. "If you're honest," he said, "you'll agree there's little difference between the two."

"Then I fear I must spend my life among the savages," she said lightly. "No ring in my nose, but a tight one on my finger. Do you think I will make a charming countess? Will it become me well?"

"I doubt you would care for my opinion on that subject," he said shortly. The warm friendship between them had disappeared, and in its place was the familiar uneasy antagonism edging his voice with coolness and turning his face hard and dark.

But she was determined to have it out between them, despite his anger. "I hope he will not be a lewd, doddering old man," she said. "My lord Argyll assures me it will not be so; the King has titled enough handsome young men recently for me to have a wide choice."

"But I doubt they all have a bag of gold heavy enough to satisfy Argyll," he said, deliberately caustic. Then, after a moment, he laughed, his anger gone as quickly as it had leaped to life. "If you're spineless enough to marry to please him," he said, "you deserve no better than the fattest old fool in London."

"He is my guardian," she said, "by writ of the King."

The MacHugh shrugged, dismissing the matter. Then he said, his voice once again warm and lazy, "You've not yet told me why you came to Scotland, lass."

She was taken unawares by his question. There was no explanation she could give him that he would not know for a lie; it was evident that he was too well versed in the amenities of court life not to be aware of the obligations which should have kept her in London at a time when Argyll was attempting to arrange a proper marriage settlement for her.

She made her decision at last, unable to ignore the strange longing to have him know the truth. "I promised my mother," she said slowly, "and it was not a promise I might break."

"And Argyll agreed?"

"I asked permission of the Queen, and he could scarce object. The Queen thought highly of my mother and deemed it only proper I should respect her last wishes."

Now he knew, and he might interpret it as he wished. She would not speak to him of her own loneliness, and her foolish dream of finding happiness and gay adventure at the end of the long road from London. He would think her a child, a young innocent; he would be vastly amused at her whimsies.

But he did not tell her what he thought of the matter. He only said quietly, "We should have guessed it," and turned to look over the dark silent loch.

"We?" she repeated.

"Robert and myself," he said briefly. "Why didn't you tell him the truth when he first asked you?"

The tightness was in her throat again, as it had been that first night she arrived at Rathmor. "He made it plain he didn't care to discuss my mother," she said.

The MacHugh straightened away from the stone parapet and faced her. "Don't be deceived by Robert's bitterness," he said gently. "He's lived too long with it to lose it in a day."

Then before she could guess his intentions, he put out his hands and turned her face upward; as he kissed her his hands went under her cloak and pulled her tightly against him. He held her so close to him that his cloak fell about her shoulders, loosing a shower of snow on her hair, enclosing her in a world which extended no farther than the tightness of his arms and the strength of his body against hers. For a moment she stood quietly under his kiss; then, against every measure of her will, her arms slipped around him, warmed between the heavy wool of his cloak and his velvet doublet.

When he raised his head he smiled down at her, not releasing her from his arms. "I'd not intended that," he said gravely, "but a man who always does the wise thing has a dull time of it."

Her pulse was throbbing with an unsteady, erratic pace, and she found it difficult to breathe properly. She knew a monstrous fear that he would see all her feelings in her face; at that moment she could not bear mockery from him, or even a careless understanding.

She raised her hands and pushed against his chest, moving away from him. He took her hand, but she

paid no attention; she only knew she must put an end
to it at once. The circular stairs cut into the tower wall
were just behind her; she started down the narrow
steps, her hand still in his, and increased her pace as
she descended, round and round, faster and faster, until
she was breathless when she reached the bottom.

Alexander's gray eyes were dark with laughter.
"Coward," he said. "Once you told me you weren't
that sort of fainthearted lass."

"I must look to myself," she said. "The Lamond
sentries were of little help."

He opened the door to the hall and stood back to
allow her to enter; and there, directly before them,
stood Robert Lamond and Kate MacLachlan.

"We were coming in search of you," Lamond said
easily into the silence. "The festivities have grown quite
dull with neither of you to set the pace."

Elspeth smiled at him, knowing well which of them
had given greater notice to her absence with Alexander
MacHugh. "Sir Alexander took me for a walk along
the walls," she said, hoping her cheeks were not
stained a betraying red, and took her father's arm.
"You've not asked me for a dance yet, and this my last
evening at Rathmor."

Lamond shook his head. "I've an old wound that
aches like a fiend the instant I so much as consider
dancing. But Alex will have to part with you for a
moment or so. I think we've a few things to say to each
other."

Kate MacLachlan's heavily lidded eyes studied Elspeth's face with a languid regard that missed no slightest detail. "You look most charming, mistress," she
said softly, and took Alexander's arm.

Elspeth noted the possessive gesture. Let Kate have
him, she thought, and welcome; but his dark face wore
a faint scowl and she wondered if he disliked to be
searched out by any woman, even one so ravishing as
Kate MacLachlan.

Alexander bowed to Elspeth, forcing her to look at

him again. "We've said our farewells," he drawled. "I'll see you at Inveraray, lass."

She did not doubt it; he'd visit Inveraray when and if he pleased, no matter if all the Campbells in Scotland were to guard over it. "I look forward to the pleasure," she said coolly, and then found she could not resist answering his smile. She watched for a moment as he walked across the floor with Kate. "She will annoy him one day," she said casually, "if she doesn't learn to curb her jealousy."

"She's never before faced so formidable an adversary," said Lamond, and chuckled. "I imagine Alex would be more amused than annoyed, if he ever paused long enough to think about it. He takes the ladies far less seriously than they'd like to believe."

Elspeth agreed, but she did not say as much. "Did Duncan speak to you?" she asked.

"Aye, he said something of your leaving tomorrow. I tried to dissuade him, but he seems to think it high time you made the acquaintance of your Campbell kinfolk."

She looked at him from beneath her lashes. "Then you consider it safe for me to leave Rathmor?"

"Safe? I doubt you'd be in danger anywhere in the Highlands. We may be quarrelsome, but we'd not take it out on a lass."

She was not misled by his words, as blandly innocent as Alexander's the morning of the hunt when she had confronted him with her certainty that she was being held at Rathmor against her will. But whatever their reasons for bringing her to Rathmor, they must have satisfied their curiosity about her, else they would not be relinquishing her so easily to Duncan.

"I meant safe for you and Alexander," Elspeth said demurely. "I've not been blind to your suspicious minds. Why else would you have kept me here so long?"

He looked neither chagrined nor guilty. "Why else indeed?" he said, smiling. "My dear Elspeth, you have an active imagination. I claim only a father's affection for a daughter he has long wished to see."

Their eyes met, and Elspeth looked into the frosty blue depths of his and longed to speak of the small lonely grave by the chapel. But she did not dare; she could read no assurance in his face that his words were sincere.

"I will miss Jean," she said. "I've come to be exceedingly fond of her. May she visit me at Inveraray?"

"I fear we seldom venture so far abroad," he said lightly, "but you will always be welcome at Rathmor."

She was not surprised at his refusal. "I shall take you at your word, sir. I should like to visit Rathmor again."

"You may always take a Gael at his word, Elspeth."

But his cool eyes were no warmer than before, and he still spoke to her as a casual visitor, no more and no less a stranger than the day she saw him first. It was, she thought, a vastly difficult matter to please a Scot.

Her eyes fell on Alexander MacHugh, standing across the room; he was laughing at something Kate had said, and he did not appear to be annoyed. The kiss was already forgotten; he had merely been amusing himself, when all was said, and Elspeth was not such a goose as to imagine she had pleased him—the black rogue—for even that fleeting moment. A kiss was only a kiss, the world over; she had best forget it also, and take care not to flatter his conceit by allowing him to guess how expert she thought him at the art.

Ꮗ 6 Ᏸ

ALEXANDER drew on his boots impatiently, brushing aside his man's clumsy attempts to aid him. He buckled on his belt and sword as he crossed the room, grabbed his jacket from a chair by the door, and cursed softly under his breath at the darkness beyond his room. He slid his hand along the stone wall as he went down the stairs, shouting as he ran, and by the time he reached the level ground of the bailey several torches had been lighted in the guardroom.

In a short time the entire castle of Fraoch Eilean was aroused; the bailey gradually filled with Mac-Hughes, jostling and stamping in the biting cold of the hours just before dawn. There was a great deal of good-natured cursing, but most of the men had been dressed by the time the MacHugh gave a second shout. Indeed, the loud halloo and clattering of hoofs outside the gates of Fraoch Eilean a short while before had wakened all the garrison; no man who had ridden long with Alexander MacHugh could have failed to be alerted by the urgency in that sound.

"Christ's blood, what's the excitement now?" Simon joined Alexander and Gavin at the bottom of the stairs, yawning widely. "One dark morning, Alex, you'll find your throat slashed for pulling such a bastardly trick." He grinned and gave Alex a hard punch in the ribs. "You've been bellowing around like an ill mannered stallion. Couldn't it have waited until the sun came up?"

Alexander gave Simon only a brief glance, making

certain he was ready to ride; then he strode toward the kitchen and left Simon and Gavin to trail behind. He took a cold joint of beef from the cook and leaned against the door to eat it quickly and wash it down with ale. Simon followed suit, content to fill his stomach before hearing the bad news, if such it might be.

"We've guests at Ardoon," Alexander said finally. He swilled the last dregs of ale from the tankard and wiped his mouth.

"Important guests, I trust," Simon observed laconically. "My manners are a good deal cruder than yours. Only Jamie Stuart himself could command such concern from me at this ungodly hour."

"Hendry will hardly polish the silver trenchers for these guests. They're Campbells, fifty strong, camped inside the walls." Alexander grinned faintly at Simon's low whistle. "How they came to be within the walls is beyond my ken, but I'll wager Hendry is finding little pleasure in fashioning an excuse for me."

"The fool," Gavin said coolly. "Was the messenger from him?"

"Aye," Alexander said. He slapped his gloves against his legs impatiently; his heavy black brows were drawn across his face. "He's pulled back into the keep, and as yet they've only exchanged polite compliments on the weather and MacHugh hospitality."

"They could be Cawdor's men," said Simon, talking around the food in his mouth. "He'll have every Campbell in Scotland out to take revenge, brother." He felt immeasurably better after eating, even to the point of seeing humor in the vision of the brawny Hendry retiring behind nine feet of stone wall while Campbells overran the castle like insects. "Mark my word, you'll be finding them behind every tree. I'd not be surprised if you discovered one under your bed some dark night."

"In his bed, more like," said Gavin, grinning, "if he has his way."

Alexander paid them no attention. This might be

Argyll's line of battle, subtly and shrewdly drawn in the sands beside Loch Awe; to serve his purpose he needed only the word that the MacHughs had marched against the Campbells, the Earl being in London and forswearing any blame. And march they would, with no other alternative, if Hendry had been provoked into fighting. The fiery cross would pass through the clan, calling the MacHughs to avenge so unwarranted an attack; before a week passed the land of Argyllshire would be soaked with stout red blood, and Argyll would obtain another writ of treason from the King. On the other hand, the tactics smelled strongly of a runaway raid, that old game invented by a bored Highlander to enliven the dull prospect of approaching winter.

Simon was watching him closely, despite his apparent unconcern. Alexander knew the lad did not want a fight with the Campbells; but holy God, no MacHugh had asked for such a thing. It was to be, or not; they must make the best of it.

"Let's have a go at it," Alexander said finally, slapping Gavin's shoulder. "I'll strangle every Campbell in the country with my bare fingers if they've gone before we arrive, snickering at their wit. Men have been hanged and quartered for less."

The men had eaten and were ready. They waited for orders, faces hard and grim under their light helmets. They were prepared for anything which might lie beyond the ride; but it was enough to be riding out into the night with their Chief and their eagerness was betrayed by the alertness of their bodies and the high tension that hummed invisibly between men and horses.

Alexander swung into the saddle. He took one long look at the men behind him and spurred his horse through the gates, splashing through the shallow water covering the stone causeway. It was high tide and Fraoch Eilean rode like a ship of war beyond the shore; in recent times the narrow causeway had been built to insure passage for horses at all times, but when the

first MacHugh built the castle and named it Heathery
Island, the natural moat of sea water had rendered the
fortress inviolable and unassailable against all comers.

It was still as unassailable, Alexander thought with
a warm pride, as a thousand MacHughs could well
make it so, and Ardoon no less.

The night was dark, with a taste of snow in the wind
from the hills, but when Alexander drew rein on the
slope above Ardoon the gray battlements were faintly
discernible against the crimson dawn sky. He waited
for the MacHughs to halt in a circle around him and
was pleased he had timed it so well; another thirty
minutes would see broad day, but as yet the banks of
the loch were gloomy with night shadows. The castle
was quiet, which meant no fighting had begun; doubtless the Campbells thought him still away in the hills
at the hunting and were in no hurry.

He gave his orders in a clear low voice, repeating
them once. The gates would be opened and the portcullis raised, since it was operated from the keep and
Hendry was expecting them. Alexander, with half the
men, would ride straight into the courtyard, depending
on the element of surprise to get them through the encamped Campbells to the far side of the walls. After a
pause, Gavin would lead the remaining men inside,
making a line across the gate to block any escape.

Gavin caught his eye briefly, long enough for the
glint of amusement in his eyes to be reflected in Alexander's face. The men saw and understood, and a low
grumble of laughter moved among them. The more
fools they, if the Campbells had pulled away from
Ardoon before dawn, leaving the castle with naught
but MacHughs inside it. But caution was the wisest
course when dealing with a Campbell, jest or no'.

Alexander held up his hand, then raked the stallion
deeply with his spurs. The horse sprang forward, moving at a gallop down the slope; the massive walls rose
above him, and as he reached the open gates he could
see the small fires within the courtyard and the dark

figures stretched on the ground. The Campbells had not left; they were brazenly encamped in the bailey of Ardoon, and Alexander raised a harsh swelling shout in his throat. It was echoed behind him in a deafening roar; and as the horses clattered at full speed through the gates the noise was ear-splitting enough to freeze the blood of the boldest Campbell.

The prone figures around the fires came to life as the horses reached the narrow passageway leading to the courtyard, but their sentries had not been alert enough to give a prompt alarm. Alexander's horse scattered the embers of a fire, throwing the coals over the closest men, and the Campbells parted in confusion before the advancing line of horsemen.

Alexander felt the soft give of a body as it fell away from the stallion's hoofs, then he was on the postern wall and wheeled sharply. He had not touched his sword, although he had loosened it in its scabbard in readiness, and now he waited calmly for the rest of his men to rein in beside him. The Campbells were still in the utmost confusion; the yard seemed packed from wall to wall with frightened horses and a cursing, stumbling mass of men. Alexander grinned as Gavin brought his men into the castle with a fierce shout. He kept his hand firm on his reins to steady the stallion in the turmoil; the black head tossed and strained at the bit, the wide nostrils quivered, the powerful forelegs lashed the air violently. Tammie was trained to the sound of battle; he would prefer to be away in the thick of it, disdaining the calm role of onlooker.

The surprise was complete. The Campbells were neatly hemmed, as they so well deserved, and not a drop of blood had been lost in the effort. They quickly realized their predicament; the hubbub died away into a sullen silence as the swords were slipped back into scabbards and the dirks which had flashed so hastily were slowly returned to boots and belts. They moved together to the center of the yard, the muttered curses dwindling into complete silence.

One Campbell finally stepped forward, the dark scowl on his face emphasized by his clenched fists. "I might ha' known a MacHugh would resort to such trickery," he said harshly. "I demand ye move the men from the gate and leave us proceed."

"Demand, Campbell?" the MacHugh said lazily, resting his elbow on his saddle pommel.

"I shouldna like to ha' to fight ye, Alexander Mac-Hugh," the man continued stubbornly. "Order the men awa'."

The MacHugh let his gaze move slowly over the Campbells. They were clearly visible in the diffused light of dawn, and there were slightly less than the fifty Hendry claimed. Some wore leather, but most of them boasted steel jerkins; the entire lot wore helmets, and here and there he could see a heavy claymore weighting its owner. They were all heavily armed, and their sullen scowls as well as their weapons attested their guilt.

The MacHugh looked at the Campbell before him with a scornful contempt, until the man dropped his eyes angrily.

"I tell ye, 'tis a shameful trick, bearing down on peaceful men as they sleep. Is it the sort o' hospitality ye offer, MacHugh?"

There were loud jeers from the MacHughs, silenced quickly as Alexander raised his hand. "I might tell you," he said, his words falling distinctly and coldly into the silence, "that you're damned fortunate we didn't slit your throats first and then send you home, slung across your saddles."

The Campbell tightened his jaw, fighting for control. The men around him moved uneasily; there was a low curse, suddenly bitten off.

"We only stopped for the night——"

"Only a stone's throw from Kilchurn?" Alexander interrupted curtly. "I fear we must limit our hospitality these days, Campbell." He made a quick motion with his head. "You may march through the gates. I'll order my men aside."

The Campbells moved to their horses, but the hard voice cut through the air like a sword. "Without the horses. A good walk around the loch will whet your appetites."

The man who had acted as spokesman turned, his face twisted with rage, but he checked himself when he looked at the MacHugh. "Ye'll hear of this," he blurted. " 'Tis a dangerous practice, stealing horses!"

"A practice to my liking," said the MacHugh, "when I've no need to step beyond my own gates. You'd best begin walking before I change my mind."

The men moved their horses to one side, forming a passage. The Campbells jostled one another through the gates, followed by loud jeers and whistles; they did not turn once they were outside the walls, but strode down the sand beside the loch with rage and hatred in every stiff line of their bodies.

Alexander dismounted, stretching his shoulders gingerly beneath his jacket. He looked at Simon and grinned. "Happy, lad?" he asked. "My sword is still clean and no harm's been done. You might as well have stayed behind in your warm bed."

The brothers looked at each other for a moment. Then Simon shrugged. " 'Tis your affair, brother" was all he said.

At the foot of the stairs Alexander confronted Hendry, his face red and worried. The captain of the garrison made a ludicrous sight, standing there with a sheepish grin, his bare sword in one hand while his plaid bulged with the two heavy pistols he had thrust inside the garment.

"Alex, I'm willing to hand ye my sword." His voice was awkward and ashamed. "I'd never ha' dreamed a Campbell could trick me into hiding awa' like a woman, forced to send for aid to defend my own fort."

Alexander laughed. "I gave you orders not to fight, man. You did well to retire till we arrived."

"They came up asking for shelter for the night and I refused. But they haggled and argued, seeming to be friendly enough, and I saw naught to do but let them

in and send word to ye what I'd done." Hendry
breathed an audible sigh of relief that he was escaping
so lightly. "They claimed they were returning to Kilchurn from a foray wi' several lame horses, that they
couldna make the extra miles."

Alexander chuckled, looking at the sleek, freshly
curried horses being herded into the stables. "I'll wager
they haven't had a decent run in a week. We'll not
have stables enough if we keep acquiring Campbell
horseflesh."

"Someone to see ye in the keep," Hendry said. "He
came in less than an hour before the Campbells, and
I've na doubt they suspected him to be in these parts."

Alexander raised his brows in a question, but the
rough voice shouting from the guardroom identified
itself on the moment.

"Christ's wound, Alexander, have you rid yourself
of those pestiferous Campbells? The devil with it, a
man can't take his rest anywhere in Scotland but he
must smell a whoreson of a Campbell beneath his
nose!"

Alexander threw back his head and laughed. Now
he knew why the Campbells had talked their way into
Ardoon; there was no' a Campbell living without a
suspicious mind and an eye cocked for a rich reward
of clinking gold pieces.

"Before God," he said, grinning, " 'tis Jamie Mac-
Donald!"

And behind him the MacHugh clansmen set up an
affectionate and boisterous shouting that rang from the
old dun walls and came near to frightening the dawn
away for the better part of the morning.

2

The wind blew fiercely from the north, drifting snow
across the tracks leading to Fraoch Eilean; but the
great castle lifted its walls scornfully above the cold

sea waters, boasting its massive strength against the bitter winds and the swirling snows. It had witnessed many winters and would hold against as many more; before it stood the protecting ramparts of the Grampians, those mighty hills forming the Highland line, and behind it was the sea. It feared no challenge of nature or man, and its arrogance was only intensified by the futile onslaught of a winter blizzard.

Inside the thick walls, bright fires sputtered with flurries of snow drawn down the chimneys by the drafts. The wind rattled the small windows, high in the walls, and the gray stones of the floors were damp and cold to the touch. But the great hall was warm with the pungent smells of browning meat and peat smoke, of steaming clothes and boots spread before the fire to dry, of the sweating men who crowded around the large kegs of ale. The fireplaces at both ends of the hall blazed with tremendous logs; there were shouts of loud laughter, a snatch of song, an occasional scuffle as youthful tempers flared under the strain of being too long indoors by a warm fire.

In the smaller hall of the keep beyond, Alexander stretched his booted legs to the fire and reached for a tankard of ale.

" 'Tis more than a man deserves," he said cheerfully. "They took away your last snip of dignity, Jamie, forcing you to flee for your life in the dead of winter." He grinned at the man seated across from him; he wore a ragged brown doublet, stained and dirty, and a pair of goatskin brogues which had been mended often and carelessly. "By Jesus, they might have left you a decent pair of breeks. You look like a common reiver after a bad night at dice."

James MacDonald shivered, despite the warmth of the fire. The memory of the long flight from Edinburgh was uncomfortably vivid. "I could overlook the loss of my baggage, but I'll not forgive the knaves for stealing my books." He sighed, shaking his head sadly. "A magnificent collection. I shall miss having them at my hand at Dunyveg. As for fleeing in the dead of winter, I had a great advantage. Who but a Highland man could pass through the Grampians in such miserable weather?"

"Who but a MacDonald," Alexander corrected him. "You were wise to come here, Jamie. If you'd sent word from Keppoch's country, I doubt I'd have ventured forth to see you."

"You MacHughs were always a lazy brood," MacDonald said placidly. "D'you know, Alex, that I had a valued copy of Montaigne in my trunks when Tullibardine seized my baggage? I wonder if he'll give it the proper appreciation; the man is illiterate, I've heard."

"I can see how you spent your six years on Castle Rock," Alexander said, a trace of amusement in his voice. "Tell me, did you read of a battle plan to gain Dunyveg for you?"

He knew the moment had arrived to make the situation plain between them; the MacDonald had spent the last two days recovering from his flight from Edinburgh, and now he could waste no more of his precious time.

MacDonald gave him a reproachful look. "Battles are won by strategy."

"You've had a lengthy time to perfect yours. What's it to be?"

James MacDonald was silent for a time. He was a small man, almost dwarfed by the high carved back of the chair; his dark hair had been cut unskillfully after his escape and it stood in short tufts on his head, giving him an odd look of continual surprise. But his shoulders stretched against the dirty doublet; they seemed large for one so small, and the powerful muscles of his forearms showed no flaccidity after his long imprisonment. Alexander remembered ruefully the hours he had once spent attempting to best MacDonald's strenuous sword arm; the man could wield a mighty claymore with a single hand as if it were no heavier than a light rapier.

"Colkitto is at Eig Island," MacDonald said finally. "I shall begin there. Then we shall take Islay and Dunyveg. Coll sends word he has more than a thousand MacDonalds with him; it will be a fair start."

"D'you propose to oust Cawdor and his cannon with your bare hands?"

MacDonald waved in a negligent gesture. "I shall send the cross through Kintyre and the islands. A hundred cannon could not withstand my MacDonalds, and Cawdor will flee for his life when he hears we are descending on Islay. You shall see."

"I hope to God I do see it," Alexander said soberly.

"You sound dubious." MacDonald crossed his legs, wrinkling his nose in distaste as he caught sight of the dirty brogues. "Do you believe we have a worthy foe in Cawdor?"

"You'll have little trouble with Campbell of Cawdor."

"What is it, then?"

Alexander shrugged. "You're taking on a large task, Jamie."

"One thing shall follow another. I can better plan my campaign from Dunyveg than from a miserable cell in Edinburgh."

"True MacDonald logic," Alexander said, grinning. "I take it you have no intention of being ousted from Dunyveg as easily as Angus MacDonald. God's truth, Jamie, the MacDonalds will celebrate from Mull to Skye when they hear the word!"

"I was not pleased to learn that Angus was taken prisoner to Edinburgh. If I'd waited a week, we could have fled the town together."

Alexander was thoughtful. "Can you outguess the King, Jamie?" he asked quietly. "I trust the walls of Dunyveg will be stout enough to withstand the royal wrath."

MacDonald's face was bland. "He's only a Stuart, lad."

"He considers himself King of Scotland. An unfortunate affair, but we can do little to change it now."

The MacDonald looked into the fire, his eyes flaming like the logs on the hearth. "The Lords of the Isles have never been subject to Scottish kings, Alex. The Somerleds knew no laws but their own; they were great kings before Scotland existed, and there's no Stuart living can claim that royal line." He looked at Alexander with a proud anger. "The days are not so long past when the weak kings of Scotland knelt before the Lords of the Isles, pleading for favor and aid."

"We can't all be kings," Alexander said easily. "I imagine Jamie Stuart intends to hold his throne against all comers."

MacDonald looked at him sharply from under his heavy brows. "Tell me, Alex, have you come to a decision? This talk of the King sounds little like you. God's foot, have you become too loyal a subject to be interested in the rebellious MacDonalds?"

"I've no love for the King," Alexander said calmly, "but I've begun to think of the affair as extremely perilous. Don't push me into a decision; a hurried answer might not be to your liking."

MacDonald stared at Alexander, his eyes narrowed. Then he laughed loudly. "Holy God, you're a canny Scot! You'll do, lad, you'll do." He was obviously pleased.

"I may find myself with a rebellion of my own, James, once Argyll returns and takes a look around." Alexander was well aware that the MacDonald's shrewd eyes were silently appraising him, measuring the extent of the changes of the last six years. Alexander was no longer the young lad who had asked frequent advice of the crafty MacDonald Chief; he was six years older in experience and intelligence than the young MacHugh who had served in the MacDonald household as a foster son. He was the Chief of Clan MacHugh, a powerful noble in his own right. He was no longer a novice.

"In that event, we shall be sharing the same misfortunes," MacDonald said smoothly. "Do you quibble over the definition of the word?"

"Scotland grows weak from too much rebellion, James, no matter how you define the word. If I'm forced to march against Argyll, the same coin will apply to me, but I'll still care little for it."

MacDonald put his finger tips together. "We are at cross purposes, lad. The word rebellion is too loosely used these days. I've no plans to take arms against the King; I'm only fighting the injustices done my clan in the King's name."

"A thin line between the two, Jamie. I doubt the King will label it anything but high treason."

"D'you believe I'll sit by idly while he appropriates all the Islands, urged on by Argyll? He'd see us ruined, wiped from the map of Scotland like the MacGregors before us. I'll not submit to him like a nesh woman!" MacDonald hit the arm of his chair with his fist. "I'll not hand over my clan as if the King deserves anything he sets his dirty mind to have!"

Alexander's face was intent and grave. "James, think carefully of the hornets' nest you're stirring. Mayhap Jamie Stuart would be content to have done with the MacDonalds; mayhap he cares little for what he's begun. God knows he has no army and less money to raise one. He must give his authority to Argyll to use as Argyll sees fit, and no Stuart can stomach that with ease. But what if you succeed? What the MacDonalds do, any clan in Scotland may also attempt. No matter their grievance against the King, they'll resort to the sword to gain their ends." Alexander held the MacDonald's eyes for a long moment. "Jamie Stuart will not allow you to succeed, no matter his dislike of Argyll. It'd be the first nail jerked loose from his throne; the rest would soon follow."

The MacDonald sighed. "I see the point, Alex. Christ, I'd not like to see Scotland torn by strife again.

But what would you have me do? I'm damned no matter my course."

Alexander laughed. "I'd lie if I said I had no sympathy for your cause." He shrugged. "When Argyll jumps me, I doubt I'll stop to quibble."

"You must consider your clan," MacDonald said. "I know that, and I'll stand by your decision."

"This much I can tell you," Alexander replied slowly. "If I cannot see my way to involving my Mac-Hughs, I'll ride with you alone."

The room was silent. MacDonald stared into the fire; when he finally spoke his voice was rough with emotion. "I cannot deny it, Alex; I wanted to hear those words above all things. I don't need your men. I'll have enough, once the clan is at full strength, and I've no wish to imperil other clans in such a hazardous undertaking." He added bluntly, "But I need you."

He did not elaborate, being a man who cared little to spread his innermost thoughts for all to see. But MacDonald had not been isolated in Edinburgh Castle; he had heard tales of the young MacHugh Chief, related to him with respect and admiration ofttimes tinged with awe. The lad was a swordsman and fighter of great repute, but his most valuable asset was his ability to lead men. The MacDonald cause was desperately in need of leaders, men the caliber of Alexander MacHugh, whose very name would bring men flocking to his banner.

"I'll be leaving for Eig Island immediately," the MacDonald said. He stood up, appearing much taller as he stretched. "I'll not strain your hospitality. Keppoch and I had best give ourselves time to reach the coast without worry of pursuit."

Alexander hoped the young Keppoch would be able to leave. He was attempting to match Gavin and Simon in the consumption of raw Scots whisky while the dice game, begun that morning, still progressed in high good humor. "We've been missing the fun, James," he said. "God's son, you're a long-winded jack."

"A man in my position must find amusement in less expensive games," MacDonald said wryly. "My pockets may be empty, but my tongue needs no such vulgar incentive as gold. Keppoch could use the same ruse; I'll vow he'll be stripped before he quits."

"Aye, Gavin will fleece him properly." Alexander looked at MacDonald's ill-fitting and ill-smelling attire. "Jamie, allow me to give you the loan of some decent clothes. I can't endure your smell much longer."

"Let's see to it, then. I feel I've been wallowing in a pigsty." The two men walked to the door and Mac-Donald held out his hand to Alexander. "I'd like your word on it," he said, "that you'll not leave Fraoch Eilean in the event Argyll gets wind of your decision. I'll not jeopardize your clan."

Alexander took his hand. "Come, Jamie, a man can't spend his life cowering under the bed sheets." He added, amused, "I suspect you're no' so concerned over my clan as you'd like to appear."

MacDonald frowned; the young MacHugh was growing too canny for his own good. "Do you think anything can be done for Angus?" he asked casually.

"It'll do him small harm to have a taste of Campbell justice," Alexander said blandly. "Next time he'll make a better fight of it."

"Surely," MacDonald agreed. "But I need him, Alex."

"Then I'd best plan a trip to Edinburgh. Can you spare me a good man or two?"

MacDonald nodded, pleased. "I'll send you word. It'd be well to wait; they'll put a heavy guard on him at first." Angus was as good as freed, MacDonald thought with satisfaction, and if he himself had sent for the MacHugh at the start, he'd not have spent six lengthy years planning his own escape from the Rock. But he had his pride then, as now, and said no more than, "My thanks, friend."

"The winter's a dull season," Alexander said lightly, "and I've been wanting a bit of entertainment."

MacDonald had heard other rumors. "What of the lass from London?" he asked, careful to sound the proper degree of indifference.

Alexander laughed. "You should have seen her when I rode to Inveraray last evening. I had it in mind to complain to Glenurchy about the Campbells we found at Ardoon, but I doubt I accomplished my purpose. God's love, the lass has a temper."

"Gave you the blame, did she? Well, there's a Campbell for you."

"She had a notion I showed too little respect for Glenurchy," said Alexander. "I talked to him from my horse instead of being properly announced. Christ, I could scarce take all my men clattering into the hall, and they deserved to hear." His grin widened. "I'd have come to better terms with Glenurchy if she'd not flounced into the courtyard, holding her nose in the air over my uncourtly manners."

MacDonald shook his head. "I'd keep away from her, Alex," he said, then stopped. Matters were going well; he had no desire to stir the man's quick temper.

But Alexander ignored the reference to the lass. "Let me know how the campaign progresses, Jamie," he said. "You've only to raise your clan, take the islands, defeat Cawdor on Islay, and retire behind the battlements of Dunyveg before Argyll comes down from London. 'Tis no task at all that I can see; by Jesus, if you don't finish it in short order, I'll know you for the weak-assed prison felon you are."

His countenance was so bland and unconcerned that for a brief moment, as was always the case, MacDonald was almost tempted to believe him serious.

"And if the worst happens," Alexander continued, "remember 'tis better to be hanged for a damn good reason than for none at all."

There was no answer to that, for either of them.

{7}

THE day had grown dark and heavy with night. Beyond the thick walls of Inveraray the wind keened around the towers, heaping the stone ledges with light snow.

Elspeth's bedchamber was warm and fire-lit, and fragrant with the scent of rose and musk. The crimson bed hangings glowed in the light of the flames; the wax tapers on the dressing table were slim white spears, reflected like stars in the mirror, and against the wall the shadows were slanted long and soft.

Elspeth was seated on the gold damask stool before the fire, her feet tucked under her skirts. Holding a velvet robe on her lap, she regarded it with a slight frown and wondered if it would be too daring for Jean's trousseau. It was a glorious thing, loomed in the Netherlands and fashioned by an expert Paris seamstress; it had been lined with soft sable skins and gathered with a jeweled girdle, and she could not think it anything but the finest gift for a bride, no matter how shy.

She held the fur against her cheek for a moment and struggled to lose the faint sense of depression that swept over her. She had not seen Jean, or Simon, or Gavin, since she left Rathmor Castle; she had seen Alexander MacHugh only once, when he rode into Inveraray to speak to Duncan on the matter of some wayward Campbells. And it seemed likely she would not find suitable occasion to ride to Rathmor for the wedding.

Argyll was returning to Scotland sooner than she had

expected him. Duncan had said, even before the word came from London, that James MacDonald's escape would mean Argyll must hasten home before the Mac-Donalds had taken all western Scotland and marched straight to the gates of Inveraray. Elspeth would soon be facing his cold eyes and hearing his cold voice; the brief hours of freedom were almost at an end.

She rose quickly and threw the robe on the bed. She could not endure the close warmth of the room another moment; she longed for one clean breath of air, blown sweet and cold with Highland snow. It was foolish to mope by the fire, dreaming over a piece of velvet cloth; she would not be betrayed into self-pity by such sentimental fancies.

She ran down the steps to the hall and pushed open the door at the top of the courtyard stairway. But the air was not clean there; it smelled faintly of smoke and food from the kitchen and the more pungent odor from the stables across the yard. She decided on the moment to go to the postern gate and persuade the guard there to open it a slight crack for her; but suddenly her eyes fell on the open gates and she stood quite still.

On the far side of the courtyard, before the stables, she saw the black stallion, dancing restlessly as a groom attempted to draw him into the open door of the stable. Katherine MacLachlan was still mounted; her hood had fallen back and the torchlight glinted brightly on the dark red of her hair. Alexander MacHugh stood beside her; Elspeth could hear his deep voice as he lifted him arms to help Kate dismount. They were both dusted with snow, and Alexander had removed his helmet; his dark hair looked rumpled, and he had pushed back his cloak as if he hated to be encumbered with it.

They walked together across the court, Alexander holding Kate's arm as she lifted her skirts to climb the stairs. Elspeth wished she might back out of sight, but she lifted her chin and went through the door to meet them at the top of the stairs.

Alexander bowed briefly, one hand resting carelessly on the hilt of his sword, and Elspeth's eyes moved involuntarily from his dark head to the line of his shoulders under the cloak and doublet. She had forgotten, since she saw him last, how tall he stood and how proudly he held himself.

Kate lifted her cloak to shake it free of snow. "We met outside," she said, her voice very gay, "and Alex insisted I come in out of the snow." She laughed up at him, her eyes slanting and her mouth vividly red in the white face. "I'm flattered you should offer to escort me to Lachlan, Alex, but we must leave soon or I might be forced to ask hospitality of you at Fraoch Eilean. 'Tis almost night."

Elspeth said, "I'm happy to see you again, mistress. How did you leave my father and Jean?"

"Jean is sewing furiously on her wedding gown," Kate said. "I promised her I'd return in a few weeks to help plan the festivities." She smiled again and swept past Elspeth to the door of the hall. "Come along, Alex, I'm near frozen."

Elspeth waited for him to follow Kate; she could hear the bright laughter as Kate greeted Duncan in the hall.

But he did not move. "I came to see you, lass," he said. "Where can I talk to you?"

His gray eyes were as unreadable as ever, his smile as slow. She stared at him for a moment. "I'm sorry, sir," she said sweetly, "but I've more urgent matters to consider at the moment."

She moved past him and ran down the steps to the courtyard. After a brief pause she heard the door close behind him, and she breathed a sigh of relief that he hadn't followed her; she was not certain her resolve was so strong that it would withstand both his power of persuasion and her great curiosity.

Gavin had joined a group of Campbell men outside the mess where the men-at-arms and retainers ate their meals. She wondered if he might be uncomfortable in the midst of so many Campbells; but she remembered how coolly he had faced the garrison at Duncraig and decided all MacHughs must wear their pride like a coat of mail.

When she caught his eye, Gavin strolled across the yard to join her. "You're outnumbered, Gavin," she said. "Is your sword unloosed and ready?"

"I kept my back to the wall," he replied. " 'Tis a trick I learned at an early age."

"Didn't Simon ride with you?"

"He's at Rathmor," said Gavin. "We see less of him than when he lived in London." His head was bare and his hair was shorn quite close, a handsome style if somewhat unfashionable; it seemed more fair than red in the torchlight. "Did Alex find you?" he asked suddenly. "He must have important business with you to ride out in his foul weather."

She looked up at him innocently. "He's in the hall with Kate MacLachlan. I've no desire to speak with him."

"He'll not like that," Gavin said bluntly.

She shrugged her shoulders, and it was a careless gesture so like Alexander himself that Gavin could not help laughing. "He'll be hard to live with," he said. "He's not often crossed by a lass."

"He's old enough to know how it feels," she retorted, putting her hands behind her. "I've never known a more conceited man."

"Well now," said Gavin, "he has his faults, but I'd not call conceit one of them. 'Tis only that he proves himself right more often than the next man."

"Does he never make a mistake?"

"Aye," said Gavin, and grinned at her. "But he's the first to admit it. On the whole, he's not inclined to haggle over small things."

"All MacHughs swagger," she said, "and I've yet to see if you've anything to back it up." She changed the subject abruptly. "Gavin, may I see Tammie?"

He shook his head decisively. "He doesn't take to strangers even when he's in good humor, and now he's away from home and in an unfamiliar stable."

"I only want to look at him," she pleaded. "He's in a stall, isn't he? You can talk to him while I look from outside." She smiled at him persuasively. "He's such a splendid animal, Gavin, and I've never seen him close at hand."

Gavin weakened. "If you'll keep quiet and let me do the talking. He came from England the wildest brute I've ever seen, and Alex must train him a bit more for polite company."

The stable smelled warmly of horses and hay and oiled leather; Tammie was in the back, surrounded by empty stalls as though the grooms feared to risk Campbell horses in too close proximity. He was standing quietly, but at the sound of footsteps he lifted his head and moved uneasily. Gavin began to talk softly before he entered the stall and at the sound of a familiar voice the black nostrils ceased to twitch.

Elspeth waited until Gavin was in the stall, rubbing the silken black nose gently as he murmured Gaelic endearments. Then she lifted her skirts and climbed up on the broad crossbar of the stall, resting her arms on the upper plank. Tammie was more than beautiful, she thought; he was as proud and scornful as if he had never known the humiliating mastery of bit and reins, as if he should still be roaming wild and free over the hills, bowing to no will but his own, acknowledging no master but himself. No one looking at Tammie needed to be told of ancestry and breed; he was a superb, magnificent aristocrat of a horse, and she admitted unwillingly that he was a proper horse for Alexander MacHugh.

"I'd like to ride him one day," she said softly. "All alone, only myself and Tammie."

"I thought I told you to keep quiet," Gavin said, his hands on the reins.

"He didn't move a muscle when I spoke." She continued to talk quietly to Gavin, prepared to stop the instant the horse became restless again. But he stood calmly in the stall, nuzzling Gavin occasionally as if silently amused at the fear exhibited by more cowardly men.

"You see, he's not so fierce. I'd wager I could have him eating from my hand were I to see him daily." She wanted to reach out her hand and rub the dark velvet of Tammie's head, but she was not so foolish. One day she would do it, and moreover, one day she would ride him. "I believe Alexander invented the story of Tammie's dangerous nature only to give the impression that he's a braver man than most," she teased Gavin. "God's love, he's not above such a trick."

"Aye, I spend all my leisure hours teaching him to be more illbred and nasty than myself." Alexander's voice came from behind them, lazy and amused.

Gavin's hands continued their slow movement along Tammie's neck. Elspeth didn't move, but her face began to burn hotly. She wondered how long he had been standing behind them before he spoke; she wondered if she had forgotten to pull down her skirts, if he could see the undignified way she was perched on Tammie's stall.

"I can see your affairs are most urgent," Alexander said casually. "Forgive me for searching you out to make certain."

She could see herself as he had found her, climbing a broad crossbar in the stables and chattering foolishly with Gavin. She stared mutely at Tammie and Tammie obligingly stared back.

Gavin walked out of the stall without speaking and she heard his footsteps retreating down the length of the stable. There was nothing to do but climb down; she couldn't hang there indefinitely, waiting for Alexander to leave.

She sighed and lifted her chin. "Well," she said, subdued if not repentant, "Tammie is surely a horse to be proud of."

"Tammie will be pleased by your admiration," he said gravely. "Were you coming back to talk to me?"

She could not think of a courteous excuse quickly enough and he saw the answer in her face. "Then I'll not annoy you further," he said curtly. He turned, waiting for her to walk ahead. "After you, mistress."

Gavin was right, she thought; the MacHugh was not accustomed to being crossed by anyone. It pleased her irrationally to know she could anger him so easily. Faith, he amused himself often enough by treating her in the same fashion.

She took a few steps, pausing by him to say, "I'm surprised Duncan would allow you in the stables. Have they chained all the horses to the walls?"

He put his hand on Tammie's stall, effectively blocking her line of escape. He looked down at her, not touching her, and she focused her eyes on his black velvet doublet and the embossed leather of his sword belt.

"You don't seem eager to see me, lass," he said thoughtfully. "I'm beginning to regret my cold ride from Fraoch Eilean."

She felt a quick flash of irritation. "D'you believe I've done nothing but pray for the sight of you, sir? I've had enough to occupy my days, even without the great honor of your presence."

"Then I should have come sooner," he said, as if her words had convinced him. "Is that why you're sulking?"

His face was too close above her; she could not think properly. "I am not sulking," she said clearly. "It would have made little difference to me if you'd not come at all."

"I thought it would be wiser to stay away," he said. "Wiser for us both. But now I'm not certain that I care whether 'tis wise or not."

Her eyes widened, but he did not explain further. His face was stubborn and unsmiling. He put his hands on her shoulders; she could feel the hard grasp of his hands through her cloak.

"I came tonight because I'm leaving for Edinburgh shortly and my affairs there are likely to keep me for some time."

"But, sir," she said quickly, "you run the risk of meeting Argyll on the road. Haven't you heard he's on his way to Inveraray?" She smiled, meeting his eyes. "Are you running away, Sir Alexander?"

His hands tightened on her shoulders. "You're well aware of the jest in that," he said, with a touch of exasperation. "I'd like a promise from you before I leave, Elspeth."

She had never thought her name lovely until she heard him say it, his warm Scots voice lingering softly over the word.

"I'll ask the promise first," she said, surprised.

"Stay away from Rathmor until I return," he said, "and if Duncan returns to Balloch after Argyll arrives, be sure you go with him."

She couldn't hide her amazement. "You're being most mysterious. Do you think I'd have a choice? If Argyll wishes me at Inveraray, there'll be no question about it." She added coolly, "I'll visit Rathmor whenever I please. My father assured me I'd be welcome there."

"I ask it for your safety," he said impatiently, "not because I've a notion to order you about."

"I don't understand," she said slowly. "Why should I be unsafe at Rathmor?"

"I've no time to explain the matter. I want your promise."

"Only if you'll give me a sensible reason," she insisted.

"Don't be a little fool," he said roughly. "Why do you need a reason?" She moved slightly and his hands tightened; his gray eyes blazed dark and stormy. "I don't trust Argyll, and while he's in Scotland you've no business at Rathmor. That's reason enough for you."

She shook her head; she would not promise. "Is that

why you wanted to talk to me?" she asked, curious, trying to think the matter through.

He looked as if he'd like to shake her. "Not entirely," he said. "Now that you've reminded me, there was something else I intended to settle with you. Only a small matter, but not deserving to be overlooked."

Before she had more than a faint warning from his words, his arms reached for her, pulling her hard against him. He held her there for a moment; she could feel her heart pounding wildly as his hand moved briefly over her hair, then tilted her face upward. She couldn't catch her breath; his eyes were too near, his mouth too close above hers, his arms too relentlessly hard and strong as he lifted her above the floor.

"Once wasn't enough," he said evenly. "You'll not run away this time."

She tried to move her head, but his hand held her face and his mouth came down on hers. After that first moment she lost all desire to struggle; she had no will to resist the urgent demand of his lips, nor could she escape the hard strength of his body, the steady thudding of his heart against her, the ungovernable happiness which swept through her like a flame when he touched her.

But when he raised his head, she saw his face was as ungentle and stubborn as before. "Will you give me your word?" he asked sternly.

I surrender too easily, she thought desperately; I am as helpless under his skillful touch as Kate MacLachlan must be. "No," she said flatly. "May I go?"

He stepped back, his eyes searching her face. He started to speak, then changed his mind and said briefly, "Aye."

She turned and walked through the stable, past the horses in their dark stalls, through the doors to the windy coldness of the courtyard. When she reached the stairs she paused, seeing that Gavin and Kate stood above her and were not yet aware of her presence.

"I don't think I care for your advice," Kate said sharply. "I have no reason to spend the night at Inveraray."

Gavin shrugged. "As you wish, Kate."

As if she could not bear diffidence from any man, Kate smiled suddenly and put her hand on Gavin's arm. "Do you dislike me so much?" she asked softly. "I've done nothing to you, Gavin. Why do you treat me so cruelly?"

Beside Elspeth, Alexander laughed roughly. "Kate, stop practicing your wiles on Gavin. The man has no use for women."

Kate's poise was undisturbed. "Any woman would accept the challenge," she said lightly. "Do you think I'll ever win his affection?"

"See to the horses, Gavin," Alexander said. He smiled at Kate, but he did not look amused. She let her languid gaze rest on him for a moment, then looked at Elspeth.

She always appears, thought Elspeth, at such a moment as this; and behind that beautiful face she is forever plotting how to use the moment to her best advantage. Damn the woman, and Alexander MacHugh with her!

Gavin brought the horses and Alexander held his hand for Kate to mount. Elspeth had no desire to watch Kate's triumphant exit; she turned to the stairs, and in so doing surprised a look on Gavin's face that he had not intended anyone to see.

She was shocked for an instant, then dismayed beyond measure. Gavin had an eye for Kate himself; she saw it in the set of his jaw as he watched Kate with Alexander, in the way his eyes went darkly blue and cold.

"Gavin," she said to him, and he turned. "I'll not be seeing you again soon."

"Are you pleased to have done with the MacHughs?" he asked. "I imagine you'll find the company at Inveraray dull enough after a good taste of it."

She answered idly, "I warrant a pair of unprincipled ears might hear a few matters of interest now and then."

He had a disarming grin. "Well now, it were a pity not to gamble a small sum when the dice are favorable," he said. "But take care you retire from the game before you've lost all your winnings." He added quietly, "We could use an ally, but not at too great a risk."

He stood beside her for a moment longer, and when Elspeth looked up she found Kate's eyes on her again. She was studying Gavin and Elspeth with an odd intentness, her eyes going from one to the other, quite forgetting to mask her interest with the usual sleepy smile.

"Good day to you, mistress," Elspeth said. "And you, sir," she added, looking at Alexander for a brief moment. Why does Kate keep staring at us, she thought angrily. Does she think to keep all the men in Scotland safe from my charms?

She looked at Gavin and smiled. "Stay out of the clutches of the Edinburgh lassies, Gavin," she said. "You've no chance with the kind of wench who gives her favors freely to the world."

When he laughed, she turned and ran up the stairs, letting her own laughter fall behind her as it willed, on Kate's pale face and Alexander's black scowl, on Gavin's amused face.

Gavin and I are much alike, she thought unhappily; we have fallen among unseemly company. Alexander makes love to me for his own purposes, and Kate smiles on Gavin only to salve her vanity. It were better if we forgot our unruly hearts and listened to the hard cold logic of our minds.

But she did not know that the MacHugh raced the stallion to Fraoch Eilean until the ground thundered with his passing, leaving Kate far behind with only Gavin for company; and that later when he saw Gavin alone in the courtyard, he said roughly, "Christ, if Argyll uses her ill while I'm gone, I'll see him in hell before I've done with him."

"Then she didn't give you her promise?" Gavin asked blandly.

The MacHugh laughed shortly, his anger burned down to a dangerous quiet. "You know the answer to that," he said. "I only hope Glenurchy sees the danger and uses his head."

"She's important to Argyll," said Gavin. "He'll treat her well enough."

"He might use her in one of his foul schemes. She knows nothing of the man's plotting against Robert."

"Why couldn't you persuade her to stay with Glenurchy?" asked Gavin. "God's foot, Alex, have you lost that charm of yours so early in life?"

Alexander gave him a shove and they wrestled goodnaturedly in the courtyard, urged on by the clansmen around them. Then Gavin was downed with one skillful movement and Alexander held his shoulders to the ground.

"Let me up," said Gavin, "you win again." He added, "Kate is waiting for you."

"Aye, Kate is waiting," Alexander said, and his eyes met Gavin's for a moment. "Stay away from her, lad," he said quietly. "I know the way to handle her."

Gavin nodded. "She's not for me," he agreed quickly, but he turned away to hide the bleakness in his eyes.

2

Kate dropped into a chair and held her feet to the fire, pulling her skirt away from her ankles. " 'Tis a long ride, Alex. Call for wine and we'll celebrate the end of it."

When he returned, he leaned an arm on the lintel and stood looking down at her, a quizzical smile on his face. "Now tell me, Kate, what in God's name are you doing out in such weather?"

"I couldn't bear to wait till spring to see you, sweet," she said lightly. "Not even a winter snow could keep

me away." She pushed her hair away from her forehead; the curls were damp and darkly red where the
snow had drifted under her hood.

A clansman brought cups and a bottle of claret;
Alexander poured her a long draught, then one for
himself. He swung one booted foot idly. "When does
your father expect you at Lachlan?"

She laughed quickly. "I sent him word I'd arrive as
soon as possible," she said, "but I neglected to tell him
when I'd leave Rathmor."

"You twist the man around your little finger, Kate."

She crossed her slender ankles, resting them on the
brass fender, and was rewarded by the quick approval
in his eyes. "All men are fools, Alex. Even yourself."

"Aye, I'm as easy for you to manage as Kenneth
MacLachlan. 'Tis your red hair, lass."

"That's a pretty lie, but I like to hear it." She gave
him a slow smile which turned the corners of her eyes
upward in a dark line of lashes. "What have you been
doing since the Yule? I've missed you."

"Dicing with Sim and Gavin and sleeping the clock
around."

"If I didn't know you so well I might believe you."
She rested her head against the chair and closed her
eyes. "Were you too lazy to venture a ride to Rathmor? Or have you been spending your time at Inveraray?"

She realized immediately that she should not have
mentioned Inveraray; he would only be amused at such
a childish display of jealousy. She kept her eyes closed;
she could hear him moving to the table, then the slight
gurgle as he poured more wine. He walked back to the
fire before he spoke.

"You are here now," he said. "I've saved myself a
cold ride."

She smiled at him again, letting her gaze move
slowly over his brown face and the white shirt, unlaced
at his neck. His eyes were clear slate-gray, his skin
stretched smooth and brown over the high cheekbones;

the corners of his mouth were firm even as he smiled at her. He didn't appear to have spent the last weeks sleeping and dicing; he looked as hard and brown and muscular as ever. He is too alive, she thought; he takes so much of living that he leaves nothing for less fortunate men.

"You're most ungallant, Alex. I shouldn't have stopped. You don't deserve to have things come to you so easily. Especially women."

"But you can't include yourself in that general term, Kate," he said lazily. "You're a most unusual woman, and I doubt you'd come to any man easily." He grinned at her. "So you missed me? D'you want me to believe there was no one at Rathmor to entertain you?"

It was true: she had missed him to the point of desperation. But she'd never acknowledge such a thing; curse the man for seeing too much as it was, no matter what one said or didn't say.

"I was bored to distraction," she said lightly.

"We must remedy that lamentable situation," he said, and leaned over to put his cup on the table. She waited, but when he spoke again he turned the conversation abruptly. "When do you return to Rathmor? I imagine Jeannie will keep you from being bored, Kate. You may spend your time advising her on the foolish ways of men."

She slanted her eyes at him again, looking through her lashes. He was the most provoking man she had ever known, and perhaps that was partially the secret of his appeal for her. But eventually she would discover the way to manage him, the subtle attack which would reach beyond his guard of self-assurance and wariness.

"An exciting prospect," she murmured. "But I'm thankful they've at last come to an agreement. They're a dear pair."

"Aye," he said, "Sim's a fortunate lad."

"I trust he won't forget it, once he's secured her properly." He looked at her quizzically and she shrugged one shoulder. "I fear he'll be like all the rest. In a few months he'll begin to look for a son, forgetting all his romantic notions. Jeannie, being an obliging lass, will hurry to present him with a braw lad, and that will be the beginning of the end for her. She'll grow old and tired before her time, weary from bearing a bairn a year, while Sim amuses himself with younger and more eager wenches. She'd best enjoy her wooing and her wedding; God knows she'll live on the memories for a long time."

"Such bitterness, Kate. What have we done to deserve such a wretched charge?"

"Do you deny it?"

He looked at her directly, smiling faintly. "It'd be a cold man who'd take a wife only for the sake of the sons she'd bear him, Kate. Yet the matter is of major importance, I can't deny it."

"What of yourself?" she asked casually. "Do you intend to pick your wife as you would a brood mare?"

"A fascinating suggestion," he said, his eyes glinting with laughter. "Would be kind enough to turn, madam, so that I might judge the width of your flanks? And may I check your teeth, and the firmness of your chest and forelegs? Come, don't be stubborn; a man can't purchase blindly."

"Alex, stop jesting," she protested, laughing. "I'm quite serious. You know you should be thinking of heirs before Simon."

"Such talk of weddings and sons," he teased. "It takes only the hint of a marriage and women begin to get all sorts of notions."

She was almost angry with him. "You have a worthy heir in Sim, but that's a lukewarm affair. You've waited a long time, Alex. Have you found no one to satisfy you on both counts?"

"Both counts, Kate?"

She made a quick gesture with her hand. "One who'll give you both sons and pleasure, of course, since you refuse to take one without the other."

His eyes were grave then, despite his smile. "You've

caught me, Kate. I'm an extremely cautious man when it comes to the lassies."

She felt an astonishing boldness and dared finally to say the thing she had been worrying over for so long. "I know you too well to be fooled by that, sweet. You've already made your choice."

He did not speak for a long time, but his eyes were steady on hers. "It took a great many words to say that, Kate," he said at last.

She made an effort to keep her voice casual, matching his. "She'll never bring you anything but danger. Certainly you'll have no security, and perhaps nothing left to bequeath to your sons, once you have them. Argyll will ruin you if you spoil his plans for her."

"What man looks for security, Kate?"

She could tell nothing from his voice. "Only a fool refuses to consider the matter."

"Then we're back where we began. All men are fools, you said, and that includes myself." His voice was cool. She dropped her eyes, knowing she had gone too far, had flaunted her understanding of him too frankly.

He smiled suddenly, the swift smile which changed the hard lines of his face so completely. "If you can think of nothing more pleasant to discuss, I'll toss you back out in the snow," he said. "You know too much of men to call them fools to their faces, Kate."

She answered his smile and stood up slowly, holding her hands to the fire. She had not lost yet, she refused to hand him over to another woman without a fair fight. There was still something between them, else he would have been completely finished with her long before.

Yet it was an impossible situation. Even when she was in his arms, knowing the intense pleasure he gave her as a lover, she could not be certain if he received as much as he gave. Some part of him seemed to be withdrawn, kept apart and secret in his innermost being, and it was that deliberate reserve which tantalized and tormented her to the point of insanity. It was that which she longed to possess above all things, that invulnerable bit of his mind and emotions which would be known only to one woman, and to that woman for all of her life.

Thus far she had found only one way to center his attention on her, if only for a short while. It was not entirely satisfactory, for mere physical relationships seldom were, but at least she could hope that something more significant might evolve from it. She felt her pulses pounding hotly behind her eyes; it would be a splendid thing to carry Alex's son within her. A fierce, wondrous thing to feel it stirring there below her heart, part of the MacHugh that would always be part of her.

The thought brought a small tender smile to her lips, and she forgot the pity she had felt for Jeannie Lamond. To love a man and be fortunate enough to bear his sons—a woman was born for that above all things. It was something to hope for desperately, but she'd not waste her time on prayers. Such things did not happen because one prayed for them; they were the results of shrewd planning and perhaps the careful exploitation of a careless moment. Let the Lamond lass from London flutter her lashes and boast of her virtue; Kate MacLachlan would show her that a victor needed more than a pretty face and an innocent soul.

"What are you thinking, Kate?" Alexander asked softly.

Her voice was husky when she spoke. "Do you think I'd tell you?" She turned to him with a laugh, ridding her voice of that betraying emotion. "I was thinking that Fraoch Eilean is warm and comfortable, the company charming, and the thought of a cold ride in the morning extremely distasteful. But I must retire soon if I plan to reach Lachlan by nightfall tomorrow."

"Then we mustn't waste our time," he said. "There's a warm fire above, Kate. D'you want to dry your clothes?" He gave her a teasing grin. "I'd not like to have you ill from riding through the snow."

Their eyes met and held, and Kate watched as the

dark pupils of his eyes slowly obliterated the clear gray.
"You're so thoughtful, Alex," she murmured. "I think
I would like that very much." She turned toward the
door leading to the apartments above.

"Shall I send a woman from the kitchen to help
you?"

She paused with her hand on the door and threw
him a smile over her shoulder. "It won't be necessary.
I need no maid."

He stood there by the fire, watching her until she
closed the door. She picked up her skirts and moved
slowly up the curving steps, her head tilted and her eyes
narrowed.

She hated to give herself to him so carelessly and
frankly. She hated his assurance and his unhesitating
certainty that she would not deny him anything, but
more than that, she hated herself for making it so easy
for him. From the first she had let it be plainly understood that he had only to ask; strange how certain she
had once been that such a casual approach was the
only way to hold him. It was more than dangerous
now; she had not been alone with him since Elspeth
Lamond came to Rathmor, and she suspected he would
not have allowed her to stop at Fraoch Eilean this
night if some quarrel had not passed between him and
the Lamond lass. But this would be the last time he
would find it so easy; perhaps, she thought, perhaps
the next time she would have a much more powerful
weapon at her disposal.

She closed the door of Alex's bedchamber behind
her, not locking it. The fire was burning brightly on
the hearth and she began to shed her damp clothes
immediately, spreading them across a chair which she
pushed closer to the fire. Then she walked to the bed,
taking the satin blanket which lay folded at the foot of
it and wrapping it around her.

There was no mirror in the room, nor anything that
would serve her as such. But she needed no mirror;
she picked up two square brushes from the chest at the

foot of the oversized bed and began to brush her hair, leaving it shimmering and deeply red against her white shoulders. She held the blanket away from her and looked down at her white skin, triumphant in the knowledge that it was more silken to the touch than the satin blanket. The muscles of her stomach were flat and smooth, curving into the small thighs and slender legs, and the transparent creaminess of her shoulders and breasts was touched with pale gold from the firelight. She could find no flaw in the loveliness of her body, and knew a deep pleasure that he could not help but be pleased with it; it would be weapon enough for the moment.

She heard him on the stairs and then the door opened. She turned to face him, holding the blanket loosely about her. He came toward her with his quick, sure strides, and she moved her head slightly, letting the cloudy mass of her hair move over her shoulders with a sound like a whisper in the silence.

He picked her up and carried her to the bed, none too gently, and the blanket fell away from her body. He stood above her for a moment, looking down at her with the small smile still curving his mouth.

It was enough, she thought proudly. It was enough to have him looking at her for that one moment with his eyes stained almost black and his face warm and intent. His hands touched her shoulders and she closed her eyes, suddenly realizing that it would always be enough. No matter how she schemed to win him in the future by denying him, no matter how calmly she decided that this would be the last time, she knew she could never deny him anything.

He would never need to do more than merely ask.

❦ 8 ❧

ARCHIBALD Campbell, Lord Lorne, the Earl of Argyll, arrived at Inveraray Castle on a bitterly cold and windy March day.

He arrived in a nasty temper, cursing the miserable weather, his wretched mount, his sore muscles, the MacDonalds and the outrageous fate which had sent him from London in such a vicious season of the year.

The voyage to Scotland had been wild and stormy, and although the Earl did not profess to be a sailor, he had been more than a little humiliated when he fell violently ill the hour his ship put out from London harbor and did not recover until he had been several days on dry land in Edinburgh. The ride from Edinburgh had been even less comfortable, with the freezing rains and snow rendering the trails almost impassable and the wind howling about his head as if all the demons in hell had been let loose to welcome him back to Scotland.

Inveraray Castle adjusted proudly to the return of its master; the gray walls and battlements seemed to soar higher into the sky with added prestige and arrogance. The banner of Argyll flew above the castle, proclaiming to the world that the Earl was again in residence. The MacCailean Mhor, the Chief of Clan Campbell, had returned from London, and all Argyllshire hummed with the news.

The word spread rapidly through Scotland and in a short time a procession of guests, kinsmen and curious neighbors began to stream through the broad gates of

Inveraray. Elspeth was soon at her wit's end to find room for all of them; the guest apartments were crowded to the rafters almost immediately, forcing the late-comers to satisfy themselves with hastily prepared beds on the floor of the great hall. Even the most important and honored guests found themselves reluctantly sharing their couches.

There were numberless Campbells, so many that Elspeth began to wonder if Scotland would be large enough to hold the lot of them in another generation. Some of them were openly triumphant at the news of Argyll's mission to Scotland; it was no secret that the Earl had been appointed by his Majesty King James to deal out the most appropriate punishment to James MacDonald, who had recovered the island of Islay and was preparing his campaign to wrest Kintyre from the Campbells. Others were more pleased to be enjoying the hospitality of the Chief again, after such a lengthy time of existing on their private purses. The Earl could deny neither his larder nor his roof to any Campbell who asked for either, and they flocked to Inveraray to take advantage of that ancient Highland code of enforced hospitality.

The Earl was kept occupied for long hours at a time behind the closed doors of the library, while men came and went with dispatch cases and important Highland chieftains waited patiently to speak with the King's Lieutenant of the West. Duncan was at Argyll's side continually, so that Elspeth was left alone to cope with the problems of feeding and sleeping so many unexpected guests.

But she was grateful to receive a respite; by the time Argyll sent for her she had grown almost accustomed to having him at Inveraray.

"He'll not notice," she told Duncan, "but I'd best dress as if I were being presented to Jamie Stuart. Sometimes I suspect Argyll thinks of himself as a king."

She chose a gray crushed velvet gown with a magnificent petticoat of silver and muted rose stripes, and ordered her Campbell maid to brush her short curls carefully and cover them with a cap of twisted pearls. But her surmise was correct. Argyll paid not the slightest attention to her appearance.

She found him seated behind his massive table, which was piled untidily with papers and dispatches, and he greeted her with only a slight wave of his hand before returning to his work as if she were not in the room. He looked extremely preoccupied and ill-tempered, apparently indifferent to any problem which did not concern the immediate task of raising an army to march against James MacDonald. But Elspeth was not so easily deceived; she was well aware that Argyll's air of absent-minded absorption in the matter at hand meant nothing at all. Unhappily, his mind was not limited to a single undertaking; he had an indefatigable ability to engage in a dozen pursuits at the same time, no matter how time consuming and momentous, without losing sight of a single unimportant detail.

She settled herself in a chair by the fire and listened to the scratching of his quill on the parchment. He wrote with his customary haste and disregard for legibility, forcing the quill across the paper with great impatience.

She noted his embroidered doublet of green velvet and the flash of the ruby ring on his thin finger as his hand moved across the paper. He looked as stylish as ever, even to the jewel-crusted belt which held the slender dagger at his waist, and she wondered if the Campbell clansmen had been properly impressed with their lord's magnificence. Somehow the importance of fashionable clothes and jeweled swords seemed greatly lessened when one crossed over the Grampians into the Highlands, where a bright tartan carried more honor and prestige than a family coat-of-arms and men were inclined to fight with more fury and gallantry after they had tossed the greater part of their clothing aside. It was an amusing thought, but Elspeth could not conjure up a vision of the noble Argyll flourishing his sword against an enemy with his bony shoulders exposed to the elements and his unpadded knees showing bare beneath a plaid.

She jumped at the unexpected sound of his voice. "How do you like Scotland, my dear?" He looked up abruptly and she thought that his eyes were as cold and intent as ever, despite the thin smile on his face.

She shrugged. "Duncan has been most kind."

He folded the parchment and sealed it, pressing his ring into the warm wax. "Scotland seems to have agreed with you. I don't believe I've ever seen you so blooming." He pushed a pile of papers aside and folded his hands on the table, sighing. "Well, we meet again under unexpected circumstances, Elspeth. I had not thought to see you before you returned to London."

"One can never foresee the duties of a King's Lieutenant," she murmured.

"How true, my dear. 'Tis a miserable chore to chase down the King's escaped prisoners, but a task which holds some small promise of reward if successful. And I intend that it shall be successful." He dismissed the subject. "I had hoped you might return to London in the early summer, but you understand that it will be impossible for you to return alone. I've closed my house on the Strand and Lady Anne will retire to Suffolk for the summer months. However, I hope we shall sail for London together no later than the autumn."

She asked him about her friends in the gay London crowd around the court, thinking as he gave her his brief, laconic answers that she actually cared very little about the lot of them.

Argyll leaned against the back of his chair, resting his chin against two languid fingers. "I anticipate a lively season for you when you return. I gather you have been deeply missed by your friends."

Elspeth was faintly surprised that she felt nothing more than a vague curiosity about those people with whom she had spent most of her life. She remembered how desperately she had missed them at first and how lonely she had been for the court life. But that was before she had grown to know the hills and braes of western Scotland; before she had ridden like the wind over rainswept moors and eaten by a campfire; before she had tasted the sweet wild freedom of this dark and austere country.

"You have a brilliant future before you," the Earl said, his eyes on her face. "With the proper marriage, of course, and the right friends. I think we shall go far together, Elspeth."

He would see to the proper marriage, despite rebellions or wars or feuds; and she had long accepted it as the cross any single young woman must bear. But the thought of it suddenly came near to choking her. The proper marriage meant a rich, dirty old Earl with pawing hands, or a fuzzy-cheeked young peer of the realm who would be easy to rule, both financially and politically. And the proper friends, under the supervision of the Earl, and the correct manner of fawning at the Queen's elbow and overlooking the royal liberties taken by the King. Such a brilliant future, such a bright and glorious life to look forward to! She wanted suddenly to cry, but she dared not let him see even the hint of a tear.

He sensed that she was not listening and dismissed her with his customary curtness. "Would you be good enough to send Duncan in?" he asked, taking up his quill without looking at her again.

Elspeth found Duncan in his office, working on a heavy book of figures. She repeated the Earl's request, noting the quick frown which sprang to Duncan's forehead; but he went at once, with no more than a reluctant sigh.

At least she would have a few months of grace. And if only the MacDonalds proved to be more of a chore than the Earl anticipated she would have even longer, for if Argyll could not end his campaign before winter, he would be forced to delay in Scotland until the spring.

But the months were so few, she thought wearily. Such a short space of time in a person's life, such a few short months to be free and happy and young. It was too brief an escape, and she knew a sudden longing to have Alexander MacHugh beside her to shrug his wide shoulders and laugh with her about the matter.

2

Duncan stood before the fire patiently, waiting as Argyll thumbed through the stack of letters and messages before him on the table.

"I have the letter from Atholl here, somewhere in this infernal jumble. In the name of God, Duncan, have we no one in Argyllshire with a decent hand?" Argyll flung the papers away from him in a quick burst of temper. "I'll go mad with much more of this! I'm no clerk to waste my time poring over letters and figures. Surely there is a single Campbell other than myself with some slight degree of education!"

"I'll see to it," Duncan said calmly. "Someone should have been found before now."

"How does Elspeth spend her time?" Argyll asked bitterly. "Do you suppose she could spare a few hours from her embroidery? God's blood, I've more important things to do!"

Duncan warmed his hands behind him at the fire and regarded Argyll with an impassive calm. "Elspeth has her hands filled, cousin. There's more to having an army of guests at Inveraray than throwing open the gates."

"Then find some lad to do the work." Argyll ran a thin hand over his forehead, erasing the small frown between his eyes. "We've still a tremendous amount of work to be done, Duncan. I can't find the letter from Atholl, but there has been some misunderstanding about the money. He claims to have no message from the King, and until such order arrives he refuses to part with a single mark."

Duncan fingered his chin. "That's a sorry tale. Surely the King sent word before you? A man can't be expected to raise an army on credit." He added, "Why didn't you bring the money with you?"

The Earl laughed shortly. "Bring money from London? James is subsisting on his English lords; he'd not dare ask them to support such a venture. No, the only money to be turned against a Scot must come from Scotland. As far as England is concerned, any brawl in Scotland is a family affair; they'll have nothing to do with it."

"An unfortunate state of affairs. I assume we should be honored to share our poverty with so royal a beggar as King James."

"He's a Scot before he's a king." Argyll said succinctly. "But there's money to be had in Scotland, if we keep our wits about us. Atholl must be persuaded, Duncan. Gently, of course, so that he'll be followed by more stubborn individuals." He put his finger tips together and gazed at them thoughtfully. "You're much better at that sort of thing than I, cousin. You also have more friends in Edinburgh."

Duncan shrugged. "I'll not guarantee the results. No one has money to spare these days. You would have been wise to have approached the King before leaving London. He'd find it a deal easier to persuade his friends to part with their gold."

"I don't want your advice on matters pertaining to the King, cousin," Argyll said abruptly. "You need not question my wisdom on that score."

"Then I trust he agreed to reimburse you the amount you spend from your own pocket?"

Argyll frowned impatiently. "Aye, he agreed. D'you take me for a fool? As for that, God knows, I've little enough to spend, and that is precisely the reason you must go to Edinburgh. Cawdor is there at the moment, bleating angrily to the heavens, but I've no reason to think that will harm your purposes. Indeed, perhaps he'll arouse some little indignation in certain corners, enough to frighten the cowards into parting with a bit of coin. God's bones, 'tis not my quarrel alone, and I'll not bear the brunt of the expense alone!"

"Cawdor will have little to give," Duncan remarked. "He's lost his gold as well as his dignity."

Argyll's voice held nothing but contempt. "The fool should have waited. I knew it was an impossible venture from the start."

Duncan dropped in the chair before the fire, studying the toes of his boots. "It was a fair attempt," he said easily. "He had no idea James MacDonald would be allowed to escape from Edinburgh or that so many MacDonalds would rally to the cause."

"Only a half-wit would suppose that the MacDonalds would sit idly by while a Campbell took Islay." Argyll slammed his hand on the table. "If Cawdor had waited till we could join forces, the entire campaign would be less ticklish."

"I've a good deal to do in the north, Argyll. I think I'll stay at Castle Campbell, rather than in Edinburgh."

"An excellent idea. You'd best not take another's word for the number of Campbells available to be mustered, Duncan. We'll expect a good thousand men more than we'll see unless we take care to round them up." Argyll eyed Duncan closely. "I am depending on you entirely. I've no other to send who could bear such a responsibility."

"I'll promise no results," Duncan said flatly. "But I'll do my best." He drummed his fingers against the arm of his chair. "I think I shall take Elspeth with me. She deserves a change."

Argyll nodded. "As you say." He leaned back in his chair, a finger resting lightly against his mouth, and his eyes narrowed thoughtfully. "Duncan, perhaps we've overlooked a detail which might prove vastly important."

Duncan gave him a quick glance, but said nothing.

"No doubt Atholl would respond gallantly to such a comely wench. I've been slow of wit, cousin. Ofttimes a pretty face can persuade more quickly than a sword."

"Then she'll remain at Inveraray," Duncan said bluntly. "I'll have none of that."

Argyll's thin face mirrored his surprise. "You're being over virtuous, Duncan. D'you not agree she should give her services to the cause when they are so desperately needed?"

"I'll not go to Edinburgh at all in such circumstances. You must depend on my ugly face alone, or else send someone else to see Atholl." Duncan spoke quietly, but the dangerous steel beneath his voice warned Argyll that Duncan Campbell, second only to the Earl in the Clan Campbell, was not a man to be trifled with.

"I see you've grown fond of the lass," Argyll said slowly. "Are you placing sentiment before the clan, Duncan?"

"Only you would accuse a man of slighting the clan by protecting his women." Duncan's voice finally betrayed his anger. "I'll not quarrel over it. The lass is my kinswoman also, and I'll have a say in her welfare."

"Perhaps it will be best," Argyll said, shrugging. "I've great plans for her after our return to London. The girl cannot be trusted to be entirely discreet; I'd care little to have her the cause for scandal." He had a sudden thought. "Duncan, I have no intention of allowing you to spoil my future plans for her."

"And I've no intention of spoiling them," Duncan replied. "So long as you treat her with some consideration."

"She has a strange popularity in London, and if I'm fortunate I'll manage a wealthy marriage. Surely you can't complain of that, Duncan, as thin as our purses have become?"

Duncan gave Argyll a direct, searching look. " 'Tis the usual thing," he said. "If you can discover a decent husband for her, I'll not quarrel over his bag of gold."

Argyll changed the subject abruptly. "Tell me, Duncan, how do we stand in Argyllshire? I've heard many tales in London and I like the situation little." He stood up and walked to the window, placing his hands under the folds of his doublet. "D'you believe we'll have trouble while we're away dealing with MacDonald?"

"Tales have a way of sounding dire in London. I know of no trouble in Argyllshire."

Argyll looked out toward the sea and shivered slightly in the draft. "It might be the very opportunity Lamond has been waiting for."

"You're begging for trouble. Lamond has no desire for a quarrel; he's a peaceful man, and the only trouble you've had with him you've begun yourself."

Argyll turned quickly. "Surely you realize that Lamond must be subdued?" he asked sharply. "I have only the interests of the clan to guide me."

"Lamond has never been dangerous to the clan. You can't deceive me, Argyll. I've lived a good many years longer than yourself, and I'm no fool."

Argyll forced a thin smile to his mouth. "This is no time to be quarreling over Robert Lamond. I'll attend to the matter at another time." He turned back to the window. "What about MacHugh?"

"I'd venture to say he cares for peace as much as Lamond does," Duncan replied noncommittally.

"Peace, peace! To hear you, there's no man in Scotland who would lift his sword unless attacked." Argyll's voice grew as thin as his smile. "I heard in Edinburgh that the MacHugh is giving no small consideration to joining MacDonald. If that is true, we're in luck."

"I've heard the rumor."

"I've taken enough insolence from the man. We'll have the MacHugh lands soon, Duncan. We've deserved them over long."

"D'you intend to take all the Highlands?"

"No man foolish enough to join forces with a rebel has the right to hold land," Argyll said unpleasantly. "MacHugh has been a thorn in my side for more years than I care to remember. He's a rash young man and a dangerous Chief to be residing so close to Inveraray." He turned from the window, his shoulders hunched under the velvet doublet which was not protection enough against the wind blowing around the thin panes of the window. "They'll learn, they'll learn. One day they'll wake from their brawling and wenching to discover that the only two names of importance in Scotland are Campbell and Stuart. There's no room for a score of kings in the country, Duncan."

"Only two?" Duncan smiled faintly, resting his chin in his hand as he looked at Argyll.

"One in England and one in Scotland, my dear cousin." Argyll walked to a table beside Duncan's chair and reached for the narrow-necked silver bottle of wine. He poured the deep red claret into two small glasses and the firelight caught in the Venetian crystal like the flame of diamonds.

"To the success of your mission," Argyll said, raising his glass. "We've all the islands of Scotland to gain for the Campbells if we succeed, Duncan, but I'd not give a pound Scots for all of Argyllshire if we fail."

Duncan finished his wine at a single draught and stood up. "I hope Scotland will be pleased to have a Campbell king," he said, and Argyll's face flushed at the amusement in his voice. "I'd suggest you wait to try the crown for size, cousin. It might be possible that James MacDonald has just such an idea in mind."

"You are fond of jesting," Argyll said coldly.

Duncan walked to the door. "I'll get the money if there's money to be had," he said. "But I'll remind you of one thing, and you'll do well to remember it. As far as MacDonald is concerned, I'll give you all the aid within my power. But once you turn your unsavory scheming toward Robert Lamond, you'll receive no aid from me." He added calmly, "And I doubt the Mac-Hughs will submit peacefully while you attempt to ruin their Chief. The man is worshipped by his clan and has gained powerful friends in Scotland. Perhaps you might defeat them, cousin, by burning them out, but it would take a lengthy time to best the MacHughs with the sword. And I'll not aid you with a single man to accomplish it."

Argyll's face paled, leaving his mouth straight and white with rage. But when he spoke, his voice was almost indolent.

"Once MacDonald is out of the way, I'll have no need of your aid. I think myself more than capable of handling both Lamond and MacHugh."

Duncan shrugged. "You're treading a narrow precipice, cousin," he said. "Take care you don't lose your footing."

The door slammed shut behind him and Argyll stood motionless at the table, still holding the crystal glass of wine. He put it on the table slowly, noting absently that the smoldering ruby on his finger was the exact same shade of crimson as the wine.

God's wound, he had trod a narrow precipice since his birth; and now, after years of planning, he stood ready to gain a goodly portion of western Scotland to his banner. Each single incident in his life led to this triumphant moment, and the men who had schemed against him would soon be tasting the bitterness of defeat.

The Campbell kinsmen who, during his minority, had been rash enough to attempt to poison him and thus gain his inheritance for themselves; Campbell of Lochnell, who had played so treacherous a part when the Earl received his first royal commission at the age of eighteen to subdue the Catholic Earls of Erroll and Huntley, and by his betrayal saw the Earl defeated at Glenlivat and thrown into Edinburgh Castle; the fools who, throughout the Earl's life, had tried by every foul means to limit his rise to power. Aye, he'd see them all fawning at his feet ere long; and by good fortune, Jamie MacDonald would be among them.

Argyll moved the glass back and forth on the table, watching the delicate crystal flare into sparkling flames in the reflection of the fire, and his eyes were narrowed and thoughtful.

[9]

I T was a wet night. The city of Edinburgh had withdrawn behind closed doors and shutters, abandon-
ing the streets to the dark wild night. The cold rain
slanted before the wind, fingering itself in violent gusts
against the tavern signs, creaking them uneasily above
the streets. The damp salt tang of the sea was in it, a
sharp reminder that spring had not yet warmed the
cold reaches of the North Sea beyond the Firth of
Forth.

The infrequent lanterns hanging against the walls
swayed in the wind, their dim candles sputtering fret-
fully. Shivering linkboys huddled in doorways and
under tall stoops, seeking protection from the bitter
rain. The steep wynds and closes plunging down from
High Street were swept bare by the wind; even the
most disreputable rogues preferred the comfort of their
home fires to roistering about town on such a miserable
night.

Two riders turned into High Street at the Tron
Church. They rode slowly up High Street toward the
Castle, their horses making a dull clatter against the wet
cobblestones. They kept well to the center of the thor-
oughfare, avoiding both the garbage in the overflowing
gutters and the dark entrances of the narrow wynds
which twisted away from the street.

The tall Market Cross, the rallying spot of all Scotland, loomed just ahead, but on this stormy night there
were no loiterers around its massive octagonal base.
Just beyond, the tower of St. Giles Cathedral was dark

against the sky, and the riders turned to make their way through the Luckenbooths which almost blocked the street. They rode past the old Tolbooth, ignoring the high turrets and gables of the infamous prison.

Gavin pulled his cloak closer about his shoulders and felt beneath it to make certain his pistols were dry.

"I'd be easier in my mind," he said, "if we'd not left the others behind."

"We're almost there," the MacHugh said absently, his eyes searching the black depths of each close as they passed. He was unfamiliar with the tavern Montgomerie had named, but perhaps it was wiser; they wanted no unnecessary gossip. "Would ye have the entire mob of them clattering down the street behind us?"

"They were in a fair sweat to come along." Gavin could see no advantage in having a company of men, expressly chosen for their skill with the sword and pistol, if they were always left behind to warm their heels by the fire. Numbers gave a man a sense of security, even when riding on his own land in the Highlands, and surely there was no spot in all the west of Scotland which smelled so unpleasantly of danger and evil as the dirty, dark streets of Edinburgh.

"I'd have a brawl on my hands within the hour. They're not accustomed to town life." The MacHugh added sternly, "And you may keep your temper to yourself tonight. No insults, Gavin. Keep your red hair under your bonnet and your mouth shut."

Gavin grinned; he'd admit there was little in life so enjoyable as needling those cowardly Scots who believed a man born north of the Grampians nothing more than a cattle thief and reiver of the lowest sort.

"This is it," Alexander said suddenly. The tavern was shuttered against the night, but thin slivers of light fell across the close and illuminated the sign above the door. He gave the close a quick scrutiny and was satisfied; after riding through the archway, he dismounted by the door.

"I'll not be long," he said to Gavin. "Keep close by the door."

Gavin drew the horses to the wall, escaping the rain by standing under the protection of the upper floors which protruded like inverted stairs over the street.

The MacHugh pushed open the door and entered, pausing a moment on the threshold to get his bearings. A hallway ran toward the back of the tavern, while to his left, stairs mounted to the private rooms. The brightly lighted, noisy common room of the tavern opened to the right. It was surprisingly crowded for such a stormy night, smelling pungently of damp clothes, browning meat, ale and unwashed bodies. A yellow-haired serving girl hurried across the room, her tray overflowing with tankards of ale and wine, and her shrill giggling joined the rumble of laughter from her customers. At a small table directly before the door, two ill-clad ruffians were loudly arguing over a game of dice.

The MacHugh stood in the doorway, shaking his cloak free of rain, until he spotted the Earl of Montgomerie at a corner table. He strode across the room, neatly side-stepping the frantic taproom drawers with their trays, and pulled out a chair at the table. He sat down with his back to the wall, then turned his shoulders so that he could observe the door.

"A charming place, Montgomerie," he said.

The Earl of Montgomerie flushed, his round face looking hurt and unhappy. "I thought it most prudent to meet here. We'll not be so easily recognized."

"I hope I didn't spoil your game," the MacHugh said, amused. "I should have skulked through the back door, dagger in hand."

Montgomerie's face grew redder. "I see no jest in it. I take a great risk in coming here tonight."

"Then don't look so guilty about it." The MacHugh caught the eye of the serving girl and held up his hand. "You're too nervous. Any man looking this way would swear you were scheming to assassinate the King."

Montgomerie gulped and reached for his glass of wine. He downed it with a single swallow and struggled to compose his face. "Damn it, MacHugh, I'm not an old hand at this sort of thing!"

"That's more than obvious." The MacHugh grinned at the girl and her eyes widened with pleasure. "A short ale, lass," he said, and added, as she hesitated, her eyes moving over his face and helmet, "Now, if you will."

She dipped him a quick curtsy before she sped across the room, but when she returned with his tankard of foaming ale she lingered by the table. The MacHugh grinned again and threw a coin on the table; the girl tossed her yellow hair over her shoulders and bent over the table to pick up the coin.

"Thank ye, sir," she said softly. She stopped briefly at his elbow to tuck the coin down the front of her bodice.

"I waited a quarter hour before that wench served me," said Montgomerie. "How do you manage it?"

The MacHugh took a deep draught of his ale and regarded the Earl of Montgomerie over his tankard. The man was evidently serious with his idea of prudence; he wore a plain brown velvet doublet and his dark cloak carefully covered the sword at his side. He wore no jewels on his fingers, as was usually the case, and the leather purse at his belt was quite thin. Nothing betrayed that this was the son of the Countess of Montgomerie, Alan Menzies, more recently Lord Balfour, the Earl of Montgomerie, by writ of King James. Small wonder the man was so nervous, with such a shining new title to keep untarnished and clean.

"A fair wager she hails from the Highlands," the MacHugh said finally. "She noticed my crest."

Montgomerie was not appeased. "Why did you have to wear it?" His pale-blue eyes held an ill-concealed anxiety as they rested on the eagle's wing in the MacHugh's bonnet and the silver crest which glinted in the light. "Someone will recognize you."

The MacHugh shrugged. He felt a quick irritation

which died away as quickly. Montgomerie was no coward; if he seemed overly cautious, he had good reason for it. Whatever aid he gave the rebel Mac-Donalds, for whatever reason, he gave it at the risk of his own neck. And the dangerous habit of risking his neck was not so familiar an occurrence to the Earl of Montgomerie as it was to the Highlanders with whom he would lay his plans that evening.

The MacHugh finished his ale and glanced toward the door. "Where are the others? I haven't much time."

"They should be here now, unless they've had a change of heart." Montgomerie's voice was strained. "I'm not sure of MacDougal. He should have reason enough to be interested in our plans, but he's offered no advice." Montgomerie stared at his wine glumly.

The MacHugh turned his tankard idly in his hands. Aye, Sir John MacDougal of Dunolly had reason to be interested in the scheme to free Angus MacDonald from Edinburgh Castle. What better reason could a man have than the memory of the old days when a MacDougal bore the same titles of Lord of Argyll and Lorne that Archibald Campbell flaunted today? God's love, there were few men in Scotland without a grudge against the Campbells.

"He intends to wed one of Glenurchy's daughters," Montgomerie said uneasily. "I hope he carries no tales."

"MacDougal will stay with us," the MacHugh said flatly. He was not pleased with the prospect of depending on Montgomerie for the success of their plans. The man's nervousness alone would give them away. Instead of spiriting Angus from the Castle the lot of them might find themselves keeping him company in his damp cell.

The door of the tavern opened in a flurry of rain and wind. The MacHugh finished his ale quickly. "The others have arrived," he said carelessly to Montgomerie. "Shall we join them?"

"Do you think we should leave together? It might be noticed."

"Holy God, Montgomerie, use your head! Can a man no longer tip ale with his friends without attracting suspicion? Your guilt shows on you like dirty linen."

Montgomerie could not resist a quick glance at the spotless white ruffles at his wrists. "You're right, of course," he murmured. He coughed apologetically and started across the room. The MacHugh tossed a few coins on the table, threw a brief smile to the serving girl, and followed Montgomerie.

The two men had already given their orders to a serving boy and were discarding their wet cloaks as Montgomerie and Alexander entered the private room at the head of the stairs. MacDougal came forward, his hand outstretched.

"Alex, it's good to see you. When did you arrive?" MacDougal's long, serious face brightened with a rare smile.

"A few days ago." Alexander took MacDougal's hand, pleased to see the sober-minded Dunolly again. "How is the lass, John? Is she convinced yet?"

"Willing enough." MacDougal smiled. "But the Campbells are too occupied with other affairs to be concerned with mine. I must await my turn."

The other man stepped forward and MacDougal presented him. "Sir Donald MacPhee, kinsman to Malcolm MacPhee of Colonsay."

The MacHugh gave Donald a long level gaze before bowing briefly; he knew well enough that Malcolm, Chief of Clan MacPhee, was one of James MacDonald's most ardent supporters, and the presence of young Donald emphasized the importance of their plans.

"The MacHugh," Donald said quietly, his eyes curious. He was young, barely out of his teens, but his cold eyes and the uncompromising set of his mouth showed plainly the lad had not gone untouched by the harsher demands of life. The MacHugh felt his hopes rising.

"I've heard many things about you, MacHugh," Donald said, pulling out a chair. "I hardly expected to meet you in such circumstances, but I'll confess I'm happier to know you're with us."

The MacHugh grinned. "If you heard them from Jamie MacDonald, I'll waste no more time. Name the place and weapons and we'll have done with."

MacPhee's icy eyes warmed slightly. "I've been forewarned, sir. I trust our swords will always be on the same side of a quarrel."

Montgomerie dropped into a chair, his face unhappy again. "Can't we get to the matter at hand?" He paused as the serving boy entered the room with his tray of tankards and waited until the door had again closed behind him. "I've more calls to make tonight."

MacDougal looked around the table. "We're in luck," he said. "Campbell of Glenurchy is in Edinburgh."

"Glenurchy here?" Montgomerie's eyes widened; he tightened his hands on the arm of his chair. "You call it luck? Are you a complete fool, MacDougal?"

MacDougal stared at him coldly. "I spoke to him this morning. It appears that Argyll is short of funds and Glenurchy is here to persuade his friends to part with their gold." He laughed shortly. "He even approached me." The MacHugh and Donald MacPhee laughed with him. "We should consider ourselves fortunate that they are too concerned with obtaining credit to give any thought to Angus MacDonald now. The task will be easier for us." He looked at Montgomerie again, distaste in his voice. "I have no intention of hiding at the sign of a Campbell, trembling in my boots with fear."

Montgomerie looked perturbed. "He'll discover the plot sooner or later."

The MacHugh rested his chin on his hand and regarded Montgomerie silently, and MacPhee sighed softly.

"As long as he doesn't discover it before Angus is safe in Islay," said MacDougal, "we've nothing to worry us."

"Do you know the plans?" Donald said to the Mac-Hugh.

"Only that it might be possible to get to Angus." James MacDonald's letter had merely asked if the Mac-Hugh would contact the Earl of Montgomerie in Edinburgh. He had not mentioned sending Donald Mac-Phee, though such strategy could be expected from the wily MacDonald. But Montgomerie was not yet explained and the MacHugh gave a faint nod of his head in the Earl's direction. "Money problems?" he asked MacPhee.

MacPhee nodded. "The MacDonald has been fortunate in his choice of friends," he said shortly, a hint of laughter in his voice. The MacHugh felt an amused sympathy for the Earl. A man in Montgomerie's position, with a newly acquired earldom to protect and finance, deserved a certain admiration for refusing to shun his former friends, but he was likely to find himself in embarrassing difficulties when he befriended such a crafty old rebel as MacDonald. Doubtless the MacDonald was practicing a gentlemanly sort of blackmail, a devious occupation at which he excelled.

"What will it be, MacPhee?" Alexander asked abruptly. "A rope over the rocks? That's been tried too often for comfort. Angus would probably prefer to stay inside the Castle."

"His lordship," MacPhee said smoothly, with a nod in Montgomerie's direction, "has convenient friends. A well-placed bribe, a cell left unlocked, a new guard who will not recognize the prisoner. Angus will walk out of the Castle."

The MacHugh's tongue found his cheek. He looked at Montgomerie and said gravely, "Do you play dice, m'lord? 'Tis a fair occupation to pass the time in a castle cell."

"Occasionally," Montgomerie said evenly. "Do you think . . . is there a possibility that something will go wrong?"

The MacHugh looked at Donald and raised his

brows, and Donald grinned. "I'm afraid his lordship has led a sheltered life, sir," he drawled. "Fate must have been unco' kind to him."

Montgomerie reddened at the implication. He hit his hand against the table, palm down. "I'm not concerned over my own welfare! How do you propose to get Angus MacDonald out of Edinburgh? Do you realize your heads might soon be decorating the spikes on the Tolbooth? Have you no sense of caution?"

The MacHugh said, "So many questions, m'lord," and laughed softly. Montgomerie looked at the men around the table, but he found nothing in their impassive faces to encourage him. He could not reason with such men. Their disregard for danger seemed almost like contempt; they were nonchalant to the point of insolence. The Earl of Montgomerie realized suddenly that his apprehensions were out of place in this company. To a Highlander who lived his life in peril and danger, fear was a disastrous and fatal emotion; the proper caution would be observed before the first move was made, and beyond that a man failed or succeeded by his wits and his sword arm.

MacDougal broke the silence. "We intend to take Angus to Dunolly until we can get him safely to Islay, Alex. I'll wait in Dunfermline. McPhee will be outside the city."

The MacHugh grinned. "And I'm to escort the man through Edinburgh. I should have known you'd save the most interesting task for me."

Donald MacPhee's voice was low. "Aye, you're to get him out of Edinburgh. You're to see that he arrives at Dunolly without mishap. MacDougal and I are to take orders from you."

"Simple enough," the MacHugh said laconically, his mind moving ahead to weigh the possibilities of getting a well-known prisoner out of the city. "Then you will deliver him to Jamie, MacPhee?"

"I believe that MacDonald hoped you would take

complete charge," MacPhee said slowly. "From Edinburgh to Dunyveg."

"Alex, I don't like that," MacDonald said sharply.
He put his tankard on the table and leaned toward the
MacHugh. "This is not the time, 'tis too soon."

"I won't be riding to Islay for a few weeks," the
MacHugh said, his eyes on Donald MacPhee. He spoke
casually, but the message was plainly there for Mac-
Phee to carry to James MacDonald. "Simon is to be
married in May, and I must be there. My brother and
heir, MacPhee."

MacPhee understood. An heir was of greater importance to the Clan MacHugh than the MacDonald rebellion; the MacHugh could not ride into battle until the
future security of his clan was well determined, for a
man, even one so legendary as Alexander MacHugh,
did not always return from battle.

"We can meet later to discuss the details," said the
MacHugh.

MacPhee relaxed visibly. "Where are you staying,
MacHugh?"

"I have a house in the Cowgate."

Montgomerie jumped nervously. "D'you mean you're
staying in your own house, openly?" he asked incredulously.

The MacHugh was growing weary of the Earl's
trepidations. "Can you give me a good reason for not
doing so, sir?" he asked curtly. "Any one of the men
with me would be immediately recognized as a Mac-
Hugh." His voice became dangerously quiet. "A Mac-
Hugh is not ashamed of his name, Montgomerie, nor
does he fear it will be disgraced by his actions." He
turned away from Montgomerie's glare and spoke to
MacDougal. "I must see Glenurchy, John. Did he tell
you how long he would be in Edinburgh?"

"Only a few days," MacDougal answered. "He's
only just returned from escorting his kinswoman, the
Lamond lass, to Castle Campbell beyond Stirling. I

didn't see them, but I understand they spent a short while in Edinburgh."

The MacHugh felt a quick relief; the lass was safe with Duncan, then. MacDougal smiled. "I'm beginning to think we both have an interest in Campbell affairs, Alex."

"A lass is always sufficient to stir a bit of interest," Alexander said lightly. "Even with Argyll guarding her bedchamber."

"No doubt it makes the game more interesting, but I don't envy you. The odds are most assuredly against you, Alex." MacDougal laughed, but the frown deepened on Montgomerie's face.

"I've heard of the beauteous wench," he said, his words holding a slight sneer. "You'd best stick to your serving girls, MacHugh, and keep well away from Argyll's fair kinswoman. I'll wager Argyll will have her bedded soon enough, if he can find a fool with enough gold, but you'll not be that man."

The MacHugh stood up slowly, pushing back his chair with his boot. "I tire of your advice, sir," he said, his voice hard. "Nor do I care to have Mistress Lamond insulted in this company. I'll have your apology."

There was complete silence around the table. The MacHugh's words were low and deliberate, but his gray eyes were almost black with anger.

Montgomerie hesitated. "I owe no one an apology."

"Montgomerie!" MacDougal warned, getting to his feet. He had known the MacHugh a lengthy time, and he knew that dangerous tone of voice. MacPhee sat quietly, looking at Alexander MacHugh.

"Your temper is too hasty, MacHugh," Montgomerie said stiffly. He felt his own anger stirring. "I had no idea you felt so strongly about Mistress——"

"Hold your tongue," the MacHugh commanded flatly. "I'm waiting for an apology." His hand went to his sword.

MacDougal spoke. "I'm sure his lordship meant no harm, Alex."

The MacHugh said nothing. Montgomerie's eyes moved from the MacHugh's face to the scabbard at his side, where the thin, wicked blade of the sword showed several inches. He wished he had kept his mouth shut. He could point out that even the MacHugh might not speak so insolently to the Earl of Montgomerie, but it seemed extremely unwise at the moment. The Earl was no coward, but he felt himself a fool. Facing a hot-tempered Highlander was folly enough; facing Sir Alexander MacHugh, his hand already resting on his sword, was perilous to the point of imbecility.

"A brawl in a public tavern is a degrading affair," the Earl said heavily. "MacDougal is right. I meant no harm." He swallowed his anger and bowed briefly. "Your pardon, sir."

There was a sharp, metallic click as the MacHugh slipped his sword back into the scabbard. The sound was loud in the silence. Montgomerie regained his composure and turned to the other men, ignoring Alexander MacHugh. "By your leave," he said. Then he remarked haughtily to the room at large, "You may contact me when your plans are completed." He stalked across the floor, his cloak swinging behind him, and the door slammed.

MacDougal sighed and dropped into a chair. "He's a fool, Alex, but we must use him. For the love of God, don't run him through before we get Angus out of Edinburgh Castle!"

Alexander laughed shortly. "He's no fool, John. Only a gentleman who keeps questionable company with wild Highlanders. He should know better."

"You have dangerous habits, MacHugh," Donald MacPhee said thoughtfully. "Tell me, sir, do you make it a daily affair, challenging the King's peers?"

"His earldom doesn't keep him from jangling on my nerves," the MacHugh said lightly.

MacPhee toyed with the pearl-handled dirk at his side. "Might I ask about the lady in question? The Mistress Lamond?"

"You may ask, but small good it'll do you." Alexander fastened his cloak unhurriedly and grinned at MacPhee. He walked to the door, pulling on his gloves. "I'll see you tomorrow, MacPhee? My lads will be anxious to hear any news you've brought us from Jamie MacDonald."

MacPhee nodded. He was beginning to understand why James MacDonald placed such faith in the Mac-Hugh.

"I'll be leaving the city in the morning, Alex," Mac-Dougal said. "I'll be at the Black Horse Inn in Dunfermline."

Alexander stood in the door. "If anything goes wrong, John, you'd best go to Dunolly immediately. You can swear you went straight there from Edinburgh."

" 'Tis no graver risk for me than for yourself," Mac-Dougal said quietly. "I'll not avoid my share of the blame."

"None of us will be taking the blame," said the Mac-Hugh. "Angus can write from Islay, explaining that he flew over the Castle walls on the tail of a MacDonald gull. We'll see you in Dunfermline town, MacDougal, and if you value your life you'll save us some of the blude-red wine."

The door swung closed behind him and the two men heard his quick strides on the stairs. He was whistling the old ballad of Sir Patrick Spens, and the gay tune seemed to linger behind long after the door of the tavern had slammed loudly in the hall below.

❦ 10 ❧

THE MacHugh spent the next few days in his town house in the Cowgate, laying careful plans with MacPhee. His men were instructed to stay close to the premises, and they passed the time at dice and cards in the library. If the enforced idleness grew more boring by the hour, there were no audible complaints. The men who rode in the MacHugh's company had learned long before that only a man willing to be proved a fool questioned the Chief's instructions.

One warm afternoon Alexander and Gavin rode down the Cowgate toward the Grassmarket. They had decided to wait no longer. The Earl of Montgomerie had notified them that all was ready and a messenger had left for MacDougal in Dunfermline. That evening, shortly after dark, Angus would leave Edinburgh Castle and step into a waiting sedan chair, which would carry him to the Grassmarket. Alexander would meet him there and, if all went according to plan, they would leave the city by the West Port, trusting their movements would not attract suspicion in the crowds which would still throng the Grassmarket at that hour. MacPhee would be waiting on the road beyond the city, ready to draw any possible pursuers in another direction.

Alexander rode past the old Magdalene Chapel, now a meeting place for the craftsmen who belonged to the corporation of the Hammermen, and turned into Candlemaker Row, a steep street which shortly emerged in the Grassmarket.

He glanced down the street to his left toward the Greyfriars' Church, marking it as another line of escape in the event that something went amiss at the West Port. Or they could ride down the Cowgate to the south back of the Canongate. He hoped it would not be necessary; he had no desire to be cornered in the dubious sanctuary of the Royal Park.

The Grassmarket was the city marketing place for flesh, wool, timber and corn. Stacks of heather and straw blocked the street; great shanks of beef and mutton hung from bloody poles extended before open booths; on every side the countrymen who had swarmed through the West Port that morning offered their wares with a deafening rivalry.

Alexander and Gavin dismounted and led their horses through the crowded square. They gave careful attention to the wynds and closes leading from the Grassmarket, but neither of them looked up at the great bulk of Edinburgh Castle, towering directly over them. They climbed through Bell Wynd to High Street, mounting to ride down the Lawnmarket toward St. Giles. The crowds grew larger as they approached the cathedral; the booths and krames clustered around the church and lining the street had displayed their wares in the open, taking advantage of the unusually sunny skies.

Alexander reined his horse abruptly. Outside a tiny jeweler's shop a groom held a large light bay. The man wore his vivid Campbell livery with a conscious pride, ignoring the dirty urchins who scrambled to pluck at his velvet doublet.

"I'd not thought of it till this moment," said Alexander, "but it would seem only proper for me to purchase a trinket for the lass."

"Which lass?" Gavin dismounted and took Tammie's reins. "The one I'm thinking of might throw it back in your face." He grinned at the thought, finding it more than entertaining. "Go waste your gold. There's always the chance you might find a more appreciative lass, if she'll not have it."

The jeweler's krame was small and dark after the brightness of the street. The only patron was Sir Duncan Campbell of Glenurchy, gazing reflectively at a richly carved gold ring which rested on a square of black velvet. He looked up as Alexander entered.

"MacHugh, I need your advice," he said. "The man would cheat me of my teeth if he only dared to sell them again for a neat profit. I've been away from Balloch a lengthy time and had best return with a bauble or two. D'you think this would seem too large for my lady's hand?"

Alexander looked at the ring, then pushed it aside and pointed to a diamond brooch in the form of the Thistle of Scotland.

"Then a bright bauble for her newest gown, Glenurchy. She'll be much happier with it."

Glenurchy frowned. "I've no doubt of it. And my purse will be lighter by several pounds Scots. I find I've changed my mind, MacHugh. Take your advice elsewhere."

Alexander grinned and leaned against the table. " 'Tis no wonder you're so close with your gold, being in the city to beg it from others." He turned the brooch over in his hand, watching the sparkling flash as the gems caught the light from the open door. "A lass always prefers a trinket that sparkles. A man has only to tell her that it matches the shine of her eyes."

Duncan opened his leather purse reluctantly and dropped several gold pieces on the velvet cloth. "I'll have to beg a goodly amount to cover this loss. I admit defeat, MacHugh. You know more of women than I. Tell me, what business do you have with Brodie? I trust you'll allow me to offer you the same kindly advice?"

The jeweler hopefully lifted a slender chain of dark red rubies for the MacHugh's inspection. Duncan nodded, pleased.

"Ah, Brodie, 'tis a beauty. Give him your gold, Mac-Hugh, and I'll have had my revenge."

Alexander shook his head and picked up a small golden circlet, attached to a similar one by a delicate chain. The bracelets seemed too tiny for even the wrist of a lass; they jingled together as he held them. "My lass will like this fair enough, Glenurchy. A jingle is as pleasing as a sparkle."

Inside one gold circlet the words "Fear na ye" had been inscribed; in the other, "My ain true luve."

"A pretty sentiment," said Alexander. He paid Brodie and pocketed the bracelets. "No need to spoil a lass with rubies and diamonds till you have her properly wed."

Duncan laughed and they walked together into the sunlit High Street. Duncan paused at his horse. "What mischief are you plotting, Alexander? This is the first sign I've had of you, and I've been in the city well past a week. The ladies are grumbling that you've been leading quite a cloistered life. 'Tis most unlike you."

"If I have your word you'll not spread the gossip, I'll tell you," Alexander said gravely. "I'm being true to a certain lass. 'Tis a sore trial to my soul, but I must avoid the pitfalls of temptation."

Glenurchy snorted indelicately. "I know of no lass in Scotland with so pious an influence. Well, no matter; I'll get the truth of it in time." He mounted his horse and held the reins loosely over his arm. "But I might tell you, Alexander, that I left my best horseflesh behind in Argyllshire and hid my womenfolk well away from Edinburgh. I took no chances."

"You may sleep soundly, Duncan," Alexander said, grinning again. "I've no designs on you."

Duncan returned the grin and wheeled his horse, followed by his groom. The crowds made way for the large light bay and Glenurchy cantered easily down High Street, his erect carriage and powerful shoulders attracting as much attention as the magnificent horse he rode.

Gavin rode thoughtfully beside the MacHugh. "I like that man, Alex. I find myself overlooking the plain fact that he's a Campbell."

Alexander laughed. "'Tis just as well there's only one Glenurchy. We'd have a dull time of it, and that's a fact."

2

Beyond the West Port the Queensferry road curved under the shadow of Edinburgh Castle, then dipped steeply to the Water of Leith. The MacHugh rode through the sleeping village of Dean, his men clattering noisily behind him. There were no shutters opened in alarm, no challenges from the night watchmen. The populace of the little town by the Waterside had become accustomed to the sound of hasty riders spurring their horses along the road to the ferry, which crossed the Firth of Forth and led straight into the Highlands.

When the village lay behind in the night, the men quickened the pace to a hard gallop. Angus MacDonald was not yet safe. Sixteen miles stretched between Edinburgh and Dunfermline; the alarm would have been sounded at the Castle long before the MacHughs reached the ferry.

A thick haar had drifted up from the sea in the late afternoon, mercifully obscuring the road in a soft white mist and muffling the sound of hoofs. Somewhere ahead in the damp fog MacPhee was waiting impatiently beside the road; in a wayside Dunfermline tavern, John MacDougal was readying his men and horses for the long ride to Dunolly.

So far the plans proceeded without mishap. Montgomerie had managed his part of the plan without arousing suspicion; the proper guard, with an eye to a heavy purse and a glib tongue to deny any such greed when questioned later, had been approached and found agreeable, and the actual escape from the Castle had

been no more difficult for Argus than finding the stout
doors between him and freedom unlatched and unguarded during the few minutes when most of the garrison was at the evening meal. The curtained sedan
chair awaiting him had taken him swiftly to the Grassmarket, where he donned a MacHugh plaid and lost
himself in the center of the horsemen riding behind
Alexander MacHugh.

The guards at the West Port had not been curious;
there was nothing alarming in the departure of a Highland chief, his "tail" of men riding behind him. Mac-
Phee must have gone through the gates only a short
time before, but if the guards wondered at the heavy
traffic on the Queensferry road at such a late hour, they
were not inclined to broach the subject to a company
of hotheaded Highlanders.

There were no signs of pursuit. The riders crossed
the Almond Water at Cramond Bridge, and Alexander
spurred Tammie to a faster pace, blessing the thick haar
which covered their flight and yet thinking that a bit of
moonlight would have speeded the ride.

The rider which suddenly emerged from the mist
directly before them startled both the MacHugh and
Gavin, riding close together. It was no peaceful traveler
proceeding to Edinburgh; no sane man would have
ridden that dark road alone. The MacHugh reined his
horse instantly and the stallion reared his forelegs
wildly in the air.

The man shouted his identity immediately and the
MacHugh answered. It was a MacPhee, his voice hoarse
and winded.

"We ha' an ambush ahead, MacHugh," he gasped,
slipping from his saddle. "Cawdor's men, beyond Dalmeny Church!" He paused for a moment to catch his
breath. "Sir Donald sent me to warn ye. Make a circle
to the ferry. They dinna know ye be on the road."

Angus MacDonald's voice came out of the darkness
behind Alexander. "Damn Cawdor!" he exploded. "We

can't leave MacPhee to fend off a band of whoreson Campbells, MacHugh!"

The MacHugh clansmen were silent. MacPhee was a MacDonald supporter, he had aided James Mac-Donald to recover Islay from Cawdor. This was Cawdor's petty form of revenge; at the last moment their careful plans were to be ruined, the evening's work would go for naught because of Cawdor's unwitting interference.

The MacHugh considered the new twist of affairs briefly, then gave his orders to Gavin. "Take a dozen men and circle through the woods. Get Angus to Dunfermline as quickly as possible." His hard voice cut off Gavin's protests, and he added flatly, "You're to stay with Angus until he gets to MacDougal, Gavin. We've come too far to be outdone now."

Angus MacDonald said nothing. The MacHugh was right; if Cawdor's men knew nothing of the escape from the Castle, there was no need to uncover the fact that Angus was free and riding with the MacHughs. He wheeled his horse and left the road with Gavin; before the horses had crossed the ditch the MacHugh had spurred his horse ahead.

He had ridden less than half a league when he heard the unmistakable sounds of battle: the harsh clang of swords, the whinnying of frightened horses, the rough shouts of men fighting in close quarters. The glimmer of light became clearer; someone carried a burning torch high above his head to distinguish between friend and enemy.

The MacHugh did not hesitate. Silence was not important, for the mere sound of approaching horses might momentarily confuse the Campbells. His men rode close behind, their swords unsheathed and their targes held securely before them. They could not use their pistols for fear of cutting down MacPhee's men, but once they drew closer there was no difficulty in distinguishing the bright MacPhee tartan.

The MacPhees were completely surrounded, fighting

desperately in the center of the road. Alexander plunged into the fight without pause and the Campbells turned to face the new enemy which had appeared so suddenly out of the darkness. Now that aid had reached the victims of their ambush, they would undoubtedly scatter and flee, but Donald MacPhee was still in danger. It would make little difference to Cawdor if his enemy were not brought to him alive; if he were killed outright there would be fewer difficulties later.

The MacHugh's blade was up and on the swing, and he gave a slashing cut against the nearest horseman and the Campbell tumbled from his saddle. A heavy blow fell against his targe, but the MacHugh urged the stallion ahead. The confusion was so great for a moment that he lost sight of MacPhee; when he saw him again the young clansman was fending off one Campbell with his targe and matching swords fiercely with another.

The MacHugh had almost reached Donald MacPhee; he leaned in his saddle and swung his sword toward the Campbell on MacPhee's left, a terrible backhanded blow with the edge of his blade that meant certain death for the unfortunate enemy who could find no guard for it. The man fell, the gushing blood staining his clothes; and MacPhee turned to back toward the stallion while holding off the remaining Campbell.

Then there was a faint arc of light, followed by complete darkness. Someone had downed the man with the torch. At the same moment the MacHugh felt the jostle of another horse against Tammie. He turned swiftly, just before the torch curved down into darkness, but he was not quick enough. He saw the rider briefly in the instant before the light was extinguished, then felt the sharp stab of pain in his shoulder. Another blow descended on his targe, knocking it from his arm, and the numbness began to spread through his body.

He heard MacPhee shout, but the sound was far away and muted; the noise of steel clattering against steel faded away slowly, until all was a dull silence around him. He felt himself falling and put out his arms to grasp the stallion's neck, but his hands seemed to encounter nothing but soft wet air which engulfed him in a blackness darker than the night.

3

The MacHugh opened his eyes to a ring of grim, anxious faces.

A single candle guttered and flickered, shedding a dim light from somewhere above him; he could see, beyond the circle of faces, the gray stone of a vaulted arch. His head was pillowed on something soft, a cloak or jack, but beneath his hands he could feel the cold clammy touch of stone. He was in Dalmeny Church, then, and there was no sight of a Campbell.

MacPhee knelt beside him. "You took a bad one in the shoulder, sir," he said quietly. He held a flask in his hand and the MacHugh raised himself on his elbow to take it. The pain was quick and sharp in his shoulder and arm; he could feel a heavy bulge of peat moss padded against the wound, beneath his shirt. The whisky was raw and burning, but it seemed to clear his head.

It cleared his vision enough for him to see Gavin's face, oddly pale and serious under his red mop of hair. Gavin spoke quickly when he saw the MacHugh's expression.

"We waited at the ferry," he said. "When you didn't come, I sent a man to see if you needed help." His voice held no apology for disobeying orders. "I should have known better than to leave you at all."

Alexander found himself smiling, despite the pain. "I'll hold you to blame for this, man." He sat up slowly, looking for Angus MacDonald. They were all there, gathered around the small space on the stone floor where he had been lying. His helmet was beside him; he picked it up and slipped it on, using only his right hand.

"Thank God 'tis my left shoulder," he said shortly. "Let's ride, MacPhee. We'll be caught if we linger the entire night."

They moved back as he stood up, using a broad stone pillar for support. Angus MacDonald stepped forward, frowning. "Ye can't go far with that shoulder, MacHugh. Why don't ye ride back for Edinburgh with Gavin? I'll make it to Dunfermline."

"I've nothing to do in Edinburgh."

MacPhee didn't speak. He handed the MacHugh his sword and the broad targe with the MacHugh arms embossed in steel across the surface. The men went out into the darkness; there were low murmurs as those outside were told the orders.

The MacHugh slung the targe over his shoulder and Gavin buckled it. He walked toward the door, counting the steps to himself until he reached the firm support of stone. The nagging pain seemed to move across his chest, shortening his breath.

MacPhee's quiet voice came from behind him. "I'm sorry, sir," he said simply. "I didn't intend to draw you into it."

"Unless you were the man who skewered me, you've no apology to make," the MacHugh said briefly; he could not waste his breath with words. Tammie was just outside the church; Alexander mounted, with Gavin's help, thankful that the stallion had come through the skirmish without a scratch.

They had lost valuable time in the church, but there was yet no sound of pursuing horsemen. They rode slowly to the ferry, crossing the Forth in the thick mist which still hovered close to the earth.

Before Dunfermline was reached, the MacHugh called a halt. His shoulder and arm had begun to throb incessantly, irritated by the steady motion of the long ride in the saddle. He felt light-headed and giddy from the loss of blood. He had ridden with his right hand on the saddle pommel, giving the stallion his head along the road.

At St. Margaret's stone he reined his horse and held up his hand so that Gavin could pass the word back to the men. He slid from the saddle and leaned against Tammie, taking a deep breath to quiet the uneven beating of his heart.

MacPhee cantered up beside him and dismounted. He unbuckled the flask from his belt and held it out to the MacHugh. "Take all of it," he suggested. "I'll replenish it with some of MacDougal's blude-red wine."

Alexander downed the whisky with a single gulp and the fiery liquid seemed to blunt the edge of the pain. He returned the flask to MacPhee and wiped his mouth with his arm.

He had made his plans, but he was not certain MacPhee would agree with him. "We'll leave you in Dunfermline," he said slowly. "You must explain to John MacDougal. The two of you will have to take Angus to Dunolly." He added, with a trace of amusement, "I doubt I'd be of much aid to you."

"You must stop in Dunfermline, sir," MacPhee said. "One of us will remain behind until you're able to travel to Argyllshire."

"Don't be a fool, MacPhee." It was growing more difficult to keep his words distinct and separate. Alexander motioned to Gavin. "It would only endanger all of us. They'll search Dunfermline no later than tomorrow. None of us must be there."

MacPhee protested. "Where will you go, sir? You can't ride much further. I'll not leave you like this."

Alexander looked at Gavin and attempted a grin. Gavin understood suddenly; he laughed aloud. "God's body, Alex, why didn't I think of it? Your brain should be muddled, not mine!"

MacPhee looked at the two of them and shook his head. "I don't like it. You'll need attention for that shoulder."

"You shall meet MacDougal in Dunfermline, Mac-

Phee. I'll take my men straight through the town. We'll ride for Dollar."

"Dollar?" MacPhee repeated incredulously. " 'Tis a fair twelve miles from Dunfermline! And you'll never escape recognition in such a small village."

"I don't intend to remain in Dollar," the MacHugh said carefully. He turned to the stallion and Gavin held out his hand. Alexander mounted slowly, holding his left arm against his body.

"I'm going to Castle Campbell, MacPhee," he said, and his tone did not invite more argument.

MacPhee shrugged. Only the MacHugh could suggest such an irrational thing and make it appear quite sane and logical. MacPhee knew he could not dissuade the man, but he hoped desperately that the MacHugh had not misjudged the lass for whom he drew his sword against the Earl of Montgomerie.

"Then I'll wish you every good fortune," he said, putting out his hand. The MacHugh's grasp proved to be as firm and strong as if the man had never been wounded. "We'll meet again in Islay. Is there any message you'd care to send Jamie MacDonald?"

"None until I see him," the MacHugh said. He shook hands with Angus MacDonald, who had ridden up beside them. "A fair ride to Islay," he said cheerfully, then wheeled his horse with his good hand on the reins and rode toward the dim lights in the distance.

The town of Dunfermline sat bestride a hill overlooking Pittencrieff Glen. The MacHugh led his men down the High Street of the town and took the track to the northwest which led by the Cleish Hills to Dollar. He did not turn in his saddle to wave a last farewell to MacPhee and Angus MacDonald; it took all his concentrated effort to stay erect in the saddle. The ride to Castle Campbell stretched interminably ahead; he had a faint suspicion he would never be able to walk into the castle. The thought was amusing, despite the piercing agony of the hole in his shoulder. The lass from London would enjoy the sight of the MacHugh being carried into her fortress, feet first.

The track to Dollar was rough and narrow. The stallion took the rocky ground and unexpected holes with his usual dexterity, but each jolt and sudden swerve seemed to shake the MacHugh until his nerves were small burning flames. The salt beads of sweat dripped into his eyes and ran cold against his mouth; he discovered he had bitten his lips with his teeth until he could taste the blood on his tongue. Finally he leaned forward, bracing himself by putting his arm around the pommel of the saddle and resting against the horse. He did not look, but he was aware that Gavin was riding abreast, so close that Gavin's foot in the stirrup occasionally brushed against his.

When they reached the dark sleeping village of Dollar, the mist had lifted, leaving the night clear and cold. Alexander gave his orders in an uneven voice to Gavin. The men would spend the rest of the night at Dollar; if they could find no inn to take them, they would suffer little from a night in the open air. It was a habit with them to prefer the sky above and their warm plaids beneath to the dirty, cramped accommodations of a village inn.

He and Gavin would ride alone to Castle Campbell; he would send further orders by Gavin on the morrow. If they did not hear from him, they were to proceed immediately to Fraoch Eilean. He had no doubt the men would ignore the last order, but he was too weary to be firm.

He remembered very little of the trip to Castle Campbell from Dollar. He looked up at the dark sky once, seeing the stars blurred and wavering before his eyes, and the effort almost cost him his balance. He tightened his grip on the saddle, fighting the urge to roll from Tammie's back to the comfort of the hard, unmoving ground. The motion grew as wallowing and reeling as the lift of sea waves during a storm; he felt sick and dizzy with the constant undulation of the stallion's stride.

The approach to the castle was along the bed of the burn, climbing through a narrow, towering canyon which grew steeper and more arduous by the step. Gavin dismounted and led the MacHugh's horse, securing his own to a heavy boulder beside the trail.

When the dark walls loomed above them, Alexander said, "Go ahead and test our welcome." Gavin disappeared into the darkness, his boots making a great noise on the rocky path. Alexander slumped in the saddle, not daring to dismount for fear he would lose his footing on the treacherously narrow path. It seemed hours that he waited there in the night; he cursed the delay silently, even though he knew that the garrison must be aroused before the gates would be opened.

Finally he heard Gavin's voice at his elbow, coming from a hazy distance. "They've opened the gates. Can you make it that far?"

The MacHugh dismounted, sliding off his horse. Gavin put his hand under Alexander's good arm and guided him through the darkness to the oblong square of light that fell from the open gates of the castle. Alexander stumbled as he reached the guard standing in the passageway and immediately felt another steadying hand.

Gathering his strength, he shook off their support and stood erect. His mind was as fuzzy and dull as the pain was relentless in his side, but his eyes immediately focused on Elspeth Lamond, standing in the courtyard before him. She was wearing a velvet robe over her night clothes and her hair was a bright gold in the light; behind her he could see the Campbells of the garrison gathering in the yard, hastily clothed and slapping their arms together in the chill of the night.

He had caused quite a stir, Alexander thought vaguely, and wondered why the guard had called the lass from her sleep. To identify him, mayhap, and it'd be no more than he deserved if she declared she had never set eyes on him before.

He shook his head stubbornly to clear his vision. "Lass," he said hoarsely, "I find myself at your mercy."

He attempted to grin at her, but a sharp stab of pain moved up before his eyes in a burning curtain. He stumbled the few steps to the stone wall which led from the gates to the courtyard and leaned his good arm against it, letting the paralyzing darkness sweep over him in successive waves. Beyond the immediate circle of pain he could hear her voice, urgent and alarmed, yet oddly reassuring.

"Gavin, how far have you ridden since it happened? Take the other side, I'll help you get him to a bed." Then he felt her hands on his left arm, gentle and unhurting. She spoke curtly to a Campbell, ordering him out of her way. "Don't touch him, I'll manage. Through the door ahead, Gavin, then turn to your left down the corridor."

Alexander was conscious of an unreasonable pride in the lass. She'd not turn frightened or hysterical, nor wring her hands in a squeamish manner at the sight of blood. Aye, she'd make a bonny wife for a Highlander; he must remember to tell her.

He sank into the merciful softness of a feather mattress, letting the dark night settle over him at last. The last thing he remembered was the sound of her voice, speaking over his head to Gavin.

"You'd best find yourself a bed, Gavin. You look weary enough to drop." Then she added softly, "Don't worry about the big bairn. I'll not leave him."

With those incredible words in his ears, the Mac-Hugh finally surrendered to the pain he had been fighting for such a lengthy time. He was safe. His lass would tend his wound.

❧{ 11 }❧

ELSPETH tossed her needlework on the table beside her chair with an impatient frown. She put her thumb to her mouth, annoyed at her awkwardness with the needle.

"I've pricked myself again," she said plaintively. "My finger resembles a sieve."

Gavin MacHugh turned from the window and smiled. "You may as well put it aside," he said. "It'll be of small good to you, splotched with blood."

Elspeth stood up and walked to the window, thinking as she did so that she had done nothing all morning but pace from her chair to the window and back again, like a caged animal too restless to stay in one spot.

Gavin moved to give her room and she looked out at the mist-covered Ochils, rising in desolate heights beyond the window, at the dizzy fall of the chasm below the walls of Castle Campbell. It was already April; spring should be tinting the skies deeply blue, the dawns and twilights should be pale lavender and gold, the air should be soft with the promise of fair weather. But she doubted if spring ever came to Castle Campbell; surely there was no time when the surrounding hills were not shrouded in gloom, when the burn waters were not dark and ominous in their rocky beds, when the sky was not heavy with clouds.

The two streams below the castle were named the Burns of Sorrow and Care; they were aptly named, she thought, and it was most peremptory of the first Campbell proprietor to change the name from the Castle of Gloom. It was a dismal castle in a grim, melancholy land, certainly as gloomy a place as she had yet seen in Scotland.

"God's love, 'tis gloomy enough to drive one mad," she remarked. "I can't see why the Campbells ever desired such a dreary fortress."

"I doubt they considered the beauty of the spot," Gavin said cheerfully.

Elspeth looked down at the steep drop below the window. "Aye, I'd hate to be storming the place. But I think I'd dislike even more to be besieged on top of this desolate hill."

"Alex feels the same," said Gavin. "He's more than pleased he'll be on his feet in another day or so."

Elspeth was silent. She stared at a high spur of the Ochils which rose across the deep gulch, knowing now why Gavin had come in search of her.

"Why don't you go and cheer him up?" he asked casually.

Elspeth said in a small voice, "I didn't think he should be disturbed."

"He's quite recovered now. You haven't been near him since his fever dropped." He added with a small smile, "He's been asking for you."

Elspeth had a sudden memory of the desperate fear which had surged through her when the MacHugh walked unsteadily through the gates of Castle Campbell that night, his brown face pale as he tried to smile at her, his jack and shirt stained crimson with blood. She could not forget how oddly young and vulnerable he had looked lying in the center of the wide bed, gray eyes closed and his mouth tightened against the pain, his face too white beneath the dark wet hair.

"The wound was deep," she protested. "I thought he should have his rest."

Gavin said nothing, but she could feel his intent gaze on her. "I don't know why I can't be sensible about him," she said miserably. "I can't abide the man, I

find him more intolerable each time we meet. Yet I
can't seem to think clearly about him at all." She drew
a deep breath and met Gavin's level eyes. She did not
know why she should be speaking so to the MacHugh's
own brother; but once before, when she asked him at
Rathmor if he considered her a spy for the Campbells,
he had spoken the truth to her at a time when she
knew a great need for it, and the liking between them
had grown into something akin to understanding. He
would not abuse her confidence, she was strangely
certain, and it was a great relief to speak her mind
plainly.

"What is it about him that gives me such a fever,
knowing he's so near, under the same roof?" She
laughed bitterly. "How amused he'd be if he knew."

Gavin's face was grave. After a moment he said, "Do
you think you can deceive yourself for long?"

"I'll be much happier," she said slowly, "if I can
continue to deceive myself till I leave Scotland. 'Tis a
miserable affair, and no good will come of it."

Gavin leaned his elbows on the casement. "You may
be safer," he said bluntly, "but I doubt you'll be happier."

She answered quietly, "It isn't my own safety I would
consider."

"So you're worth a few bags of gold to Argyll," said
Gavin, "and he'd sell his soul to the devil for a few
English pounds. Still and all, it shouldn't keep you
from giving Alex a bit of your time. Would you care
to be shut up in that small room with only my ugly face
to keep you company?"

She laughed at him, admitting defeat. "I'll see him,"
she said.

She smoothed her skirts absently as she climbed the
stairs. Earlier in the day she had walked for a long
while along the battlements, watching the mists whirl
and twist as the morning wind blew them back to the
hills. She had not worn her farthingale: it was too
pleasant to feel the heavy velvet skirts billow away

from her body, to let the chill edge of the wind wet her with the damp mist. She had thought of many things, walking there in a world which touched the clouds, hearing nothing but the cry of a bird on the wind and the muffled tread of a sentry somewhere beyond her.

She had thought of many things, but the thinking of them had come no clearer. Her mind had seemed like a jewel chest filled with bits of bright stones and chains of gold and silver, hopelessly entangled, and only when she pushed all thought away and let herself feel nothing but the wind against her face and the wet fingers of the mist did she find some measure of happiness within herself. Yet the thoughts returned and the mists disappeared with the wind, and the slight happiness was as fleeting as the sound of a bird cry above the Ochil hills.

She found Alexander playing an indifferent game of chess with one of his men. The board rested on the coverlet of the bed between them and Alexander was propped on his elbow with several fat pillows at his back.

The clansman stood up and stretched when he saw her; he was obviously grateful to be relieved at his post. "I'll gladly leave him to you," he said. "No man deserves such punishment."

Alexander laughed. He was wearing a thin white linen shirt, open almost to his waist to allow room for the bandage which stretched against his shoulder. He had lost some of his tan, she thought irrelevantly, and the hollows beneath his high cheekbones were deeper, but his eyes were clear and bright with impatience. He looked very strong and alive, and very pleased to see her.

The clansman left them, closing the door softly behind him, and Elspeth took the chair he had vacated, pulling it away from the bed.

Finally she said inanely, "Gavin says you'll be on your feet soon."

"If I'm not," he said cheerfully, "I won't be responsible for what I might do." He added gravely, "I hope you're properly ashamed, ignoring me for so long a time. Have you been hiding away in the stables, talking to the horses?" She flushed, and he laughed. "Or mayhap you've been scouring the floor. It was most impolite of me, dripping blood all over Campbell Castle."

"At least we know now that you've got blood in your veins," she said. "Ordinary red blood, the same as any man."

"What a disappointment for you. Did you think it'd be nothing but cold water?" He said hopefully, "If you weren't sitting so far away I'd give you better proof that it's not."

She looked at him warily. "Duncan will be back from Edinburgh tonight," she said. "He'll be pleased to see you so much better."

"More pleased than he was to find me here," said Alexander. "And are you pleased, lass? You haven't seemed too anxious about me."

She avoided his eyes carefully, wondering how much he remembered of the first nights after he came, when she stayed by his bed until she fell asleep with her head on the covers beside him.

"I've been busy," she lied, but it was an ungraceful lie.

"That excuse is growing threadbare," he said.

She gave him a quick glance from under her lashes and saw that he looked as amused as he sounded.

"You're an obstinate wench," he said suddenly. "D'you never retreat an inch? What must a man do, after fainting dead away at your feet and begging for help? God's foot, I've run out of tricks."

She tried not to laugh. "Is that why you allowed a Campbell to run you through?" she asked, curiously. "I should have known you'd have a fair excuse for it."

"How did you know it was a Campbell?"

"Gavin told me," she answered innocently.

"A lot of good it did me," he said. "You have no sense of appreciation." He regarded her thoughtfully. "I'd forgotten I brought you a small bribe from Edinburgh. 'Tis in my pocket, if you'll look in the press."

She hesitated. "I don't care for bribes."

He made a quick motion as if he would throw back the covers. "I'll fetch it then."

She stood up hastily, and Alexander shrugged and settled back. He knew, of course, that her curiosity was too aroused to let the matter pass. She found the bracelets in his pocket and held them lightly in her hand.

"They're lovely," she said softly, amazed that he would bring her a gift. How did he know that he would ride to Castle Campbell, or that a sword wound would keep him there for several days?

"I confess I bought them for another lass," he said, "but since I'm here you'll do as well. If you'll come here, I'll fasten them for you.

"Thank you, I can manage."

"Such meager gratitude," he remarked cryptically. "I'll take them back if you must be so prim." He leaned on his elbow, grinning at her. "I believe I'm having a relapse because of your stubbornness. You'd best come here before my cut breaks open."

" 'Tis nothing but blackmail," she retorted. "Gavin said it was almost healed." She added, "And you'll not have them back again. You said I might have them."

"You'll be as safe as with a bairn, lass. I'm too weak to lift my arm. I want only to smell you," he added blandly. "Gavin's balsams and plasters have an unpleasant scent and I've smelled nothing else for days."

She studied him intently, seeing a familiar gleam of mischief in his eyes. She walked slowly to the bed and looked down at his dark hair, restraining a sudden impulse to touch it; she was much closer to him than was wise.

"Sit down," he commanded, taking her hand with a

strong grasp and pulling her down on the edge of the bed. "Now give me the bracelets."

As he took them, she noticed something inscribed on the inside of each. "What does it say?"

He fastened them around her wrist and said something in Gaelic, his voice warm and lazy.

"I'm not so proficient at Gaelic," she confessed.

"You'd do well to learn," he said. "Few people in the Highlands speak anything else. 'Tis not so difficult. It has a lilt in it, like a music, once you know the meaning of the words."

"Tell me," she said, "in English."

"One says 'Fear na ye,'" he said. "The other says 'My ain true luve,' but don't let your yellow head swell out of all proportion." She looked up and saw that he was smiling again. "Since the one says so boldly that you've no need to fear, it will undoubtedly protect you from all harm."

"If I had naught to depend upon but a gold bracelet," she managed at last, "I'd be most desolate."

His hand was resting on her wrist, covering the bracelets. "I have a jeweled dirk at Fraoch Eilean, lass, and I can see it would be a more appropriate gift for you. 'Tis a miniature, given me by King Jamie when I became Chief, but it would more than serve your purposes." His gray eyes moved down from her face. "Small enough to slip in your bodice, and I'll wager it'd be a weapon enough to protect you from any barbaric Scot."

Elspeth could not keep back a laugh. "A likely place for it," she murmured.

"You have a delicious smell," he said. "Paris?"

She nodded, wondering what woman had taught him to recognize a Parisian scent. "And you've an educated nose," she said.

"If you'd come a bit closer I might identify it exactly."

Her eyes widened. If she were an inch closer she would be against his bandaged chest. He meant just that, and his hand slipped from her wrist to her arm and tightened, drawing her down.

"Please don't," she said faintly, and he took his hand away so quickly that she almost fell over.

"I'll not force such a stubborn wench," he said softly. "D'you want me to ask you politely?" The laughter was still in his voice, but his eyes were warm and intent. "If the answer is no, that's the end of it. 'Tis getting to be a wearisome affair, having you always angry with me."

She didn't want to be stubborn. She wanted to forget Argyll's cold eyes which hid so much and betrayed so little; she wanted to put aside thoughts of the wealthy English marriage to be arranged for her, and the hatred between Argyll's Campbells and the Mac-Hughs.

"Elspeth," he said, "look at me."

She raised her head, her eyes guarded, hoping he would not be able to read her miserable thoughts.

His eyes looked straight into hers. "Don't look like that," he said gently. "Has anything happened since I saw you at Inveraray? Have I made you very angry with me?"

She looked down at her skirts, wine-red like the color of crushed strawberries. "Why did you ask me to stay close by Duncan?"

He was silent, then he took one finger and raised her chin. "There were many reasons," he said, "and I'll not go into all of them. But I told you I don't trust Argyll. While the MacDonalds are up, he'll be busy enough, but he's far too clever to have only one scheme in his head. And I've a small interest in his schemes concerning you."

An idiotic happiness flooded through her like a hot liquid. "It would matter little to him," she said. "He'll not allow you to interfere."

"That's to be seen," he said briefly.

But the strange sense of mystery, of ominous affairs just beyond the circle of her knowledge, that she had felt so strongly since first meeting him, was yet alive and worrisome inside her. He knew certain matters which vitally concerned her, she was certain of it, and yet he had no intention of telling her anything.

She had yet another question to ask and she put it bluntly. "If you've no fear of Argyll, why did you think it wise to stay away from me?"

"You're an inquisitive piece of baggage," he said lightly. "If you don't know, I've no reason to tell you." He smiled and added, "I might say I was wary of a fair Campbell from Queen Anne's court."

"I am still that," she said quietly.

His eyes moved over the gray crimson gown, left carelessly unbuttoned below her chin, and rested on her hair. Elspeth remembered suddenly that she had not brushed it since her walk on the battlements.

"I like you best when you look most like an urchin," he said unexpectedly. "Have you been out in the wind?"

She wanted to tell him how it was with her, but she could not. She could not tell him that when she was with him she was not a Campbell, nor a Lamond, nor a lady of Anne's court, only a rebellious lass with wild blood which sang in her veins till she felt afraid of nothing in the world. Nor could she find the words to tell him how strangely she liked the wind wailing around the parapets of the castle, and the mists touching her face, or how free and strong she felt when she was alone in that high world above the earth.

She said only, "I walked on the battlements."

He made no comment, but somehow she was certain he understood. Indeed, she felt as if there were nothing about her which he did not know and understand; it had been that way from the beginning.

"I can see I'll have a difficult time of it," he said at last. "I can't match wits with the Earl till you make up your mind. All these months in Scotland and I've yet to bring you to my way of thinking. 'Tis the first time I've waited so long for a wench, and I'm not certain I'll last much longer at it."

She could feel all her pride ebbing away, dissolving the barriers she had so carefully erected between them. "I'll make up my mind when I please," she said, "and I know nothing of your way of thinking. You've never told me." Then she put out her hand, quickly so that she couldn't change her mind, and rested it against his face.

He didn't move. Her hand seemed to burn where it touched his face; she could feel the muscle tighten along his cheekbone, but she could not force her hand away. Instead she moved it until she could feel the short dark hair at his temples. She had wanted to touch it for such a lengthy time.

"God help you if you don't mean it," he said quietly.

He put his hands on her shoulders and drew her down against him; she could feel the thick bandage, rough and clean, on her face. He held her head under his chin, against his throat, and his other arm went around her, holding her so close that she could feel the pulse beating in his throat. For a long while he didn't move except to tighten his arm whenever she stirred.

She said softly, "Your shoulder should not be treated so."

"Don't say anything, lass," he said. "Be quiet."

His voice was deep and warm and his hand moved over her hair slowly, almost as if he weren't aware of doing it; she wondered what he was thinking. But she was drowsy and happy, content to stay there forever and feel his hand on her hair. He encircled her with his tenderness, his gentleness, so apart from everything hard and ruthless about him; this was his way of charming her, like magic, into quietness and submission.

Then he turned her face up and kissed her, and her drowsiness was gone in an instant. His mouth moved to her throat, her cheeks, her eyes, and back to her lips.

"So you'll make up your mind when you please," he said, low. "D'you think you know my way of think-

ing well enough now?" His voice had laughter in it
again. "Does it please you?"

She found a small voice somewhere inside her. "You
have a forceful way of telling it," she said.

"I'll say it more plainly, if you must have words.
Be as stubborn as you like, lass, but I'll wait no longer
than I choose."

Despite his smile, she knew he was not teasing her.
He said the words gravely and he obviously meant
them. She stared at him for a moment, searching for
something to say in the face of so deliberate a challenge.

She rested her chin in his hands. "I am not one of
your clansmen," she said distinctly, "to be ordered
about at will. Nor one of your Highland wenches, eager
to fall into your arms like a ripe apple."

He raised his dark brows and waited, his grin deep-
ening.

"You know well enough that Argyll will decide
whom I shall wed, and I have grave doubts that he'd
consider you a desirable prospect."

She thought she had squelched him fairly, but he
was not perturbed. "Were we speaking of being wed?"
he asked bluntly.

A warm flush began at her throat and spread over
her face. She had not been wary enough, after all; she
had not expected he might still hurt her so easily.

"Any Highland wench," he said, "would have more
pride than to allow herself to be bartered off by the
Earl at his discretion, in the manner of one of his prize
mares."

He laughed mockingly, and she thought with despair
that his moods were like quicksilver, as contradictory
and unruly as a mountain burn.

"One day you'll have the courage to forget your outraged virtue and admit you were meant to be loved,
like any woman." His eyes moved over her slowly,
deliberately. "And by the MacHugh," he added curtly.
"From the day you were born, lass, and till the day

you die. You'll find nothing of shame in it, and more than a little happiness. I cannot speak of being wed in these miserable times, but that's a small matter and one day I'll attend to it properly. Now I can only remind you that it will take more than your foolish pride or Argyll's weak sword to change my mind."

She knew suddenly why he would not speak of being wed; if the rumors were true, he would soon be riding to join MacDonald in the south, riding to a battle from which he might not return.

"You've enough confidence in yourself," she said. "Is it an unwritten law in Scotland that anything you want is yours for the taking?"

"You were born to disregard laws, lass," he said lazily. "I'd not have you any other way. And I might find it in myself to forgive you for being so contrary about so important a matter."

She walked to the door, knowing she could not think clearly until she was away from him. She paused and said, "I thank you for the bracelets. Or would you like them back?"

He laughed. "I don't want them back," he said. When she opened the door without speaking, he added, "And my thanks for being so able a nurse. I'd wager even Kate MacLachlan would scarce have treated me so tenderly."

She slammed the door and sped down the stairs, stopping abruptly to remove the gold bracelets from her wrist. But they jingled together like tiny bells, a gay and wayward sound that was extremely cheerful. It would be a pleasant way to annoy the Earl, she reflected, when he was boring her with one of his long tirades.

And somehow it was vastly comforting to remember the words incribed inside. The MacHugh had said, "Fear na ye," and no one in all Scotland would deny the words had the sound of a charm in them.

❧{ 12 }❧

DUNCAN Campbell stood with his back to the window, studying the MacHugh. "You intended it this way," he stated flatly, and the MacHugh's shrug seemed to confirm his words. "You're too canny for me, Alex. I've been used quite shrewdly for your purposes."

"Have it your way, Glenurchy."

Duncan could not help but be amused at the man's audacity. Alexander had been cleared of any implication in Angus MacDonald's escape from the Castle on the strength of his presence in Castle Campbell, and Duncan was certain the young MacHugh had foreseen just such a fortunate misconception.

"So you rode the entire distance from Dalmeny," said Duncan. "Could no one in Dunfermline attend your wound? Or Stirling?"

"Come, Duncan, I'll think you begrudged me my return to good health. Would I have traded Elspeth's healing hands for the grimy paws of some village smith?" The MacHugh smiled charmingly. " 'Tis enough to make an injured man ride twice the distance. Besides that, I reckoned that you owed me some restitution for allowing your kinsmen to attack the Mac-Hughs so brazenly."

"Cawdor? You've no proof of it."

The MacHugh shrugged again, expressively, and Glenurchy suspected the man could produce sufficient proof with little trouble. Cawdor had played the fool again; there could be no doubt of that. But it was not so much the method by which the MacHugh had cleared himself of implication in MacDonald's escape which disturbed Glenurchy—although he was certain that Alex had been at the bottom of that remarkable episode, he thought the man deserved credit for possessing a cool wit which could not be outdone—no, it was the reaction of the Earl of Argyll which disconcerted Duncan Campbell. He was forced to admit that for once his cousin was in the right.

"Argyll is fuming," he said, "and I must find a reasonable explanation before I ride to Inveraray. Since you're canny enough to think circles about me, d'you suppose you might conjure up such an explanation for me?"

The MacHugh's grin was quick. "The Earl fuming, Glenurchy?" he drawled. "God's body, that's cheerful news. I had no idea he'd hear the news so soon."

"I received a most disagreeable message from him just before I left Edinburgh. He's in such high dudgeon that I'm surprised I didn't hear him without benefit of a written message."

"Because Elspeth was kind enough to dress my wound?" Alexander shook his head sadly. "The man has a black soul, Duncan. He should attend Kirk more often."

The MacHugh was sitting on the edge of a table, swinging his boots idly above the floor. Duncan Campbell stared at him, thinking that Argyll had greatly underestimated the caliber of his opponent. "A rash young Chief," he had called the MacHugh, dismissing him as ill-qualified to match wits with the indomitable Earl. Aye, he was both rash and young on the surface, Duncan admitted, but there could be no more deceptive a scabbard for the hard, well-tempered steel which lay beneath. Duncan sighed, dropping his stare to the floor at his feet. Scotland had great need of such men as the young MacHugh Chief; Duncan found himself wishing he could discover just such a rash young man among the Campbells.

"The Earl is more than a little offended that Angus MacDonald has eluded his grasp. I take it he finds it hard to believe that you had nothing to do with the matter. D'you intend to stick by that ridiculous tale?"

"Argyll has a suspicious nature," Alexander said innocently. "It was a bit of bad luck that I happened to leave Edinburgh on the same night that Angus flew the cage. My streak of misfortunes began the moment I decided to forego the pleasures of Auld Reekie, Duncan. Had I been happily seducing a fair lady that evening, I would never stand accused of such a dastardly trick as aiding a MacDonald." He added, "And I'd not have been skewered by a wayward Campbell."

Glenurchy shook his head. "That's another deplorable affair. Argyll is well aware of your reputation with the lassies." His brows drew together and he gave the MacHugh a level scrutiny. "As am I, Alex, and I don't like it."

"I am pleased that his lordship would so nobly defend a lady's honor," Alexander said, but some indefinable quality in his voice proved the mockery of his words. "My intentions are no less honorable, Glenurchy."

Duncan realized with exasperation that he could not argue with such a well-turned phrase, as courteous as it was misleading. But he would have the matter clear between them, honestly and fairly. "I'll not stand by and see the lass hurt," he said quietly.

The small smile which touched the MacHugh's mouth did not extend to his level gray eyes. "You'll not see her hurt by me," he said briefly.

Duncan nodded. "I insult your honor by asking such a thing. But you must know Argyll's plans for her." He would not have spoken of it, but he remembered the bracelets he had seen on Elspeth's arm that morning, the jingling bracelets he had watched Alexander purchase in Edinburgh.

"Have you no say in the matter?" Alexander's voice was cool.

"I am a Campbell, Alex, and must follow the decisions of my Chief. You can find no argument with that sentiment." Duncan sounded weary. "D'you believe me a piece of stone, that I could find no affection in my heart for such a lass? I'd use every means within my power to keep her safely in Scotland, away from his influence, but he's her guardian and I've little power where the lass is concerned."

Alexander looked thoughtful. "The man will have greater favor with Jamie Stuart once the MacDonalds are defeated."

"Aye," Duncan agreed heavily, "and never doubt he'll not make the most of it. God's truth, I've no call to be speaking of my Chief in such a manner, Alex. But the man galls me beyond endurance, and that's the plain of it."

Duncan Campbell thought of his beloved Balloch and Finlarig, the massive strongholds guarding the vast Campbell lands to the north. Any honest man would find pause to bless his God for such possessions, for such an unequaled opportunity to strengthen the heart and body of Scotland. Planning better methods of farming to increase the yield of each barren acre, seeking for peace among the clans, striving for prosperity and a decent mode of living for each of his clansmen— those were satisfying and equitable goals for a Scot to hold in his heart.

But there were more selfish goals guiding the men who cared more for the gold in their purses and the titles after their names than they did for the whole of Scotland. If the men so motivated bore another name, if they were ancient enemies, a man could properly scorn them. He could fight them with all the weapons at his command, declaring openly that such traitors deserved not the smallest portion of Scotland nor any of its honors. But how did a man fight the evil in his own house? How could he protest the guilt of others when his own clan harbored the same miserable greed?

Campbell of Glenurchy was not aware that he stared

so bitterly at the MacHugh; he was thinking that he was in a devilish spot, forced to fight an eternal battle between loyalty and honesty.

At last he came back to the present problem. "Do you join MacDonald?" he asked bluntly.

The MacHugh did not hesitate. "I've come to that decision," he said.

"I had hoped you would not. You cannot dream that MacDonald will succeed."

"Does the success of a cause determine a man's loyalty, Duncan?"

Duncan Campbell seemed a powerful figure, standing easily erect with his large shoulders outlined against the window. He wore a heavy broadsword, as if in contempt of the new lighter swords, and his broad hand looked more than capable enough to wield a massive claymore with the same dexterity. But he suddenly felt very old and tired, a soldier whose vigor and courage had slowly ebbed from his body, leaving him with an old man's fearful thoughts and a sword which was no more than a sham at his side.

The MacHugh had spoken quietly, but Duncan Campbell would not soon forget those brief words. He longed to be as young again as the young chief who faced him, young with all the strength and confidence which prompted such words. It would be good to be among the untamed, the incautious, to know that bold pulsing of blood once again. Above all things, he would like to taste again the fierce pleasure of offering one's sword without reservation, of daring to venture all for the sake of a brave cause, no matter how hopeless.

He said heavily, "He'll not stop with you. Your clan will suffer."

"When I go, Duncan, I go alone."

Duncan shook his head. "Alex, you're the Laird of MacHugh. Your banner is famous throughout Scotland. It matters little if you ride without your clan. D'you dream Argyll will not be able to turn it against you?" He scowled blackly, disliking to be a warning voice. "I trust the lass has naught to do with your decision?"

"There's no lass in the world so bonny," Alexander said curtly. "You'll not find me such a gallant fool. And I doubt that Argyll's defeat would aid her chances." He smiled at Duncan. "I'll take the risk of it. I've great admiration for Jamie MacDonald, and I could scarce ignore such a golden opportunity to plague Argyll. God's foot, the man will soil his clothes."

"You'll plague him, make no mistake about it."

"On the face of it, Argyll's task would seem a simple one," Alexander said. "He thinks to rule Scotland by subduing James MacDonald for the King. But I dislike to see a man gain so much so easily. 'Tis bad for the vanity." He gave Duncan a direct, level glance. "You're a shrewd man, Glenurchy. Think the matter through for yourself. MacDonald alone is easy prey, I can't deny it. But do you think Argyll has given enough consideration to the risks of stirring up the clans? I doubt Jamie Stuart would care to face the whole of the Highlands rallying around a united standard."

Duncan's eyes narrowed. "Is that your scheme?"

Alexander shrugged. "I've no scheme beyond a reasonable amount of foresight."

"I'd not believe you'd attempt to rouse the clans to rebellion."

"I imagine Argyll would hold the credit for that dubious honor."

"By marching the King's army against MacDonald?"

"I speak of his grudge against the MacHughs," Alexander said emphatically. "A commission of fire and sword may seem brave and final on a scrap of royal parchment, but 'tis slightly more difficult to enforce. Argyll won't find the MacHughs so easy to tame as the MacGregors!"

Duncan flushed. It was a stain upon the Campbell name, that hounding of the MacGregors. After arresting the Chief of Clan MacGregor by treachery, Argyll had hunted the clan with fire and sword till all of Scotland had shuddered at the bloody affair. Duncan could not deny the injustice of the laws passed by Argyll, refusing any MacGregor the right to carry a weapon, forbidding use of the very name under pain of death, allowing any Scot to kill a MacGregor without fear of punishment. It was a terrible thing, a thing to shame a man with the memory of it.

"I did not approve of it, MacHugh."

Alexander's face was hard. "You bear the name Campbell. You administer the estates in Glenurchy which belonged to the MacGregors." He spoke harshly, his hot temper rising quickly. "MacHugh lands will never fall into Campbell hands after such a bastardly fashion, Duncan. Once was enough for Scotland."

"Damn it, man, speak of something else before I forget our friendship!" Duncan's hand went unconsciously to his sword.

" 'Tis a friendship which stretches thin at times," Alexander said grimly. "I am too constantly reminded of an old saying in the Highlands. D'you remember it, Duncan? 'From the greed of the Campbells, good Lord, deliver us!' "

"We were speaking of the MacDonald campaign," Duncan said, restraining himself with an obvious effort.

"Aye," the MacHugh said flatly, "I was warning you that Argyll might find it difficult to persuade the Mac-Hughs to abide by a decree of fire and sword, even if he procured one from the King. If the MacHughs send the cross burning through the Highlands in protest of such an indignity, you may rest assured they'll not stand alone."

"God's body, you've as much vanity as Argyll!"

"Vanity, Duncan? You know the temper of the clans as well as I."

"Aye," Duncan said slowly. "I was forgetting how cannily you judge men. So you believe Argyll will face a wide rebellion if he crosses the MacHughs?"

"I'm no prophet," the MacHugh said calmly. "But

neither is Jamie Stuart. And he's in no position to tempt such a cruel fate."

Duncan Campbell had lost his anger. His admiration for Alexander MacHugh grew each time he saw the man. "Do you think to bluff me?" he asked curiously. "I carry no tales to Argyll."

"I'd not consider it amiss if you dropped a small hint," Alexander said, grinning. He slipped from the table and took his sword and belt from a chair. "It might cause him to hesitate before acting rashly."

" 'Tis a bloody thing to contemplate," Duncan said thoughtfully. "Would you stir up the clans to war?" He added hopefully, "I've not seen all the Highlands flocking to MacDonald's banner."

"There's a bit of a difference," Alexander said. "My clan is not marching full strength against a royal army, nor have they ever lifted their swords against the throne. There's no just grievance can be charged against them that would warrant a punishment of fire and sword." He laughed shortly. "But I find reason enough to ride against Archibald Campbell, and I'll stir the clans against him if the need arises."

"You've a reckless sword, MacHugh."

"I've a clan to protect," the MacHugh said flatly.

"If you were any other man, I'd have drawn my sword against such insults. But I'll pass it by; I've no desire to cross blades with you like some ill-tempered lad." Duncan sighed and turned to the window, resting his weight on his hands. The room was silent; the MacHugh poured a flagon of claret.

"Wine, Duncan?"

"I'll admit to a thirst. But leave it now, Alex." Duncan moved one hand slightly, as if he had no patience for wine at the moment. "Shortly before I rode to Edinburgh I journeyed through a portion of your land which borders on Argyll's."

Alexander rested his boot on a chair and studied the claret in the narrow silver flagon. He said nothing, but his brows drew sharply together.

"I needed no mark to distinguish between Campbell and MacHugh land. 'Tis so apparent even a bairn could note the difference." Duncan swung around to face the MacHugh. "How do you do it?"

" 'Tis a simple thing, man, and I've naught to do with it." Alexander smiled, no longer wary. "The good Lord sees to such matters. The birds sing louder, the trees are taller, the stags are fatter and the flowers bonnier when the ground below is no' a Campbell's."

"You've a prosperous estate, MacHugh. I saw little of poverty, even in the rudest stone hut."

Alexander shrugged eloquently. "All MacHughs are poachers and reivers. They see no need to starve when Argyll's land furnishes them with game and his stables afford them with valuable horseflesh to be sold at market. We ha' a school for the teaching of such matters, Duncan."

"Stop your pesting, Alex. Tell me the way to manage it; I could use such a method myself. God knows it pleases me to see a man's clansmen living in comfort and plenty."

The MacHugh downed his wine and placed the flagon on the table with unnecessary force. "They've little enough. Would you deem a warm plaid and a full stomach good fortune? 'Tis no more than any wretch deserves."

"But a deal more than the ordinary man possesses," Duncan said impassively. "Do you turn every coin back to your clan? I should think it'd leave a thin purse for yourself." He ran his hand over his chin and regarded Alexander gravely. "You'll have no gold for your sons."

"My sons will have a stronger heritage than gold," the MacHugh said curtly. "I'll not rob my clan to line their paths with velvet. They'll find their own gold, Duncan, and be better lads for it."

Duncan's eyes gleamed under their shaggy brows. "Then I'm to believe the Laird of MacHugh denies himself to give to his clansmen? 'Tis hard to believe of a young man like yourself. What of the dicing and wenching? I see no evidence of the frugal life."

Alexander threw back his head and laughed. "By all that's holy, when I enjoy such pleasures my Mac-Hughs do the same. Ha' you no' heard of their wild reputations?"

"Is display against your principles?" Duncan asked idly.

"The greed of one man can take the food from a hundred bairns," Alexander replied brusquely. He did not care to continue the conversation. "Do you spend your time prying into the affairs of others?"

"There was no need to pry," Duncan said quietly. "I had only to speak to your MacHughs."

"Then I fear they've misled you, Glenurchy." The MacHugh placed his hands on his hips and leaned against the table. "A contented clansman draws his sword quicker. 'Tis as simple as that." He laughed lightly. "You might practice it on your Campbells. God knows they need some spur to urge them forward."

"I would it were so simple to gain their devotion. You're a wise man, Alex, for one so young."

Alexander shrugged the matter aside. "Stronger than the laird are the vassals," he said, quoting an old Gaelic phrase.

Duncan smiled dryly. Of all the men who paid lip service to that nobel sentiment, he would that more lived their lives by it as did the young MacHugh. But it served little purpose to question the man, keeping in mind the sweet lass Elspeth and, if the truth were told, his own desire to have the Campbells and MacHughs closer in friendship and mayhap marriage. The very qualities which so pleased Duncan were those which Argyll would despise in Alexander MacHugh; there could be no possible hope that the two would ever become reconciled.

"Well now, I've been put off my subject," he said finally. "I still face the Earl's wrath for sheltering you at Castle Campbell while all Edinburgh searches for the rogue who spirited Angus MacDonald away from the Castle."

Alexander took a long step and slapped Duncan on the shoulder. "You're a man of wit, Duncan. If you fail to make the matter clear, you're no Campbell."

"If I'd any wit left me, I'd leave it to you to make the matter clear."

"Then send his lordship to Fraoch Eilean," Alexander said promptly, "and I'll take care of it."

"He'd never overlook the bitter taste in his wine, no matter the vintage," said Duncan. "No, that's scarce the proper way of it."

"Then find your own answers," said the MacHugh, grinning. "I've problems enough without adding yours to the lot."

Duncan harbored a faint suspicion that the Mac-Hugh was more than a little amused at the situation. God's love, the man surely gave the lie to any foolish belief abroad that a Scot was naturally dour and grave. He'd laugh in the face of the devil, and no doubt expect that black-hearted gentleman to give the same in return.

⤝ 13 ⤞

THE trip from Castle Campbell to Inveraray seemed endlessly long and boring to Elspeth. She rode with her maid, surrounded by the bristling spears of Campbell men-at-arms; and out of unwarranted concern for her, Duncan led the way at a leisurely amble which grew increasingly irritating to everyone.

The men curbed their impatience and exercised their horses by galloping ahead to join the outriders, but Elspeth was forced to ride quietly, chatting to her maid of inconsequential matters and struggling to keep awake in the sun. She plodded along, reining her restive chestnut to an apathetic walk and cursed silently and fluently. Occasionally she dismounted, for the mere diversion of walking, and strode along the trail, kicking her velvet skirts out of her way with an unrestrained vehemence.

The MacHugh politely ignored her for the entire journey. Whenever the group halted for food or a night's rest he immediately appeared at her side, holding his hand courteously to help her dismount. He brought her food and offered her wine from his flask, but he gave her maid the same consideration. Beyond those small attentions Elspeth saw little of him, and he did not seek out her company.

During the day he rode far ahead on black Tammie, conversing at length with Duncan Campbell. The steel helmet at his saddlebow caught the sun like a bright mirror, a distraction which drew Elspeth's eyes each time she raised her head. His MacHughs rode directly behind him, their lances bearing square banners which unfurled in the wind to show crimson castles and fesswise blue crosses blazoned across a field of white.

On the last afternoon, Elspeth watched the sun dropping toward the hills and knew they were nearing Loch Fyne. Soon they would reach Fraoch Eilean and the MacHugh would leave them; she wondered if he would trouble himself to bid her farewell. As if in answer to her thoughts, the MacHugh wheeled the stallion and cantered back along the track, sitting his horse so easily that no one would guess he had been recently bedded with a serious wound. He did not seem wearied from the journey; his face was darkly tanned from the sun, for he had not once worn his helmet, and his shoulder muscles stretched against the steel mesh doublet as if it were no heavier than linen.

When he reached Elspeth he turned and rode beside her, resting his arm on his saddle pommel. "I hope your fatigue is not a burden, lass," he said. "The end is almost in sight."

"Your consideration overwhelms me, sir," she said coolly. It was difficult to control her voice when she met his eyes; he had known all along how bored and restless she had been, with no one to entertain her but the Campbell woman who spoke little but Gaelic. He had not even sent Gavin back for company, as if he would punish her properly for spurning his own during the last few days of their stay at Castle Campbell.

"Duncan wishes me to ride ahead and send the outriders on to Inveraray with word of your arrival," he said innocently. "Would you care to exercise your mare?"

She swallowed her anger; the prospect of a fast ride was too tempting, and she would have her revenge in time. She turned the mare to the side of the track and rode slowly past the Campbell escort. When she reached Duncan she smiled and lifted her hand.

"Stay close by Alexander," he cautioned. " 'Tis

MacHugh land, but I'd not like to have you riding alone."

She touched her whip to her horse. The MacHugh drew abreast and they rode together along the trail, but Elspeth pointedly ignored him and they rode for almost a league without speaking. They came even with the four advance horsemen too soon; Alexander gave them their orders and they spurred down the trail, leaving Elspeth with a vague disappointment because the ride had been so swift.

"Shall we ride on?" Alexander asked gravely.

"Duncan expects us to rejoin him."

"We might wait at Fraoch Eilean," he suggested. He waited for her decision, holding his reins loosely, and Elspeth fought a weak struggle within herself. " 'Tis only a short distance," he added.

She knew it could not be far; she could smell the salt of the sea in the soft wind and taste it on her lips. "Give me a length or two and I'll race you on even terms!"

He gave her more than a length. Elspeth was well down the next hill before she heard Tammie's thundering hoofs behind her, but she knew instinctively that she would need no less than a league's start to outstrip that black brute of a racer. Still, the mare was a graceful thing, lifting above the ground as though she had wings shod to her hoofs.

The MacHughs pulled even with her and they pounded over the rocky ground abreast; long before they reached Fraoch Eilean the stallion was forging ahead, held back by Alexander's insistent curb on the reins.

They drew rein in the woods before they reached the gates of the castle. The towers were dark and foreboding above the trees, warning any travelers on the trail that they were trespassing on the native heath of the black MacHughs and should exercise the proper caution and respect. But Elspeth turned her back on the haughty gray walls of the MacHugh's stronghold.

"One day you'll forget your scruples and I'll be left far behind in a cloud of dust." She gave Tammie an approving glance. "Unless you'll make me a gift of one of Tammie's offspring."

"I've been tempted too many times for comfort," he said, "to leave you behind in a cloud of dust. Better, a thick fog of it."

"Why have you hesitated?" she asked sweetly. "I've noticed you're seldom ruled by your courteous instincts."

"I must protect Tammie's vanity," he said, and walked his horse toward her.

She moved backward, not trusting him. " 'Tis strange you attend to everyone's vanity but your own."

"You've a shrewish tongue, lass. You'll never find yourself a husband." He put his hand on her arm and the warm touch of it raced through her blood. "Will you attend Jean's wedding?" he asked abruptly.

"I'd not miss it," she answered, and hoped Argyll would not prove her wrong. "I trust I have your permission to return to Rathmor?"

He grinned. "Aye, I'll be there to make sure you do nothing foolish."

Her anger was quick and hot, a culmination of all the irritation and wretchedness of the journey from Castle Campbell; and the knowledge that it was a childish rage, aroused by nothing more than his constant teasing, only made her angrier.

"I cannot find words," she said clearly, "to tell you how odious and insufferable I find you."

"Words, lass?" he asked, and his hand tightened on her arm. "Must you find words? I need none. 'Tis plain enough if you've the honesty to face it. Hate me if you like. Hate me and curse me till you've no more strength for it. Then ask yourself if you'd have it any other way." His voice was low and demanding. "Would ye find any pleasure in submitting like a frightened sheep? D'you think to keep your mind and heart guarded by an iron girdle as you would your maidenhood? God's death, love's no' so cowardly and weak a thing!"

"I don't love you," she said inadequately.

"It matters little if you name it love or hate," he said. "You cannot separate your feelings in wee jars and label them accordingly." He dropped her arm and Tammie moved a few feet away, tossing his head impatiently. "As long as you keep reaching for a thing, lass, it'll stay alive in you."

She was not surprised by the intensity of emotion in his eyes, in his strong, harsh voice. She knew only that he was right again. The thing between them, that had been there from the very beginning, could never be rigidly confined within the ordinary bounds of love or hate; it was too violent, too unruly, too contradictory. Aye, he was right, always right. She would not have it any other way. She would not relinquish the challenge, the aliveness of it for all the polite and lukewarm swooning in Scotland and England.

"You've a deft way with words," she said.

"I like a lass with spirit," he replied. "The same as a horse."

"Aye," she retorted, "so you may break them alike to your will."

"I'd no' break Tammie to my will," he said slowly, "even if I could. And since I know that I cannot, I value him above all things."

"I trust Tammie holds you in the same esteem."

"We have an understanding of a sorts," he said, grinning, "but whether we love or hate each other the more is a moot question I'd not attempt to answer."

Elspeth looked squarely at the wicked gleam in Tammie's eyes. "You've a healthy respect for each other," she admitted. "Mayhap, being two of a kind, 'tis easier to read the other's intentions."

"A point which applies not only to horses," Alexander said promptly.

Elspeth held her reins firmly; beyond the woods the jangle of harness and bit grew louder as the Campbells approached Fraoch Eilean, and the chestnut mare skittered nervously in anticipation.

"I hope you'll not languish away from boredom before I see you at Rathmor," said the MacHugh. "I'm afraid I'll not be able to enjoy the Earl's pleasant company with you."

"His lordship will be crushed at the news," she said. She added flatly, "His company may be many things, but I have never found it boring."

"And seldom pleasant," Alexander agreed. He laughed down at her. "Use some of your temper on Archibald," he suggested calmly. "I see no reason why I should always bear the brunt of it."

"He cares little for spirit," she said. "He prefers his women weak and cowardly."

The MacHugh shook his head sympathetically. "I told Glenurchy the man has no heart. You'd best take him to Kirk with you more often. Of course, that would mean mending your own sinful ways. Is it too hard a price to pay?"

She glared at him, but could not keep from laughing. Then Duncan and his men turned the bend in the trail and came upon them, and the MacHugh said his farewells briefly. He merely lifted his hand to Elspeth and turned the stallion toward Fraoch Eilean, his men charging after him with evident pleasure to be home and rid of their Campbell companions.

Elspeth rode beside Duncan the few remaining miles to Inveraray. The great gates were standing open in anticipation of their arrival and the courtyard was crowded with soldiers and clansmen. There was a sense of haste about the castle; the neat piles of weapons in the guardroom and the predominance of heavily armed clansmen spoke clearly of the feverish preparations for war. The messengers were still arriving and leaving with dispatch bags; the unfamiliar tartans of some men in the courtyard were evidence that the Earl intended to muster his army from all of Scotland.

Elspeth dismounted and trailed disconsolately behind Duncan as he climbed the stairs. The Earl of Argyll met them at the door of the great hall; his velvet doublet and starched linen ruff were as neat as if he had been attending the King, so that Duncan and Elspeth felt more than a little wilted, dusty and unkempt.

"Dear cousin, I am thankful you have arrived safely. I warrant it was a most unpleasant journey." He turned to Elspeth and held out a languid hand; the ruffles at his wrists fell delicately over the thin fingers. "May I speak to you, mistress? It grieves me to discuss trifling matters before you've rested from your journey, but I fear I'll be occupied later."

Elspeth shrugged wearily and followed him into the hall. Duncan closed the door behind them and removed his helmet with a slight sigh. His mail seemed to weigh heavily on his shoulders; his face was lined with dust and his hair fell damply over his broad forehead. Elspeth smiled at him encouragingly; if they were being called to answer for their misdeeds, at least they would stand trial together.

Argyll led the way into the library. A small fire burned on the hearth, for it was cool within the castle despite the warm sun outside. Elspeth dropped into a chair; she slipped off her red velvet cap and ran her hands through her short hair, knowing well that if she looked she would see the Earl's brows raised in fastidious horror. He abhorred untidiness, having told her frequently that he considered it a mark of slovenly character inexcusable in a lady and deplorable in a gentleman.

"Elspeth," he said, his voice chilled, "must you ride through Scotland dressed like a—" he hesitated before finishing coldly— "like a wanton?"

Elspeth tried to look innocent. Her new riding habit was cut like a man's doublet, snug and tightly fitting, and the skirts were divided so that she might ride astride with maidenly decorum and modesty. But she had removed the jacket in the warm sun on the trail, leaving her shirt unlaced at the neck, and if it seemed indiscreet it had proved vastly comfortable.

"My lord, I did not think to disgrace you. It was so dreadfully hot in the sun."

He was not misled by her smile. "In the future, mistress, you will confine such unmaidenly conduct to your bedchamber. It ill becomes a woman of your rank."

"Faith, there's small difference in rank on your Scots trails." Elspeth sighed. "The sun burns and the dust suffocates all, with a lamentable lack of respect for the circumstances of birth."

" 'Tis a cross you must bear," Argyll said irritably.

Duncan moved impatiently. "Have you nothing more important to speak of, cousin? If not, leave us retire."

The Earl smiled thinly. "I have many matters of importance to discuss with you, Duncan, but they will rest well until a more opportune moment. I've no wish to anger myself now with thoughts of Angus MacDonald." Neither Duncan nor Elspeth spoke and Argyll continued, "I shall be pleased to hear your explanations of that miserable affair later."

Argyll's sharp eyes moved over Elspeth slowly, contemptuously. She did not move under his scrutiny, but a slow anger stirred inside her. She had come to expect his contempt and dislike, for he treated everyone in the same fashion. But there was something more menacing in those cold eyes, something triumphant, as if the small defiance of dressing to displease him was laughable and piteous, as if there were no defiance, not even of the spirit, which could not be stamped out by a single motion of his languid hand.

"When you are wed, Elspeth, I trust your husband will instruct you in the proper manners expected of a gently bred wife."

"I've been instructed most adequately, sir," she said, "by Queen Anne and the ladies of the court. Do you think to improve on such authority?"

Argyll flushed. Elspeth knew it had ever rankled in him that the English considered a Scot peer, no matter how ancient his earldom, the most unpolished and rustic of nobles. He had taken the brunt of many barbed jests about the crude manners fostered in un-civilized Scotland, and if the jests were common and ill-bred in themselves, they nevertheless struck home with Argyll, who had learned the proper amenities only through hard appliance and humiliating experi-ence.

He glowered at Elspeth. "I question the authority of any such scandalous women as I found in London."

"For the love of God, will you leave the lass be?" Duncan exploded. "We're in no mood to haggle over manners and clothing. Come to your point, man."

"Your trip to Edinburgh must have been singularly unsuccessful, Duncan, for you to return in so foul a temper." He waved Duncan into silence. "I have news which should please you both."

Elspeth looked at him warily. The man might have oil on his tongue, smooth and slippery enough to change the very sound of his words.

"I've received word from London," the Earl said. He looked directly at Elspeth. "I have found you a husband, mistress."

She could do no more than stare at him. She had expected it and dreaded it, but the actuality jolted her as if she had never heard the word before.

Argyll ignored the silence which greeted his news. "I have done my best to treat you well," he went on, toying with the ruffles at his wrist. "I expect no thanks, but in time you will learn to appreciate the affection and esteem I have shown you."

Duncan cleared his throat. "Who is the man, Argyll?" he asked harshly.

"We are most fortunate. I have arranged a betrothal between Elspeth and Walter Kildare, Earl of Luns-don."

Elspeth controlled her face, but she was not so

successful with her voice. "Walter Kildare?" she repeated faintly. "I can scarce believe it."

"Did you believe I'd chose an unpleasant man of revolting habits for you, my dear? I think you've no trust in me." Argyll shrugged his shoulders and sighed. "The young man has come into a large inheritance recently. Besides that remarkable good fortune, the King has appointed him Master of the King's Horse, a position of some prestige and remuneration. Come now, tell me I've treated you most nobly."

Elspeth studied the fire behind Argyll. She could think of nothing to say. She thought of Walter Kildare, the kind young lord who had felt so ill at ease in the roisterous world of the court. She had imagined prospective husbands of every loathsome description and character, but she had never once dreamed the one might be Walter Kildare of the gentle voice and courteous manners.

Duncan broke the silence. "Do you know the man, lass? What sort of gentleman is he?" He added kindly, "If you do not approve, we'll not rush to it."

"A fatherly thought, Duncan," Argyll said calmly, "but the matter is settled. Lunsdon has agreed without settlement. 'Tis an amazing good stroke of luck that he's demanded no impossible dowry."

"Settled?" Elspeth echoed. "How long have you known?"

"Will ye wait till the MacDonald campaign is ended?" Duncan asked slowly."

Argyll ignored Elspeth's question. He examined his velvet shoe carefully. "Lunsdon wishes her to return to London by the summer's end. I intend an elaborate affair, worthy of such a match, and she will need time to prepare for it."

Duncan looked at Elspeth again. "You've said nothing, Elspeth. What think you of Walter Kildare?"

"He is a dear lad," she said shortly. She needed time to think, she must accustom herself to the thought. Betrothed to Walter Kildare, and a winter wedding in London; faith, she could no longer avoid thinking of it.

She stood up and looked directly at Argyll. "It is well I have till the end of summer," she said flatly. "I've made plans for the next month. My sister—" she emphasized the words plainly—"my sister is being wed to Simon MacHugh, and I intend to visit Rathmor for the ceremony."

Argyll surprised her by smiling faintly. "It pleases me to have you win the affection of the Lamonds," he said coolly. "I've no objections; visit them whenever you like."

He lied so easily that she could almost be persuaded he meant it. But she looked at his eyes, slate-gray and hard, and wondered what purpose he had for hiding his hatred for Robert Lamond. She did not like it; she did not care for the cool confidence in his voice or the ready lies on his tongue.

"Why don't you ride to Rathmor with me, my lord?" she asked idly, not looking at Duncan. "Sir Robert would be pleased to have so honored a guest at the festivities."

"I should be delighted," he said, "but I've the small matter of a war on my hands." He added smoothly, "I must depend on you, my dear, to bring me news of your family when you return."

She saw it was no use; his lies proved nothing beyond the certain knowledge that he intended harm for both Robert Lamond and Alexander MacHugh, and that much she had known for some time. His malice was calculated to a fine degree, hidden behind a great wall of deceit and trickery; and because he trusted no one and was outguessed by few, it was seldom possible to prepare for his attack until it happened. And then it would be too late.

⟨ 14 ⟩

JEANNIE Lamond had her spring wedding beneath the blue skies of Argyllshire. The skies remained fair and clear, the thorn trees in the garden below the castle became white clouds of blossom, and the Lamonds and MacHughs began to gather from the whole of Scotland.

For days before the ceremony the walls of Rathmor Castle rang with the boisterous festivities which inevitably attended a Highland wedding. It was a gay occasion for all concerned, since the marriage had the hearty approval of both clans. Each morning and evening the pipers strutted before the castle and shrilled their salutes to the chiefs present at Rathmor for the wedding. The young lads from the surrounding countryside matched their skill at archery, wrestling and fencing, often daring the cold waters of Loch Awe for swimming contests.

Rathmor's great kitchens were well stocked, the wine cellars filled to the beams, the ancient arms in the hall polished to a brilliant sheen. The dancing lasted beyond midnight each night, and the silver flagons were filled and refilled with pause only for the weary who took to their beds with the dawn.

It was a bonny wedding for a bonny bride. On the day of the ceremony Jean stood in the center of her bedchamber and allowed Elspeth and Katherine to dress her in her wedding gown.

"Sim will never recognize you." Kate laughed, lacing the satin bodice. "He'll be certain we've changed brides."

It was true; Jeannie no longer seemed to be a slip of a child. She was so beautiful that it took one's breath away to look at her face, and that was as it should be for a bride. Her hair was like dark smoke about her shoulders; the lustrous white satin gown emphasized the tiny waist and the lovely curves of her breasts. She wore a slender chain of diamonds about her neck, and their glow seemed to catch in her eyes and linger there like twin stars.

"Have you seen Sim?" she finally asked, a break in her voice.

"He's as pale and dour as a bridegroom should be," Kate assured her. "Alex has him in charge, so I'm sure he'll be dressed in time."

"Pale?" Jean asked vaguely. "Dour, Kate? Why should he be?" She turned quickly, a sudden frown between her eyes. "Do you think he's changed his mind"

"You silly goose, all men are miserable when the day arrives."

Elspeth added solemnly, "Aye, Kate is right, sweet. And there's a reason why he wasn't allowed to see you this morning. One look at your white face and poor Sim would have ridden for home, swearing all the way you'd both made a terrible mistake."

Jean laughed and the color returned to her cheeks. "You're both daft," she said happily.

She was ready then. Kate patted her cheek cheerfully and Elspeth gave her a quick kiss, both careful not to muss the fluted satin ruff which lifted from the jewel-crusted bodice.

She moved slowly down the stairs, hearing the faint rustle of her train as loud as thunder in the silence. There was her father, standing beside Alexander; the two of them looked quite stern, but Alex dropped one eye in a deliberate wink as she gained the courtyard. She smiled tremulously, because he was almost as dear to her as Simon, and so when she looked at Simon for the first time on their wedding

day there was a radiant happiness for him to see in
her face.

Simon wore a doublet of crammesy velvet, lined
with white; the sleeves were elaborately slashed in
the Spanish style and heavily embroidered with gold
thread. Alexander's dress sword hung at his side,
supported in a velvet scabbard with tassels of gold,
and the jeweled MacHugh crest blazed in the sunlight. It would be Simon's now, and the gift of it
signified the blessing of the Chief of Clan MacHugh
on the marriage.

Simon looked grave and very proud as he stood at
the door of the chapel, waiting to take her hand and
lead her into the holy place where they would stand
before the minister of the Kirk. But his eyes softened
as she walked across the courtyard, then he smiled.

The words of marriage were spoken in a low, unhurried voice by the black-clothed minister, but they filled
the ancient chapel and sounded well beyond the open
doors to the courtyard, where the guests were standing who could not squeeze inside.

Elspeth stood beside her father and Gavin, hoping
she would not cry. The sun fell softly through the
open door, striking Jean's bent bead as she said the
solemn vows with Simon MacHugh. A happy bride
the sun shines on, Elspeth thought wistfully; it seemed
too much happiness to look on without tears, and
tears would surely be an ill-omen in the midst of so
much joy.

She raised her eyes suddenly and looked across
the chapel to Alexander MacHugh. She found him
looking at her, his eyes quiet and darkly gray. She
could not turn away; somehow, in that holy place
there was no place for deceit. She could not lie to
him; her feelings must be in her eyes for him to see,
as clearly as they could hear the voices of Jean and
Simon plighting their troth.

The MacHugh did not take his eyes from her face
for the rest of the ceremony. His face was expression-

less and unsmiling, and he seemed aloof and distant in his elegant velvet and satin doublet. But Elspeth suddenly remembered the evening before, when she had watched him at a vigorous game of shinny. He had been wearing a kilted plaid, as had the other Lamond and MacHugh lads, and a pair of sheepskin brogues. He had looked like any young clansman, except that his wide shoulders and great height set him apart from the others.

The game was composed of two opposing teams, each endeavoring to drive a ball to a certain point on either side. It had seemed a bruising, dangerous game to Elspeth, with the heavy clubs flourishing wildly in the air much like swordplay and the players fighting over the ball as if it were the Crown of Scotland. The children screamed with excitement, the pipers chrilled loudly and the spectators yelled encouragement until the uproar was earsplitting.

The MacHugh had shouted and laughed as loudly as the smallest boy. His team had gained the ball after a desperate struggle, and he brought it to Elspeth as she stood on the hill above the field. He had offered it to her as the winning knight in a royal tournament might honor his lady by presenting her his trophy. He had laughed up at her, his face wet and dirty, and his boyish, triumphant air had touched her oddly.

She would have to tell him today. She had been foolish to wait; the task grew more difficult each day.

The ceremony was ended at last, and Jean and Simon walked together up the narrow aisle and through the doors. Elspeth followed them slowly, knowing without turning her head that Alexander was directly behind her, his hand now resting lightly under her arm.

Neither of them spoke, but Elspeth felt his presence like a physical thing; she could not move, she could not walk away from him, yet it was like a sick pain beneath her stays to feel him so near. Finally they were separated in the crush of well-wishers and clansmen who had jammed the courtyard. The crowd soon began to gravitate to the great hall, where the banqueting tables were laid for the lengthy feasting which would follow, interspersed with entertainment, until well into the next day.

Elspeth did not see the MacHugh for a long while. When she finally caught sight of him, he was in a far corner of the hall with Simon and Gavin. They were laughing, their flagons raised in a toast, and she thought the three of them looked happier than she had ever seen them. Plots and intrigues and battles were put aside, away from their thoughts, as if such violent affairs had no place in Rathmor Castle on Jeannie's wedding day.

Elspeth wandered into the small hall beyond, finding it even more crowded. She saw Kate MacLachlan, surrounded by a dozen admirers, and nodded briefly. Kate had been surprisingly friendly during the last few days, but one never knew what thoughts lay behind those slanted eyes.

She rested her arms on the casement of the window in the alcove where Jean's harp sat, covered in black velvet. Beyond the castle the hills were growing green with spring; the sky was a soft blue, washed clean with the warm May sunlight.

She wondered what Walter Kildare would be doing in London. Ordering his wedding clothes from his London tailor, mayhap, or riding for his country estates beyond London to inform his family of his approaching wedding. Doubtless it would be another shock for them, after the Earl's recent inheritance and his good fortune at court. They would probably think Walter more than foolish, taking a wife so soon after acquiring his sudden wealth. Any sensible English family would prefer that their money be turned back to the land they had struggled so long to preserve, rather than see it spent on a foreign bride. And a poor bride, with no dowry to speak of, a bride from

Scotland, the land of murderers and ruffians. They would be less than friendly to her, and small wonder.

Elspeth sighed, her eyes on the peaceful quiet of the hills beyond Rathmor. Walter Kildare did not belong in the world of London, but neither would he care for the Highlands of Scotland. He loved his rolling English fields, marked in neat patterns by stone fences; his ancient manor house, whose lovely gardens stretched to the lazy river below it; his pleasant and secure life as a country Earl, with friendly neighbors and respectful tenants who touched their forelocks when he rode abroad on his wide lands.

"Do you find Jean's wedding such a sad affair?"

Elspeth did not turn. Alexander joined her at the window, leaning on the casement beside her.

"Any single lass will weep at a wedding," she said lightly. "Perhaps 'tis a matter of pride."

"Hoping the next will be yours? Are you so anxious to be wed?"

Elspeth looked at a faint wisp of cloud rising above the hills like a bit of white thorn blossom blown upward by the wind.

"Don't plan your wedding too soon, lass," he remarked casually. "The MacHughs will be recovering from this one for some time yet."

There was small chance the MacHughs would be celebrating Elspeth Lamond's London wedding. It was a perfect opening to tell him, but she could not make the words come.

"When do you leave for Islay?" she asked instead.

Alexander was silent for a long moment. He turned slightly, and she knew his eyes were on her face. "I've nothing to keep me," he answered quietly, "now that Sim is wed."

"Then you'll be riding soon?" She would not face him. She kept her eyes on the tiny cloud till it disappeared into a larger one.

"Aye." His voice lowered, even though the heavy velvet hangings of the alcove prevented their voices from carrying beyond them. "D'you understand why it must be this way?"

She looked at him then, waiting for him to say more. His dark blue doublet turned his eyes the color of the blue-gray mist which drifted on the horizon above the sea. The lines of his face were hard and firm, and his mouth was unsmiling. He looked as she had first seen him, on that long-ago day when they met by the black loch in the hills; but now there was something else in the depths of his eyes, something in the tone of his voice, in the way his velvet sleeve brushed against her hand on the stone casement.

"I must go, Elspeth, or I would not. It began before you came to Scotland, and I must finish it before I can think of other things."

"Such as?" It was a foolish question, but it would gain her more time.

"Do I need to tell you, lass?"

She looked at his shoulders, blocking out the crowded room, and her eyes rested on the golden pendant which hung around his neck. The Thistle of Scotland was worn with age, rounded on the edges until the outline blurred into the pendant.

She said finally, "Will you return before fall?"

"The answer to that lies with Jamie MacDonald. I'll stay no longer than necessary." His voice was stern, as if he had asked himself the same question and found no answer. "We're being most serious for a gay occasion. Have you eaten?"

She shook her head, then raised her eyes to meet his, knowing she could not wait for another chance.

She said carefully, " 'Tis possible I might be in London by the time you return."

He raised his dark brows, but he said nothing.

"I must prepare my trousseau." She paused, then lifted her chin and looked at him directly as she finished on a quick rush of breath. "I'm to wed Walter Kildare, Earl of Lunsdon, before the year's end."

The silence was complete. Even the voices in the

room behind them seemed to fade away into a faint murmur. The MacHugh did not move; when he spoke at last his voice was controlled as ever.

"And you agree to such an arrangement?"

"I have no choice. As my guardian, Argyll arranged the settlement." She repeated the words, "I have no choice."

How could he understand? There was no possible way to explain, in all the world, why a woman must marry one man when she loved another. There would never be words to explain to the MacHugh—the MacHugh, who abided by no decisions but his own, who knew no law but the seal of his King, who defended his rights at the point of his sword.

She knew he would be angry; she was prepared for the hot rage which blazed in his eyes.

"Do you remember what I told you at Castle Campbell?"

Aye, she remembered. And she could feel the bracelets at her wrist, one with the words "Fear na ye" inscibed inside. "What would you have me do?" she asked slowly. "Argyll has made his decision and Duncan does not object. They are my kinsmen, they have the right to plan my future." The dull ache in her throat proved the lie in her words, whispered silently that such things were wrong, were unbearably false and cruel.

"I had begun to think you were losing that foolish pride," he said, his voice roughened with anger. "Did you have no choice, or did you prefer to make none?"

The sarcasm in his voice was like a slap. She clenched her hands against her skirt; it was growing difficult to keep back the tears.

"At least I can be thankful it will be Walter Kildare."

He put his hand on her arm. "Did you know him in London?"

"I knew him quite well. He is a pleasant young man." His fingers tightened on her arm, but she did not flinch.

"D'y think you love him?" he asked harshly. "Look at me and tell me you love him!"

He knew, he had known for a long time, and she could not lie to him. He laughed, softly and triumphantly. "You see, lass, you love me. And yet you believe I'd allow you to belong to another?" His eyes darkened, more black than gray. "D'you intend to leave while I'm away and can do nothing to prevent it?"

"You could do nothing in any case," she said wearily.

"Are you too weak to protest when he forces you into marriage with a man you don't love?" he countered flatly. "Like a paid wench, selling her favors? God's blood, mistress, I find it hard to understand!"

Elspeth wrenched her arm away from his hand and stood back. "It'd be useless to protest," she said desperately. "Please leave me, I don't care to speak of it." She could not endure it any longer. If he did not soon go away she would be in tears. But he did not move, and she stamped her foot childishly. "Go away. You've no right to speak so to me!" He had never once said he loved her she thought wildly, he had never committed himself so deeply.

She would have left then, for he showed no inclination to move. But she looked beyond him and saw Kate MacLachlan coming toward them, her emerald gown moving like green waves about her feet as she walked.

Kate smiled at Alexander. "You look like a thundercloud, Alex. People are beginning to wonder why you two are so solemn. Such a strange way to behave at a wedding, standing in a corner and glaring at each other." She tapped her fan gently against Alexander's doublet, then unfurled it before her face.

"And you are a curious busybody," Alexander said easily. "Do you know the proper way to behave at weddings, Kate? If I told you, I'm certain you'd refuse my suggestion."

Kate regarded him over her fan, lowering her lashes until her dark eyes were almost hidden. Her shoulders gleamed like pale satin above the deeply cut bodice of her gown, and the burnished red of her hair was incredibly brilliant against her white skin and the sea-emerald gown. It was a daring gown, worn to please men. Worn to please one man, Elspeth corrected herself, and that man Alexander MacHugh.

"Would you be desolate if I refused? I'll decide for myself after you've explained." She took Alexander's arm, turning to smile at Elspeth. "If it seems proper to Alex, I'm certain it would seem quite improper to anyone else. Will you forgive me for stealing him away?"

"He is yours, Kate," Elspeth said lightly.

Alexander bowed briefly. He did not smile, nor did he apologize for leaving her so abruptly. "By your leave, mistress."

She watched as they walked toward the doors to the great hall. They made such a handsome pair together that people turned to stare. Kate MacLachlan would be an excellent match for the MacHugh; her family would be overwhelmed with such good fortune, and it was plain to see the woman loved him to the point of madness. But the thought was so distasteful that Elspeth could hardly bear it. She wondered if the MacHugh had ever told Kate that he loved her; it was doubtful, else the wench would have snared him long before.

She waited for a lengthy interval, then followed them slowly into the hall and slipped into a chair at the high table beside her father.

"You look weary," he said, his cool gaze warming as he looked at her. "Has it been an exhausting day for you?"

She smiled and said only, "It was a lovely wedding."

"Aye, it was that. Rathmor has waited many years for a wedding like Jeannie's." He was silent, looking at the pale wine in the goblet before him; and Elspeth wondered if he was remembering another wedding, the one which had never taken place at Rathmor. Mayhap his thoughts had gone further yet, to the small grave in the hills, where lay buried all his dreams of seeing a son grow tall to bear his name.

At the far end of the table Jean and Sim were raising their goblets with Alexander and Kate. Elspeth took the plate which her father had heaped with meat and fruit, but the sight of so much food only lessened her appetite. She toyed with the silver knife for a long while, but she could force nothing past her lips but a few sips of wine.

The afternoon dragged into dusk; the clansmen began to light the candles on the tables and along the stone walls. The pipers played continuously and the celebrating guests showed no signs of tiring. But at last Jeannie stood up, amidst a chorus of wild cheers and toasts; she curtsied to Simon and left the hall, followed by Kate MacLachlan. Elspeth knew that her place was also with Jean.

The turret at the far end of the great hall led up to the bridal chambers. Robert Lamond had moved his apartments to another tower, for only Jean and Simon would sleep in the privacy of the south turret on their wedding night.

Kate was hastily divesting Jean of her wedding gown when Elspeth entered. The room was warm and scented, softly lighted by white tapers which smelled faintly of rose and musk. The bridal bed was spread with satin sheets and a maid was warming them with silver warming pans which had been filled with hot coals.

Jean's heart-shaped face was pale and serious; she stood quietly before the fire and allowed Kate to undress her, but her lips quivered as though she might turn and flee at the slightest provocation.

Elspeth went to the small table by the bed and poured a goblet of clear Rhenish wine. "Here, pet, drink this. Perhaps it isn't wise after so many toasts, but it will warm you inside."

"It can't warm me where I'm cold," Jean whispered, but she took the wine like an obedient child and sipped it slowly.

"Only Sim can do that." Kate laughed, but Elspeth frowned at her quickly. Kate shrugged and handed Jean the filmy bit of lace gown which had been spread across the bed.

"Now the robe, Kate," Elspeth ordered calmly. "You'll find it in the press."

It was the exquisite crimson velvet robe which Elspeth had given Jean. Jean slipped her arms into the sleeves and hugged them close to her body, and the crimson brought the color to her cheeks and halted the trembling which threatened to spread from her mouth to her hands.

Elspeth took a deep breath. She looked around her at the warm room, at the candles smelling of rose and the satin bed sheets gleaming in the soft light. She looked at Jeannie, happy and frightened and lovely beyond words, waiting for Simon MacHugh. She thought of the soft, velvety darkness of the room when the last boisterous guest had left and the candles had been extinguished.

She suddenly felt as if she were stifled, unable to breathe in the suffocating warmth of the room. She gave Jean one helpless look, gathered her skirts in her hands, and fled down the stairs toward the hall.

2

Simon had left the high table, surrounded by laughing, jesting men, both MacHughs and Lamonds. Presently they would take him up the turret stairs to the room where Jean waited, and the age-old custom of bedding the new couple would take place.

Elspeth had almost gained the doors to the small hall when she saw her father glance in her direction; but she ignored his questioning look and fled through the small hall, finally reaching the tower door and the sanctuary beyond.

She wrenched open the brass-studded door, but as

she held her skirts aside to enter she caught a glimpse of Alexander MacHugh, pausing in the door across the room. It gave her a moment of panic that he had seen and followed her, but she slammed the door and ran up the curving steps. The light was dim, for the only lantern was just beyond the turn above her, and she cursed the fullness of her skirts. She could not lift them high enough; her feet stumbled over the stiff petticoats and she put one hand against the stone walls to keep from falling.

Below her the door opened and closed. He caught up with her as she reached the first landing; she would have opened the door to the retiring room, not attempting to reach her bedchamber above, but he put out his hand and took her arm.

She turned to face him, forcing her voice to calmness. "I did not ask your company, sir."

His face was hard. "Why did you run away? Jean needed you with her; I saw her face when she left the hall."

She did not answer. He looked at her for a long moment, and then flung her arm down with an abrupt movement which made her wince.

"Can't you bear the sight of her?" he asked harshly. He put one hand on the hilt of his sword, the other on his hip. "Perhaps you're retiring to dream of your own wedding, mistress." He laughed, and it was not a pleasant sound. "Do you regret you'll not be so eager a bride as Jeannie? Or is the prospect of your husband's heavy moneybags compensation enough?"

"I hate you," she said. "Take your vile thoughts elsewhere."

The small candle in the brass wall lantern flickered a dim light across his face. He cursed under his breath, bitterly; without another word he picked her up in his arms and started up the next flight of stairs. There was no room for her to struggle; he moved up the narrow circular steps sideways, his sword scraping against the wall.

A thin sliver of light showed under the door of her

bedchamber. The door was not securely latched and he kicked it open with his boot. Light flooded from the room onto the stairs. Maggie, the Campbell maid, sat up drowsily in her chair by the fire; she settled her dust cap on her head and stared at them with bewilderment.

The MacHugh indicated the door with a nod of his head, "You're not needed now."

"Maggie, don't leave!" Elspeth began to struggle, but his arms were like steel bands around her.

"I cannot obey the both of ye," the woman said dryly.

"Make haste, woman!" The brusque authority in the MacHugh's voice left the maid no alternative. "Go below to the retiring room. Your mistress can call if she needs your aid."

The maid hesitated no longer. She gave a brief curtsy and left the room; the MacHugh walked over and kicked the door shut with his boot. He put Elspeth on the floor beside him, still holding her with one arm, and pushed the bolt firmly in place across the door.

Elspeth asked quietly, "Do you find pleasure in handling me so rudely, and in my father's house?"

He laughed shortly. "He knows I am here."

He relaxed his hold on her arm and she moved across the room, shrugging her shoulders. She dropped her fan on the dressing table and unfastened the gold bracelets slowly, ignoring him with an assurance she did not feel. Her heart thudded violently under the velvet bodice of her gown; she was breathing more rapidly than she would care for him to know.

She realized too late that he could see her reflection in the mirror. She met his eyes in the glass, wishing she could hurl the mirror in his face.

"Are you frightened that I'll ravish you, mistress?" He smiled strangely. "Don't be disappointed if I deny myself that pleasure. I like my wenches eager and willing. And I'd not like to spoil your virtue for Lunsdon; he'll be cheated enough as it is."

She refused to give him the satisfaction of an answer.

"So you find me too rude to your liking? Doubtless it will be a relief to return to London, where your admirers swoon over the scent of your gloves and woo you with pretty sonnets. And gold, of course."

He paused and she turned. "Are you quite finished? You must be drunk, sir!"

"Did Walter Kildare approach you in such a delicate manner? D'you fool yourself he's man enough to make a woman of you?" He put his thumbs in his belt and laughed. "Aye, I'm more than a little drunk. 'Tis no small aid when a man has an unpleasant taste in his mouth."

"You've known since I came to Scotland," she said, "that I was to be wed at Argyll's discretion. Why don't you leave me alone? Are you never satisfied?"

"I'm satisfied," he replied flatly. "I have an extremely high regard for myself, which is more than I can say for my opinion of you." He added, "I misjudged you, and I find it a bitter thing to take. I never believed you'd submit to Argyll's unholy schemes so meekly."

"I'm to marry Lunsdon," she said carefully, fighting her anger, the hurt inside her, the aching that would not quit her blood. "It will be so, whatever your opinion of me."

He crossed the room to her in two quick strides, taking her shoulders in a relentless grip. "Marry a man you don't love? Holy God, I'd sooner kill you!"

"Do you think I'd be a happier bride," she asked, "if I saw my father ruined, and you put to the horn and outlawed? You've no need to curse me. I'd not be the one to suffer if I defied Argyll."

His eyes had not left her face; his hands were bruising her shoulders. But when he spoke again his voice was drained of all anger. "You fear for me, lass?" If the thought amused him, he did not show it. "Does Argyll think to have you wed while he's still in Scotland?"

"He'll join me in London before the wedding," she said.

"I trust the MacDonalds will oblige his lordship by ending their rebellion before the appointed date."

She kept her eyes on the dark blue of his doublet, so close to her face. "Please leave me," she said, feeling a weariness beyond endurance. "You make it much harder to bear."

He looked at her without speaking for a long moment, then dropped his hands. He turned and walked to the fire, propping his boot on the fender. Standing there deep in thought, his wide back to her, he yet dominated the room so that she could not move or take her eyes from him.

At last he turned to face her, feet wide apart and his thumbs hooked in his belt, the firelight tracing his dark head in bold relief.

"We've had no holy words said over us," he said quietly, "but you belong to me, and I need no minister of the Kirk to sanctify my actions."

If he had spoken a tender word, or shown her any gentleness, she might have been able to withstand him, to keep her determination and resolve. But he did not attempt to charm her, he used none of the persuasive magic he could so easily summon to his command. He stood before her, silent and proud, his face closed against her, his mouth ruthless and hard. He would never force her to his will; he would ask nothing of her. Whatever she gave, she would give freely and gladly; however she came to him, she would come of her own accord.

She remembered how he had told her that one day she would forget her outraged virtue and admit she was meant to be loved by him, for all her days. He would have it so, damning Argyll and Walter Kildare; or else he would not have her at all. The space between them stretched incredibly wide, and she must cross it alone under those intent gray eyes, not knowing what she would face at the end of it; for if she made no move, he would walk through the door and out of her life, and for all the lonely years ahead she would have nothing but her foolish pride and fear for him to comfort her.

She took one step, and then another, and still he did not move. She thought of Jean and Simon, in the warm, sweet-scented turret room; of Walter Kildare, choosing his wedding clothes at his London tailor's; of the golden bracelet bearing the lilting words with the sound of a charm in them, "Fear na ye."

And she lifted her chin and walked toward him, knowing suddenly that the foolish pride of self would be nothing at all beside the fierce pride of loving him.

"Did you know," she said, her voice not quite steady, "that the Kirk fines those who would find their own pleasure, and it unsanctified?"

She had reached him then; and her eyes met his and saw at last the cold there disappear into warm laughter. "The Kirk may keep its envious nose out of our affairs," he said.

The clock on her dressing table ticked loudly in the silence; she could hear her heart pounding with the same agonizing rhythm. He had not touched her, nor moved toward her.

"I've been told a lass is always shy on her wedding night," he said gently, "and you are." He put a finger against her cheek softly and then took it away. "Also very frightened, but I hope you're not that."

She stared at him, hearing his words repeat in her mind like the endless tinkle of a music box. Her wedding night, he had said; and the tenderness in his voice touched her as no vow he might have given her before the stern God of the Kirk.

"Did you think I'd beat you?" he asked, and grinned. "Perhaps I shall yet, for keeping me waiting such an ungodly time."

He took her face in his hands, his strong fingers feeling the contours of her face and moving to touch the short silken curls. Elspeth felt the tears burning, wetting her lashes, and she closed her eyes; she had never known such happiness, and mayhap it must last her for a lifetime, beyond all the dire events conspiring to separate them.

"My lass," he murmured, against her face. Then his hands were on her gown, pushing it away from her shoulders. He found her mouth and kissed her, a long kiss, and the touch of his hands burned against her skin and flamed inside her.

"Aye, you shall have your wedding night," he said, low. "And you'll remember it always, for you'll have no other."

3

Elspeth woke slowly, reluctant to leave the deep contentment of sleep. She stretched lazily, wondering why she had awakened so suddenly, and blinked in the bright shaft of sunlight which fell across the bed.

Then she sat up quickly, remembering everything at once. The room was empty. There was no sign of the MacHugh. The sun was high, which meant she had slept most of the morning, and she felt a vague surprise because the maid Maggie was not there. A warm fire burned on the hearth, but her bare shoulders were cold.

Then she heard spurs clinking against the steps outside the door and realized the sound must have awakened her, but she was unprepared when the door swung open without a single knock of warning. She made a desperate attempt to pull the sheets about her shoulders, but it was too late.

The MacHugh closed the door behind him. A glint of mail showed beneath his leather jacket and he carried his helmet in his hand. His dark cloak reached almost to the spurs on his tall boots; it swung back as he walked to reveal the pearl-handled pistols at his belt. He was ready to ride. He was leaving.

Elspeth could think of nothing to say, even if she could have managed her voice.

He took a bright tartan shawl from Maggie's chair

and tossed it Elspeth. "You look blue with cold, lass," he said, smiling. "Did you sleep well?"

"Very well, thank you." She wrapped herself in the shawl and gave him a small tentative smile. The Mac-Hugh strode to the side of the bed and looked down at her. "Is it very late? I didn't intend to sleep away the day."

He sat on the side of the bed, adjusting his sword. "You needed the sleep. I fear I kept you awake most of the night." Her face turned warm. He was smiling, his eyes on her face. "I sent Maggie for your breakfast," he said. "I'd join you, but I've lingered too long."

He was really leaving her. He was riding for Islay, and she might never see him again.

He seemed to read her thoughts. "I cannot explain why, but I must go." His voice was amused. "I've no choice."

He was using her own words. But when the Mac-Hugh used them they sounded so inevitable, so irrefutable. He must ride to join MacDonald; he must go into battle for a cause which was not his. When he spoke, she did not question such friendship; that would come much later, when he had gone.

He stood up abruptly and walked to the window. There he stayed for a moment, thinking, then came back to the side of the bed.

"In the event you must leave for London before I return," he said, "send word to Rathmor or Fraoch Eilean. Simon will see that the message reaches me."

"Argyll might force me to go before he marches his army south," she said slowly. "But I doubt he'll see any reason for it. And once he leaves, it will be easier to disobey him."

He looked down at her, his face grave. Then he sat down again, his brows drawn together in a scowl.

"He's too canny to underestimate your intelligence." He was silent for a moment. Then he drew off his leather gloves, slowly, and Elspeth could see the heavy ring on his right hand. The MacHugh took it off and held it in the palm of his hand.

Elspeth felt unexpected tears spring to her eyes. "No, Alex," she whispered, "I cannot take it."

He took her hand and put the ring in it, closing her fingers around it. She could feel the raised crest on the ring, the crest of the Chief of Clan MacHugh.

"You've only to show it to a MacHugh, lass," he said quietly. "If you cannot show it, send it. Promise me you'll do it, whenever you need aid.

Her voice was unsteady. "Alex, I cannot involve your clan."

"You're my lass," he said, low, "and they would gladly die, to a man, if they thought it would keep you safe for me."

The sunlight had disappeared. The small room seemed dark and gloomy. She could not speak for the tears choking her throat; she longed to put her head on his shoulders and weep, her arms holding him so tightly that he could never leave her. But she could not. He would hate her tears, he would be scornful of her clinging.

As if to prove her right, he laughed suddenly. "Come, haven't you a kiss for your departing warrior? You're giving me a glum farewell."

She held the ring tightly in her hand. "I should think you'd have had enough, sir."

"I'm so weary from kissing you I can scarce face the day's ride," he said cheerfully. "But enough? Hardly, when I've only begun to teach you the proper way of it."

She gave him an unexpected push, but he recovered his balance and caught both her hands. "I'll agree 'tis most sinful and exciting to make love in broad day, but I've no time for it." He laughed at her, keeping her hands still under his strong grasp. "You're impatient for more, now you've had a taste of it, but you must wait your turn, lass."

She tried to pull her hands away, but she only succeeded in loosening the shawl. It dropped from her shoulders and she stopped struggling against him; when she raised her eyes to his, he was no longer laughing.

He bent his head and kissed her, slowly, and stood up. When he released her hands she made a motion to gather up the shawl.

"No," he said softly. He looked at her for a long time, his eyes moving over her slowly, as if he never wanted to forget the picture she made for him, sitting in the center of the bed with her hair tousled and her mouth still soft and warm from his kiss.

Then he smiled, the incredibly brilliant smile which turned his dark face warm and tender. "My ain true luve," he said. "You'd best wear the bracelets so you'll not forget it."

He was gone. The sound of his spurs against the turret walls. Elspeth did not move; she listened till she could no longer hear the faint jingle of spurs; then she listened to the silence which followed.

She thought suddenly that she might see him leave. She threw back the covers and looked wildly for her robe. She could not find it, she would miss seeing him. Then she saw a bit of yellow velvet on the opposite side of the bed. She threw herself across the bed and grabbed the robe from the floor.

She had a difficult time finding the sleeves; then she found she could not see the ground from the high window. She dragged a chair across the floor in desperation, cursing silently as the robe snarled under her feet.

At last she could see, standing on tiptoes on the chair. The MacHugh was in the saddle, bending slightly to speak to Simon. Their hands met in a brief clasp, and she could see that they were smiling. Then the MacHugh wheeled his horse. He rode without looking back, followed closely by Gavin and his men; the plumes in their steel helmets fluttered in the wind like bright banners aloft against the blue Scots sky.

Elspeth put her hand against her cheek. The heavy gold ring was warm to the touch, as if it still held the heat of his blood within the metal. She kept it there, touching her face, and gazed at the road long after he had disappeared from view, until not even the sound of hoofs could be heard against the castle walls.

{ 15 }

ELSPETH raised her head from the book and watched Argyll as he tossed his gauntlets on the table and adjusted his sword. She said nothing, but she put her finger in the book to mark her place and waited for him to speak. He was angry; his face was pale and his left eye twitched slightly, and each movement he made seemed carefully controlled.

"I leave for Duntroon, Elspeth," he said abruptly.

It was no news to her; she had known for the past week that he would take horse for the south this morning.

He wore full mail beneath his cloak; it was the first time Elspeth had seen him in battle dress and she was forced to admit that he looked much more a man in steel armor than he did in velvet and satin. Indeed, he looked most forbidding and dangerous, if one overlooked the droop of his narrow shoulders under the weight of his mail. She wondered if he would collapse under the strain; perhaps he would resort to the old custom of using a hook and derrick to lift him from his mount. She dropped her lashes so he could not see the amusement in her eyes.

"May you have a pleasant ride, sir," she murmured.

"I assure you my ride will be most pleasant," the Earl said brusquely. "I have not talked with you since you returned from Rathmor, mistress. I understand you enjoyed yourself immensely at your sister's wedding."

Elspeth placed her book slowly on the table. She wondered what purpose he had in bringing up the matter; it had been weeks since Jeannie's wedding.

"Aye," she said, "it was a grand wedding. My own will be more elaborate, I've no doubt, but I fear you cannot match Jean's for plain beauty."

He would not allow her to put him off the subject. "I have no wish to discuss weddings with you, mistress," he said. "I would speak to you about your behavior since you have resided at Inveraray."

She raised her brows and said nothing.

"I feel a great shame for you," he continued thinly, "and more shame for my own name, that you would abuse my hospitality in such a manner. By God's hand, you've become so insolent a baggage that I can scarce find the words to describe my displeasure!"

"If you would explain, sir," Elspeth said slowly, "I might better understand this talk of shame." She searched her mind for an explanation. Who could have told him, how had he found her out? Did Argyll have spies in Rathmor, in Robert Lamond's own fortress? Elspeth remembered she had heard it said once that even the Earl's candles had long ears.

"I have come from a most interesting conversation with Mistress MacLachlan. The woman knows a good deal of your activities; you should be more wary of your friends."

So Kate had been the informer. She had ridden into Inveraray the evening before on her way to Lachlan, but she showed no inclination to hurry away. "She is no friend of mine," Elspeth said flatly.

"I am certain of that. Perhaps all your Scots friends will prove as false." Argyll clasped his hands behind his back. "I could call you a number of ugly names, mistress, and you could scarce flinch. Are you like a bitch in heat, that you must satisfy every man in Scotland?"

Elspeth's face flamed. "Your rudeness grows out of bounds, sir."

Argyll silenced her with a cold stare. "I care little about your amorous writhings. But I give you a last warning, and I advise you to heed it well. You will not spoil your approaching marriage with such degrading behavior."

Elspeth stood up, her hands clenched against her skirts. "The degradation lies in your own mind, m'lord." She added coolly, "And in Kate MacLachlan's, where it began."

"It matters little where it lies," he said curtly. He took his gauntlets from the table. "I'll have no more of it. You sail for London on the *Queen Bess,* leaving Leith within the week. I have sent a letter ahead to Lunsdon, informing him that you are arriving. You will reside with his family until I join you, and it will go ill with you if your behavior in London is as indiscreet as it has been in Scotland."

Elspeth returned his stare without dropping her eyes. She would give nothing away; Alexander MacHugh had taught her a great deal about masking her thoughts.

"As you will, m'lord," she said carefully. "Is Walter's family now in London?"

"For the coming winter season and Lunsdon's wedding. Another small matter, mistress. Your obvious passion for the MacHugh pleases me little. 'Tis well you will not see him before you leave; I'm aware the man is no longer in Argyllshire. He has long tormented me, and your ill-timed affair with him only strengthens my resolve to subdue him properly." The Earl smiled, with little mirth. "I must admit that you are quick to find succor in a strange land, Elspeth; I had no idea you would find a victim to your charms so readily. My hopes for your marriage have been considerably brightened. A woman who can sway men to her will so quickly will have little trouble managing the docile Lunsdon."

She ignored him. "You give me little time to prepare myself for the journey."

"I think you need little time. You will sail on the *Queen Bess* without fail, mistress. I am taking the precaution of leaving several of my trusted clansmen to escort you to Leith."

"What shall I use for funds in London?"

"Duncan will advance you a small amount. It must suffice you until I have arrived in London to settle the final details between myself and Lunsdon."

"Final details? Do you mean he will bear the cost of the wedding? And my trousseau?"

Argyll shrugged. "We cannot quibble over such matters. Either the man pays for your favors or he goes without them. I can afford no wedding."

She looked at him with distaste. "I am astonished that Walter Kildare agreed to such an arrangement."

"The man is a fool," Argyll said. "You are fortunate."

"And you, m'lord," Elspeth said shortly.

He pulled his cloak about his shoulders and walked across the hall, turning at the door. "Remember that I have done with warnings. Your misguided lover is now in Kintyre, casting his lot with that of a forsworn rebel. He is also a fool, and I seldom find it difficult to deal with fools. You will learn in time that they are easy prey, easily defeated. And if you are wise, you will spend your energy preparing for your future as Lunsdon's wife, rather than warming the bed of any brawny young man who stirs your passion."

He hesitated a moment, regarding her impassively. "I might add, mistress, that I do you no ill favor in sending you from Scotland at this time. For your own safety it would not be wise for you to remain longer."

There was more than contempt and anger in his voice; something like triumph lay beneath the cold words, and a great satisfaction she did not understand.

"I know of no threat to my safety, sir," she said carefully, and prayed that his love of boasting would now betray him.

"Did you know I intend to have you declared your father's eldest child and therefore heir to his properties?"

She stared at him. "I'm not his legal heir," she said. "He'll fight any such scheme."

The triumph moved into his narrow eyes. "He'll have no fight with the King," he said coolly, "and a child born from handfast is quite as legitimate as any other."

She said nothing, but her mind went back to that strange suspicion directed at her from the first moment she had landed in Scotland. She had been stupid not to have guessed his intentions but the MacHughs and Lamonds were as canny Scots as Argyll himself. They must have known of his plan from the beginning.

"I have information that Lamond intends to produce another heir," Argyll said casually, his eyes never leaving her face. "He thinks to disprove the death of your brother, after so many years. A shrewd move, I must admit, but I doubt the King will place credence in the tale."

For a lengthy moment Elspeth thought she could not stand; the blood seemed to drain from her body, leaving no breath of life to keep her spine straight and her face expressionless under those relentless eyes of his.

"I cannot imagine where you heard such lies," she said finally, steadying her voice with a great effort. "The bairn died; I saw his grave with my own eyes."

"So you knew there was another child," Argyll said with an odd satisfaction. "When did you discover it?"

She would never tell him, nor would she ask how he had learned that closely guarded secret. She only knew she must find some way to get the news to Robert Lamond. "He is dead, that much I can tell you," she said.

"He is alive," Argyll countered flatly. "I know it for the truth." He smiled, and she thought she had never seen so unpleasant a look on that thin face. "Did you not hear some whisper of the scheme while at Rathmor, mistress? I find it hard to believe a curious woman would know nothing of such incredible trickery."

She shook her head numbly. "I think you're mad," she said. "It cannot be true."

He shrugged. "It matters little whether or not you believe me. But you might consider your position if aught befalls the man, whoever he may be."

"If he is alive," she said slowly, "the Lamonds will keep him so." She added, "Do you know his identity?"

"Your faith in their ability is commendable," Argyll said, "but hardly wise. If any ill fortune removes him from his position as heir, I foresee your Lamond kinsmen might well hold you to blame." His cold voice went on and on. Aye, the man was mad, and the merest hint of the evil scheming behind that bland face was enough to turn her blood cold in her veins. "Don't fail to sail on the *Queen Bess*," he repeated. "I want you out of Scotland and married to Lunsdon. We need both his title and his gold, and mayhap you will come to be grateful for his protection." Then he said curtly, "I am not so much a fool that I would tell you his identity, my dear Elspeth, even had I discovered it. I want no interference from you in the matter."

The door slammed behind him and his sharp voice rang out in the courtyard below. Elspeth stood where he left her, her brows drawn together thoughtfully. The numbness had disappeared, and in its place was a determination as cold and implacable as Argyll's own. She did not trust him; his tongue ever lied more easily than it spoke the truth, and she could not believe he would have mentioned so fantastic a matter unless he knew all to be known about it. And if he knew more than he had told her, there was one other who had spoken to him in greatest secrecy and might well be the source of his information.

She found Kate MacLachlan in the library, seated on a settle beside the fire. She wore a dark brown velvet gown with a wide white linen collar which lay flat against the bodice, an amazing style recently initiated in London to combat the old discomfort of stiff ruffs. Her red hair was pulled back tightly under a white cap and veil; she looked most demure and solemn.

"Kate," Elspeth greeted her pleasantly. "How neat you look this morning." She moved slowly across the room, letting her yellow satin skirts rustle against the carpet. She fingered the gold bracelets at her wrist, and they gave her vast comfort and courage. "I would I had your knack of appearing so neat and retiring."

"D'you mean it as a compliment, sweet?"

Elspeth returned the smile innocently. "Dear Kate, I'm certain a man looks for such qualities in a woman."

She walked to the fire and lifted her skirts to rest her foot on the fender. "My lord Argyll has arranged for me to sail for London at once, Kate," she said. "Isn't it a shame that I must leave so soon?"

Kate widened her eyes. "Aye, a shame. We'll miss you dreadfully."

"I must begin my wedding preparations."

"Then you will also miss Alex again. Faith, that's a lamentable thing. He'll regret not telling you farewell."

Elspeth heard the gates of Inveraray clanging shut after the departing Campbells. The noise of horses grew fainter as they rode along the trail leading south. She looked at Kate steadily.

"A most lamentable situation, Kate," she said. "But I'm not certain I intend to sail for London."

Kate's hands moved slowly over her skirts, then she clasped them together. Her voice was slightly husky when she spoke. "I fail to understand your meaning. D'you mean to disobey the Earl?"

Elspeth shrugged. "He is a quick-tempered man and likely to make hurried decisions which mean little. I gather he has heard a bit of unfortunate gossip, and you know, Kate, how a man reacts to whispers and rumors." She looked at Kate and smiled. "Men are like small lads, jumping to hasty conclusions."

Kate's eyes were not so wide. "I cannot believe you would ignore his orders. He is a cruel man to cross."

"Your concern for me touches me, Kate."

"Then you will not leave Inveraray?" Kate asked slowly. "What of your wedding plans?"

"There are many men in the world, Kate. Oh, not so charming or so wealthy as Walter Kildare, but with other qualities which I might find endearing after a time. But, of course, not sailing at once will scarce cancel my wedding plans. There will be no ceremony in any event until Argyll is back in London."

"I fear you are making a mistake, Elspeth. Perhaps the Earl will change his mind."

"Which Earl?" Elspeth asked quietly.

Kate looked almost angry. "Lunsdon," she said shortly. "A man is never secured till the vows have been spoken."

Elspeth said pleasantly, "You are right, Kate."

Kate was silent for a long time, then she raised her dark eyes. "I think you are unwise, sweet, but perhaps that is a failing common to women. I, too, have been unwise. That is why I would have you do nothing rash. I know how it is to pay the penalty for a heedless moment."

"Unwise, Kate? I would never associate such a word with you."

"I have confided in no one," Kate said sadly, "but perhaps you are a friend who will understand."

Elspeth could not help admiring the woman's ability to turn from one false emotion to another; she fully expected to see tears streaming down that pale face in another moment.

"Aye, I am the most understanding of friends, Kate," she said, and despised herself for being also a hypocrite.

"I am with child," Kate said slowly, "and now I must bear the shame and scandal of a single misdeed."

Elspeth's heart began again to beat slowly and unsteadily. She had not expected it, she had been too unwary. Kate's dress had four pleats across the skirt and Elspeth counted them for a second time to be sure. She looked at them until she could depend on her voice and her face.

"I can scarce believe it," she said at last. "Who is the man, and why have you not been wed before now?"

"I dislike to tell you, Elspeth," Kate said softly. " 'Tis Alex, and we've not been wed because he does not know of it yet."

"Alexander," Elspeth echoed, for something was expected of her. She struggled to find words which would not betray too much. "When did you discover it, Kate? Have you sent him word?"

Kate smoothed her hair under her white veil. "I became certain only recently. I doubt I'll send him word now, for a man in battle should not have his thoughts and anxieties elsewhere."

"Don't you think he will wed you," Elspeth asked carefully, "when you tell him? Surely no man would leave a woman to bear a fatherless bairn."

"Aye, he will marry me," Kate said, her voice sweetly firm. "He is far too chivalrous to put me aside. You are kind, Elspeth, to accept my confidence, but pray keep it to yourself. 'Tis not a thing one cares to have bleated to the countryside."

"No, I imagine it is not," Elspeth remarked calmly. She regarded Kate deliberately, letting her eyes move from the red hair and white face to the amazingly tiny waist beneath the brown velvet gown. Kate flushed and folded her arms across her waist.

"You lie, Kate MacLachlan," Elspeth said bluntly. "You do not carry his bairn."

Kate's eyes narrowed. "Look all you please. 'Tis not a thing you can prove by sight."

"Nor is it the way to snare the MacHugh," Elspeth said contemptuously. "What would you do when he discovered it to be a lie? Or d'you dream you might conceive on your wedding night and smooth the matter over later? 'Tis an underhanded way to catch yourself a husband, Kate, and I doubt Alex would be amused by it."

"You cannot know how things stand between us,"

Kate said smoothly. "We have an understanding which
has lasted a lengthy time; he is a man to be attracted
by a pretty face, but he has always come back to me
when he tired of another."

"You are not exceedingly canny," Elspeth observed
flatly. "If he has bedded you so often, he should have
reason to suspect that others have also been as fortunate."

Kate's white face turned even paler with anger.
"Take heed, mistress," she said, low. "I dislike such
insults."

"Such a virtuous rage, Kate," Elspeth said calmly.
"Did you not reason the matter out? You were always
available to warm his bed, but God's bones, a man
can scarce marry all the indiscreet women who would
blame him when they find themselves with child!"

Kate's eyes blazed like the fire behind her. "You'd
best sail for London and make the most of your marriage to Lunsdon," she said. "Indeed, I believe you've
no other choice, whatever you think of my affairs.
You'll not be able to interfere."

"I pity you, Kate," Elspeth said, "for I know how
it goes with a woman when she loves a man. But if
you were the lass for him, he'd have wed you long
ago. And since he did not, I feel no pangs of remorse
because he has chosen me."

Kate would not admit defeat. "He has no choice. He
cannot prove whether or not I lie, and he would never
forsake me without being certain!"

Elspeth did not like to do it, for she considered it an
unfair advantage, but she wanted it clear between
them. She put her hand to her neck and lifted the
heavy gold ring from the folds of her bodice, holding
it out so that Kate could see it plainly.

" 'Tis unfitting to quarrel over a man, Kate," she
said. "I think you lie, but if Alex is to be a father, he
will know it. He is not so much a fool that he'd not
remember when it might have happened. And if you
tell the truth, it will prove itself in time." The ring
caught the light on its jeweled crest. "But you are

wrong when you say he has no choice. And I think we will leave the matter to him."

Kate stared at the ring and her face seemed about to crumple. "I cannot believe—he did not give you his ring," she whispered incredulously.

"Aye, he gave me his ring," Elspeth said, "but if he were to change his mind, I'd not attempt to hold him to me by lies." She added, suddenly finding herself without bitterness, but only with pity and a great distaste, "Nor would I put another's life in jeopardy, and barter my soul to one like Argyll, for love of a man."

Kate did not move. Her eyes were startlingly dark and wide; and the tiny spark of fear in their depths could not be disguised.

"Did you think to aid your cause by selling your secrets to Argyll?" Elspeth asked softly. "Did he pay you well, or did you receive nothing more than his promise to send me away from Scotland? God's love, Kate, you hold your worth cheaply!"

The silence in the library was complete. Kate MacLachlan did not speak or move. She seemed held in a spell, frozen with some dark emotion within herself, so powerful and violent that she could not turn away from it.

"Alex will find you out, Kate," Elspeth said quietly, "and when he does, I'd not care to be in your place."

They looked at each other for an endless moment. It was true, then; Kate had been the informer. Elspeth turned away at last, not wanting to gaze longer on the black hatred caught in the frozen witch's eyes of Kate MacLachlan, standing in defeat.

But as she walked slowly up the turret stairs, Elspeth knew a miserable jealousy which brought quick tears to her eyes now that Kate could not see her. She counted on her fingers, hating herself as she did it, and thought of Kate's flat stomach and small waist.

She did not trust Kate, the woman had no soul. But one could never prove or disprove a thing merely by looking at a tiny waist and counting the months backward.

Ꮗ16Ꮙ

THE MacHugh dismounted in the hot sun. He slipped off his helmet and wiped his damp forehead with the back of his gloved hand. He tossed the reins of his horse to a MacDonald standing close by and strode into the cool dimness of the stone hut.

"Jesus!" he said shortly. He shrugged out of his leather jack, leaving it on the dirt floor where it fell. "I'm prepared to steal me a MacDonald kilt."

Donald MacPhee stood up and stretched. He grimaced and lowered his arms again; one was tightly bound with a bandage and supported by a scarf tied around his neck. He had removed his steel mesh doublet and wore only a shirt and breeks, but his high leather boots were still dusty from the road.

"Warm? The discomforts of war, to be borne with patience." He grinned at Alexander and indicated the rough table beside him, where the maps and dispatches had been pushed aside to make room for wooden trenchers and tankards. "It took you a lengthy time to subdue your share of the Campbells. I've been waiting to eat."

"You call this a war?" Alexander asked. He looked at the dried meat and coarse black bread on the trenchers. "You call this a meal?" He returned MacPhee's grin, then threw his helmet on top of his jacket and ran his hand over his short dark hair. "God's body, how did you return so soon?"

MacPhee sat on the lower bench beside the table and stretched his legs before him. "Competence, MacHugh," he said, "accomplishes miracles."

Alexander laughed and sat down at the table. He unfastened the flask from his belt and poured a goodly portion of wine into a tankard. "How does it go, lad?" He looked at MacPhee's arm.

"A bit of stiffness yet," MacPhee replied with disgust, and flexed the fingers of his right hand.

"Give it rest," the MacHugh said easily, helping himself to bread and meat. "You want no permanent stiffness in your sword arm."

"I'll take a turn with Gavin tonight," MacPhee said, "and loosen it up."

"Did you meet no resistance? You look well pleased with yourself."

"Only one injury, a MacDonald who got in the way of a nervous horse." MacPhee told Alexander briefly of the day's events. He had taken the small Campbell settlement to the north with little difficulty. His company of MacDonalds had surrounded it, attacking from four sides. The Campbells had laid down their weapons after one look at the rough MacDonalds as they charged down the hill.

"I've no doubt of it," Alexander said, grinning. It took a stout heart to withstand the sudden terror of a MacDonald raid. It was a fearsome sight when one did not expect it; indeed, even if one knew the exact moment the MacDonalds would come charging over the hills, the knowledge would scarce take the edge of fright away. The MacHugh had selected a group of his most spirited and venturous MacDonalds, training them to lead the attack on their swift Highland ponies, a crude cavalry tactic which had been remarkably effective. They galloped into the charge with their spears held before them like a row of steel spikes, followed by the foot troops who discharged their pistols and then brandished their blunt axes above their heads as they ran, screaming their battle cries until they sounded like a thundering horde of wild men swooping down from the skies.

"You've taught them well," MacPhee remarked.

The MacHugh shrugged. "They were born with it. 'Tis only a matter of showing them the proper way to spend their energy. They're apt pupils when it comes to new tricks of raiding."

"Do you know any more tricks, sir? God's bones, we'll have all of Scotland for the MacDonalds."

"Why stop at Scotland, man? Shall we take our MacDonalds down to London and frighten the trousers off Jamie Stuart?" The MacHugh washed down the salty meat with wine. "When I've gone, you'll be the one to think up tricks, and I'll warn you not to tarnish my reputation."

The young MacPhee was silent for a time. Then he said thoughtfully, "Discipline is excellent. I've had no trouble with looting or burning. You might tell me how you do it; I fear once you leave I'll not have so easy a time with them."

The MacHugh spoke curtly. "I'll not have them scorching the earth behind them; Jamie MacDonald wants more than burned towns and ruined crops when he takes over. You'll find no trick in it, MacPhee. Make them obey your orders."

MacPhee suspected there was more to it than that, but he said nothing. They had swept up from southern Kintyre, taking all before them with few battles and fewer injuries; it was an accomplishment which had proved both the MacHugh and his leadership, and the MacDonalds were not inclined to quibble over his orders.

"And how did it go with you?" MacPhee asked casually. The MacHugh's eyes were tired, the lines of his face etched with dust.

"No better than I expected," the MacHugh said briefly. "Nor worse, thank God."

"Did you leave Gavin to finish up?"

The MacHugh nodded. He looked around the rude shieling, thinking that they might have had the foresight to sequester one with some form of bed. The hut was at least clean and without vermin, but the bare dirt floors held nothing more than two crude wooden benches and a table.

"Were they troublesome?"

The MacHugh brought his gaze back to MacPhee. "They've been under seige for more than a week. 'Tis a lengthy time when no preparations have been made for it." He was pleased; the last Campbell stronghold on MacDonald land had fallen, and now that Mac-Phee had taken his objective there was nothing else to be done beyond securing the peninsula with a wide circle of sentries.

He stood up and removed his doublet, stretching his muscles gingerly; his head almost touched the roof of the hut. He walked to the doorway, leaning his shoulders against it, and looked out across the small glen. A few MacDonalds were lighting fires for their evening meal, and the small pin points of light spread across the gentle rise of land like fireflies in the fading dusk of the day.

"Jamie MacDonald must have been saying his prayers nightly," he remarked. "I'd give much to know the reason for Argyll's delay."

MacPhee spoke behind him. "Mayhaps he's had difficulty arming his hired soldiers."

"The man I sent north reports the Earl still at Duntroon," MacHugh said. "He has a fair number of men, MacPhee. Enough to retake Kintyre, I'll wager."

"Retake Kintyre?" MacPhee said, frowning. "Do you mean it?"

"MacDonald is spreading his army too thin. He'd have been wiser to remain on Islay; not all the Campbells in Scotland could have driven him out." The MacHugh had carried out his orders with a minimum of men and supplies; he had taken Kintyre by strategy, not by bloody battle, and he had gained invaluable time for James MacDonald. But he did not like the look of it. He did not like the rumored number of Argyll's men, nor the unenviable chore of guarding the entire peninsula against his attack.

He shrugged and grabbed his jacket from the floor. "I stink of too much war, man," he said. "Will ye join me?"

He did not wait for an answer. He strode through the clansmen gathered about their fires and made for a small rise in the land. From the slope he could see the rough waters of the ocean foaming against the shore. The sea wind was growing chilled from the tossed spray and the approaching evening, but the Mac-Hugh tossed his clothes and boots on the sand and ran for the water, hitting the first wave with a clean dive. When he came up, shaking the water from his eyes, he saw that MacPhee was close behind him. They were both excellent swimmers and spent the better part of an hour in the water, until the first evening star and the cool night breeze reminded them that the MacHugh wanted an early start on the morrow for his ride south to Dunaverty Castle.

A gutted candle shed its flickering light in the hut when they returned, and Gavin was putting away a good meal of dried meat and wine.

" 'Tis all secured, Alex," he reported. "They made no more struggle, and I gave them permission to go to the fields, as you said. They'll have food enough."

"Good," the MacHugh said briefly. He cared little for the thought of women and bairns being without proper food and water. "You'd best get some sleep, lad, we leave early." He took a heavy plaid from his saddlebag and left them, going outside to roll up in his warm plaid beneath the stars. He disliked the confining stone walls and thatched roof of the hut; he preferred the night dew below him and the dark Scots night, sprinkled with stars, above him as a roof.

The MacDonald clansmen, preparing for the night, greeted him as he strode through the encampment; it did not take light from the fires for them to recognize his tall powerful figure. It pleased them that he would forego his shelter to join them in the open, for it was a thing they had known few commanders to do.

The dozen MacHugh clansmen who had ridden to Kintyre with the MacHugh as his personal guard waited until their Chief was breathing steadily, then crept closer to station themselves in a circle about him. They wrapped their plaids about their shoulders and settled their swords at their sides with great care to be silent, for it took only a slight noise to bring the MacHugh to his feet, sword in hand. They sat there in the darkness, hunched under their plaids, and prepared to wait for the dawn.

The MacHugh pillowed his head on his arms, drowsing, and grinned to himself in the darkness. He could see the dark figures of his men, stationed at a proper distance from him, and it touched him oddly. He also felt a certain amusement, for a Highlander, even a Chief, who could not fend for himself without a guard was in poor straits. The MacHugh had spent many nights in the open, alone, with nothing to guard him but his ears and his wits, and it pleased him to do so. But he was content to let the men play out their little game.

A high wind was blowing off the sea, cold and damp after the hot day, and his plaid was warm and comfortable about him. His sword was at his side, where his hand could close on the hilt at a second's notice, and his dirk lay within the blanket under his arm. He had his weapons, his friends, and a good night's sleep ahead, and he was content.

He was asleep before he finished the thought.

2

The MacHugh and Gavin rode into Dunaverty Castle well before noon and found it bustling with an air of urgency and importance. The highest Chiefs of the MacDonald clans were under its roof, an honor calling forth the utmost in ceremony and deferential reverence. The clansmen mingled in the courtyard and outside the walls, their bright tartans proclaiming them men of Glencoe, Glengarry, Keppoch, or ClanRanald. Since no branch of the MacDonalds admitted the superiority of any other and refused to recognize any chieftain as supreme Chief, there was continual bickering among the clansmen. But the MacHugh knew well that the good-natured grumbling and quarreling disappeared the instant the MacDonalds faced a common enemy. Theirs was an argument of long and ancient standing which would undoubtedly go unsettled for many more years; and the entertainment derived from it extended to the highest ranks, where MacDonald chieftains were equally inclined to lift a tankard of ale or draw their swords over the question.

Alexander dismounted and climbed the stairs, with Gavin behind him, and was stopped at every step by enthusiastic clansmen who recognized his crest. He greeted them absently, thinking that the great number of troops at Dunaverty must mean that James had drawn a good portion of his army across the Sound of Jura to Kintyre. He was prepared for Argyll, then, and the MacHugh felt some of the grim weight lift from his mind.

He had reached the door of the hall before he remembered that it might be more courteous to bathe and shave before reporting to Jamie MacDonald and his chieftains. He considered the matter a moment, then shrugged his shoulders.

"God's love," he said, meeting Gavin's amused eyes. " 'Tis no time for priggishness. They'll take us as we are, else we'll damned well invite them into the field for a few weeks."

"Aye," Gavin agreed. "I overlooked the importance of bringing my satin trousers along. They'll think us reivers of the lowest sort."

"The better to deal with Campbells," the MacHugh returned promptly, and strode ahead into the hall.

The men seated and standing around the huge fire turned in surprise. James MacDonald was seated at the table in a high chair which seemed to tower over his head. When he saw the MacHugh he jumped to his feet and met him halfway across the room.

"Alexander," he said, slapping him on the shoulder. "I talked to the man you sent ahead only an hour ago. I had no idea you'd follow him so soon." He walked with the MacHugh to the table, plying him with questions. "How did you leave the Campbells in the north? Any word of Argyll? How have you fared with my MacDonalds?"

The MacHugh greeted the other MacDonald chieftains, noting that the atmosphere in the hall was heavy. He had interrupted a heated quarrel, and several of the men greeted him absently as if their minds were still elsewhere.

"Have you eaten, Alexander?" MacDonald turned to the young Keppoch, who was scowling darkly, and the MacHugh did not miss the curtness of the order, "Find food for the MacHugh, Keppoch."

Keppoch shrugged and left the room. The MacHugh sat down at the lengthy table and accepted the wine handed him by James MacDonald.

"I'll speak of my appreciation later, Alex. Now it will suffice to say the sight of you has never pleased me more. The news has been excellent; we owe more to you than we will ever be able to repay."

MacDonald of Glengarry spoke, his voice as haughty as ever. "You've done well, MacHugh," he said reluctantly. "It leaves us in a humble position."

The thought of the imperious Glengarry feeling humbleness was more than amusing. "Keep your compliments, Glengarry," the MacHugh said, grinning. "I've no need of them, and I know it must pain you to part with them."

Glengarry laughed. "I'm grateful then, if you would have me honest," he said, "and I need not be humble to tell you so."

Keppoch returned with a clansman who carried a large tray heaped with hot food. The MacHugh and

Gavin fell to with energy; they had ridden light in order to assure swiftness, and the MacHugh had allowed little time for killing game. One's appetite soon palled under a steady diet of dried meat and oat bread. .

"Tell me, Alex," MacDonald said finally, "what news do you have of Argyll? I've sent scouts beyond you, but they've not returned. Is he still on Loch Crinan?"

"From the reports of my men, he's still mustering his army there," the MacHugh said. "He'll move soon; 'tis growing too close to autumn."

"Aye, he'll move soon," MacDonald agreed, "and we must be prepared for him. I've sent Malcolm MacPhee of Colonsay to Dunyveg. He's to remain at Islay till he receives word that we need his forces. I'd not trust Argyll to overlook the idea of attacking Islay or Jura first."

The MacHugh raised his brows. "Where do you expect him to strike?"

Glengarry spoke again. "From the sea," he said explosively, "whether it be Islay or Kintyre. I've word he's outfitting galleys."

James MacDonald scowled at Glengarry. " 'Tis reasonable to think he would prefer to march into Kintyre," he said flatly, "before he'd sail his entire army down the coast. Mayhap he intends to use the galleys to attack the Islands."

ClanRanald raised his head, his dark eyes brooding. "Aye, and he might intend to attack both the Islands and Kintyre."

The MacHugh's tongue found his cheek. He looked around him at the angry MacDonalds, quarreling among themselves. "And he might intend to attack you from both sides of the sea," he said, tossing a bone into the scramble, "cutting between you. A neat strategy to trap your forces."

There was silence, then a loud murmur as all the MacDonalds decided to speak at once. James MacDonald silenced them with his harsh voice.

"Peace! Let me hear the man." He looked at the

MacHugh. "Glengarry thinks we stand at a great disadvantage in that event, having the entire peninsula to protect. It would be impossible to scatter our forces along the coast, and well nigh disastrous to split our army more than we've already been obliged to do."

The MacHugh shrugged. "If you have sufficient warning, it will take you no longer to draw your men into a line of battle than it will take Argyll to disembark an entire army and attack." He added bluntly, "He has a goodly number of men, James. Make certain you have the warning in time."

"I agree, Alex, that we must keep a close watch on the sea. Still, I believe that Argyll will attack by land. I have information from Colkitto in Jura, learned from men he sent to the mainland, and we can scarce disregard it. If we must watch the sea, we must also keep a close watch by land, and we cannot forego one for the other."

The MacHugh's face was unreadable. "Aye, Jamie," he said, "you'll do well to watch sharply in all directions." He did not trust the man Colkitto, but he would not venture that opinion in this company of hottempered MacDonalds.

"How have you fared since you last sent word?" James MacDonald asked.

"Less than a half dozen casualities," the MacHugh said briefly.

There was a low murmur around the room. Keppoch's dark face lightened with admiration. "By Jesus, Alex, the MacDonalds have never taken so much with so little bloodshed!"

Glengarry seemed dumfounded. "No more than a half dozen?" he repeated. "D'ye speak the truth, man?"

"Count them yourself, Glengarry," the MacHugh said curtly.

Glengarry reddened. "I meant no question of your words," he said bluntly. He lapsed into silence, pondering the news that all the north of Kintyre had been taken so easily. Then he stood and walked around the table. He held out his hand, speaking with a respect which softened his harsh voice. "We've argued before, MacHugh, and we'll argue again. But I'll not forget your services to the MacDonalds." He shrugged his broad shoulders. "You may depend on me if you ever need aid yourself."

The MacHugh smiled. "I can think of no man I'd rather have on my side of a fight, Glengarry. My thanks." He added gravely, "I've developed a fondness for your Glengarry men, if not for yourself."

Glengarry laughed. "At least we speak our minds, and I'd prefer it." His scowl around him gave evidence of his dissatisfaction with the MacDonald council of war.

All the MacDonalds laughed but Keppoch, whose thin face was still perturbed. "Dissension in the ranks," he said to the MacHugh. "D'you believe quarreling dogs ever win the joint of meat?"

The MacHugh thought that such a question could only be answered by the haughty MacDonalds themselves, but he said, with a trace of amusement, "Aye, Keppoch, if there are enough dogs and a big enough joint of meat." He turned to James MacDonald. "I'll speak to you later, Jamie, and hear your plans for me. At the moment, a hot bath seems vastly more important than your campaign."

He turned and walked from the hall. Gavin walked beside him down the stairs to the courtyard; both men were silent. The early-afternoon sun had broken through the clouds, striking the gray parapets of Dunaverty Castle and touching the turrets with gold. The spears and pikes of MacDonald men-at-arms in the courtyard glittered brightly and the tartans made a brave show of color in the sun. Above the castle the MacDonald banners unfurled in the wind, as proud and valiant as the men who would bear them forward in the press of battle.

"It will be a good fight," the MacHugh said slowly,

"but at this moment I'd not wager a mark on the outcome."

Gavin was grave. "You gave them little advice, Alex. They stand in need of one cool head."

"Jamie will keep them in line," the MacHugh said. "I'm not here to tell the MacDonalds how to fight their battles, Gavin. If the case were reversed, I doubt I'd appreciate interference."

"If that were the way of it," Gavin said flatly, "you'd need no advice."

The MacHugh laughed. "Don't be too certain of that, lad." He walked down the steps, his good humor restored by the thought of the battle ahead, whatever the outcome. "If we fail," he said quietly, "we will still have fought nobly for Jamie's cause. It looks to be a fight to warm my heart."

"Aye," Gavin said, and grinned, "if they give you half a chance you might carry the day alone. But leave a Campbell or two for my clumsy sword."

They kept up the banter, as they had always done, but their thoughts were grave and speculative; the prospect of seeing the proud MacDonalds humbled before Argyll and their cause defeated was not so incredible that they could push it from their minds with a lighthearted jest.

{ 17 }

THE *Queen Bess* sailed from Leith harbor on a bright August morning. Shortly before noon a group of riders entered Edinburgh by the Water Port and rode up the Canongate. At the Netherbow Port they turned into St. Mary's wynd, following it until they reached the Cowgate. They cantered easily down the Cowgate, for few citizens were abroad in the streets; the sun was hot at noon and the townspeople dedicated the midday hours to relaxation indoors.

The horsemen turned into the courtyard of the shuttered MacHugh house. The gates swung closed behind them, and after one glimpse of the bright-red Mac-Hugh tartan, the curious neighbors went about their affairs with no further interest. A maid, sweeping the steps of an adjoining house, stared at the riders until the gates hid them from her view. She recognized Simon MacHugh, but she had never seen the slender lad who rode beside him. It was not Sir Alexander, for a truth; she wielded her broom dreamily, wondering if one day she might be fortunate enough to see the famous Chief of MacHughs, if only from a distance.

Inside the small courtyard, Simon MacHugh dismounted and held his hand for his companion. The lad slipped easily from his saddle, ignoring the proffered hand, and looked about him with considerable interest. He was shorter than Simon; the plumed hat which shadowed his face reached only to Simon's shoulders.

He smiled at the men around him, waiting for them to dismount. Then he put his thumbs in his wide belt and swaggered across the yard toward the doors of the house, looking up at the tall windows above him with unconcealed delight, like a country lad seeing the wonders of Edinburgh Town for the first time.

Simon laughed behind him and followed him up the steps. "You'll not find it extremely elegant," he announced solemnly. "But Alex spends little time here, and when he's in the city he prefers to spend his gold on women and wine."

The lad shrugged, waiting for Simon to unlock the doors. "Give me a hearty draught of ale, man," he said carelessly, "and a wench to warm my bed, and I care little for elegance." He put his hand on Simon's arm and added, with exaggerated gravity, "But make certain the wench is clean and doesn't tend to giggle when she's had a few rounds of ale."

Simon shouted with laughter, and the men behind him looked at the slim lad with affection and walked their horses toward the stable as if they were loath to leave his company.

The house was musty and dark, but cool after the heat of the ride. Simon rummaged through a massive sideboard in the hall until he found a candle. "We'll find wine in the library," he said, and led the way. The furniture was covered with linen, for the house had not been occupied for several months. The shuttered windows were boarded across from within, but dirt had blown through the cracks to pile thickly on the sills.

Simon stuck the candle in a brass holder on the library table and held it above his head to light the candles above the fireplace. The room was not so dusty as the rest of the house, since Simon and his men had been there earlier in the day.

"I lifted this from Alex's best stock at Fraoch Eilean." Simon examined a goblet and shook his head ruefully. "God's foot, it'll have to be superior vintage to kill the taste of the dirt."

"I'll not quibble over a bit of dirt. Hand it over. I'm fair parched."

Simon poured the wine from an oblong silver flask. "I brought it solely because I believed you'd be fainting in my arms by now."

Elspeth stretched her legs before her and surveyed the dusty toes of her boots. They were too large, and she could feel a small blister on her heel. She pulled off the wide-brimmed hat and ran her fingers through her hair with a sigh of relief.

"Liar. You knew I'd love it." She laughed at him and took the wine. The dust rose in clouds about her as she settled back in the chair, and she smiled happily. Dust, dirt, blisters, heat—nothing could mar her pleasure. She was free, she had not sailed on the *Queen Bess* for London; she was sipping wine in the Mac-Hugh's Edinburgh house with Simon, and the day seemed wondrously fair and bright.

Simon was thoughtful. "Something is lacking," he remarked, gazing at the specks of dust floating on the wine in his glass. "We're missing some small trifle, which escapes my mind at the moment."

"Aye, a very small trifle. We have no host."

Simon looked up and smiled. "He'll curse when he finds he's missed the fun."

"It's only just begun," she said. She lounged easily in the chair, resting her wine glass on the wide belt at her waist, and considered the Earl's wrath. But the future would take care of itself; she felt no regret for what she had done.

Simon looked at her, slim and impudent in her man's doublet and shirt, and wished that Alex were standing there in his place.

"He's well out of it," Elspeth said. "At least Argyll can't hold him responsible for this."

"Argyll needs nothing more to hold against the Mac-Hughs. I can detect Alex's subtle touch in every piece of news from the south."

"But I've acted on my own, and I'll not have him blamed for it. I'm glad he's not with us."

Her voice was not entirely convincing and Simon

did not answer. The MacHugh himself could not have dreamed up a more amusing way to defy the Earl. She had slipped away from the Leith docks after her Campbell escort turned back to Edinburgh; when the *Queen Bess* sailed for London, Elspeth was riding boldly into Edinburgh, only a few minutes behind Argyll's men. When they felt sure the roads would be clear of Campbells they would leave for Rathmor; once there they would decide on Elspeth's next move.

Alex would have been vastly entertained by the idea. And somehow Simon felt that Alex should have been with his lass today, riding up from Leith in the bright sunshine of an August morning. He should have been there to laugh as she swaggered about in her breeks and boots, imitating a brash young lad. He should have shared the outrageous mischief in her face because she had outwitted the Earl on the first move. God's love, the lass must have been born under Alex's own star.

"Simon." Elspeth's voice was suddenly small and quiet. "You mentioned the news from Kintyre. Has it been good?"

Simon hesitated. "So far." He studied his wine. "Argyll must have arrived on the scene by now. I've had no word during the past few weeks."

She could not ask him, but the question was in her eyes.

"We see an occasional rider going north," he went on calmly, "otherwise we hear nothing. I've had no direct message from Alex." He smiled at her. "He seldom bothers with such matters."

Elspeth stared at the small slivers of light escaping through the closed shutters. The room, lighted by candles, looked dim and unreal when the courtyard beyond the window was flooded with sunlight. It was like the pale, quiet world beneath the sea, cool and melancholy as the sands washed by long fathoms of green water.

"The MacDonalds haven't a chance," she said

abruptly. "Argyll has half the Campbells in Scotland with him, as well as the hired soldiers recruited by the King."

"I know." Simon walked to the shuttered window, then back to the table. He leaned against it, running his hand over his dark hair. "It was Alex's decision, Elspeth. He'll take the risks as they come to him; I doubt he'll be unprepared."

Elspeth had thought to keep her secret until she reached her father at Rathmor, but now she was not so certain it was the right thing to do. She did not understand Simon MacHugh, who had returned to Scotland from a favorable position at court to persuade Alexander to keep the name of MacHugh unsmirched, and when his advice was not heeded, remained behind while his brothers rode out to war. She was not certain she approved of him, or trusted him. But there was so little time left; the secret was no secret if Argyll knew of it, and mayhap Simon would know the proper course of action.

"Simon, I think we'd best ride to Rathmor at once," she began quietly. "Argyll knows my brother is alive."

She could not have anticipated the effect her words would have on him. He lifted his head and stared at her, his handsome face gone pale and taut. For a long moment he stood so, his hand still lifting the goblet of wine he had intended to put to his mouth.

"In the name of God, how did you find out about him?" he asked at last, his poise shaken for the first time since she had known him.

"Argyll told me," she said impatiently.

"And how did that devil discover it?"

She shrugged, for the excitement touching her was too private a thing to share. It was true then; the bairn had not died, he did not lie in a lonely grave in the hills beyond Rathmor. He was a grown man, of twenty years as herself; somewhere under the same skies her brother walked alive and tall, and mayhap one day she would meet him face to face. She did not like to carry tales, but her hatred for the women who had betrayed her brother was too violent to be concerned with principle.

"Kate MacLachlan," she said bluntly, "but I've no idea how she knew."

He gave her a sharp glance. "She didn't get it from Alex," he said. "He's far too canny for her."

Her eyes rested on him, long enough to bring a deep flush to his face.

"I can see you've no high opinion of me," he said, "but before God I didn't give it away. Not even Jeannie knows."

"Then Gavin," she said reluctantly, remembering how he had looked at Kate that day in the courtyard at Inveraray. "Someone told the woman."

Simon looked amazed. "Doesn't Argyll know his identity?"

She shook her head. "He would not tell me, but I suspect he knows."

Simon drained his glass. "He knows, right enough," he said flatly. " 'Tis Gavin, and I'd wager my life Kate suspected the moment she saw you two together. You're very alike, you know."

Elspeth put her hand across her eyes. She had not dreamed it would be Gavin; she had thought of some lad hidden away in a friendly clan, frightened for his life, a stranger to her and his clan. But it was Gavin with the cold blue eyes so like her father's and the dry wit she had become so fond of matching; and he had ridden south with Alexander, straight into Argyll's hands.

Simon slammed the door behind him and Elspeth heard his voice in the hall as he spoke to his men. She took a deep breath. After a moment she ran down the hall and through the door to follow him.

Simon's men were already in their saddles. Simon was putting on his helmet, his face set with anger. He turned when he saw her and came to the steps.

"I can't leave you here, Elspeth. You'll have to ride

to the Grassmarket with us. We can find a decent inn for you thereabouts." He shut and locked the doors behind her. "You'll be safe there, till I can send for you."

"I'll not sit behind in an inn," Elspeth announced calmly. "I'm riding with you to Rathmor."

"Don't be a fool, lass."

Elspeth gave him a level stare. " 'Tis more my affair than yours, Simon MacHugh." She saw her horse, held by a smiling MacHugh. She pushed by Simon and spoke to the clansman. "I've no sword," she said sweetly, eyeing the brace of pistols he wore. "It would appear more normal if you'd give me the loan of a weapon."

He gaped at her. She held out her hand impatiently. "Hurry, man, I've no time to quibble!" She added persuasively, "Not even a lad rides with no weapon at all. 'Tis only for the appearance."

The man gulped and looked about him for assistance. There was none forthcoming; the other clansmen averted their eyes. He had no choice; he took one of the heavy pistols and handed it to her.

Elspeth thrust it into the leather belt at her waist and mounted quickly, wishing they would stop staring at her. She wheeled the horse and grinned at Simon, standing on the steps as if he had taken root there.

"Simon, must we ride without you? God's love, we could be there while you're still gathering your wits!"

Simon shrugged his shoulders and looked at his men; they had been pleased at the little scene there in the courtyard. He could see their verdict in their eyes. Let the lass ride with them. She was a Lamond, and she had already snubbed her nose at the Earl of Argyll once that day. And Simon knew that each man of them had seen the MacHugh's golden ring suspended on a chain around her neck. That was enough, more than enough. The lass could keep the pace.

Simon mounted quickly. The group rode through the gates into the Cowgate and turned toward the

Grassmarket. Beyond the West Port of the town they took the road west. Once they were well away from the town, Simon put his horse into a faster pace. Elspeth was riding abreast; she spurred her horse and threw him a quick smile.

The sun was warm on her head and the wind blew cool and sharp against her face. Above the road, beyond the trees, the sky was a clear blue, as deeply blue as a mountain tarn. Here and there lighter blue-gray trails of peat smoke rose lazily into the sky from cottages hidden among the trees and caught in the high wind to become faint streamers of cloud.

She sat her horse lightly, adjusting to the steady pace with the ease of a natural horsewoman, and wondered why women had ever allowed themselves to be forced into clumsy sidesaddles. She had never before felt so free, so alive, so intensely happy. She had no petticoats and skirts to restrain her, no conventional whalebone and buckram, no gentlemanly concern over her welfare. She felt like a young lad in reality, pounding full tilt through an August day, knowing no greater joy than merely being alive at such a moment.

It was a heady wine. The dust was soon caked on her boots and breeks and the sun became hot and wet on her face, but she took no notice. She had a good horse beneath her, companions she would not exchange for King James and all his court, and the day was bright and fair.

She resolutely pushed the thought of Argyll to the back of her mind. She could now guess at his motives for allowing her to travel to Scotland. Once she had unsuspectingly gained the confidence and affection of the Lamonds, he would find it easier to establish her as Robert Lamond's legal heir, and if his plans had been upset at the discovery of Gavin's identity, he had quickly formulated a scheme to take care of that small obstacle in the way of his success. It was a bitter thought and she had no proof that Argyll intended such a thing, but she admitted it sounded much like him. She also felt certain that the MacHughs had carried her to Rathmor so precipitously in order to protect Gavin; they must have felt a great necessity to know if Argyll had somehow learned of Gavin's existence and sent her to Scotland to discover what she could of the matter. It explained the hostility and suspicion she had felt at Rathmor, and the cool reception she had received from her father; it made quite clear Alexander's displeasure at her eternal questions. Now she could see the danger she had brought to their plans; knowing nothing of Argyll's schemes, she could yet have stumbled across the truth and unwittingly given the secret away.

But they would warn Robert Lamond, and beyond that she refused to think. Gavin was with the MacHugh, when all was said, and she could not believe harm would come to Gavin as long as Alexander was alive to fight beside him.

At sundown they paused to eat, but Simon ordered only a brief halt. Elspeth slipped from her saddle and stood beside him; she wiped her face with her gloves, but there was no way to remove the streaked dust. She stretched her arms gingerly under the sleeves of the doublet and leaned against her horse.

Simon gave her a quick glance. "Tired?"

"So soon?" She dismissed it with a slight smile and a shrug. "I'd never admit it. We've a good distance to ride yet." She eased her foot in the roomy boot, feeling the blister still painfully apparent on her heel. "Simon, I'll not stay at Rathmor. It'd be most unwise."

Simon was silent, for he had been pondering the same question. Robert Lamond's position was precarious enough without adding more fuel to the blaze.

"You've a garrison at Ardoon."

"Jean is at Fraoch Eilean, Elspeth. She'd be desolate if you refused to stay with her." Jean would be desolate, Simon thought wryly, and Alex would be furious if the lass got herself into more trouble.

"Fraoch Eilean is much too close to Inveraray. If

you think it more proper, Jean could join me at
Ardoon?" She had a sudden thought and her eyes
crinkled in a smile. "D'you deplore my free use of
your hospitality? I might ride to Lachlan to pay Kate
a lengthy visit."

"Alex might find some slight amusement in the
thought, but I'd not recommend it. Not if you value
that pretty throat."

When they had finished the light meal, Simon
mounted. "Tighten your belts if you feel a bit of
hunger," he announced to his men. "We'll not halt
again." Simon felt sorry for the lass; no doubt she was
weary to the bone. He looked at her and smiled. " 'Tis
remarkable what a long ride will do for the waistline."

Elspeth wheeled her horse, speaking over her shoulder. " 'Tis an insult to hint that my waistline needs
such an aid," she said, laughing. "We'd best be off."

The MacHughs exchanged looks. It would take the
night to reach Rathmor, a goodly stretch of riding for
even the hardiest clansman, accustomed to riding long
and hard on light rations. No matter how plucky the
lass, she would never last the ride without aid.

The clansmen decided the question among themselves. They had no need for words; the solution was
more than obvious. "Aye, she's game enough," a
sturdy MacHugh remarked to his companion, riding
close abreast. They nodded, smiling, and the man
reached into his saddlebag, pulling out several pieces
of dried meat and a small bone flask. The other clansmen saw and understood.

So, during the long ride through the cool Scots
night, Simon grew increasingly impatient at the frequent and numerous stops requested by his men. One
was nursing a cramp in his leg, another discovered that
his saddle girth had almost worn through, and yet another deemed it necessary to examine his horse after
he stumbled into an unexpeceted hole. During each
halt the dry meat and flasks were passed to Elspeth
in the dark; thinking that the men were kindly sharing

their rations, she ate and drank gratefully, and the strength seemed to flow back into her body with each halt.

The MacHughs knew it was a day and night to be remembered a long time; and a ride they would recount again and again around the hearth, until their listeners would tire of the familiar details. They had ridden with the Chief's lassie, and they would tell how she had stayed with the arduous pace as well as any man. For they had determined it so, or else were resolved that they would fall back with her.

And when Elspeth rode into Rathmor she sat her saddle as straight as when she rode out of Edinburgh, to Simon MacHugh's exasperated amusement and his men's fond pride.

It was a sad farewell they gave her. They grinned at the slim, dusty lass for the last time, knowing she would be dressed in satin when they saw her again, and swaggered off to the kitchens to appease their empty stomachs.

2

"You might have told me," Elspeth said reproachfully. "Are you still suspicious of me? Do you believe I'd have given it away to Argyll?" She added, depressed, "He found you out, in any case, and Gavin is in as much danger as if he'd not lived his life in disguise."

Robert Lamond did not seem concerned. "Simon will warn them in time," he said, "and although I'd suspect Argyll of anything, we've no proof he intends harm to Gavin."

Simon had ridden south that day, after a brief sleep, taking with him a few hand-picked MacHughs. But Elspeth was not comforted; a battle pended in Kintyre, and no one could blame the Earl of Argyll if a man riding with the rebellious MacDonalds met with an unfortunate accident.

"Why did Alex take Gavin with him?" she asked wearily. "Why couldn't he have stayed behind, like Simon? Surely he had as good a reason; he's your heir, your only son."

Lamond smiled. "If we'd chained him, mayhap, or broken his sword arm, we might have persuaded him to stay behind." He had not lost his brusqueness, but Elspeth found she had grown accustomed to it, and could detect the affection behind it. "But I'd not keep him safe behind walls, lass," he added. "He'll be a better man for a bit of danger now and then; I'd not have it otherwise."

"I fear he's learned a few tricks from Alexander," she retorted. "Danger is no more than a pleasant diversion to them. Faith," she added, exasperated, " 'tis only the ones waiting behind who suffer."

"The way of all women," Lamond said, shrugging.

She knew him too well by now to be angered. "Aye, we must ever weep at being left behind," she said lightly. She took the MacHugh's ring and held it tightly in her hand. "Would it please you if I prefer Alexander to the Earl of Lunsdon?" she asked, and tried not to wonder if he cared a fig who she married.

He met her eyes and smiled again. "Then you've come to a different opinion of him? When we last spoke of him, you seemed to think him exceedingly unpleasant."

"Well," she said ruefully, "he soon taught me to feel differently."

Lamond folded his arms on the table between them. "It would please me immensely," he said unexpectedly, to have both my daughters married to MacHughs."

"It will protect you from any claims," she said innocently, "that I am your second eldest and heir after Gavin. I imagine that MacHugh would keep a firm hand on my ambitions."

"So you know about that," Lamond said, looking vastly amused. "But you mustn't grieve over your reduced fortune, lass. Alex spoke for your hand some months past; he asked for no dowry, but I'll not have my daughter wed without a mark to her name. I've arranged for you to receive a certain amount of gold by the year, and the larger part of your portion will be a share of land equal to Jean's."

Elspeth could not speak for fear the quick tears behind her eyes might be betrayed in her voice.

"Now that our little plot has been discovered," Lamond went on calmly, "I'd like to clear up a few matters between us. I'd not like to have you thinking ill of your mother, and yet I could not speak plainly before for fear all her plans would have gone for naught." He spoke with little emotion, but his eyes looked back on another year and other lass, and the bleak set of his face was a pain at Elspeth's heart. "She left me because she feared for my life, and it was at her insistence that Gavin was fostered out to another clan. I could not dissuade her; she was a Campbell, I a Lamond, and the ill feeling between the clans began long before our time. There was no happiness in her heart that she might bring ruin to my clan."

"Why did she never tell me?" Elspeth whispered.

"Only the midwife knew," he said, "that Louise bore two bairns that night. She deemed it the only safeguard to keeping him safe for me." He hesitated, as if to find the proper words to explain so incredible a scheme to her. "It is the usual way in the Highlands to foster the eldest son to another clan. It keeps the bonds of friendship closer, and teaches our sons the value of living with others. But it is seldom kept secret, and I would not have agreed to the plan had I not been aware of the bitterness felt by Louise's family. The Campbells would not accept our marriage, even though handfast has long been considered a legal union, and they swore to avenge the insult I had given them by bringing her to Rathmor." He added very quietly, "They would have fought me and my clan in armed warfare to take the lad from me, if only to deprive me of a son and heir. That is why she left me, and why she left her son behind to be raised in the only measure of safety we could devise in the urgency of the moment."

"I can scarce believe the Campbells held you in such hatred," Elspeth said quietly. "Was there no way she might have remained at Rathmor?"

Lamond pushed back his chair and walked to the fireplace, leaning his arm against the stone lintel. "I would have fought to the death for her," he said, "but she would not have it so. I could not hold her against her will. She had courage enough for herself, but her fears for me outweighed all else." He added flatly, "As for the Campbells, their hatred feeds on greed, Elspeth, and they'll see the Lamonds hounded like the MacGregors before they've finished."

"Not while you live," she said, lifting her chin.

"And not while I've a daughter who can gentle the MacHugh and outwit Argyll at one and the same time," he replied.

"Alex is far from gentled," she said, laughing, "and to our grief, Argyll has more than one trick at hand."

But the gloom had been dispelled and they were closer than ever before; and whatever the future held for her, she knew it would be splendid to face it in such company as the MacHughs and Lamonds.

She rode to Ardoon over Lamond's protests, and Jean joined her there to remain until word came from Kintyre; and it was at Ardoon that she at last came to terms with herself.

Ardoon was the MacHugh's stronghold, the castle where he was born. In this place he had lived as a small lad, watching as his father's clansmen rode out to battle, listening to their boisterous tales around the fire. Elspeth thought of the woman who had mothered Simon and Alexander MacHugh and wondered if she had been lonely in the wild valley of wind and water and towering peaks. Faith, the woman had been loved by the Chief of MacHughs, she had birthed two fine sons. What more could any woman desire?

And Elspeth walked the battlements in the company of the woman who had come there before her so many years ago, feeling the presence of all the proud Mac-Hughs who had known those old gray walls and towers. Above her, the triple summit of Ben Cruachan overhung the loch like a thundercloud; and the hills lay piled against one another, more purple than the heather, bluer than the still loch waters, lifting against the heart-shaking blue of a summer sky. It was no longer the Scotland of rain and mist, and whaups crying before a high wind; it was an enchanted place, touched with magic, as if each moor and hill had taken to itself the gay wild lilt of the Gaelic heart.

She was pleased that Jean understood and did not ask foolish questions when she disappeared for hours at a time and left Jean to her embroidery.

"You were born in the Highlands," Jean remarked sagely. " 'Tis coming back to you now, no matter that you've always been away." She nodded her head like a wise child. "And you'll not forget it, however far you may go."

"And if I stayed," Elspeth teased her, "I'd doubtless go mad from the lonely place, and weep a sea of tears, wishing myself back in London."

But it was only a game she played with herself, to ease in some part the aching fear that she might in truth be forced to leave this place, as her mother had done before her.

Jean did not mention Argyll, and neither of them referred to the Earl of Lunsdon, waiting in vain for Elspeth to arrive in London. But they frequently spoke of Alexander, for there was little chance they might avoid his name while living under the protection of his banner at Ardoon. Wherever they turned in the castle they met a MacHugh clansman, standing unobtrusively at the door or walking several paces behind. When Elspeth ventured from the gates, she soon discovered that MacHugh sentries were stationed in a tight circle around the castle.

Elspeth spent many hours exploring the countryside around Loch Awe; but since she was never allowed outside Ardoon without an escort, her most constant companion was Walter, the MacHugh bard whose hereditary place was beside his Chief at all times. He was displeased that the Chief had left him behind, but he found that lamentable situation bettered somewhat when he could be in the company of the fascinating lass who wore the Chief's ring around her neck.

Walter's favorite occupation was recounting old legends and ballads to Elspeth, telling her the glorious history of the clan with rhyme and song. The two of them would sit for hours before the fire in the hall or on the green banks of the loch, the old poet growing eloquent before his rapt audience. Occasionally the piper joined them, and the skirl of the pipes sounded over the water and challenged old Cruachan himself as he glowered overhead.

The afternoon that Duncan Campbell rode to Ardoon Elspeth was beside the loch, stretched full length on the grass while the piper shrilled merrily on his pipes and Walter, the bard, nodded his gray head to the tune.

Duncan reined his horse and sat quietly watching. Elspeth was wearing her breeks and boots, having grown inordinately fond of such freedom of movement, and her hair was carelessly tied back with a ribbon. The two clansmen wore the red tartan of MacHugh, crossed with green and dark blue, and their short kilts blazed color against the blue of loch and mountains.

"Dugald," Elspeth said suddenly, gazing thoughtfully at the piper, " 'tis an amazing stroke of good fortune that he left you behind."

The pipes were instantly silent. "I dinna ken why," Dugald said stiffly.

"You've nothing but a jumble of shrieking sounds in that bag. Not the smallest resemblance to music." Elspeth rolled over and looked at the blue sky above her.

"Think of the dreadful confusion of a battle, Walter," she said to the bard, "with Dugald's screeching notes fighting among themselves as fiercely as the MacDonalds and Campbells. God's breath, even the MacDonalds would flee, sure the very hounds of the devil were howling at their heels!"

Dugald laughed and Walter agreed gravely. "Dugald's no' so bad when he has a wee bit o' ale under his belt, lassie. But all sober he ha' the sound o' the whaups in his pipes."

"Better the noise o' a bird than to croak like yourself," Dugald retorted calmly. "Ale or no, ye sound the same."

Duncan Campbell interrupted. "Both of you may seek a bit of ale," he ordered, dismounting. "I'd like a word with Mistress Lamond."

The two clansmen turned abruptly. Elspeth sat up, pushing back her hair, and stared at Duncan.

"I didn't hear you approaching, Duncan," she said finally, smiling a little.

"Your guards heard me," Duncan said easily. "I had a devil of an argument persuading them to let me pass."

Dugald and Walter turned toward the castle without a word, recognizing Sir Duncan of Glenurchy and the Campbell tartan he wore. They could do no good, caught as they were by surprise, but they hastened to give Hendry the alarm.

Elspeth stood up and dusted the seat of her breeks. She thought unconsciously of curtsying, remembering in time that it would appear most ridiculous. She put her hands behind her back and looked up at her kinsman.

"How did you find me out?" she asked innocently. "Or were you looking for Hendry?"

Duncan shook his head in exasperation, keeping back the smile which would have come so readily to his mouth at the sight of the lass. "Your maid has a large conscience, my dear. Why did you do it?"

"Did you come to drag me back to Inveraray?" she asked him by way of an answer. "Do you intend to lock me in the dungeon and push my food through the bars?"

"I came as soon as I found you were not on your way to London, as I have thought these past days. I can hardly believe you'd deceive me so, lass."

Elspeth sighed. "I feared Argyll might accuse you of having a hand in it."

"I had no idea you felt so bitterly about the marriage. You showed no displeasure that Argyll chose Lunsdon. I was with you when you learned the news, Elspeth, and you didn't protest then."

"No, I didn't protest. One does not always say the plain thing to Argyll."

"Then you've no intention of marrying Lunsdon?"

"I've no such intention."

Duncan shook his head. "I fear Argyll's rage when he hears the news. He's counted heavily upon it."

"I'll not marry to pay his debts," Elspeth said doggedly, "no matter his rage. If he would harm me, then he must."

Duncan scowled darkly. "You know I'd never allow him to harm you. You've nothing to fear from him."

"I'll not lean on you, Duncan," Elspeth said softly. "Would you have him take away your Balloch and Finlarig? Would you be a man with no land, no titles? He'd manage to do it, if you crossed him."

"And the MacHughs?" Duncan asked. "Do you deem it better that they should take the blame?"

"I have thought of that too, many times." Elspeth looked at the castle beyond them. Would Argyll burn those ancient walls in his rage? Would he ruin the MacHughs, as he intended to ruin forever the proud clan of MacDonalds?

"You have no weapons with which to fight Argyll," Duncan said, his eyes also on the great bulk of Ardoon. "Alexander may be unable to help you. God knows he will need all his wits about him to face his own future, in the event Argyll obtains a letter of fire and sword against him. He'll be an outlaw, Elspeth."

"Why did he go, Duncan?" she asked quietly.

Duncan chose his words with care, flicking his whip against his leg. "The honor a man carries in his heart cannot be explained, lass," he said slowly. "Nor can you measure the courage of a man who will not betray his friends, even though he faces disaster himself. We've no right to question, unless we have known the same dilemma and acquitted ourselves with the same integrity."

"You admire him for it," Elspeth said. "I think you would do the same."

"I pray that I would," Duncan said briefly.

"If Argyll outlaws him, we will take our chances together."

"And if Argyll is unable to outlaw such a popular chief, even though he rides with MacDonald?"

"I will thank God for it," Elspeth said, low, "and I will not jeopardize him further by using his hospitality."

There was sympathy in Duncan's eyes. He remembered Elspeth's mother, and the day he had seen the dull pain in her eyes because her love for Robert Lamond endangered his very life and clan. A thing is never finished, he thought wearily; women must always suffer, as men must forever heed that harsh master in their hearts, responsibility.

"If you remain," he said carefully, "Alexander might not allow you to leave. He has a way of disregarding danger."

She saw the wisdom in his words, for she also knew the ways of the MacHugh. "I promise you, Duncan, that I will return to Inveraray if he comes home safely, with no mark against his name." She added slowly, "But if he is outlawed, I'll take the same penalty. I'll not leave him."

Duncan smiled, although his heart felt the weight of knowing the lass might face such a dismal future. But mayhap it was not so black; the pair of them would make a good thing of being together, outlawed or not.

"Then I've accomplished the purpose of my visit," he said. "I'm happy to know you are well. And well protected, if those surly MacHughs who stopped me are any indication."

"Did Argyll tell you I have a brother?" Elspeth asked quietly, watching him closely.

Duncan's face hardened, "Aye," he said briefly. He added, with a conscious attempt to reassure her, "It came as a shock, after all these years of not knowing, but I'm more than pleased with the news. He can keep an eye on you now, and my conscience will be greatly eased."

She reached up to kiss his cheek. "He's in the south, with Alexander," she said lightly, "but I shall believe them safe until I hear otherwise."

"I pray to God they'll be safe," Duncan said curtly. He mounted, looking down at her with a fierce scowl. " 'Tis a hard world for a lass," he said glumly. "I would I had you safe at Balloch, away from men and wars."

Elspeth smiled. "I'd be bored beyond measure," she said, and he leaned down to grip her shoulder affectionately. Then he raised his hand and wheeled his horse; Elspeth stood watching, her hand seeking the hard solid comfort of the ring hanging on the chain around her neck.

Aye, she thought, women must ever wait and steel their hearts against loneliness and fear; and the men would go riding out to war as long as the blood ran hot and proud in their veins. It was indeed a hard world, but she would not have it otherwise, not so long as Alex MacHugh drew breath in it, and her beside him.

⟬ 18 ⟭

AFTERWARD, when he spoke of the matter, Simon MacHugh admitted to a vast amount of good fortune in reaching Alexander and Gavin. But as he rode south, keeping to the back country and well away from any trail or village, he was thinking less of good fortune than of the more immediate urgency of slipping through Campbell territory without being halted. There was no question in his mind but that he would succeed in his mission; he must succeed, not only in escaping Campbell detection but in reaching Alexander in time to warn him that the game was up and Gavin discovered. Whatever happened when that had been accomplished, Simon no longer cared or dwelt on, for loyalty ran deeper in him than any superficial desire to further his own career as a younger son of the house of MacHugh.

Aye, he thought, loyalty, that most irrevocable of clan codes, was a point of honor more fiercely and tenaciously held than a man's life; the rudest clansman seemed to be born with it in the marrow of his bones. Simon felt he was no less a MacHugh for having spent more time in London than most Highlanders could endure; and as he rode the long miles toward the south, he hoped his inactivity over the past years would not hinder the task before him. A good fight was brewing, and with any luck he would soon be in it; an enraged Campbell would be a more bitter test of his swordplay than the fashionable fencing he had enjoyed in London.

He sent his MacHughs back once he had reached the dangerous line which marked Kintyre to the south; it would prove easier to move in secrecy if he were alone. He waited until nightfall before he ventured on, and after a hasty meal of wine and dried meat he felt sufficiently fortified to make his way past several quiet villages which might or might not be harboring a company of Argyll's hired soldiers.

Simon was not halted by any challenging Campbells, and reached the MacDonald lines well before dawn. But to find the MacHugh in the midst of the MacDonalds proved to be the most difficult part of the entire journey.

"Aye, he was here an hour past," a MacDonald of Glengarry told him, and offered a hot meal from the iron pot suspended over the fire. Simon shook his head and went on, but each clansman he asked could only say he had seen the MacHugh that day but had no idea where he might be found.

The MacDonalds were busy at the morning meal, their helmets and targes laid aside, jesting among themselves and eating with such gusto that there might not have been a Campbell closer than Inveraray. And so far as Simon had been able to determine, there was certainly no Campbell army advancing southward, else he would have encountered some sign of it during the night.

When he finally found Gavin and the MacHugh, they were just beyond Dunaverty Castle. The MacHugh was teaching a MacDonald clansman the trick of a certain slashing backhand cut with the sword; he was bareheaded, wearing a white linen shirt open at the neck instead of mail or leather jacket, and in the heat of the summer day he had exchanged his breeks for trews of MacHugh tartan.

Gavin saw Simon first and his face grew still and grave. He motioned to the MacHugh; Alexander turned at once and, seeing Simon there so unexpectedly, could not school his face quickly enough to hide the questioning concern.

"Simon!" he said, striding toward him with his sword still in hand. "What the devil brings you here?"

The three of them walked apart from the crowd of clansmen, and Simon waited until there was no chance they might be overheard.

"I had no choice," he said. "I've news you won't like, and it seemed important you should know it at once." He looked at Gavin and said quietly, "Argyll knows the truth, lad."

There was a long silence. Alexander turned and leaned against a tree, looking up at the high towers of Dunaverty. "How did he discover it," he asked, "and when?"

Simon drew a deep breath and looked away from Gavin. "He learned from Kate MacLachlan, but I've no idea how long he's known."

Gavin did not speak. He looked at the ground, his face inscrutable; but the thin scar curving his cheek seemed to stand out more plainly than ever.

"Does he know it is Gavin," asked Alexander, "or merely that the lad lived?"

"I think he knows," Simon answered. "If Kate was canny enough to ferret the lie in the tale of the bairn's death, she'd not stop till she discovered the whole truth."

Alexander sighed. "Well, we've known it would come, sooner or later. But I'll admit I didn't think Kate had learned so much." He shook his head slowly. "We've seen too much of her, mayhap. I should have kept her well away from Fraoch Eilean."

Simon said quickly, "I'd say she guessed simply by looking at Gavin and Elspeth together. None of us gave her any hint of the matter. And it was no secret that there was a lad; anyone could have found the grave."

"We'll soon know how much she discovered," Alexander said. "If Argyll stands sure that Gavin is the lad,

I doubt he'll wait long to make his next move." Then he said evenly, "And how is the lass Elspeth?"

"Kate put a knife in Elspeth's back at the same time she betrayed Gavin," Simon said. "Argyll ordered her to sail from Leith this past week."

Alexander's face turned hard and closed. For a moment he didn't speak, then he said lightly, "You're indeed the bearer of sad tidings, Sim. The devil himself would be more welcome at the moment."

Simon grinned. "I can't see you suffer, brother, much as I'd like to," he said. "The lass didn't care to sail. She's at Ardoon, waiting for you to cease your games of war and come back to her eager arms."

He told them of the ride from Edinburgh then, glad to see that Gavin had recovered his poise and was listening with a faint smile on his face.

When he had finished, Alexander said, a hot flash of pride in his eyes, "She's a braw lassie."

"Does she know?" Gavin asked slowly.

"She gave me the warning," Simon said. "I gather Argyll boasted of the matter before her. But she didn't know it was you, Gavin, until I told her."

Gavin grinned slightly. "Was it a shock to her?"

"I should rather imagine she found it so," Simon said cheerfully. "But she took pains to appear pleased."

The MacHugh shrugged; he gave Gavin a light shake. "Well, you're no MacHugh but a Lamond now, lad. Will you leave for Rathmor at once?"

"And miss the sport?" Gavin said promptly, and the bleak shadow disappeared from his eyes. "God's foot, you'll not get rid of me so easily."

"There's no saying what Argyll has in mind," Alexander said. "He'll have his eye on you."

"We'll be ready enough for him," Gavin said.

The MacHugh looked at Simon and said quietly, "And you, Simon?"

Simon held his eyes for a long moment. "I'd like to stay," he said as quietly.

"You're my only heir," the MacHugh reminded him,

as if it were his duty, and an unpleasant one. "A battle is no place for you."

Simon was firm. "We'll take our chances together. I'd be of little good to the clan if aught happened to you."

The MacHugh said, " 'Tis your own neck you're risking, man. Have it your way."

But he was obviously pleased, as was Gavin; and Simon hoped desperately that he would acquit himself well enough to gain their respect as well.

2

The bards would long sing the tale of the battle fought between the MacDonalds of the West and Argyll's Campbells. Argyll came down on Kintyre from the sea, both east and west, and James MacDonald was not warned in time. The doughty MacDonalds were driven from the peninsula to the islands from whence they came, on a day when the very sun turned crimson as if bloodied by the scene it shone upon.

And behind all the songs, and the weeping laments, would be the sounds and images of that day. The battle began like all battles, with a scattered shout, the faint snap of a distant pistol, the loud piping growing in strength from all sides; and before long, the hard impact as the first long wave of steel bit against steel, and the shrill yell of clan slogans rending the ear to the clamor of that first sweeping attack.

The MacHugh, holding to Glengarry's right, fought with the strength of a dozen men, but he could not be everywhere. Simon and Gavin were with him until the end of that long day. Neither of them would forget, nor would the MacDonald's who fought with him, how the MacHugh rallied the men behind him to renewed strength, holding them against repeated Campbell attacks, how he lifted his voice in a gay shout, urging all those who were men enough to move forward with him,

To Simon, the MacHugh's sword was a thing alive, a flashing blade of fire that sang with a whistle of steel; no man could stand against him long on that August day.

Once a Campbell shouted, "Get the red-haired Mac-Hugh," and the fine rage of the MacHugh's sword carried that Campbell to death on the instant and threatened those with him until they backed away. Then Simon moved up, and Gavin; the three of them cut a wide circle around them that did not readily fill again when the Campbells saw their fallen comrades and the high swing of the MacHugh's sword.

But the battle was lost. The MacDonalds made one fierce charge at the beginning, but it failed; and there was little hope that another might succeed. James MacDonald bowed to the inevitable; his force of Mac-Donalds was spread too thinly over Kintyre and the islands, and not all their courage and loyalty would hold against the superior Campbell force. And so he gave his command to retreat in good order, and sent word to his chieftains and to the MacHugh that the day was lost and he intended to fall back to Islay.

The MacDonalds gave way slowly, holding the line until their Chief was safely away. Then they would put into execution their well-planned strategy of retreat, whereby many a Highland force withdrew from certain disaster to rally again in circumstances more favorable. The men would finally scatter, filtering away from the scene of battle until the Campbells were left facing no enemy but the dead and knowing no certain victory but the possession of the land on which they stood.

It was not ignominious defeat, for there was no Mac-Donald who lived that day who did not believe with intense faith that Jamie MacDonald would strike again, with a stronger force and a greater chance of success, whenever he felt the time to be ripe. The day had gone against them, but a MacDonald was not defeated until the last man bearing the proud name had vanished from the face of Scotland.

The MacHugh stood in the shadow of the trees, his sword still unsheathed in his hand, and said his farewell to James MacDonald.

"God be with you, Jamie," he said quietly, and his dark face, dusty and streaked with sweat, was yet charged with the high spirit of the battle. "We'll hold for you as long as possible."

James MacDonald was unutterably weary, but he smiled at the MacHugh. "All is not lost, Alex," he said evenly. "Once I reach Islay we'll make a better showing." He held out his hand and the MacHugh shifted his sword to take it in a firm grasp. "My thanks are too great to be shown by mere words," said the MacDonald, "but I'll not soon forget what you've done for us." He shook his head, as if wondering where the flaw had been in his plans. "If we'd had more than one of you, the day would have gone differently."

The MacHugh reflected that he often disagreed with James MacDonald. He sometimes believed his motives less than unselfish, he knew him to be a polished and wily ruffian of the highest order, and yet his affection for the man had increased during the time he had ridden under the MacDonald banner. It was a thing which could not be explained, but the MacHugh accepted the bond between them as a natural and binding thing, growing out of friendship and clan loyalty; and so it would always be, whether in defeat or victory.

"Send me word if you need me again," he said. "We've not finished with Argyll yet."

MacDonald nodded. "We'll need your sword, Alex, as long as the MacDonalds stand." He grinned, although it cost him considerable effort. "God's love, I hear you took on the number of a regiment for yourself. Did you get a chance at Argyll?"

The MacHugh shrugged. "Not all my prayers availed me," he said. "He kept well out of my way. Jamie, hurry with it. I'd not like to have you overtaken on the water."

"You sinner," MacDonald said. "If we'd been more

God-fearing we might not be fleeing for our lives." He lifted his hand to the MacHugh. "You've no need to hold longer, Alex. Get yourself away while there's time; I've a good enough start to reach Islay safely." Then he said, "God speed you," and turned away quickly.

The MacHugh stood motionless until MacDonald had disappeared with the men who would go with him to the islands. Gavin and Simon waited with him, silently contemplating the difficult task ahead of eluding Argyll's men.

The MacHugh sheathed his sword and turned to Gavin. "Where did you hide the horses?"

"Close enough," said Gavin. "But do you think to ride through the Campbells? I can think of better ways to give myself over to the bastards."

"I'll not leave Tammie to some whoreson of an Englishman, or even to Argyll," said the MacHugh. "Go and fetch the horses, then we'll discuss our next move."

Gavin disappeared into the woods, and the MacHugh and Simon moved to a more secluded spot beneath the trees and sat down to await his return. The sounds of battle were faint and distant to the north; doubtless the fighting had been reduced to scattered skirmishes, and before long the Campbells would come charging through the woods in search of more MacDonalds. But there was a little time left to them; Argyll would not advance until he was certain he rode into no trap of MacDonald's making.

Simon sighed slightly. He felt the weary depression that came with the battle's end, with the silence after great confusion and the inactivity after hours of desperate struggle.

"Well. Gavin is safe," he said finally, but his voice betrayed his fear for him. He leaned back and pillowed his head on his hands. "They tried for him and failed. Did you hear them single out this red head?"

"Safe for the moment," said the MacHugh. "I'll be-

lieve him safer when we're well away from Argyll."
He laughed softly. " 'Tis now I reap the benefit of my
reputation as a cattle reiver, Sim. Can you fade from
sight on the moment and slip through the hills as easily
as a fox eluding the pack? Did they teach you those
tricks at Whitehall? If not, by Jesus, we'll be leaving
you behind."

"At the moment, I feel much like a badgered fox,"
Simon said. "But this is my first battle and my first
retreat, so don't blame me too heavily."

The MacHugh grinned. "The taste of defeat is gall-
ing, I'll grant you, but we made a fight of it." He added
bluntly, "We're not tasting death, like those Campbells
we left lying behind us, and I'd not exchange my defeat
for all their cold victories."

"Aye, we're alive," Simon said, and was pleased to
find his voice steady and firm again. He answered his
brother's grin. "I hope you intend to keep us so."

The MacHugh chewed at a blade of grass. If he was
weary, he did not show it; if he was depressed and
grim over the turn of events, his dark face gave no sign.
He rested easily on the ground, as though to regain his
energy for the problems still ahead, wasting little time
on regrets. Simon felt a renewed strength by merely
looking at his brother, so unconcerned even in defeat;
and he reflected that many a man before him had
known that confident assurance of the MacHugh's and
been cheered and comforted by it.

Gavin slipped through the trees with the horses and
stood looking down at the two men. "Do you remain
here at your leisure?" he asked, amused. "I hear enraged Campbells somewhere in the background, and
I'll be on my way. No mighty heroics for me."

The MacHugh stood up. "I hope your stomachs are
settled," he said, stretching. "Do you feel able to brave
the cold waters of the sea? I've not had my feet on
a ship in a lengthy time."

"A ship?" Simon echoed, his face blank. Gavin said
nothing, knowing the MacHugh too well.

"Well now," said the MacHugh, "hardly a ship, when all's said. But it will hold us, and the horses, and I'd prefer it to donning a Campbell tartan and trying to stroll through Argyll's army. I'd never be mistaken for a Campbell. My face is no' villainous enough."

"Where is the boat?" Gavin asked.

"To the east," the MacHugh replied, "and well hidden, if the MacHughs I left to guard it were resolute enough to stay away from the fighting. We'd best be to it; I gave the men orders to scatter with the MacDonalds and make their way home when the going is safe enough, and I'd as soon do the same before it's too late."

Simon felt a faint scorn for himself that he had ever doubted they would escape. The MacHugh had hoped for victory, and he had fought like a demon for it; but he had also foreseen the situation was defeat and failure on the turn of the dice.

"I am content to follow, brother," he said cheerfully. "Jeannie awaits me, and I've had my fill of battle for the while."

The MacHugh looked at Gavin. "And you, Lamond," he said, "do you approve of the plan of action?"

Gavin grinned at the unfamiliar form of address. "I've been a younger MacHugh too long to change on the moment. I'll not question your authority."

They started toward the eastern coast, and the sun dropped behind a dark bank of clouds and no longer shone on the fair land of Kintyre, once again under the banner of Argyll. The MacHugh thought of James MacDonald and hoped he would reach the welcoming wall of Dunyveg on Islay without mishap; and he thought of Elspeth Lamond at last, allowing himself that pleasure for the first time in many long and clamorous hours.

⊰{ 19 }⊱

THE MacHugh found her on the shore of the loch below the tall walls of Ardoon. She sat on a large boulder which had dried to a pale gray in the sun. Her arms were clasped about her knees and her head was tilted, as if she loved the touch of the wind on her face; and he knew that could he see them, her eyes would be as blue as the loch at her feet.

Then, as he watched her, she turned slowly, with some instinctive feeling that she was no longer alone. She looked directly at him and her eyes widened. Neither of them spoke. Elspeth slipped her boots from the rock and stood on the sand, but she did not move toward him. She leaned against the boulder, her eyes on his, and the silence was broken only by the faint wash of waves against the shore.

Alexander walked slowly across the sand. He gave her a careful scrutiny, from her polished boots and tight leather breeks to the open neck of the white shirt, where his gold ring rested in the hollow between her breasts.

"You make it devilish hard for a man," he said quietly.

She didn't speak. But she straightened, away from the boulder, and planted her feet firmly apart in the sand as she looked up at him.

"I must confess to a small bit of sympathy for the unfortunate Argyll," he went on, his gray eyes glinting with amusement. " 'Tis seldom the commander of an army finds himself so rudely treated in his home camp."

"He doesn't know," she said in a small voice.

"But I know," he said calmly, "and I find it a most difficult situation."

She should have been warned by the lazy tone of his voice, but she could think only that she had abused his hospitality, that he was displeased to find her at Ardoon.

"Difficult to remember that I am supposedly a gentleman, and that you are a poor, mistreated lass who seeks protection behind my honor." His gaze was grave and innocent. He propped one booted foot on the boulder. "A helpless and destitute woman always stirs the most gentlemanly instincts in a man. As I said, 'tis devilish hard."

"I doubt I would trust your gentlemanly instincts overlong," she retorted, sure of herself at last.

"Nor would I," he agreed, his eyes moving over her again, slowly. He liked the look of his lass, dressed as a lad. "Since I cannot say in all fairness that you are mistreated, helpless or destitute, I'd have little argument with my honor."

Elspeth leaned against the rock. "Did Gavin ride to Ardoon with you?" she asked quietly.

"Aye," he said. "I'd not have the courage to face you, were it otherwise."

She could not prevent a small sigh of vast relief and gladness that they were home again, and the two of them safe and alive.

"Did Simon reach you?" she asked then. "And how did the MacDonalds fare against Argyll?"

"Sit down, lass," he said, "and we'll talk of it." He made a swift, unexpected movement and lifted her to the boulder. Her face was level with his then, and their eyes met and held. The MacHugh smiled and leaned toward her, a small flame flickering in the dark depths of his eyes; he put his hands on her shoulders and kissed her.

The sun was warm on her hair, as warm as his lips against hers, and the feel of his physical nearness, after so many days of loneliness, was a joy so sharp and intense that it was almost a pain. But he took his mouth away too soon, so that she felt somehow cheated, and the laughter in his eyes brought a quick burning to her cheeks because she knew he understood.

"We've much to settle between us," he said, the grin spreading to his mouth, and she felt the old urge to leave the imprint of her hand on his face.

"Is MacDonald successful?" she asked quietly. "That would be wondrous news."

The MacHugh shook his head. "No, lass, Jamie MacDonald was not successful."

She stared at him, seeing at last his dusty boots, the leather jack showing the hard wear of the campaign, the unmistakable lines of weariness etched on his dark face.

"You've come straight from the battle," she said faintly, and her heart turned over. "Is all lost? Do you flee from Argyll's army?"

He rested his hand lightly on the hilt of his sword, a gesture so much a part of him that he was unconscious of it. "The battle is lost, and MacDonald has retreated to the islands. But I'd not say it was the end of the world, lass."

He gazed at her, and for all her life she would remember how proudly he held himself in defeat, how his eyes warmed with laughter despite the heavy weariness touching him, how unconquerable his spirit remained in the very face of disaster.

"Alex," she said softly, "will you be outlawed?"

He shrugged his wide shoulders. "I imagine Argyll will have his revenge on MacDonald's supporters in one way or another."

She turned to look at Ardoon, rising above them against the blue sky, knowing she could not force herself to say the words while she looked at him.

"I've put myself deeply in your debt," she said, "but I'll be leaving now that you've returned."

"You've less trust in me than I imagined."

"I promised Duncan, and myself, that I'd not use your hospitality as a shield." She looked at him then, seeing his chin tighten with stubbornness at her words. "I'll return to Inveraray, and when Argyll arrives I'll handle him in my own way. This time it will be my battle."

The MacHugh considered her vastly capable of handling any man, even the Earl of Argyll, with spurs sharper than anyone would reckon for; but he did not tell her that he had no intention of leaving her to tend to the matter alone.

"And if I'm put to the horn?" he asked quietly.

"I'll be most desolate," she said. "But," she added cheerfully, "I've no doubt we'll make good fun of it."

He was silent, his eyes on the soft curve of her cheek and the impudent, tilted chin. If he were outlawed, his titles and estates forfeited, with nothing left to him but his clan and his sword arm, the lass would not hesitate to throw in her lot with his. It was an unforced, voluntary loyalty that stirred him oddly, as did her careless boast that they would make good fun of it if such a thing were inevitable.

" 'Tis a hard life, lass, if a man is forced to it."

Her eyes laughed at him, clear blue and unafraid. "I'd not wonder," she said.

The MacHugh thought it small wonder that he had loved her from his first sight of her. She was gay and lovely and hot-tempered, to be sure, with a beguiling way of turning sweet as sugared wine; and before God she had more than her share of arrogance and pride. But reflected in her direct blue gaze was a courage as unflinching and honest as a man's; it was a thing he had searched for all his life and never found till now.

"When will you be leaving?" he asked, his voice low.

Her cheeks grew hot, but she raised her head and met his eyes fairly. "I'll ride before night," she replied honestly, "else I might find it too easy to change my mind."

He threw back his head and laughed, and the sound echoed back from the castle walls.

"Spoken like a true wench," he said. He took her elbows and swung her from the boulder, lifting her high above his head until her hair fell about her face and shone as bright as the yellow whin in the sun; and it was like the night at Rathmor when he danced with her in the great hall and whirled her in the air until they were breathless with laughter.

Then he put her on the sand and took her hand. "If we've only the afternoon," he said, "we'd best make the most of it."

He strode down the shore of the loch, swinging her hand, and Elspeth matched her strides to his. He stopped once and picked up several small pebbles, skipping them across the surface of the water. Elspeth did the same, proud that she threw as straight and true as a lad. "You're no' so adept," she boasted, and wrestled good-naturedly with him until he pinned her arm around her and kissed her firmly, putting an end to the matter.

They roamed over the moorland above the loch, laughing like two children enchanted with the bright day and the sweet wind off the loch. They climbed through a purple carpet of heather to the crest of a slight hill, and Alex pulled her down beside him. They rested there, looking below them at the blue expanse of water with its green islets.

"Do you like the thought of fathering a bairn?" she asked abruptly.

He was so still that she turned to face him. He looked at her for a long moment without speaking, his eyes so dark they were no longer gray.

"Lass," he said quietly, and stopped as if he could say no more, but the single word was like a caress. Elspeth realized at once that he had misunderstood her, that she should never have voiced the question so bluntly. He was smiling, the MacHugh smile that lighted his face like a candle, and she had made a dreadful mistake.

"Alex, I didn't mean myself," she said quickly, her breath catching in her throat.

She turned away, so that she would not see that brilliant smile die from his brown face, and went on hurriedly, "I was speaking of Kate MacLachlan. Perhaps I should have waited; no doubt she'd prefer to give you such private news herself."

He was silent behind her. Elspeth watched a bird wheel and soar above her in the blue sky. "I apologize," she said softly. She had been more than cruel to say such a thing to him; she had been tactless and foolish, for she had not intended to question him. It was his affair, and Kate MacLachlan's, and it had been presumptuous of her to mention it.

"Did Kate tell you that?" he asked at last, and she could tell nothing from his voice.

"Aye," she answered. "I should not have asked you. 'Tis none of my affair."

He put his hand on her arm and turned her to face him. His face was grave, but the smile still lingered in his eyes. "I think you might show some slight interest without being improper," he said. "So Kate would have you believe she's to have a bairn of mine. Did you believe her?"

She returned his level gaze, not knowing what to say. "Does it matter what I believe?" Then she caught her underlip with her teeth and shrugged her shoulders. "I told her she lied," she said flatly. "She appeared flat as a board, and I'd not believe a son of yours would be so little in evidence."

The MacHugh grinned at her honesty. "Aye, she lied, lass," he said.

She needed no more; the idiotic relief swept through her. "I was dreadfully jealous," she said, low, and the quick pleasure in his face more than justified that small confession.

"I must have a talk with Kate," he said. "She takes an unfair advantage of a man."

Elspeth did not look at him. Gavin was safe, for the moment; and Kate MacLachlan would know misery enough with her conscience and her desolation.

"Does Gavin know?" she asked carefully.

"He knows," Alex said, and the dangerous edge of his voice boded no good for the woman. "At least he's cured of his passion for her. She's done us a great favor, if only she knew."

"Leave her be," Elspeth said. "It was all for love of you, and if you weren't so blackhearted a rogue, it would never have happened."

"God's foot, I can't take all the lassies in Scotland who cherish a longing for me," he said. "Would you care to share me so many ways?"

She gave him a shove, and he took her head between his hands and rumpled her short curls as he would if she's been a lad in truth. The rough touch of his hands turned to gentleness as he put his arms around her.

"Do you know the tale of Loch Awe?" he asked, and when she shook her head he told her the legend of the fairy spring high on the slope of Ben Cruachan. "The bed of the loch was once a fair valley," he said, "with shielings and fertile fields, and so long as the fairy spring was kept carefully covered, the valley was a fine home for the clans. But after generations of peace, the folk grew less careful, and one day a lass who went to draw water forgot to cover the spring when she had finished."

"It would be a lass," Elspeth murmured.

"All night," the MacHugh said, "the water spilled down the hill like a flood of moonlight, and when morning came the valley had ceased to be." He made a wide arc with his arm, and for a moment she was completely under the spell of his warm voice, almost believing she could see the silver spring of fairy water turning the fair valley into a wide loch of deepest blue, with only the highest places remaining as islands sprinkled upon the water.

"And all because of a lass," he said, and laughed down at her. "When I consider the disaster a single lass can wreak, I find it incredible the world has progressed at all."

"I know a fable or two myself," Elspeth said, "and we can't be blamed for all the trouble a man finds for himself."

'I'll wager you know no fable as amazing as the tale of a lass from London who fell in love with an unco' MacHugh," he said, and his arms tightened around her.

" 'Tis not nearly so fabulous as that of Mary Stuart, the lass from France," Elspeth whispered against his face. "I'd not presume to compare myself with her, but I confess I feel much like a queen today."

Alexander laughed softly, exultantly. "I care little for the ending of Mary's love for Bothwell," he said. "We must arrange our own legend more skillfully."

He put his mouth on hers then, and the moment seemed suspended in time, a small bit of eternity forever after remembered for the smell of crushed heather beneath them and the faint drone of bees searching for honey in the war sunlight.

But the afternoon came to an end, as all such glorious moments must, and they went down to Ardoon to speak to Gavin and Simon before the MacHugh rode with Elspeth to Inveraray.

Gavin was standing by the window when they entered the hall; and Elspeth walked toward him with her heart pounding unsteadily and her hands cold as the waters of a winter tarn high in the hills.

He smiled slightly, and the late-afternoon sun blazed in his red hair and outlined his MacHugh tartan in a brilliance like the flames of the fire.

"I should have known," she said unevenly, "that all my insults might come back again to taunt me."

"Aye," he said, "you'll have your just punishment for calling attention to my ugly face and telling the world how witless I am. At least one person saw the resemblance between us."

She looked at him for a long moment, seeing the blue eyes so like her own, the way his fair head became almost red in the sunlight, the way his hard chin lifted with an unconscious pride; and she wished, with a great sadness, that her mother might have seen him standing so.

"I find the news very pleasant," she said at last.

"Well now," he said lightly, "I hoped you'd not turn and flee to London when you found me out. 'Tis not the worst could happen to you, gaining a brother after all these years. I can keep Alex from beating you too often, and mayhap I'll be handy when you need a proper man to teach your bairns the evil ways of the world."

He took her hand in his, and she saw that his eyes were neither cold nor distant; and so knowing that he was not so unaffected as he would seem, she was vastly grateful to him for easing the strain of the moment.

"Aye, you're the one to teach them," she said. "I remember a day you drove me on a mad ride through the hills, threatening to use your sword on me if I didn't keep the pace. Is that the way you show your brotherly affection?"

"I've other ways of showing it," he said quietly, "and I'm thankful we've a goodly number of years before us to make up for the time we've lost." Then he smiled at her. "You'll be a nuisance, right enough. I've yet to see a lass who didn't bedevil a brother into madness. But mayhap I can bear the strain."

Then Alexander joined them; and Simon and Jean, with eyes only for each other, withdrew to the privacy of Jean's apartment to celebrate the good news salvaged from defeat.

"I misjudged Simon," Elspeth said to Alexander. "I thought he cared only for himself, but he proved me wrong on all counts."

He smiled. "He's a MacHugh, when all's said. Did you think he'd betray me, lass?"

"I don't know what I thought," she confessed. "Mayhap I remembered the men at court, and feared he was too much like them."

"He won his spurs in Kintyre," Alex said briefly. "I've known he was not cowardly, but my MacHughs cherished a few thoughts like your own and he's long needed to prove himself to them."

"You'll have other heirs soon," Gavin said, "and I'll wager it'll be a relief to Sim. 'Tis a difficult thing for a man to face filling your boots."

Alexander laughed, and his gray eyes looked down into Elspeth's. "What say you to that, lass?"

She smiled tremulously, but she did not tell him what she thought of the matter, nor of the fears she yet felt inside her. He was not safe, nor was Gavin, and so long as Argyll lived and hated, they would ever live in danger. Not all their pride, not courage, nor skill with the sword, would protect them from the wrath of the King or the greed of the Campbells.

No, she could not show her miserable fears, not when the two bravest men in Scotland escorted her to the evening meal, laughing and teasing her as if no battle had been engaged or lost, as if no dread prospect of being outlawed weighed upon their minds. She must be as gay, and never dare to think she might be lonely again one day without the two of them to laugh with her and shrug their shoulders at misfortune.

{20}

"GOD'S love, I've never seen so dour a company." Simon was stretched on a leather-cushioned settle before the fire, his head comfortably supported by Jean's lap. He held a pear-shaped lute of ivory and silver and plucked the strings fitfully, tilting his head to determine the correct tuning of each note.

He gave a sharp twang to one string and Jean jumped. "No more dour than that wretched lute," she said pointedly. "Do you know no melody?"

Simon sighed. "No longer a sweet bride, but a nagging shrew." He smiled up at her and commenced to play a soft melodic air. He closed his eyes, allowing his fingers to move aimlessly over the strings, and the tune changed to the slower, sadder ballad of Lord Randel.

Jean worked on her needlework, her head bent close to the tapestry. It was almost dusk but no candles had been lighted; the only light came from the hearth, where the fire was little more than a bed of burning coals. The great hall of Fraoch Eilean was gloomy and dark, and Jean would have preferred the warm comfort of the smaller hall beyond, but she dared not move or ask Alex for more light. He was sitting opposite the settle, in a tremendous chair carved with his armorial bearings; he held a silver tankard of ale, which he had not touched to his lips, and his face was dark and grave as he stared into the fire.

"Sim, can you play nothing more cheerful?" she pleaded.

He shrugged, upsetting Jean's needlework. He laid the lute on the settle beside him and stared at the smoke-stained beams of the ceiling. "My talents have seldom been so miserably appreciated."

Jean gave him a glare of exasperation and pushed his head from her lap. "Sim, do cease your nonsense." She tried to convey, in a single meaningful look, that it was no time for jesting. Alex was in a black mood; Sim should know how unwise it was to irritate the man when he was in such a stormy temper. That morning Kate MacLachlan had paid them an unexpected visit, and Jean had been astonished at Alex's anger when he saw her. They had talked for a long time in the small hall, then Kate had left as unexpectedly as she came, her face paler than ever and her slanted eyes black with anger or misery; Jean was uncertain which emotion it had been. Then, no sooner than Kate had departed, a messenger arrived with news that Jamie MacDonald had fled to Ireland and his kinsman Colkitto had surrendered on Islay and betrayed a number of MacDonald allies.

"Leave him be," Alex said unexpectedly. "I'll take care of him in a short while."

Simon grinned. "Try it at your peril, brother. Although I give it as my considered opinion that it might clear your clod of a head if it were given a few thumps against a stone wall."

Jean held her breath. Only three persons in the entire world, Gavin and Simon and Elspeth, dared to take their pleasure by deliberately provoking Alex, and Jean had never grown accustomed to the highhanded insults which so delighted the four of them.

"Sim, sooth the bairn. She's properly horrified that you'd speak with such disrespect."

Jean smoothed her face immediately; she had not been aware of frowning. Simon put his head back in her lap.

"She's nothing but a sop for your vainglorious airs," he said calmly to Alex. He relaxed, feeling the warmth of Jean's thigh against his face, although separated by several layers of satin and linen petticoats. He moved his head so that he could see her face and put one arm around her waist.

"I've suddenly discovered a great weariness," he said. "Put down that foolish needle, Jeannie, and let us retire."

Jean's face turned pink above the ruffled bodice of her gown. " 'Tis not even night yet, Simon MacHugh."

"Does it make such a difference?"

Jean stood up hastily. "I'll see to some food," she said, and fled to the kitchen. She found cooled malmsey and small meat pies thick with rich gravy, but the food did not immediately restore Alex to good humor. He ate silently, as if unaware of the food before him.

There were sounds of spurs clattering against the stone steps beyond the hall door, then Gavin strode into the room. His red hair was damp where his helmet had rested; he looked dusty and sweaty, and he apologized briefly to Jean. She smiled, still finding it difficult to accustom herself to the unexpected knowledge that Gavin was her own half brother and not a MacHugh at all.

"I've been keeping a close eye on the approaches from Kintyre, Alex," he said brusquely. " 'Tis been a dull task, but by Jesus I found it too lively today for my taste!" He put his helmet on the table and wiped his hand across his forehead. "My ears are sharper than most, else I'd be languishing by the trail with a sword through my gullet." He caught himself, remembering Jean's presence. "We drew back through the trees only in time to avoid the Earl himself, riding scorched leather for Invararay."

Simon dropped his tankard on the table with a thud and stared at Gavin. "Argyll himself? Gavin, have you been drinking?"

"I'm no' so much a fool I could miss that ugly face," Gavin retorted. "He was in a sweat, pushing his horse the limit, but I had a good enough look to know him on the instant."

Alexander said nothing for a moment. He pushed back his chair and propped his boot on the underbar of the heavy trestle table.

Then he asked curtly, "How many men with him?"

"Two score," Gavin said. "I'd stake my life on it. Unless he had more behind him. But he had no outriders before him, and I didn't wait to see if more were coming."

"Then two score it is. He'd not separate his guard." Alexander looked at Jean. "We must have a council of strategy, Jean. Would you leave us now?"

Jean left them reluctantly. She longed to know what Alexander intended, but she dared not disobey that quiet command. It would be a dangerous sort of business, of that she had no doubt; the three of them had waited Argyll's return to Inveraray with impatience. Alexander would be in better temper now; he hated inactivity above all things, and she knew he had chafed under the strain of sitting quietly at Fraoch Eilean while Elspeth waited alone at Inveraray for Argyll's coming.

Gavin sat in the chair Jean had vacated and poured himself a flagon of wine. Alexander rested his elbow on the carved arm of his chair and put his chin in his hand.

"So Archibald has left the scene of victory," he said softly. "He must consider the lass of no small importance." He grinned, but the light in his eyes was not entirely humorous. "The man must be blind with rage, venturing home with so small a guard."

Simon frowned. "I didn't expect him so soon."

"Nor I. But he is here, and Duncan is at Balloch Castle." Alexander paused; he had not imagined that Argyll would leave the south until his victory was well secured. It might be that he had accomplished that feat in an incredibly short time, subduing all the islands, but it was more likely that he intended to rejoin his army immediately after he dealt with the lass. In that event, they had precious litttle time to plan a course of action. And Duncan Campbell, thinking it would be some time before Argyll arrived, had recently departed for his castle of Balloch to attend to his affairs there.

Gavin did not like it. He had not liked the unpleasant look of the Earl of Argyll as he whipped his horse furiously toward Inveraray. "I would I hád known it sooner," he said coldly. "We could have spirited the lass away before he arrived."

Alexander toyed with his silver-handled dirk, finally wiping it with a linen cloth. He slipped it into the slender sheath at his waist. "She wanted it to be her private battle," he remarked calmly. "She asked for no interference." He shrugged, his eyes on his boots. "She'd deserve no better than to be left alone."

Gavin frowned. "Do as you please," he said, "but I'll not leave her alone to face that bastard."

Simon held up his hand. "Hold off, man," he said to Gavin. "He thinks he's canny enough to leave us here, while he rescues the lovely lady. He's too greedy for glory." Simon moved his wine flagon and used the tip of his dirk to outline a square in the moisture left on the surface of the table. "There is Inveraray," he said casually. "Stout walls, uncourteous Campbells, and Argyll foaming at the mouth. A double guard at every window and door." He rested his head on his hand and looked at Alexander. "Now be good enough to tell us," he said curiously, "exactly what you intend to do?"

Alexander grinned. If they wanted to join him, he'd not hold them back. Gavin had more than enough to urge him on, and Simon had long since ceased to worry over Argyll's disapproval. He pushed back his chair and dropped his boots to the floor with a thud. He drew his dirk again, so quickly that the two men opposite him saw it only as a dangerously sharp point which glinted in the light.

"You're in practice, Alex," Gavin said admiringly.

Alexander drew a small circle on one side of the square which Simon had etched on the wet table. "Perhaps a heavy guard at the front gate," he said. "I've yet to see a Campbell who didn't swagger with victory. They'll be swarming like insects." He drew another circle directly opposite the first. "But if Archibald was angry enough to ride to Inveraray with only two score men, he'll be too confident to post his guards in an invincible circle. This is the postern gate, lads. I'd wager my arm there'll be but one Campbell posted in that unpleasant spot, reeking of the garbage from the kitchens."

"Gavin, you can never hope to best the man." Simon was pleased. He gulped his wine and thumped the flagon on the table. "Let's be at it. I'd not like to be too late."

Alexander silenced him with a single look. "Too late for what?" he asked lazily. There was a metallic ring to his words; Simon found himself hoping that Argyll did not harm the lass in any way before the MacHugh arrived, else it would be a bloody night's work and no man could foresee where it might end.

Gavin shook his head and sighed. "D'you plan to walk in as his lordship's dearest relative? God's foot, Alex, you can't vanish into thin air once you're inside." He added, as an afterthought, "Overlooking the smaller matter that the guard might not allow you through the gate."

"How many MacHughs below?" Alexander asked Gavin.

Gavin computed the figures rapidly. "Half again a hundred horse," he said. "Less a sufficient guard for Fraoch Eilean."

"We'll not need so many. No more than two score." A slight smile touched Alexander's mouth. "It'd be an insult to Archibald." He added, "Gavin, you know the Campbell at the postern gate."

Gavin grinned. He had taken a letter or so to the lass, but he'd not go so far as to say that surly Campbell was any kind of an acquaintance.

"We'll write a letter to the lass," Alexander said. "See to it, Simon. You have a dainty hand."

He grinned at Simon, then was out of his chair and across the room. He grabbed his sword from the cabinet by the door. "Wear no mail," he ordered over his shoulder. "We've moonlight tonight." Then he turned, as if another thought had come to him. "I've no reason to say that all will go well," he said bluntly. "If I don't appear within a reasonable time, you're all to ride back to Fraoch Eilean. And in God's name, if you don't obey that order, I'll have both of you hanged by the neck till the birds will be loath to pick at your bones!"

Gavin and Simon followed him, each careful to hide his thoughts from the other. It was a bold trick, and it might succeed. Only the MacHugh would consider slipping into the fortress of Inveraray with Argyll raging within, amply guarded by pugnacious Campbells. And only the MacHugh might possibly get away with it.

If Gavin and Simon were unusually quiet, it was not from lack of confidence in the MacHugh. It was simply the plain conviction that he would be vastly amused and entertained by the events of the evening, while they would be forced to sit helplessly outside the walls of Inveraray, silent and miserable with anxiety for him.

2

The night was bright with moonlight, but the riders hugging the shadowed side of the road betrayed no glint of mail or sword. They rode at a hard gallop for a mile, then slowed their horses to a snaillike pace. Finally they dismounted altogether, leading their mounts into the darkness of the wood which lined the track. The hoofs made little sound on the thick grass, now heavy with night dew, and the bits and bridles which might have jangled had been carefully wrapped with cloth.

They slipped through the trees, dark shadows which could not be distinguished from the darkness under the branches where the moonlight could not penetrate. At last they halted, well before reaching the cleared ground beyond the trees, and the MacHugh gave his final orders to Simon in a low voice.

"I hope I'll be able to bring the lass with me," he said quietly. "But I may find the chance to chat with Argyll, and in that event it will be a while before you see us. But in no circumstances are you to show yourselves." He emphasized the words, his voice curt. "Don't get any foolish notions about coming to my aid, and don't give them a hint that anyone is around."

He settled his cloak again, wishing it were not necessary to wear it. The night was too warm, but the heavy coil of rope attached to his belt must be covered.

He gave the signal to Gavin, who moved silently along the edge of the trees, keeping well within their shadows. Alexander stayed close behind him and followed as Gavin cut into the open ground. They stood little chance of being challenged from the battlements, for the long shadow cast by the castle reached to the trees at that point.

When they reached the postern gate, Alexander drew back against the wall, pulling his dark cloak closer around him to hide his sword. Gavin rapped firmly on the gate, but not so loudly that the sentries above might hear.

They waited in the silence. Gavin was calm, but he was not so fond of his cat-and-mouse way of attack as was Alexander. Give him the brave skirl of the pipes and a hearty war cry, and he'd match his sword with any enemy beneath the sun. But he had less stomach for the dark of night, with his sword encumbered under a cloak and only his wits to keep him out of eager Campbell hands; he thought of the day he had tricked the lass at Duncraig, and remembered he'd not drawn a comfortable breath till he was over the hills with her.

Finally the narrow slit in the heavy wooden gate was

thrown back. "Who's there?" The guard did not sound overly perturbed. "Wha' d'ye want, clattering on a gate this hour o' the night?"

" 'Tis only myself," Gavin said softly. "Gavin of MacHugh, with a note for the Mistress Lamond."

The guard peered through the slit and Gavin held his face closer for identification, hoping that the news of his identity had not spread to every Campbell in Argyllshire. "The same as before," he said, in as friendly a voice as he could muster. "I'm to wait for a proper answer, writ by hand."

The guard cursed under his breath. There was a long pause, then the massive chains holding the latch began to rattle.

"I dinna ken why ye couldna come at a decent hour o' the night." The Campbell grumbled disapprovingly. "His lordship would ha' my head if he knew."

The gate swung open slowly, only a slight crack at first as the guard took another precautionary scrutiny. Gavin held his hand in the sliver of light which fell across the grass so that the gold coins in his palm glittered plainly.

" 'Tis only a letter for the lassie," he said persuasively. He grinned, remembering that Alex was beyond him in the dark, listening to this small exchange. "You know how the man is about a lass, wooing with a passion like you've never seen." The Campbell smirked and Gavin decided to embellish his tale. "I'll wager the letters you give me in return are so hot they'd warm your fingers to the touch."

The guard snickered and Gavin had a brief premonition of the devious ways by which Alex would undoubtedly repay him for this. "Come, man," he said, "if I'm not back with her answer quickly, he'll ha' me lashed."

The Campbell allowed Gavin to step inside the gates and stared at him thoughtfully. "The MacHugh wouldna give ye the lash. I'd not believe it if I saw it."

Gavin gestured impatiently. He had more confidence

now, for although the guard was young and brawny, he obviously did not possess a great deal of brains beneath that tangled mop of hair. Gavin held the letter out and the Campbell took it; he took a step toward the kitchen doors, then turned on Gavin suspiciously.

"Ye be a fool if ye believe I'd leave my post to deliver the cursed letter." He hesitated, fearing the wrath of the Mistress Lamond no less than that of the Earl. Caught between two dreadful evils, he clutched at the only possible solution. "Ye'll ha' to trust it to a kitchen maid," he stated flatly. "I'll wait here wi' ye till she brings an answer." He stepped to the kitchen door and called to a young lass busily turning a spit over the roaring fire beyond the entrance. "Come, lassie, I've an errand for ye."

The guard did not hear the slight rustle behind him. He leered into the kitchen, his mind on the possible contents of the letter and the interesting appearance of the kitchen wench, whose full breasts were loosely bound in her white bodice.

Alexander slipped into the dark passage between the kitchen and the thick castle walls. The smell of offal and garbage was almost unbearable, and he grimaced at the close dankness of the air. But the passageway was black, protected from the guard's lantern by a slight jog in the wall. Alexander guided himself with one hand, moving it along the outside wall. If he remembered correctly, the rear door of the chapel opened into the narrow walk. It would be safe enough to enter; he had little reason to believe the Earl would waste time on his knees this night offering pious thanks for victory.

His hand encountered the wooden timbers of the chapel door. It had been originally intended for an alternate exit for the priest in the old days of popery, and he hoped it was unlocked and had been used recently enough so that the hinges would not squeak loudly enough for Argyll himself to hear them.

The door was not locked and he tried it gently; it

swung open silently, and Alexander offered a fervent thanks to the conscientious maids of Inveraray. The interior was pitch black and he realized he was in the small space behind the nave. He found his way through the curtains to the front of the chapel; it was dimly lighted by two tapers in a silver sconce by the doors leading into the yard, and it was empty.

Alexander considered his position quickly. It would be impossible to cross the yard without being recognized, and the only other way out of the chapel led through a corridor to the kitchen. He searched for the door and found it tucked between two stone buttresses which supported the roof. When he reached the kitchen door he cracked the door slightly and looked beyond into the brightly lighted kitchens which stretched almost the length of the castle. Cooks were running from tables to fires, hurrying the maids and stewards; the scene was one of great confusion and haste. The Earl and his men had obviously called for food.

He noted that a circular flight of stairs led upward at the far side of the room. It seemed a devilish length of space to cross, but he had no choice. Gavin was talking to the Campbell guard at the rear door, and the Campbell's back was turned. Alexander opened the door and stepped boldly into the room. No one turned to stare at him; the browning of meat and the proper scrutiny of baking bread was of prime importance.

He forced himself to saunter slowly across the room, as if he had every reason to be strolling through the kitchens of Inveraray at such an hour. He stopped at one table and sampled a roasted pigeon, tearing off one of its juicy legs before he walked on. The cook slapped at his wrist with a wooden spoon before she looked up; when she saw him her eyes widened and she dropped a brief curtsy. Alexander grinned at her and held up the pigeon leg in triumph, and she shrugged as she returned to her task.

He held to the same careless walk, keeping a watch on the Campbell guard from the corner of his eye. It took every ounce of will power to continue toward the stairs as if nothing were amiss, and it seemed an eternity before he reached them. He dropped the pigeon bone and kicked it aside, then put his hand on the iron handrail and started up the stairs, expecting a shout from the guard at any moment.

As he turned the stairs, just before they moved out of sight above the kitchen, he saw the kitchen wench return with the letter in her hand. She had not had time to receive an answer; mayhap the Earl had ordered that no message be delivered to Elspeth.

Once above the light of the room below, Alexander let out his breath and bounded up the steps. He could hear the rattle of chains beneath him; the postern gate was being closed and latched for the night. He was thankful he had thought to bring the length of rope; it would be highly unpleasant to be forced to choose between the dungeon or a jump from the walls.

He met no one on the stairs. When he reached the upper floor he hesitated again, thinking swiftly. He must find a place to remove his cloak, for he could not accomplish anything so long as he was encumbered with it and the rope. Several doors opened off the corridor into which he had emerged, and he knew that the doors opposite him led into the library. He chose the door immediately at his left; the door was not locked, and he closed it behind him and stood there a moment in the darkness to get his bearings.

When he struck a light from the tinderbox in his pocket, he realized he had made a wise choice. This was Duncan's office, and he would not be disturbed unexpectedly. He lighted a plump candle on the massive table and looked about him, whistling softly under his breath. First he rid himself of the cloak and the coil of rope, stuffing them behind the big chair for later use. He slipped his sword an inch or so from its scabbard and returned it; he laced his jacket and removed a ring which he wore on his forefinger. He wanted no

fripperies to hinder him in the event the night did not
remain so calm and peaceful.

He leaned across the table to blow out the candle.
He hesitated, his eyes on the pile of papers on Duncan's desk. The man was a fool, he thought, leaving
his affairs so public to the eyes of any man who entered the room. Alexander grinned, wondering if his
conscience would bear the weight of a bit of pilfering.

He pushed back the chair and sat down, ruffling
through the papers. He moved the candle closer so
that he might see better and settled comfortably in the
chair. He glanced at a few pages of parchment, then
returned slowly to the first papers he had seen. He
rested his chin on his hand, his tongue in his cheek, and
whistled soundlessly.

"Holy Jesus," he said softly, "a veritable fortune of
correspondence."

A letter close to the top of the pile caught his eye.
It bore the great seal of James Stuart, King of England and Scotland, and Alexander handled it carefully. When he had finished reading it, he slipped it into
an inside pocket of his jacket, feeling no twinge of
conscience.

When he opened the door into the corridor, the Mac-
Hugh was grinning widely.

3

Elspeth stood before the fire, her head held proud
and high. Her heart was hammering unsteadily beneath
her stays and she struggled to keep her breathing even,
but the Earl of Argyll did not know these things.

He knew only that his kinswoman looked incredibly
lovely and insolent, and his rage, which had partly
abated with a draught of cool wine and a clean change
of clothes, began to rise hotly to his head again. She
wore a demure gown of dark blue over huge hoops
which floated gracefully about her as she moved, and

the color emphasized the startling blue of her eyes. Her fair hair was hidden beneath a small velvet Marie Stuart cap; she looked most demure and innocent, a calculated effect which maddened the Earl beyond all reason.

"You little fool, do you realize what you've done?" He mimicked her harshly, "I did not wish to leave for London!" He flung himself around the table and stood facing her. "God's breath, mistress, I can scarce believe you would so deliberately disobey me!"

She was silent, keeping her face calm with an effort. Perhaps, she reasoned, he would shout at her until his rage was spent, and then she might be able to handle the situation more ably.

"You've made me the joke of London. You've insulted the Earl of Lunsdon beyond repair." His voice was hoarse with anger. "D'you believe any man in England would have you now? D'you dream the King will grant you pardon for such miserable behavior?"

"And do you feel concern over my pardon," Elspeth replied calmly, "or your own?"

He took a step toward her, then restrained himself. "You are most forward, mistress, for one in so helpless a position. Duncan is not here to plead for you now, but if he were, his presence would not save you. I intend to teach you a small lesson, one which I have regrettably neglected over long."

Elspeth felt a sudden surge of anger. The man was haughtier than the King himself, and a good deal more unpleasant. She had expected and dreaded it, but now that the moment had arrived she was more furious than frightened.

"I need no one to plead for me, sir," she retorted.

Argyll's face was unpleasantly amused. "Then you will have no quarrel with my intentions, for your own objections will avail you little. Perhaps a husband such as Lord Barsdale will curb your insolence. The man has pleaded with me for your hand."

She whitened, and the Earl saw it immediately. "So

you are not so brave when faced with your punishment. I will elaborate for you. If you have found it easy in Scotland to be imprudent, you'll not find it so again. I should never have allowed you in this god-forsaken country, but I intend to rectify that unfortunate mistake at once. A lonely visit to Cornwall will be more in keeping with my purposes. I doubt your temper will remain so rash after a lengthy stay there."

Elspeth thought of Lord Barsdale, a slobbering old Earl who had frequented the court as long as she could recall. He had a filthy habit of putting his hands on any woman who ventured within his reach; he was an unpleasant old man such as she and Alex had laughed about on that long-ago evening at Rathmor. He was quite wealthy, she had heard, and his earldom was an ancient one, but not even the most grasping of fathers had been able to stomach the disgusting sight of the old man as he drooled on his waistcoat and moved his hot eyes in a continual scrutiny of bodices and bare arms.

"You will remain in Cornwall until I have returned to London to make the arrangements with Barsdale. And I doubt you will find friends there to encourage the infamous behavior you have displayed here."

"Tell me, m'lord, how do you think to get me there? And what good would it accomplish?" She stood straighter, letting him see the amusement in her face. If it were a bluff, it yet might save her. "You'll agree, sir, that few men of wealth will marry a woman when she refuses to take the vows without a dirk at her back. I doubt any man could escape the sight of your grasping fingers in the background, and Lord Barsdale is noted for his reluctance to part with his gold."

Argyll thought of the Earl of Lunsdon's fortune which had eluded him, of the long weeks he had devoted to bringing that foolish lout of a country Earl to the point of acquiescence without Elspeth to assure him of her desire to wed him; he imagined how Jamie Stuart and his entire court must be amused and entertained at his expense because the great Argyll could not handle a mere lass.

"Christ's blood, I shall make you suffer for this," he said, and his eyes blazed with a wrath of utter frustration and bitterness. He lost all sense of reason, feeling only an overwhelming hate for the girl before him who had thwarted all his ambitions and plans. "Where are your Scots lovers, mistress, who will draw their swords to protect you?" he sneered. "Or do they consider you an inglorious whore with no honor to defend?"

The ignominy of his words stunned her because it was so unexpected, and for a moment she could not think clearly of anything. But she lifted her chin defiantly, not caring to let him see that his insults might touch her.

At that instant, Argyll knew the culminating humiliation of his entire life, a life eternally fraught with disappointments and indignities, with slurs and ridicule. Argyll, of the unappealing character and appearance, stared at the slim lovely lass who faced him with no fear and no cowardice; she seemed to embody all the kinsmen who had betrayed him, all the enemies who had discredited him, all the false friends who had insulted him.

He took two steps toward her; then he raised his hand and struck her with all the power behind his long arm, and the sound was like a clap of thunder in the silent room. Elspeth stumbled under the impact, falling against the chair behind her, and her eyes widened in shock. But she did not cry out; she merely stood there, one hand against the chair and one on the cheek where the mark of his hand had left a long red stain.

For a moment Argyll was still blinded with his consuming emotions. Then he seemed to realize what he had done, and the blood drained from his face.

"Elspeth," he said, moving his hand over his forehead like a man dazed. "I ask your pardon. Before God, I did not mean to strike you."

She did not speak, but the contempt in her face

needed no words. Argyll hesitated, then he saw her eyes go beyond him and widen again. He turned quickly, for once in his life completely confused, and his blood turned to ice along his veins.

The MacHugh stood there, his wide shoulders resting easily against the door which led to the library. He held his sword carelessly, with the point touching the floor at his feet, but his gray eyes flamed with a violence so ruthless and pitiless that even Argyll could find no words to meet it.

Alexander's lazy gaze moved from Argyll to Elspeth, flickering over the red welt rising on her cheek. His dark face was inscrutable, but Elspeth thought that she must be seeing him as he looked before battle. He was dispassionate, wholly in command of himself; his nerves were so steady and alert that not a muscle betrayed that savage light in his eyes. Yet something about him, somtthing in the taut lines of his powerful body, warned that the dangerous violence was controlled by an extremely thin rein.

"Leave us, lass," he said evenly.

Elspeth moved slowly across the room, still struggling between amazement and disbelief because he had so suddenly appeared from nowhere. Neither the thick stone walls of Inveraray nor Argyll's Campbells had managed to keep him out; he was surely touched with magic, as Jeannie had once said.

The MacHugh did not take his eyes from Argyll. When Elspeth had passed through the library door he kicked it shut and slid the latch in place without moving his head a fraction of an inch.

"I should kill you, Argyll," he said, and the steel beneath his voice was as cold as the sword in his hand. "I dislike to see a man mauling a lass about. But you would scarce fit such a kind description, and I'll not dirty my blade with it."

The Earl had regained his composure. He smiled thinly, his mind working again at its normal speed. "I am unarmed, MacHugh," he said. Two Campbells were posted outside the door leading to the corridor; he considered the possibility of shouting to them and then putting the table between him and the MacHugh before the man ran him through. But he remembered that he had locked the door when Elspeth entered and ordered that he not be disturbed in any circumstances; he cursed silently and flicked the lace ruffles at his wrist.

The MacHugh seemed amused. " 'Tis a heavy door to batter down, m'lord," he said. "I doubt your men could reach you before I've finished my business here."

Argyll kept his face bland. He had lived too long by cunning and subterfuge to be unduly alarmed. Not in his own fortress, surrounded by his own faithful men.

"You're more a fool than I imagined," he said smoothly.

The MacHugh raised his sword and indicated a chair. "We shall see," he said laconically. "Take your ease, m'lord."

The wicked blade of his sword trembled, shooting sparks in the reflected glow of the fire. Argyll controlled his anger with difficulty and sat down in the chair; he would play the game as long as it pleased him, then he would deal suitably with Alexander MacHugh.

"If you will be so kind," he said, "I should like an explanation of such boorish behavior. I find it most distasteful." He added, studying his nails, "And exceedingly unwise, coming from a gentleman in your position."

"Then we shall come to the point of the matter," the MacHugh said promptly. "It would pain me to provoke your displeasure." He had not moved from the door, nor did he straighten from that careless, lounging position. "I've come to relieve you of your responsibilities in regard to Mistress Lamond. From this moment, we shall consider her in my charge."

Argyll stared at the MacHugh. "So you have come to defend her honor," he said sardonically. "How gal-

lant, and how ludicrous." He shrugged, crossing his
thin legs in their silken hose. "Such a shame that the
lady's fair honor is slightly soiled around the edges.
Hardly worth such a valiant effort, I assure you."

Beyond the tightening of the muscles in his face, the
MacHugh's expression did not change. "Such foul insults are born in a foul mind," he said casually, "and
I'd not deign to challenge you over them. But I might
suggest that you refrain from speaking so coarsely,
m'lord." He held the point of his sword in the air for
a moment, then rested it over his shoulder. "You might
tempt me to soil my sword despite my firm resolu-
tions."

Argyll moved a languid hand. "D'you hope to accomplish that without penalty?" he asked. "Your threats
fail to alarm me, sir."

"No one saw me enter Inveraray. No one knows
that I am here with you now." Alexander grinned
cheerfully. "Quite a puzzle for your Campbells, m'lord,
to find you stuck like a pig in your own hall, with no
sign of a single enemy. I foresee a most pleasant fight
among themselves, each accusing the other of treachery."

Argyll paled, but his voice was even. "What do you
want of me?"

"I've told you," the MacHugh said softly. "I'm taking the lass with me, but I'm awaiting your gracious
blessing on our betrothal."

"Fool," Argyll sneered. "I'll have you put to the
horn in less than a week. I've other plans for her, with
the King's permission."

The MacHugh's face was unreadable. "Tell me,
m'lord, have you secured your victory over James
MacDonald?"

Argyll waved his thin hand again. "The rebel has
fled to Ireland, MacHugh, and his prime lieutenant,
Colkitto, has co-operated to an astonishing degree. Before I took horse for Inveraray, the man had betrayed
several of MacDonald's close supporters." He could

see no reaction in the MacHugh's face, so he continued, "I fear to disappoint you if you thought to escape notice. The King will doubtless hold you in as much blame as MacDonald."

"I trust it will take some time to finish up the matter," the MacHugh remarked innocently. "Have you received that promised gold from Jamie Stuart?"

Argyll sprang to his feet. "Do you dare pry into my affairs, MacHugh? I'll have your head on the Tolbooth!"

The MacHugh crossed one boot over the other and regarded Argyll impassively. "I've been reading a most interesting correspondence," he said. "Letters from your Scots creditors, m'lord. God's body, I was amazed to learn that Jamie Stuart has not parted with a single pound of gold in support of your campaign. A noble gesture, sir, to pay the cost of the King's wars from your own pockets."

Argyll stood motionless, staring at the MacHugh. His hands were clenched into fists, his bony shoulders hunched under the black velvet of his doublet.

"Do you intend," the MacHugh continued softly, "to sell Inveraray to satisfy your creditors? The letters I read showed unmistakable signs of impatience. What will you use for gold, sir, now that the Mistress Lamond refuses to marry for your purposes?" The taunting voice went on and on, hurling the unpleasant truths in Argyll's face. "The King has been known to overlook trifling enmities before, Argyll. Will you risk his wrath by quarreling over gold, or do you plan to pay his waged soldiers for the length of time they've been in Scotland pursuing your personal enemies? And what of the ammunition and supplies? Will you refer your creditors to the King again and gain his eternal displeasure?"

Argyll found his voice. "If I impoverish myself for so noble a cause, MacHugh," he said carefully, "I only endear my services to my King. Once I return to London, I will have no difficulty receiving a royal decree of fire and sword against your clan." He flung the words at the MacHugh scornfully, restraining his terrible anger. "You will be ruined, MacHugh, mark my words well!"

The MacHugh laughed quietly. "Who will ruin me, m'lord? The Earl of Argyll, Lord Forlorn, fled to London to escape his Scots creditors? Jamie Stuart, cowering in the midst of his court in fear of his very life? I'll wager the King grows weary of taking the brunt of your personal enmities. For the love of God, the man cannot destroy every clan in Scotland who must feel your grudge!"

The MacHugh paused and took the sheet of parchment from his pocket, holding it so that Argyll could see the Royal Seal.

"I found proof of it, m'lord. The King has refused your petition for commissions of fire and sword against MacDonald's supporters."

Argyll's face was white and pinched, his eyes narrowed. He did not know how the miserable affair had reached such a point, but he had lost. He had lost to a cursed girl who refused to obey him, who had thrown away the fortune of gold which would have paid his creditors and returned the sheen of glory to his campaign. He had lost to an insolent chief who dared force his way into the very fortress of Inveraray, who brazenly read private correspondence, who forced the most powerful peer of the realm into submission at the point of an arrogant sword.

But Argyll would submit to no man. If his career was ended, if his dreams of glorious fame and fortune had crumbled like the coals on the hearth, if he must return to London an unpopular, poverty-stricken dupe of James Stuart, there was yet time to find some measure of revenge against the man and girl who had so defeated him.

"I'll find a way, MacHugh," he snarled under his breath, and made a quick move toward the closed door behind him.

But Alexander MacHugh was quicker. His hand closed on Argyll's sleeve and the point of his sword prodded uncomfortably in the Earl's padded doublet. "Would you leave me, m'lord?" he asked reproachfully. " 'Tis an insult to my charming company."

Argyll stiffened, but the MacHugh's strong grasp and the prick of the sword were insistent. He moved ahead of the MacHugh, suddenly aware that the man intended to shut him up in the ridiculous retiring room. The small cubicle had been planned for the convenience of ladies who wished to retire from the hall without leaving the scene entirely; it was furnished sparsely with a single chair and a small table.

"I trust you'll be comfortable," the MacHugh said. He paused at the door, sword in hand, and his face was cold. "Remember this, Argyll. I've grown exceedingly weary of this affair, and I give you fair warning. Keep well away from the MacHughs, as well as the Lamonds. And forget about the lass. You've had your chance and bungled it, and I'll not be so courteous the next time."

He bowed briefly. Argyll stood against the table, trembling with a rage and hatred for the MacHugh so malevolent and consuming that it was almost visible in the small room.

⟩ 21 ⟨

THE MacHugh slammed the door and twisted his dirk in the latch. It would not hold indefinitely, but Argyll would have difficulty dislodging it without help.

He was across the room without a sound. The library beyond was empty, as it had been when he came through it before, and he cursed under his breath. If the lass had retired to her bedchamber, they would have small chance of getting away before the Campbells were alerted by Argyll.

At the door leading into the corridor he paused, listening, but he heard nothing suspicious. He opened it quietly and came face to face with Elspeth.

"I thought you would linger forever," she whispered. She no longer wore the blue gown with its enormous hoops; she had changed to a shirt and breeks, with a leather jack which was much too large for her and swallowed her hands in the sleeves.

He grinned down at her. "Take a deep breath," he said softly, taking her hand. "The chase will soon be on."

He drew her into Duncan's office across the corridor and closed the door behind him. "You'll find a candle on the table," he said casually, and showed no impatience while the wick took intolerable seconds to catch and flare. Once the light flickered he looked closely at the latch. It was sturdy, but it would never hold under a strong battering, and they would need every minute of time they could wrangle. He pushed Duncan's massive table across the floor until it rested against the door, then he turned his attention to the coil of rope which he had hidden behind the chair. It was knotted at intervals along its length, providing a far more efficient ladder for climbing down a sheer stone wall than a smoother hemp.

He heard running feet in the hall and loud voices which grew fainter as a door slammed. "They've heard his lordship screeching," he said, and grinned at the thought of the Earl closeted in his own retiring room, screaming for help. He pushed the velvet curtains aside and looked through the window.

Elspeth joined him, and her eyes widened. It was an incredibly lengthy distance from Duncan's window to the ground. One or both of them might easily slip and fall that long way to the ground; and it would logically be Elspeth, who had never had a great deal of practice climbing down castle walls. But she said nothing. She would rather die in that unpleasant manner than to confess her apprehensions. She stood quietly and watched as he secured the rope to the stone sconces sunk into the walls at each side of the window.

"Blow the candle," he commanded quietly. They stood there in the darkness until their eyes became accustomed to it. The walls below the window were in deep shadow, but the moonlight beyond furnished enough dim light for their purposes. Elspeth stared at the rope on the stone casement; it hung there motionless, disappearing into the ominous darkness below. She took a deep breath and swallowed to clear the humming in her ears.

"I'll go first," the MacHugh said, his voice as cool and nonchalant as if he made a habit of climbing down frail, slender ropes each morning for exercise. But his hand was on hers, warm and reassuring. "Count ten before you follow, but once you begin, don't hesitate and don't look down." He added bluntly, "Make haste, else they'll pull you back up like a well bucket. The rope is strong; it'll take the weight of us both. And if you slip, I'll be below to break the fall."

"I'll not slip," she said faintly, feeling far less confident than she sounded. Her knees were beginning to grow weak and trembling, and her stomach lurched oddly. She wondered if she were going to be ill.

The MacHugh grasped her shoulder briefly. " 'Tis more simple than it seems, lass," he said, and then he was over the casement, moving down the rope. The top of his dark head disappeared, and she was alone. The Campbells were in the corridor; she could hear their shouted curses quite plainly. In a very short time they would try the door to Duncan's office and find it latched against them. She forced herself to count slowly, in rhythm with the thudding of her heart.

When she had counted ten she climbed onto the casement, and a momentary giddiness threatened to cut off her breath. She grasped the rope firmly, feeling the palms of her hands wet and slippery. She lowered her feet from the window and for one horrible minute she dangled there in mid-air, unable to move in any direction, up or down, desperately certain that she would hang there helplessly until the Campbells came to pull her back into the room. Then the rope jerked slightly and she remembered that the MacHugh was below her, climbing easily down the rope to the ground. She could not allow him to think her a flighty woman, prone to vapors and fainting spells, turning to cold stone at the most urgent moment. He would tease her unmercifully, and the thought settled her giddiness and brought a stubborn tightness to her mouth.

She loosened one hand experimentally and felt for the knot below her, hearing the pounding on the door from a far distance. Her hand encountered the knot at once, and she tightened her grip until she dared take her other hand from the window. She discovered with amazement that the rope was firm and the knots sufficiently large to afford a fair grip. It was not so difficult then, and she moved down the rope slowly, gradually increasing her speed until it seemed that she was jerking along at a tremendous pace. She slid her feet along the wall, balancing herself, and remembered Alexander's warning not to look down. But suddenly her hand felt for another knot, and her heart stopped beating for a long, agonizing eternity. The rope had ended; there was nothing beneath her but air.

"Jump," the MacHugh's voice came softly from below her. She finally summoned the courage to look down, and found that she was suspended just above his reach. It was a goodly jump, but she closed her eyes and dropped, feeling his arms go around her with a thankfulness which choked in her throat.

He lowered her to the ground unceremoniously and took her hand, giving her no time to compliment herself because she had not fallen and broken her neck after all, because she had actually managed the appalling feat of climbing down the walls of Inveraray on a rope.

He pulled her after him across the grass, moving with amazing swiftness. The shadow cast by the bulk of the castle was dark, but Elspeth was pleased that she had thought to cover her white shirt with the leather jacket. Just before they reached the shelter of the woods a shot rang out behind them, and Alexander took the last few feet to the trees in one long stride, carrying her with him as if she were no more than a rag doll.

"Run like the devil," he ordered brusquely, holding fast to her hand, and set an example by sprinting through the woods like a fleet stag. She stumbled along over roots and stones, almost falling, but he merely dragged her to her feet without a break in his stride. Tree branches swung against her face, leaving stinging scratches, and a sharp pain in her side began to spread through her chest.

She began to wonder dazedly if he intended to run all the way to Fraoch Eilean. She had almost decided that was his purpose, when the woods suddenly became alive with horses and men, merging with the dark shadows so skillfully that they were invisible from a short distance away. Alexander wasted no time with words. He lifted Elspeth to the saddle of the horse which appeared directly before them and sprang up behind her, his spurs digging into the horse at the same instant.

The dark figures mounted on the horses followed the MacHugh's lead silently, without a moment's hesitation, as if their spurs had been poised in readiness. They rode directly into the clearing which stretched from the trees to the walls of Inveraray, putting the horses into a bold gallop past the gates of the castle. Inveraray was in a state of confusion; every window blazed with light, and torches bobbled on the battlements and over the ground behind the castle walls.

It was plain there would be no immediate pursuit from Iveraray, but the riders did not slow their horses until they were well along the trail which led through Glen Aray. Then a dozen MacHughs well back to form a rear guard, while Simon and Gavin moved ahead to lead the way to Ardoon.

Alexander had not spoken to her since they began the ride. Elspeth rested her head against his chest and listened to the quiet night noises about them and the rhythmic clatter of hoofs. They rode through the velvet darkness beneath the trees and the bright moonlight which flooded the small glades, and the night wind was sweet with the scent of heather and moss, wet with dew.

" 'Tis beginning to be a habit of mine," Alexander said suddenly in her ear, "grabbing a wench by her hair and dragging her off into the night." She could not see his face, but she knew he was smiling by the lilt in his words. "But I fear the Earl is too old and senile to be amused by such a romantic notion."

"Did you harm him?" she asked, surprised that she had not even thought of such a thing until that moment and cared less.

Alexander laughed softly. "Only his pride, lass. I'd stake my life if I could cross blades with him, but I'd not take advantage of him in his own castle, unarmed and ambushed. 'Tis hardly a fair thing."

She wondered what had happened between Argyll and the MacHugh in the closed hall at Inveraray, but it did not seem vastly important at the moment. She was riding to Ardoon with Alexander, and nothing else mattered.

"We've not heard the last of it," the MacHugh said quietly. "He's plagued me all my life, and I know him too well to believe he'd surrender so easily." He laughed again. "God's love, it'd be a dull life for the MacHughs if we had no Argyll to keep us entertained. I doubt we'd care for the boredom of it."

"I have no envy for him," Elspeth said slowly. " 'Tis like a poison that eats into his very soul. He's known little happiness in his life."

She had no anger left, but only pity for the man who knew such bitterness and hatred, who could never know the happiness which had been granted to her this night. And she had learned, the instant that he struck her in anger, that he would never frighten her again. He had used her for his purpose, aye, and spent his rage on her more than once, but he had not deliberately intended to harm her. Truth, the things which lay behind his cold gray eyes and thin mouth would always be hidden by the ambition in his soul; but perhaps a man who had been born to treachery and violence could not always be blamed for the dark corners of his own heart.

When they reached the open moorland the wind was stronger. Alexander took a cloak from one of his men and threw it about his shoulders, for his own had been left behind in Inveraray. He gathered Elspeth in his arms, close against him, and she rode so until they reached Ardoon. The motion of the stallion was smooth and gentle, lulling her to drowsiness, and she could feel the steady beat of Alexander's heart beneath her cheek. His arms were strong and warm around her, holding her within the protection of the cloak, and Elspeth thought she had never known such a sense of security and peace. She wished that she could stay there forever, safe from all harm in the circle of his arms.

She was almost asleep when they reached Ardoon. She slipped from the MacHugh's arms and stretched gingerly, feeling chilled in the night air without the warmth of his body and the cloak.

Simon and Gavin were awaiting them on the shore of Loch Awe. They had dismounted, as had their men, and they were all grinning broadly at the success of the evening's raid.

"I hope," Gavin said cheerfully, "that you'll not make a habit of this, lass. Each time I see you I find myself fleeing from a panting mob of Campbells. 'Tis the most arduous wooing I've ever seen a man pursue."

Simon said, amused, "You could scarce expect Alex to choose the easiest way."

Alexander came up beside Elspeth; before she could move, he had swept her into his arms again. "Alex, put me down," she protested, furious that he would treat her so before so many smirking MacHughs.

He held her in a grip like steel, so that she could not move. His gray eyes were black in the moonlight, and he laughed down at her with the familiar lazy amusement. "I thought you had lost that temper," he said gravely, "when you prayed yourself down the walls of Inveraray."

"You once said you liked a lass with spirit," she said, "and I would please you."

And they laughed together, and she put her arms around his neck, content to give him his small victory. There would be another time when she would show him she was not to be ordered about. There would be other days, and other years; there was the whole of life stretching before them.

The MacHugh carried her through the gates of Ardoon. She could hear his men laughing behind them; and above her she saw the ancient walls of the castle, soaring against the stars, as proud and unconquerable as the black MacHughs who defended it.